TOUGH LOVE

HEIDI CULLINAN

It takes a strong man to be this fabulous.

Crescencio "Chenco" Ortiz pulled himself up by his garter straps after his father's will yanked the financial rug from under his spank-me pumps. He doesn't need anyone, yet when Steve Vance steps into his life, the prospect of having a sexy leather daddy on tap begins to take on a certain appeal.

There's a hitch when he learns Steve is friends with Mitch Tedsoe—the half-brother Chenco never knew except through his father's twisted lies. Despite his reservations, soon Chenco is living his dreams, including a performing gig in Vegas. Now if only he could get Steve to see him as more than just a boy in need of saving.

Steve's attraction to Chenco is overshadowed by too many demons, ones he knows his would-be lover is too young to slay. Yet as he gets to know the bright, determined young man whose drag act redefines *fierce,* Steve's inner sadist trembles with need. He begins to realize Chenco's relentless tough love might be the only thing that will finally set him free.

Heidi Cullinan, POB 425, Ames, Iowa 50010

First publication 2014
www.heidicullinan.com

For Saritza Hernandez, the most wonderful, amazing agent in the world. Thank you, Sary, for being my partner on this wild and crazy ride.

ACKNOWLEDGMENTS

Many, many thanks to Saritza Hernandez for being my consult, my rudder, and occasionally my sanity, to Sasha Knight and Samhain Publishing for loving this series and giving it a new home, to Scrivener for saving my ass with those secret backups in the library, to Damon Suede for both loving draft one and kicking my ass where I'd phoned it in, to Brandt for catching what would have been an embarrassing entendre. Jo, much gratitude for your continued awesome feedback. Thank you Jason B for more than I can ever say, and thanks to Daniel Cullinan for reading, commenting, doing the dishes, and being very patient as always.

Thank you to all the *Special Delivery* fans who waited so long for this book to happen, and thanks most of all to my patrons, especially Pamela Bartual, Rosie M, Marie, Kaija Kovanen, Sarah Plunkett, Tiffany Miller, Erin Sharpe, Chris Klaene, and Sarah M.

*Remember, this country was founded by a bunch
of men wearing wigs.*

—RuPaul

CHAPTER ONE

O N A STEAMY January afternoon deep in the rat's asshole of south Texas, Chenco Ortiz opened the envelope taped to his trailer door and watched the last of his cobbled-together dreams turn to dust.

Had it come via his post office downtown instead of flirting at him in the afternoon breeze, the letter would have gone unopened into the laundry basket with the rest of his mail. The unorthodox delivery threw him off his game, but the handwriting sealed his fate. After a long day of bending out the window handing people their tacos to go and suffering the Rio Grande Valley's perpetual irritation with a man named *Ortiz* who couldn't speak Spanish, the lure of *Crescencio* penciled in feminine scrawl was too much to resist.

It reminded him of home.

When Chenco had still lived in his mother's carefully manicured subdivision, she'd left notes on his door when their schedules didn't match. Sometimes the missives had been to ask him to pick up his sister, but sometimes they were simply Carmelita Ortiz's special brand of love.

You are strong and good, my son. God gave you to

me perfect. I am so proud of you, and I love you just the way you are.

Intellectually Chenco knew there was no chance this particular letter was from his mother. He'd learned all too painfully *just the way you are* was code for *so long as you stay the way I want you to be.* But today he was hot and tired, and he stank of grease and failure. He wanted the note on the door to be from his mama, saying she forgave him and he should come home. Honestly, as grisly as things had been lately? He'd take an angry tirade, so long as she spoke to him again.

Chenco opened his mail.

The letter was from a lawyer.

Dear Mr. Ortiz: As executor of your father's estate, it is my duty to inform you of the current status of your residence at 369 Charity Place in the city of Donna, Texas.

Ah, yes, the trailer. Chenco shut the door behind him, setting his keys down on the kitchen counter. He should have looked this lawyer up in Cooper's papers and sorted things out himself instead of making the guy hunt him down. He had the deed in the safety deposit box at the bank, but he supposed he'd need to file it officially. Hopefully doing so didn't cost a lot of money, because paying for the leathery old skinflint's pine box had not been cheap, and Chenco hadn't exactly started out with a trust fund.

It would be good to have the ownership settled at last. As castles went, it was a pretty pathetic one, but

Chenco had clawed his way into this heap of rust, and he had nowhere else to go. He'd take any victory he could get right now, especially over the mean old son of a bitch he'd called father.

But as Chenco read on, he went cold to his core as Cooper Tedsoe, dead and buried these three weeks, stole triumph from his son's trembling hands.

"He can't do this." Chenco's whisper, raw and hollow, echoed inside his ringing ears. "This can't be right. He said…"

Well, he'd *said*. When had Cooper ever told the truth?

How could he lie about this?

Setting his teeth, Chenco grabbed his keys and stormed to his Nova, letter in hand. By the time he drove into McAllen and parked outside the lawyer's office, he'd so girded himself with inner steel he made knights in armor look pathetic and bulky. Before the politely smiling receptionist could say anything, Chenco slammed the half-crumpled paper onto her desk. "This is wrong."

Her smile wavered. "I'm sorry, sir?"

Chenco poked his finger at the paper. "Someone taped this on my trailer door. It's a *mistake*."

A flicker of recognition and fleeting sense of sadness lit the receptionist's eyes. Without looking up, she pressed a button on the phone system in front of her. "Mr. Cuevas, I'm sorry to interrupt your meeting, but Crescencio Ortiz is here."

A whisper of sanity suggested to Chenco perhaps

he'd done this badly, but as Cuevas emerged from a closed door behind the receptionist, the last dregs of control ran out of Chenco's fingers. He shook the letter in the lawyer's face. "This is *horse shit.*"

Cuevas held up his hands. "Mr. Ortiz, there is no need for such language. I'm in an important meeting right now, but in a half hour I can—"

"This says you're giving my trailer to the—" Chenco choked and swallowed the rush of pain before switching tactics. "Is this some kind of joke? You think this is *funny?*"

The lawyer had the same look of pity on his face as his receptionist. "I would never joke about probate. I will point out also it isn't I who gives or takes anything. Our office is simply executing our client's directive. However, I understand why you are concerned. If you could wait twenty minutes—"

"Your directive is wrong. Even my father wasn't that big of an ass. This whole thing reads like something out of *The Onion.* Really, the *White Knights* of the Ku Klux Klan? As if they're heroes instead of racist, murdering assholes? Why them? What the fuck does the KKK want with my trailer?"

With a weary nod to the receptionist, the lawyer opened the door to his office and leaned inside. "I'm very sorry, Steve, but I need a few minutes. Maria will get you some coffee."

"No worries, Luis. I'll take a walk and get my own. I could use a chance to stretch my legs."

A man emerged from the office—a white man, an

inch shorter than Chenco but twice as broad and swelling with muscle. Sometimes men wore chaps and motorcycle boots as a fashion statement, but Chenco suspected there was a bike to go with this guy's gear. His shaved head, tattooed arms, and heavy leather said *badass* without so much as a stutter. The letter's invocation of the KKK still ringing in his head, Chenco retreated, blind rage giving way to wariness.

The man met Chenco's gaze and held it. He didn't threaten, but at the same time everything about him said, *Behave, boy.*

Chenco wasn't behaving. He was being an ass. Lowering his gaze in shame, Chenco loosened his posture.

He wasn't sure, but he thought he heard the white man grunt quietly in approval.

"No need to rush," Cuevas's client said as he headed out the door.

The lawyer ushered Chenco into his office, shutting the door behind them. He indicated the chair across from his desk, and when Chenco sat, he found the leather still warm from the man whose appointment he'd interrupted, the one who'd silently scolded him. When Cuevas settled into his own seat, threading his fingers together over the desktop as he leaned closer with a grim expression, the last laces of Chenco's defenses came undone.

"Mr. Cuevas. This can't be right. I put money toward the lot fees for the trailer. I paid the taxes. I paid Cooper's goddamned *hospital bills.*"

"I understand, and I'm truly sorry. Unfortunately

this does not change the contents of your father's legal documents."

Behave, boy. "Sir, his will didn't say this. I *saw* it. If he did write this, he did it after his stroke, and it can't stand up to anything."

"I'm sorry to tell you this dictate does in fact come from the valid legal will for your father, dated before his stroke." The lawyer's countenance brightened. "However, if you could produce this alternate document, and if it were dated after the copy we have on file, it might be possible to contest."

Chenco had gutted the trailer and safety deposit box after Cooper went to the nursing home. He had no letter. "Maybe he filed it with a different lawyer."

"No other will has been filed. I can provide you with the original copy, if you should care to verify this yourself, or I can provide one to your attorney."

"I don't have an attorney. I have the trailer."

"Mr. Ortiz, I'm afraid you do not."

Why couldn't the lawyer yell at him, call Chenco names and threaten him? Why was he as grandfatherly as Mr. Flores at the funeral home had been?

How was Chenco supposed to fight back?

Chenco dug his fingernails into his leg. "Why would he do this? Why would he tell me he was leaving it to me, let me pay for everything and then…"

He trailed off, arrested as terrible recognition dawned, hollowing him out as if he'd been shot from the inside. When the lawyer passed over a box of tissues, Chenco pushed them away, dragging himself from the empty cliff of hurt and shame with a shake of his head.

"No." The word felt like steel in Chenco's mouth, and he clung to it. "I haven't cried for him yet, and I'm not letting him have any tears now."

Cuevas nodded and put the box aside. "I could put in a request for an extension, using your revelation of a potential additional will as cause. I doubt the other party is in a great hurry to claim a fifty-year-old mobile home in Donna, Texas."

No, but they certainly wouldn't grant any favors to a homosexual half-Latino, to say nothing of what they'd do when they found out about Caramela. "I won't be able to find the will, sir."

"You are upset, Mr. Ortiz, and grieving. I'm sure the court will allow you ample time to exhaust the possibility of an alternate will, especially when I speak up for you personally."

Now Chenco felt like shit. "You don't owe me such a courtesy, not after how I've behaved."

Cuevas let out a huff and sat back in his chair. "I've been waiting to mitigate this damage for years. You didn't make helping you very easy. I've sent you several letters, some registered, but from your reaction I'm taking it the one I had taped to your door in the flats is the first one you've opened."

"I can't deal with this. I don't have any money saved, not after paying his—" Chenco stopped, not trusting himself to go on. His throat felt thick, his stomach raw. "I work two jobs already, but I don't make enough money to pay rent on my own."

"Do you have friends, perhaps, or other family where you can stay? Your father did have another son by his wife—"

"*God no.*" Chenco shuddered. "My older brother doesn't know about me, I don't think, but if he did, he'd kill me. If you thought Cooper hated a gay half-breed, wait until you get a load of this guy. He's been in town since the funeral, and I've worked like hell to avoid him. If I have to stay with someone, it's not going to be Mitch Tedsoe."

"I don't know the man, so I'll have to defer to your judgment. As I said, I'll file for an extension. Hopefully this gives you time to make alternative arrangements."

Chenco's stomach wasn't raw, it was rancid. "I can't pay you."

The lawyer's smile had dark edges. "Oh, you won't. The estate and its beneficiaries will receive my bill, and I intend to be thorough regarding this matter." He handed a card over the desk to Chenco. "Please leave your number at the desk in case we need to be in touch. In the meantime, don't hesitate to call if something comes up. I wish you luck in your endeavors, Mr. Ortiz."

Recognizing he was being dismissed, Chenco thanked the lawyer and returned to the main lobby, where he left his cell number with the receptionist. On his way out, he glanced to see if the man he'd interrupted was in the waiting area, but it was empty, which was a relief. All Chenco wanted to do was get out of

McAllen, head back to Donna, and soak in his tub. While he still had a tub.

The impact of what the lawyer had revealed closed over Chenco in a slow, choking fog. *The trailer isn't mine anymore.* Cuevas would buy him some time before the inevitable, but there was no way out. Cooper had seen to that. First he'd bled his son dry, then he'd left the only thing Chenco wanted to an organization who would never in a million years do anything but kick Chenco hard and fast into the street.

Was Mitch's return to the valley part of this double punch? Had he known what Cooper would do and was in town to hunt him down and finish the blow? What if Chenco hadn't run off when he'd seen Mitch at the funeral? Would he be rotting slowly into the mesquite instead of wallowing over how badly their father had fucked him over?

The thought made his feet heavy, disorienting Chenco so much he inadvertently circled the block, landing on the street parallel to where he'd parked. Slipping into the alley, Chenco wrapped himself in the darkness, sliding down the relative coolness of the brick wall as he sat on the ground and hugged himself. Three stray cats scuttled from beneath a pile of newspaper, the smallest bearing a dead rat in its mouth. From the street, sounds of lazy afternoon traffic drifted into the alley, and above him an air conditioner whirred and complained in the heat.

He should call Booker, or Lincoln. Even in a month he wouldn't have enough money saved to rent so much as a shoebox on the corner. He'd have to live in someone's spare room or sleep on their couch. Except what was he supposed to do with Caramela's things? Lincoln would let him store some stuff, but he had roommates, and Heide took up all his extra space. Was Chenco supposed to trust Booker's boyfriend not to rip Caramela's wardrobe up for fun some afternoon when he was high? Hope nobody went through his bins in the storeroom of the club?

What in the hell was he going to do?

Chenco rocked gently, taking slow, careful breaths as he soothed himself. He wouldn't let the fucker win, not now when this was the final battle. He shut his eyes and imagined Caramela on the stage of a bright, beautiful hall, the best in the world, a thousand admirers roaring and screaming her name. Yes, he'd get there, and he wouldn't let his asshole father stop him.

You are good. You are strong. You are perfect the way you are. You will figure this out, one way or the other.

Chenco murmured the words out loud when they failed to take simply by repeating them inside his head. He *would* beat this. He wouldn't let anyone stop him. He'd claw his way into the sun. He didn't know how he'd do it yet, but he'd find a way.

All those years. All the time, all the money, all the visits to the nursing home—he laughed at me. He never loved me. He never even liked me. He hated me so much he went out of his way to destroy me.

Swallowing, Chenco drew his bottom lip into his

mouth and bit, sucking on the soft flesh until it hurt, until he could focus on the pain instead of the hollow wounds inside him. He wouldn't cry. He wouldn't cry. *He wouldn't—*

"Are you all right?"

Chenco looked up, releasing his swollen lip as he stared at the mouth of the alley. The man from Cuevas's office stood there, his shaved head silhouetted against the sun. Leather creaking, he closed the distance between them and crouched in front of Chenco.

THE BOY FROM Cuevas's office reminded Steve of Gordy.

It was the facial expression, the look in the kid's eye. A hunch of his shoulder, the huddled, haunted body language, determination and grit leaking out around despair. The echo of his best friend called to Steve, leading him to the stranger.

"Are you okay?" Steve repeated the question, gentling his voice and resisting the urge to touch the young man's arm in reassurance. "Do you need any help?"

The boy's shoulders let go of some of their tension. "I'll be fine, sir, thank you. I'm very sorry for interrupting your appointment."

"That's not a problem." When the kid remained curled against the wall, clearly hoping Steve would get up and leave, Steve held out a hand. "Steve Vance. Pleasure to meet you."

The boy accepted the hand with a slight but steady grip. "Crescencio Ortiz, but everyone calls me Chenco."

"Chenco, not Chencho?"

The boy blushed. "My little sister mispronounced it, and the wrong version stuck." Letting go of Steve's hand, Chenco withdrew and wrapped his arms around himself again with a curt nod. "Nice to meet you, Mr. Vance." *Now please go away,* his expression telegraphed.

Steve pretended not to notice the dismissal. "Likewise, Mr. Ortiz."

In his pocket, Steve's phone buzzed, and he murmured an apology as he pulled it out. Canceling the incoming call, Steve opened a text window and tapped out a reply.

"Sorry. One of my houseguests needs directions."

Chenco shifted uncomfortably. "I don't want to keep you."

"Not at all." Steve eased himself onto the ground as his knees were starting to protest. He sent the text. *In the middle of something. Can you give me fifteen?*

The response came a few seconds later. *Okay aisle just keep getting lost a little hunger.* Another text came through almost immediately. *Fucking voice texting.*

Steve replied with a link to Find My Friends and gave instructions on how to use the app to locate him. When he was satisfied his friend wouldn't end up in Reynosa, he pocketed the phone and returned his focus to Chenco. "These are old friends back in town after a long absence, but they've lingered to sightsee. I don't mind putting him off a bit longer."

The look on Chenco's face said he was dubious

about the merits of sightseeing in the Rio Grande Valley. As an RGV native, Steve had to agree with the sentiment.

Chenco rubbed his arm in a self-conscious gesture. "You have your appointment, so I understand if you have to go." His tone made it clear he wished Steve would.

Probably Steve *should* go, but he couldn't bring himself to leave the alley. Partially it was remembering how upset the boy had been in Luis's office, but mostly it was the eerie way Chenco was so determined to button up now that got to him. Clearly Chenco was used to having to solve his problems on his own, to making himself okay by sheer force of will. Steve couldn't shake the desire to be the guy who made it easier, at least this one time.

"I know you'd *rather* I leave you alone, but I saw how upset you were. I can tell you still are. Humor an old man and reassure me I'm not going to read about you on the front page of the paper tomorrow."

Chenco's cheeks burned, but his body posture eased in quiet surrender. "My father passed away three weeks ago. He wasn't a very nice man, but…it turns out he was more of an asshole than even I predicted. It upset me as all."

"As I left, I thought I heard you say something about your father leaving his property to the KKK. Your home?"

Instead of replying, Chenco glanced at Steve's smooth, shaved head.

Steve laughed and touched the back of his scalp. "Wrong tree you're barking up there, boy." He could see the hesitation in Chenco's expression and decided he might as well lay down all his cards. "I'm not Klan, Chenco. They don't let gay men wear the sheets."

Chenco's expression softened in surprise. "Oh. I didn't—" He deflated the rest of the way, flummoxed by Steve's confession. "Oh." He rubbed his arms self-consciously. "Me too. I'm gay, I mean. Which is why my dad left the trailer to the Klan. To be an asshole."

"Sounds like he succeeded. I'm sorry."

Grimacing, Chenco averted his gaze. "I should have known he was only using me. I never loved him, but I thought we had an understanding, that maybe he hated me but respected me in his own fucked-up way. No chance. He did this *just to hurt me*. He knew I couldn't afford to move out of the trailer and my mother would never take me back. He was fully aware what a nasty kick in the face it was to give a gay half-Latino's only piece of security to the fucking KKK. He did it to bleed me out."

So fucking like Gordy. The comparison chilled Steve to his core. "Do you have a place to go?"

"Mr. Cuevas bought me some time. I'll find something."

Steve didn't like the vagueness in Chenco's tone. "If you have trouble, let Luis know. He can hook you up with some agencies, maybe make some phone calls for you."

"I don't want to bother him any more than I already

have.”

"Luis is a family friend—I know he'd be more upset over executing a will that helped send a kid to the streets than he'd mind being bothered."

Chenco gave Steve a hard look. "I'm twenty-four."

Steve's lips curled into a wry smile inside his goatee. "I'm forty-one. You're a kid."

"Yes, sir." Chenco's tone was wry, but his gaze slipped to the tattoos on Steve's arm.

Steve cleared his throat. "If it comes down to it, I know a few affordable places you could rent. I can talk to the landlords, maybe get a six-month discount to get you on your feet."

The offer sent Chenco's walls right back up. "Thank you, but I'd never expect anyone to do that for me."

"Likely why I offered."

"But why? You don't know me."

Steve arched an eyebrow. "You don't think someone can do something nice just because it needs to be done?"

Chenco pursed his lips. "Everyone wants something."

How did someone get so cynical at twenty-four? "So you don't have any friends who would help you simply because they like you?"

"Yes, but you're not my friend." Chenco looked away. "I'm sorry. Probably you *are* being nice, and I'm spitting in your face."

Leaning forward, Steve put his left hand on the ground near Chenco, not touching him. "You're right to be cautious of strangers. But I do want to help you if I can."

Chenco drew back. "But *why*? I'm just some guy who interrupted your meeting."

"You're a human being in need, and I can see a way I could possibly help you. That's why."

"But no one is that noble. Nobody ever helps me."

The naked yearning underneath his tough exterior, the need clawing over iron resolve, made Steve burn with an answering fire. "Maybe this is your turn to be saved."

Their gazes met and held, and Steve felt his whole being go still. Chenco had let him in, just a little, and Steve knew what a gift that was. He planned to treat it with respect, hopefully get that wall torn down some more. *Let me help you, boy.* He could see their friendship expanding in front of him, and he wanted it in a way he hadn't wanted anything in a long, long time. One more minute, one more reassurance, and he could give Chenco his phone number, maybe get Chenco's in return.

A disturbance at the mouth of the alley broke the spell.

"Monk, this is the fucking coolest app ever. It took me right to you. I'm making Ethan download it the second I see him. Oh—hey there. Sorry, didn't realize you had company."

Swallowing his irritation at the interruption, Steve pushed to his feet and gestured between Chenco and the man who approached them. "Chenco, this is Randy

Jansen, one of my houseguests. Randy, this is Chenco Ortiz."

"A pleasure to meet you." Randy extended his hand.

As Chenco accepted Randy's handshake, however, Steve realized something was wrong. Chenco looked wary again. It was almost as if he recognized Randy—except Randy didn't seem to recognize him back. Jansen was his usual cheeky self, pumping Chenco's hand harder than he should have as he winked.

Chenco looked as if he'd seen a ghost.

Randy picked up on that but played the scene as cool as he would a poker hand, deftly switching his focus to Steve. "Got a text from Sam on the way over. We might want to swing past the house before we do the grocery store. Something came up on the feed. Sam wasn't sure if it was a big deal or not, so Mitch went over to the cannery to check—"

Movement out of the corner of Steve's eye drew his attention, and he motioned Randy to be quiet. Chenco had backed away, stumbling over an upturned box.

The prickle at the back of Steve's senses morphed into full-on alert. Yes. Something was very wrong here. "Chenco?"

"You're in on it." Chenco's expression was full of hurt and pain as his gaze moved from Randy to Steve. "You didn't want to save me. You're in on it. I was right. You do have an agenda, and it's *his*."

Steve closed the distance between them. "Chenco? Who are you talking about? What's wrong?"

The boy took off like the hounds of hell were on his

heels. Scaling turned-over trash cans and scattering stray cats, Steve chased him, but the kid was younger and leaner and fueled by terror. By the time Steve got to the street, Chenco had climbed into a beat-up brown Nova and peeled away.

Randy came up beside Steve and put a hand over his eyes to shield them from the sun. "What the fuck was that?"

"I don't know." Steve played his mental tape backward, trying to find the source of what had made the kid run. Everything was fine, right up until Randy came into the alley. He turned to his friend. "It was you. He was upset at *you*."

"I don't even know the kid." Randy glared at him. "What the hell, Vance?"

"He burst in on my appointment with Luis, upset about something in his father's will. I gave them a minute to sort it out, and when I went back, I found Chenco in the alley. His dad's an ass, he's about to lose his house. He's proud and hurt and lost, and he's got nowhere to go. Now he's upset with me, and I don't know why." He caught Randy regarding him with an odd expression. "What?"

Randy put a hand on Steve's arm. "Oh, Monk. He isn't Gordy."

Steve jerked away. "I didn't ask for your analysis, Skeet."

Jansen didn't back off, the bastard seeing too much as usual. "Look. I get it. You wanted to help save him, and something went wrong you can't identify or fix. It's practically a rerun. Except you don't know this kid, and you're not responsible for him. Also, this guy seems in firm possession of all his marbles, unlike Gordy. You can stand down."

Steve's jaw hurt from clenching it. "I need to get back to Luis."

Randy caught his shoulder when he tried to leave. "Hey. Chill. I won't bring up Gordy again." When Steve gave a curt nod, Randy let him go. "So he was fine until I showed up. But it was *you* he looked at like you'd gutted his kitten. That's the pot right there, the space between me scaring him and this somehow being your fault."

Steve had no idea how to read the gap. "I'd ask Luis, but he'd never tell me anything unless he thought the kid was in danger."

"Well, you got his name, right? Did you forget your hacking skills in the hour and a half since I last saw you?"

That angle had occurred to Steve. He knew he shouldn't go there, but God he wanted to. He *needed* to fix this with Chenco. Steve longed to take the young man's pain, hold it in his hands and turn it into something as beautiful as the boy himself.

Randy put a hand on Steve's arm. "Give him a Google while I make dinner. If nothing else, maybe we can give the intel to Luis. Sound good?"

Steve nodded, but he knew there wasn't a chance in hell he'd hand this over. No matter how bad an idea it was, he'd have every electronic record on Chenco Ortiz before Jansen finished layering his lasagna.

If Chenco needed saving, Steve would be the one to rescue him.

CHAPTER TWO

FOR A WEEK after the ordeal at the lawyer's office, Chenco pretended nothing had changed. He went to work. He went to the club to rehearse. He didn't open any more mail, no matter how friendly it seemed.

He couldn't stop watching over his shoulder every time he was in public, however, always looking for signs Steve Vance, Randy Jansen, or Mitch Tedsoe had found him again.

They hadn't, but Chenco lay awake every night, cheeks burning as he thought of what an idiot he'd been, falling for Vance's trap. He'd almost had Chenco too, which was the scariest part. At first he hadn't been sure if Randy Jansen was the same guy he'd seen with his half-brother around town, but then he'd heard Mitch's name and there'd been no question.

He couldn't make out how Vance connected to whatever Chenco's brother had in store. Vance had said he was gay, but if a friend of Mitch's was his houseguest, and the guy hung out with Mitch…well, who knew what that meant. Probably it meant Steve had lied.

Except the guy was so good Chenco had almost fallen for his lines. He had to steel himself constantly against thinking maybe Steve *was* on his side somehow. Nothing would come of wallowing in his weakness. He had to be strong.

Goddamn, but he wished more than ever he could go back to his mom and cry in her lap. He pulled her old notes—he'd saved the silly messages she'd once taped to his bedroom door—out of the cedar box in his bedroom, but that was all he dared allowed himself. Her renewed rejection was the one thing he didn't think he was strong enough to take right now. Cooper could fuck him over six more ways from Sunday, but one look of disappointment from Carmelita Ortiz and Chenco would fold.

Except Chenco was running out of time. He'd done a cursory look for new places to live, and his prospects were worse than he'd expected. As time dragged on, Chenco's anxiety increased, and when he flipped through a wig catalog, trying to plan for Pride month performances, the cold depths of reality hit him— Cooper's betrayal didn't just affect him, it threatened his alter ego.

Chenco called Lincoln.

He caught his friend on the way to work—Heide had a show at Lasers, Lincoln said, but she'd finish at midnight if Chenco could meet after at the club. Since Chenco worked until nine, he agreed, and after running home to shower and change, he headed up to Edinburg to catch the end of Heide's act. As soon as he stepped into the main room, he heard the drag queen's booming, brazen voice bellowing across the bar. She was in the middle of her erotic balloon-tying act, the audience roaring as Heide gave a swollen green penis a heavy hand job.

Heide was full-on clown queen. She drew on her lips almost to her nose, and Chenco knew from bra shopping with Lincoln her tits were 36HH—HH for Heide Hole. She made them perky by special blow-up inserts affixed to the straps of her gaudy green gown. Her hair tonight was a three-foot-high fire-engine-red tower of curls set off by the tackiest gold tiara this side of a toddler beauty pageant. Her earrings were fiber-optic lilies dangling to her shoulders, matching the necklace nestled snugly in her faux bosom. Her shoes as always were stunning—six-and-a-half-inch clear stilettos with a string of dice along the heel stem, a glitter buckle, and floating disco balls in the see-through rise below the balls of the feet.

Caramela was *so* borrowing those.

Chenco settled back to enjoy the show. When she closed her final set and blew the audience a kiss good-bye after her encore, Chenco gave her a few minutes to get settled before heading through the stage door and knocking at her dressing room.

"Come on in, hooker," a clear voice called in sing-song.

Slipping inside the cramped former closet, Chenco smiled as their gazes met in the reflection of the stage mirror. "Bitch, have you been getting collagen in those lips? You look like you gave a blow job to a Hoover attachment."

Heide snorted. She sat hairless now, Lincoln's patchy mop of dull brown locks matted beneath the nylon cap as she curled her lip at herself in the glass. "Allergic reaction to new lipstick."

Chenco flattened his lips. "What did I tell you about buying out of the clearance bin?"

"Whatever." Heide pulled off one of her lashes, wincing as the last of the glue gave way. "So, go on. Rip me to shreds, skank, I'm ready."

This was their game when they saw each other work, and usually Chenco was all over it. Tonight, though, he didn't have it in him. "It was good."

Heide stopped tugging at the second eyelash and turned to Chenco with the accessory winging up toward her overly penciled brow like a demented neon caterpillar. "What the fuck." She pointed at the stool beside her. "Sit. Spill. And if you try and bullshit me, I'll kick your ass."

Chenco sat. He gave Heide the whole story, starting at the funeral. He told her about seeing his half-brother Mitch there and leaving before the ceremony started. Heide threw shade as only she could.

"What a fucking *cunt*. He hasn't been back to the valley in years, and he shows up now, lurking around waiting to jump you?"

"That's just it. I still don't know for sure he knows about me." He explained about the letter and the meeting with Cuevas.

When Heide heard about the trailer going to the KKK, she shouted so loudly and angrily the stage manager came in to make sure everything was okay. Heide shooed him back out, muttering under her breath as she wiped off the last of her makeup.

"What a *fucker*. Oh my God, I knew your dad was an asshole, but even I didn't see this coming." She tugged off her nylon cap and rubbed a wet wipe furiously around the base of her hairline. "Do you have an apartment yet? What am I talking about, you don't have any money. Fuck the apartment. You'll move in with me."

"There's no room."

"We'll make room." She was in the strange transition between Heide and Lincoln now, titless and wearing her male side's face but still using Heide's vocal tones and hand gestures. Caramela usually shut off with the wig, but Heide liked to linger.

Chenco shifted uneasily on his chair. "The lawyer bought me some time. Unless of course he's in on the scam with Vance."

"What scam? Who's Vance?"

Chenco told the story of interrupting Vance's meeting, of his finding Chenco in the alley and offering to help. "Vance kept after me, like he couldn't let it go. I was almost ready to trust him when this other guy shows up, the one I've seen hanging out all over town with my brother. God, what would they have done to me if I'd been stupid enough to believe he really wanted to help me?"

Instead of commiserating, Heide frowned. "Honey, something about this is off. You said the lawyer made time for you, cut off this other guy's appointment. The leather daddy was nice to you, and he came right out and said he was gay."

"It could have been part of the act."

"Maybe not. Maybe it's Jansen and your brother who are the assholes." Heide arched Lincoln's eyebrow to her hairline. "Or maybe your daddy lied about your brother too."

"You're forgetting the Pulitzer-level journal in the trailer detailing all the ways Mitch hates fags and hopes they all get AIDS and die."

Heide grimaced. "Fair point. Well, fuck them. I still don't think the lawyer's part of this. Nobody's come to kick you out yet, so either the KKK doesn't give a fuck about a half-rotted trailer in Donna, Texas, or the lawyer really is doing you a solid. My money's on the latter. Did you Google him?"

"Whatever. You know I don't have a computer or a smartphone."

The last of Heide slipped away as Lincoln rolled his eyes and picked up a phone from the dressing table. "What was his name? Luis Cuevas?" He punched at the screen with his index finger. "Hmm. Well, if he's fucking you over, he's in some deep cover. He's done pro bono on a few bashing cases, and he's big on immigrant rights. Looks like he does the estate and property work to pad the bank so he can save the world on the side." Lincoln put his phone down. "I'll ask around at work, but I think this will check out. Besides, why would a legitimate businessman draw out an elaborate scheme when he could laugh at you and tell you to get off his lawn when the will already had you nice and fucked?"

"Why would a father bleed his son dry, lie about his will, and leave everything to white supremacists?"

"Cooper Tedsoe wasn't a father. He was a professional cunt-sandwich." Lincoln reached for a bottle of water. "We'll look around for a place, sweetie, but if you don't find something you like, you're coming to mine. I never get laid anyway, so you can take the other side of the bed with a clean conscience. We'll put Caramela's stuff in the garage or rent a storage space."

"Oh my God, she wants to claw your eyes out so hard right now."

"Miss High-and-Mighty can surely try, but this old queen can take your skinny-assed Chiquita any day, any time. Makeup and melty shit comes inside, but her precious muff-muggers and designer mop heads can survive a bit of baking. You can let your queen fly, but she don't get to drive."

This, this right here, was why Chenco hadn't come to Lincoln straight off. He never understood about Caramela, despite being the one who'd helped her come to life. He'd let Lincoln tease him and distract him, and he'd let his friend help try and find somewhere new to call home, but as he headed to the flats and his bed, he made his queen a promise they'd only go to Lincoln's apartment if it was absolutely the only place left in the valley to go.

CARAMELA WAS CHENCO'S savior and his damnation both. He'd made peace with this duality, though it had taken many years, buckets of tears, and one terrifying night of hysterics on Lincoln's couch. On that sacred night, Caramela had risen from his ashes, and she had never let him down.

She was the reason he worked two jobs and was still broke, but she was also the reason he wasn't living some false life as an accountant or a doctor or whatever career his mother would have forced him into. She'd helped him fight Cooper, and to this day she stood ready to guard him against whatever he didn't want to face. Caramela was the reason he was free. Letting her run the checkbook seemed a fair trade.

However, as another week wore on after his talk with Lincoln, as the day Cuevas would call to let Chenco know he had to move out drew ever closer, neither he nor Caramela were happy. He still had nowhere to live, and Lincoln was starting to get annoyed at his refusal to move in. Chenco had put in some hard hours on the public library computers trying to find a new place, but nothing felt right. Nothing felt safe. He had no idea what to do, and the terror of his future gnawed at him until he could hardly stand to eat anything and couldn't sleep for more than a few hours at night.

His scheduled gig at Club 33 on Valentine's Day should have been a lighthouse, but as he began his transformation into Caramela, the yawing pit inside him was as hollow and raw as ever. He'd feel better after he performed. Even with this affirmation, his hands shook as he pulled on his pantyhose, and by the time he had the companion nylon stocking over his hair, he had to stop and swab out his pits. Several times he'd had to prop his elbows on the vanity, resting his face in his hands.

Deep breaths. Deep breaths.

Chenco complied with his own order. He felt dizzy, but some of the red edges around him began to bleed away.

There you go. Now get your shit together and put your face on. We have a show to do.

The makeup application focused him—it was difficult and full of ritual, both practical and personal. Mostly, though, Caramela saved him. She made him pick up the makeup brushes and work. She put him together even as she created space for herself to be.

Chenco left as much prep as he could to the private bathroom in the back of the club, but a great deal of getting ready simply wasn't logistically possible anywhere but at home. He waxed, but there would always be some shaving, generally in areas delicate enough on their own merits, let alone adding in acrobatics over a small and sagging sink.

Then there was the problem of makeup and hair. To complete his transformation on site, he'd need a minimum of two giant plastic tubs full of materials. Time was also an issue. He wasn't the only one trying to use the club bathroom, and Chenco's eyebrows alone took him forty-five minutes when he was at home with plenty of space and had JLo playing in the background.

It wouldn't be so bad if Caramela wasn't glam. She wanted to be the Queen of Queens, which meant she had to have the best, and getting the job done right demanded hours upon hours of work—and money. Parton liked to say it cost a lot of money to look that cheap. Whatever the dollar amount was, it couldn't come close to keeping a queen. Makeup. Costumes. Compression garments, breast forms, shoes, padded panties, and enough body glitter to choke a Westboro Baptist.

And hair. *Jesus*, the fucking hair. It was Caramela's weakness—she had to put it on before leaving the house, which meant Chenco had to hide it. Which meant he had to squash it, which made Caramela threaten to shove her stilettos into dangerous places. Their Gaza Strip was the long walk to the Nova from the house. Caramela wanted to be out and proud, and Chenco wanted to keep his teeth and his brain matter in their proper places. His neighborhood made crack dens look like Boy Scout meetings. Their peace treaty was a plastic hairnet like the old ladies wore strapped under a hoodie. It went on in the trailer and came off in the parking lot behind the empty Blockbuster Video three blocks from the highway.

Tonight Caramela didn't berate him for squashing her hair. Sensing Chenco's nerves, feeling plenty of her own, she forewent their usual tussle and invited him to focus on the careful application of liner and fake lashes, to let becoming beautiful erase his weariness.

She emerged like a sunrise, claiming his already

pretty features and making them runway-worthy. His nose became a perfect slope toward his plump, raisin-colored lips. His cheekbones were lifted and defined, with shading which begged for those soft lips to be admired. The eyes, though—even Heide crooned over Caramela's brows. They were works of art, taking thick Latin caterpillars and taming them into fine, delicate lines—not penciled, not ruthlessly plucked so he had feminine brows when he went out as a man. The other queens all wanted to know how he did it.

With a hell of a lot of swearing, seriously sore arms, and the magic combo of a watercolor brush and a washable glue stick. That was how.

Once Caramela's face was on, Chenco felt better. As he tugged on the evening's wig—eighteen inches of dyed auburn, real human hair—Caramela slipped over the last of his skin. Smiling at herself in the mirror, she touched the underside of her locks, slid her hand to her faux breast and gripped it hard as she bared her teeth.

"*Chica.* You are so fabulous, they're all gonna cry."

Spinning elegantly toward the stereo, she cued up her favorite remix, cocked her hip a few times to the opening bass, and went to work.

She sang along with JLo, communing with her goddess and the center of her soul as she selected her wardrobe. Chenco felt uneasy, so she'd give him something fierce, something to make everyone shocked and off balance, to give her space to remind him how powerful she was on the floor, how one hour of drag could right a year of wrongs in his life. This meant sequins and glitter. She selected the faux-chain-mail dress which made her look nearly naked—thank God he shaved his junk, as this outfit cut a bit close to the Spanx.

Heide had allowed the loan of the dice shoes with a promise Caramela return them without a single scratch. They went into the bag to be put on in the parking lot. The only real question remaining was jewelry. The nested silver hoops were obvious for earrings, but what necklace? What bracelets?

The silver-blue bands reminiscent of Wonder Woman's Bracelets of Victory caught her attention and went immediately onto her wrists. *That's right, hookers, I can deflect anything you shoot at me, even you, Daddy.* Speaking of Cooper—she smiled as she selected the antique pewter trefoil knot Chenco had rescued long ago from the back drawer of Cooper's dresser. Armor chosen, donned, and ready.

Ready but packed, at least as far as the shoes went, Caramela zipped the bag, her gaze falling on the drawstring sweats and hoodie.

With a grimace, she reached for the plastic rain hat. She fucking hated this part.

IN THE END Steve did have to hack to find Chenco. He asked local funeral directors about any twenty-four-year-olds who'd recently buried their fathers, but none would readily give out any information, not even when Steve asked nicely in Spanish. He should have let it go, but he hadn't been able to get the kid's look of betrayal out of his head.

Randy helped him search. They kept their project from Mitch, because he had enough going on right now.

Steve's longtime friend had come back to the valley for his asshole father's funeral, but out of some strange nostalgia he'd lingered well past his original reason for coming. Steve knew Mitch was putting things to rest, closing a circle. That his once-stoic friend would so much as consider working through his old shit was huge, and Steve credited the change to Mitch's husband. Every time Mitch came back raw from a trip down memory lane, one smile from his husband seemed to help Mitch reclaim another piece of himself.

Chenco didn't have anyone to level him. Steve wanted to change that.

Hacking didn't take long, and though he couldn't come up with a mailing address, just a post office box in Donna, Steve did learn Chenco held two jobs, one at a local fast food chain and one at a glitzy gay bar called Club 33. Randy had sniggered at the name.

"Man, that's an old one. Thirty-three?" When Steve continued to stare at him, still not comprehending, Randy pulled out a piece of paper and drew two number threes beside each other. "Look at those two numbers next to one another and think like a dirty-minded, gay twelve-year-old boy. Two asses lined up for buttsex. If you want to go all Escher, the middle of the second three can double as an itty bitty penis."

Steve rolled his eyes, but he couldn't help a little

grin too. Yeah, now that Jansen pointed it out, the two numbers did look like a couple of butts. This didn't help them find Chenco, however.

After their lack of headway with Chenco's other contacts, Steve and Randy decided to pay the club a visit and inquire directly rather than risk anything on the phone. Confronting him at a bar seemed easier than a fast food restaurant and also more fun.

They brought Mitch and Sam along because when Sam heard where they were going, he declared it the perfect way to spend their anniversary. Ten minutes inside 33, Sam started swinging his hips to the beat, smiling slyly at Mitch and dragging him onto the floor with sultry promise.

Randy cast the pair a longing look, but he let them go and went off with Steve to search. It got them nowhere. Chenco wasn't anywhere to be found.

"It's still early," Randy pointed out. "Maybe he's not here yet."

"Possible." Steve rubbed his goatee and frowned at the dance floor, trying to think. It was hard with all the damn club music.

Randy indicated the far side of the room. "Why don't I go flirt with the bartender, see what I can wheedle out of him?"

Not having any better ideas, Steve nodded his agreement and went back to scanning the crowd for Chenco, just in case.

There were quite a few patrons present for as early as it was in the evening, but a poster on the wall near him proclaimed a drag show was coming up at ten, so perhaps it'd be a draw.

Everyone seemed so young. Steve had a hard time believing they were old enough to drive, let alone consume alcohol. No doubt they wondered what Grandpa was doing glowering at them. Steve tried to imagine what he'd done on a Friday night at their age, but of course the analogy didn't hold. At nineteen, he was in the Persian Gulf. When he got home, there was no Club 33. Even at Stanford, he hadn't gone to a club like this, though there might have been a small one somewhere. His hookups had happened at the gay video store and the biker bar on the edge of town, or with Gordy. Discretion was the name of the game.

Looking out at the sea of rainbow-colored hair, raunchy clothes, and open groping on the dance floor, Steve had to admit every now and again he missed discretion.

Drag queens, though. Steve turned back to the poster. Drag queens were familiar turf. He had zero interest in putting on a dress himself, but there was something about watching a man put on a wig and heels and work a floor under punishing stage lights. Nothing said *screw you, gender stereotypes* like a queen. Drag was a man doing what society said emasculated him and yet making the act about power, control, upending of norms. Steve loved it. If they didn't find Chenco, he thought he might stick around to see how the game had changed since the last time he'd been to a show.

Caramela, the playbill read. *The Rio Grande Valley's*

Own Superstar! She was certainly gorgeous, and slightly familiar. He was still examining the poster when Randy came up to him.

"Holy shit, Monk. You aren't gonna believe this." He laughed. "Well, goddamn. You beat me to it. Here I thought I was gonna blow your mind."

Steve frowned at him. "Beat you to what?"

"I found Chenco. He'll be here later. Except you found him too. Look a little harder at the poster."

Steve grimaced at Jansen before turning back to the advertisement for Caramela. He scanned it for Chenco's name, but he didn't see it anywhere. Then something in his subconscious prickled, and he dragged his gaze to the drag queen's face. "Holy shit."

"Exactly." Randy tapped the poster. "About an hour and a half until show time. You want a drink to fortify you? I figure we can't jump him until after, anyway."

Steve stared at Caramela, who melted all too easily into Chenco Ortiz's pretty, sensual face. "Yeah, I'll take a drink."

"I'll grab you a Bohemia." Randy disappeared toward the bar.

Steve resumed staring at Caramela/Chenco. When Randy returned, he handed Steve his bottle with an *I've been thinking* expression on his face. "I flirted a little harder with the bartender when I got the drinks. Guess where Chenco's from? Donna. His trailer is in the flats."

Mitch's father had lived there. "He should be glad to be rid of the fucking thing, then. The flats are a toxic waste dump."

Randy tapped his fingers against the label of his bottle. "Something really obvious is right in front of our noses. After his show, we're going to sit Chenco down at the bar and figure this out. He's got no reason to run from me, or you, and if nothing else, the kid could use some new friends."

Admiring the poster one last time, Steve nodded his agreement, thinking it sounded like as good a plan as any.

CHAPTER THREE

CARAMELA CROSSED THE parking lot at eight forty-five, swinging her jeweled Gucci clutch as she covered the distance between the Nova and the club in powerful strides. It made her cringe that people had to see her climb out of the piece-of-shit vehicle. *Work those tips, honey, and you'll get your BMW.*

"*Caramela*," random strangers cried out, waving and laughing and blowing her kisses. She blew them back with a saucy wink and a delicate flash of her gloved hands. The security guy at the door welcomed her, telling her she was a precious, beautiful angel in Spanish. She was pretty sure that's what he said. She tossed him a *gracias* and thanked God she didn't need to fumble any further in the language.

Caramela wove her way through the throng, declining drinks and cigarettes but bestowing several flirtatious touches on her more besotted admirers. With a final wave and a promise to see them in an hour, she disappeared into the employee area of the club.

Booker lounged on the saggy green sofa in the break room, but when he saw Caramela, he rose and opened his thick brown arms to her. "*Honey.* You're gonna kill them dead."

"That's the idea." Caramela checked her reflection in the mirror, making sure she'd truly caught all the damn hoodie fallout in the Nova's rearview. "Good crowd out there."

"Yes it is." He sank into the couch, propping booted feet on a chair. "What's the lineup?"

Caramela obsessed over a lock of hair wanting to angle out instead of in. *Fucking. Hoodie.* "Let's open with 'Waiting For Tonight'."

He tucked his hands behind his head. "Smooth entrance. Okay. I'll set up some blue and purple gels. Disco ball?"

She paused, considering. "No. Well—play it by ear. Slow and steady spin, if you go for it."

"Of course, baby. What's next?"

"I want to step away from JLo for the second number, but not far, and just the once."

Booker considered this. "What about '*Puakenikeni*'?"

Caramela wrinkled her nose then shook her head. "Close, but no. Not Rowland either, not tonight. It might have to be Nelly."

"Then may I respectfully submit 'Maneater' because it makes me fucking wet."

She dug out her compact. "Just for you, baby. After, I want to do a triple threat. All Lopez."

"With 'Papi' at the end, I assume. Straight up, or remix?"

"Straight up." Chenco needed a pure, hot channel of

the good shit.

"Got it. Then…" He tapped his toe in the air as he pondered. "I'd say 'Hynoptico' for the faux finale, and 'Goin' In' for the opener to the last set." When she cast him a questioning look, he waved an impatient hand. "Yes, I'll play Flo Rida's half of the duet for you. Why do you even ask?"

"It's nice to ask." She curled her lip at the still-smudged liner. "Fuck, I'm going to need the kit."

He fetched it for her and opened it up on the arm of the couch, watching as she began the process of makeup repair. "You're in a real mood, baby."

They hadn't spoken since Booker's awkward *sorry about your dad* text after the funeral, and Caramela wondered how much to fill him in. "It was a fuck of a day. Been a fuck of a month too." She half-hoped Booker would prompt her to tell him what was wrong, but all he did was try to hand her a bottle of water with a straw. Annoyed and a little hurt at his lack of interest, she shook her head. "Can't. I already have to piss."

"You will drink this water, bitch, or I will pour it down your throat."

Pursing her lips, Caramela took the water from him. "Fine. When my teeth are floating during the second number, I'll be taking my venom out on you."

Book brushed a delicate kiss across her hairline. "When spring break comes, we're gonna kill them in South Padre. I got it all set up. And this summer, it's gonna be us taking over Filthy Divas."

Caramela made a face and picked at imaginary

things in her teeth. "Book, I'm still not sure about taking the show out of the valley. Anyway, I can't afford anything right now."

"Padre is the valley, and it's gonna be so great, you won't want for money again."

South Padre was semi-local, only an hour's drive away. Filthy Divas wasn't—it was in Los Angeles, and it might as well be on the moon. Not that Caramela—or Chenco—could get Booker to understand. If she argued too much, he'd get bossy and tell her this was his job to worry about where the gigs were. He'd pull all his BDSM shit—he loved having a daddy to boss him around, and he was convinced Chenco needed one too.

An image of Steve Vance and his triskele tattoo drifted into Caramela's mind.

She dug her gloved fingernails into her palms. *No. No daddies.* Chenco had been his own damn *papi* since he was old enough to cry for one. He wasn't giving control up to anybody again. Neither was she.

"I'm not discussing spring break. I have a show to do."

She expected him to argue, but to her surprise, he only said, "We'll talk about it later."

His quick yielding made her give in too, more than she'd planned. When she leaned into him, he slipped an arm around her waist and drew her to him. "*Se fuerte, mi reina.*"

Be strong, my queen. Shutting her eyes, Caramela drew a deep draught of Booker—sweat and spice and safe, strong man, the scent drawing into her belly and swelling out to her toes. She had a flash of Steve Vance and his heavy, heady presence, the memory of safety tinged with regret. "*Soy fuerte.*"

They argued about lights and strobes and confetti, Caramela with her shoes off and feet in Booker's lap. Other staff wandered in and out, waving to the two of them, some of them Booker's team wanting clarifications on the lighting, but mostly it was Caramela and Booker. When the set was settled, Caramela asked after Booker's boyfriend, which made him brighten and laugh and launch into stories old and new, stories of kinky sex and wild times, stories of Booker's submission and pleasure. He left out all the drug parts, which she appreciated, and the rough parts, which she worried about anyway. Caramela eased into her corner of the sofa, letting Book's beautiful voice calm her and bring her back to ground, chasing her sorrow over Steve Vance away.

At a quarter to ten, it was time. Caramela strapped on her heels, touched her necklace, and drew her focus. There was no more room for leather daddies and mysterious, dangerous strangers. There was only the queen.

WHEN CARAMELA TOOK the stage, the club roared into life. She stalked the perimeter twice, blowing kisses and drawing hearts in the air for her frenzied fans, making space for her persona and giving herself time to swell inside it. When she was ready, she saluted the light booth—Booker's signal to swing into lyrics—and away they went.

Caramela lip-synched of course, but the fans didn't care. What they loved was the illusion of Lopez on their stage, *their stage*, their club, a Lopez they could weep over and touch, a Lopez to whom they could babble fanatical praises in valley Spanish. Lincoln criticized Caramela for falling for the tawdry antics of RuPaul and incorporating them into her shows, but Caramela shut her ears whenever he started to wheeze about the perversion of drag. She didn't care what the history of female impersonation was. She only knew her act was *the bomb*.

Her fans knew it too. For the forty-five minutes Caramela took the stage, JLo came to the valley, and she had a smile for every gay boy who had ever loved her. Club 33 swelled with worship for Caramela, and she took their supplication and transformed it into the divine.

As she finished the Nelly number, Booker joined her on the stage. Feeling flirty, she ground against him, Caramela in front, Booker bearing her up, playing wet dream for hundreds of watching men. When the music switched to the opening organ of the next song, Booker grabbed a cold mic, and the crowd went wild. Booker lip-synced along to Flo Rida's command for them to put their hands up, the lights sliced the room like knives and the energy level strained the limitations of the roof.

Caramela made the movements of her body communication with the gods, and she constantly reached for thicker download cable to intensify that connection. Duets with Booker playing rapper allowed Caramela to focus on her moves, making the audience beg for more. The break from singing gave her the opportunity to collect tips too—the more she let Booker grab her crotch and ass, the more money they made. By the time the song came to a close and Booker returned to the booth, she had enough tips to get her dreaming of the thousand-dollar wig she'd dog-eared in a catalog.

The next song began, and Caramela saw Randy Jansen.

It was him, there was no question—Mitch's friend was here, watching Caramela from the front row. Jansen stared at Caramela's face and her neck, and everything in his gaze said, *I know you and all your secrets.*

Caramela faltered.

Why was Randy here? How the *hell* had he known about Caramela? What was he going to do? What was *she* going to do? The questions swirled inside her, and the opening bars of the song cranked in perpetual loop as Caramela was too stunned to shift into the first verse.

She cut Jansen a glare. *You*, puta, *are going to pay.*

He raised an eyebrow at her and remained at his post.

With a deep breath, she shoved the panic and fear into the dark corners where they belonged. This was *her* damn spotlight. She led the crowd in handclaps, riffing with patter as she strove to find her feet again. She had steel in her now, and when she felt strong enough to look Jansen's way again, she let him know in no uncertain terms what a *cucaracha* he was and how he would crunch under the force of her dice heels. Nobody fucked with her music—nobody, especially not this asshole.

As her eyes drifted across the crowd, Caramela saw Steve Vance.

He stood in the back by the bar, leaning against the wall but watching the room as if he were on guard. He tracked Caramela as she moved across the stage, seeing through her the same way Randy had. It was clear he knew she and Chenco were one and the same.

Except somehow, with Vance, everything was different.

Unlike Jansen, Steve Vance didn't feel threatening. He was the man from the alley, whose stern, quiet command could center her, whose gentle smile called to her. He didn't speak now, but he made Caramela remember how it had been in the alley. As she stared at him, all the doubts of the past few weeks seemed foolish. Steve made Caramela feel as if there was at least one safe space left in the world. He looked like he would beat down the room to keep that space of safety. He'd even beat down Jansen.

For Chenco. For her.

The crowd was used to a gap between her penultimate song and her finale, but tonight it went on too long, Caramela frozen in place, staring at Steve Vance. If she looked away, she was afraid she might drown.

Is Heide right? Are you someone I can trust, Steve Vance?

She didn't know; she had no way to find out. She couldn't move, couldn't dance, couldn't do anything but stare at the man by the bar. Any second the audience would get restless, and then it would all be over.

No control. No safety. No chance.

Steve pushed off the wall and came across the room.

The crowd's cheers diluted, cut by a murmured rush, and even as the lull in her performance was terrifying, Caramela could barely breathe for the pleasure of watching him. It was stupid, this insipid, vapid fantasy of a butch boy in gleaming leather, and it had no right to mess up her act. Yet she couldn't look away. Out of the corner of her eye, Caramela could see Booker leaning over the second floor rail, his body posture stiff with concern, but she couldn't look at him to reassure him.

It was the *fucker* Randy Jansen's fault. There was no question that *asshole* was anything but the full author of this shit.

Steve Vance strode up to Randy Jansen, and without so much as breaking his visual connection with Caramela, hauled Jansen onto the tips of his toes by his hair.

Jansen howled in protest, but when he saw Steve's face, he went still. Onstage, Caramela lost her breath.

Sexy daddy, you can haul me to my toes anytime.

As if he'd heard her, Steve stared at Caramela with the intensity of a sun. He was not a threat—she *knew* it now, like Gospel. He wouldn't hurt her. In fact, every molecule of his being telegraphed sincerity and safety.

The spell around Caramela cracked. With all the promise and passion she had, she stared Vance right in the eye as she lifted the hot mic and said, *"Baila para tú Papi."*

The crowd roared back to life, the music swelled, and Caramela danced.

She marched across the stage, collecting the tips she'd neglected at the pause, the tips which were now all but pouring from her supplicants' wallets. She collected them, but she lingered at Steve whenever she passed. It was him she moved her body for, Steve the sexy stranger who could command a room, who slayed her demons simply because he could. This was her signature song, but for the first time in a long while, her whole heart was in the performance, and she flashed Booker the sign to loop into an extended mix. He didn't just give her an extension, he gave her full-on strobe, disco ball, and rainbow gels. If he could have rigged quick confetti, he probably would have gone there too.

Caramela didn't need the disco ball—she *was* fractured light tonight. It was a rush, nearly cracking apart but coming back together for a man so hard he was practically a walking erection. She never faltered in her "Papi" dance, a blend of Lopez's moves and her own, but tonight every shoulder roll, hip thrust, every slide sizzled, spilling out onto the floor. Any whispers of danger, any sense that somehow she should remain on guard, died under the intensity of the performance, the freedom filling every cell of her body. She danced on the ashes of her father, on the sneering faces of the thugs in the trailer park, on the piercing gaze of Randy Jansen, whom she could still see writhing and cursing beneath Steve's punishing grip.

She danced for Steve, her papi tonight, and she whipped the room into such a state they didn't wait for her to come by and collect, they threw their tips on the stage. She danced until her body ached and even Booker couldn't wring out another drop of shizzle. Making one last round, she waved and blew kisses, feeling like she floated fifty feet above the club until Booker came to the gate and held out his hand.

His face was as wild as hers, full of fear and excitement. Caramela let him wrap his big body around hers, leading her through the crowd and away. Except the crush was too much this time, and her adrenaline was already starting to crash. Booker couldn't cut through, not until Vance flanked him.

Saving me again, Caramela thought, but she couldn't say anything, could hardly think for the thickness of the crowd. Her two men didn't exchange a word, only worked in concert to get Caramela to safety. Steve didn't so much as brush her arm to claim her, but Booker kept checking with Steve for direction. When Caramela had to stop to take off her shoes, Booker nodded to Steve in a silent request for help, having her lean on him until they were off and she could carry them with her free hand.

He was a goddamn rock, and sexy as fuck.

Maybe he's real. Maybe I can trust him, at least.

Caramela tried to talk herself back to caution, but it

was hard. She could smell him, standing this close, and he was good enough to eat.

Booker led them to the back, and Steve came along. Randy came too. And Mitch.

Caramela tripped, heart seizing as she saw the big, blond man fill the doorway to the dressing room. The sight was so jarring Chenco fell forward for a flash, tripped out of his composure by terror. His own personal boogeyman stood before him—a practical body double of Cooper, his mean and nasty big brother.

While Chenco wore a dress.

Chenco cut a glance to Steve, the knife in his chest twisting as he met the gaze of the man Chenco had let betray him *twice*.

There was another man with Mitch, however, a cute twink with a fuck-me faux hawk and a crude blond dye job. Chenco braced himself, ready for Armageddon, but Mitch and the twink simply stood together, looking confused as fuck, the twink's hand tucked into Mitch's arm.

What the *hell*?

In the confusion, Randy approached Chenco. Chenco panicked and Caramela took over again. She was ready to take this fuckhead down with her if need be. But Randy simply stood before her, rude and strange and dangerous, and inside, Caramela could feel Chenco wanting to cry.

No. *No.*

"*Get the hell away from me.*" Shrugging out of Booker's hold, Caramela shoved Randy into the wall.

The goddamn bastard didn't flinch, just kept staring. He looked down at her neck, and she watched something ease in his face, like he'd been trying to solve a puzzle and finally figured it out.

"You're his son."

Caramela couldn't breathe.

Randy's eyes glittered. "You are. You're his son. You have to be. Your father died last month, same as Mitch's. You live in a trailer in the flats in Donna. Your eyes wrinkle the same way as Mitch's when you're angry." Randy shook his head in disbelief. "You're wearing the fucking necklace. *You're his son.* It's the only explanation that fits. You're Cooper Tedsoe's fucking *son.*"

Out of the corner of her eye, Caramela saw Mitch pale, his whole body rigid.

He'll kill you, your brother, if he ever finds out about you. He'll string your faggot ass up on the goddamned flagpole and let you rot in the south Texas sun.

Caramela dug for bedrock strength. She and Chenco were not going down, not after all her work. She didn't care how big or mean these assholes were. She'd take them all out, one fucker at a time.

She glared at Randy.

Starting with this one.

Randy opened his mouth to speak, but Caramela swore in her broken, fucked-over Spanish, gripped the left heel of Heide's dice shoes and slammed the point with the full force of her fury into Randy Jansen's shoulder.

CHAPTER FOUR

S TEVE HADN'T SEEN a scene go to shit this bad so fast in a long time.

The bouncer who'd led Caramela offstage pulled her off Jansen, waving the second shoe threateningly as blood from the first stiletto soaked Randy's shirtfront. Sam cried out in alarm, shrugging Mitch off to run to Randy's side. He went right into nurse mode, shouting for gauze and room to get to the couch. Mitch remained still, dumbfounded by Randy's reveal.

The bouncer glanced at Steve, a blatant cry for help, and Steve relaxed, knowing now what he needed to do.

When Steve stepped forward, the man turned her over without so much as a blink and went to help Sam and Randy. For one dark moment, Caramela went hellcat, fighting Steve's grip. Hauling her roughly to his body, Steve dug his fingers into her shoulder and bent to her ear.

"Hush."

She gentled, but not all the way, not until Steve added the sharp pressure of fingernails, half-moons digging into her skin. The pain stilled her, made her relax—a little too much, though, and Steve could feel the shakes and sobs threatening to push out of the anger she'd leashed.

He lessened his grip enough to draw her back against him. "Stay with me." He turned the hold into a steady massage. "Listen."

Caramela choked on a sob, but she held it in and nodded. Yes, she'd listen.

"Jansen is an ass, and he fucked this up. Yet he's not a bad man, and you've hurt him in front of friends, friends who are already on edge. If you strike him again, you will deal with me. Do you understand?"

Her whole body tensed, and she blew angry breath from her nostrils. Steve tightened his grip, pushing his fingernails in with more authority, and she calmed down, back to the edge between cracking and exploding.

Steve had to check the instinct to brush his lips over her hair and whisper *good girl.*

He cleared his throat.

"Bleeding out Jansen will not stop what you're trying to hold back. Fear of these people is unnecessary. Mitch and Sam are good folks, Randy too. Whatever Cooper did to you, they are the other end of the map."

She almost broke—two sobs, but she swallowed them with no tears, and when the smooth skin beneath Steve's fingers began to pucker from pressure, she eased back into control.

Steve forced his attention to the room at large. Caramela seemed stable, going back to the bouncer to fold herself into his arms. Sam had Randy under control, and Sam himself was stable, at least for now. Mitch, however, needed a leg up.

The trucker stood a head taller than Steve did and was a little bit wider, but he had the same uneasy edge he'd always carried in the valley. Right now he pirouetted on a knife point. Steve grimaced, wishing Randy would have checked with him before he decided to play secret baby.

That Chenco was Cooper's son blew Steve's mind too, but there was no denying the confirmation on Caramela's face when Randy confronted her. It was the truth. It was out in the open. Now they had to deal with it, Mitch included.

"Tedsoe, we need water and probably a whiskey for Randy. In a minute Sam will need you."

Mitch nodded. He couldn't look away from Caramela, though, trying to see Chenco, his brother. Trying to see Cooper.

"*Mitchell Allen Tedsoe.* Go to the bar, get the drinks, and get your shit together."

This time Mitch gave Steve a curt, grateful nod and disappeared from the room.

A glance at the couch revealed the shoe was out. Sam held a heavy packet of gauze over the wound, watching the angry red pool beneath his hand as he shouted for more bandages. Randy was pale but conscious and reassuring Sam he was fine, telling him to calm down.

Steve caught the bouncer's gaze, indicating Caramela and the door. *She needs to get out of here.*

The man nodded in relief, surrendering her with his indifference. When Steve blinked in surprise, the bouncer only murmured something about *"Can't handle the blood, man"* and ducked out of the room.

Who tossed his friend off to a total stranger?

With no other real option, Steve took over herding Caramela. She didn't fight him—she'd slid under his command pretty hard, but she was still in character, which impressed him. Remembering the fury with which she'd landed the heel in Jansen's shoulder, he directed her patiently to find her bag and keys. She didn't put up any resistance until he led her down the hall toward the back entrance.

"Stop. *Where* are we going?" She stiffened in his arms. "You mean you're taking me *out* of here? I don't even know you."

It was good to hear *she* at least had some sense. Steve relaxed his grip so she could move away and face him. "You needed out of the room. I was going to settle for a little fresh air for now. But now that we're talking—yes, we need to work out what happens next."

She folded her arms over her chest. "Nothing happens. You can all leave me alone." When Steve only stared back at her, not in the mood to dignify this with an argument, she glared back for a few seconds then crumpled. "Why are you here? Why did you follow me? Is this part of his sick game?"

Steve frowned. "Whose sick game?"

Caramela's lip curled. *"Cooper's.* Mitch's. Whoever else is in on the fun of ruining my life."

"Mitch isn't playing any game. He had no idea you existed until two minutes ago. He'll come around in a minute. He's not a bad guy."

She was not convinced. "I have his old journals where he wrote incoherent essays full of rage and homophobia. Cooper loved to tell me how someday my big brother would come back and kick the shit out of me. This was *before* he found out about the drag."

"For the record, *Mitch* is gay."

She stilled, studying Steve hard. "Bullshit."

"No shit. Mitch is queer. Loves cock as much as you and me." Steve jerked his head back toward the dressing room. "Sam—the young one—is his husband. Randy's gay too. Hell. Every last one of us is. So you can stop worrying on that score. As for the drag thing—" Steve shrugged. "I doubt it's a big deal. He's not exactly a judgmental kind of guy. Maybe he was when he lived with Cooper and when he denied the truth about himself, but not now."

Caramela said nothing, only continued to hunch over, holding her arms over her chest.

Steve's phone buzzed in his pocket. Pulling it out, he found a text from Randy. Steve smiled. When Caramela frowned, he waved his phone at her briefly before lowering it to text back. "Jansen says he's sorry."

She shook her head in disbelief. "What?"

"Jansen can be a real ass. He knows it too." He finished his message, waited for Jansen's reply, then looked up once he got it. "He's inviting you to the house." Which was Steve's house, but he'd let the technicality slide for now. Especially since this was exactly what he wanted, to get to know Chenco, to help him. Caramela too.

Caramela didn't recoil, which was a good start. "*Why?*"

"Because he wants to meet you."

"Jansen, or my brother?"

"Everybody wants to meet you, Caramela."

The comment caught her up a little. "You can call me Chenco."

Steve raised an eyebrow. "Figured you were still in character."

"Yes, but…" She eased a fraction. "Thanks. Not many people get it."

Steve gave a curt nod. "As you pointed out, you don't know me, but if I may offer my advice—I think you should come meet Mitch. Meet all of them. You struck me the other day as someone looking for family. I'm telling you, you hit the fucking mother lode."

"I put a stiletto through the shoulder of the mother lode?"

"Well, once you get to know them, you'll realize this was probably the best way in. If you knew how Jansen introduced himself to Sam, you'd give him a matching wound in the other side."

Caramela bit her lip and smoothed her hands over her dress. "I need to change."

"Do you do this here, or at home?"

"Home."

"How about I take you, wait, and drive you to my

house to meet everyone?"

She gave him an arch look.

He gave it right back. "I think you're holding yourself together with your sequins. You shouldn't really be driving."

He expected a barrage of *you don't own me* and *who do you think you are*, but she surprised him. "You're leather, aren't you? You're one of those BDSM tops or whatever."

He crossed his arms lightly over his chest. "I take it that's a problem for you?"

"Let's just say Booker has a boyfriend into the same, and I'm definitely not interested."

Steve wanted to hear *all* about this, but not now. "Helping you has nothing to do with bondage and discipline, dominance and submission, masochism and sadism." He paused. "All right, it has a *bit* to do with discipline and dominance, but it's more about my personality than anything else. I want to give you a ride because you're probably in shock and shouldn't be driving. I'm inviting you over to my house to meet your brother who doesn't want to bash you. I am *not* suggesting anything to do with sex."

He watched her face as she digested his speech. "The stuff you rattled off—bondage, discipline, dominance…" She frowned. "You said two D words and two S words. It doesn't make sense."

Steve was about to ride her for focusing on the alphabet when the real point was he meant to reassure her, but she wavered, and he realized she'd latched on to the acronym because everything else was too scary to contemplate.

Yeah. No fucking way she was driving a car.

"Your options are," he began, his voice quiet but firm, "I drive you, your friend drives you, or I call you a cab."

"I can't afford a cab."

"I said *I'd* call you a cab. I'd foot the bill."

Her head jerked up again, her gaze heavily suspicious. "It's over twenty dollars at the rates they charge to take me all the way to the flats. Why would you do that?"

"What I've gotten to know of you so far I like, for one reason. You're Mitch's little brother, for another. I also enjoyed our conversation the other day, and I'd want to help you on your own merits as well."

She rubbed at her arms, clearly not calmed by the idea of kindness from strangers. Eventually she said, "You can drive me."

He'd been ready for her to tell him to go to hell. Pleasantly surprised, Steve pushed off the wall and came to her side. Right off they had trouble—when he herded her to the back exit, she balked.

"There's no clear access to the front this way. Also there's a lot of glass, and I'm barefoot."

"You can't go through the front. They'll mob you, and you're already about two shoves away from coming apart." He glanced around, then at her bag. "Any chance you have ballet flats in there?"

"No. My other shoes are in the car."

Steve turned Caramela gently so she faced him. "I would like permission to carry you."

"You keep messing everything up and fixing it at the same time. You scare me. You make me feel like I've gone crazy. I don't do this. I don't let total strangers drive me home then over to their house. I certainly don't let them carry me in character across a parking lot full of fans."

Steve said nothing. She let out a breath then started to crumble. Steve didn't reach for her this time. She had to make this leap herself, or it wasn't going to work.

"Okay," she said at last. "I'll do it, but explain to me exactly what's going to happen, please. I know you said you were going to drive, but can you…spell out what happens now?"

Steve spoke slowly, his voice soothing but firm. "I'm going to carry you to your car. I'll drive you to your house. I will wait while you change into Chenco, and then we're going to talk, you and me, before we meet your brother. We can do it in a neutral space, or in the car, or at a coffee shop before we head to my house." He hesitated. "Or I can drop you off and we can do the meet-up tomorrow."

"No. I'll keep avoiding." Caramela rubbed her arms and looked over at him reluctantly. "Probably shouldn't have told you that."

Yes, but she had, and her urge to confess to him made something deep and pleasing hum in Steve.

She rounded her shoulders, hunching her body into a protective stance. "I really thought you were all in on

Cooper's scam. I know you're not now, or at least I'm pretty damn sure, but Mitch…well, I've lived in mortal fear of him for years. That emotion is hard to shake off on somebody else's word."

"If Mitch or anyone else were to attempt to harm you in my house or simply on my watch, there would be some serious hell to pay. Words are all I can give you right now, but I mean them."

"All right. Your house is fine." Her hand trembled, however, when she brushed a lock of hair out of her face. "I feel a little weird. Like I might throw up or float away. Or melt into a puddle, or blow up."

"You've had a big scare tonight. You've had a hell of a time lately too, from what you told me the last time we met." He took a step closer, not touching her but making a gentle, subtle wall around her. "I'd prefer to stay with you while you change. I'll wait in the kitchen if you want, but I need to be able to hear if you go into shock, as I'm not entirely convinced it's off the table. When you're Chenco again, we'll talk and reassess whether it would be better to meet Mitch and the others tonight or wait." He pursed his lips. "If we wait, though, I don't think you should be alone."

Her nostrils flared. "I'm not *that* unstable."

Steve didn't dignify the lie with a reply.

She lifted her head and looked him in the eye— defeated, but she held his gaze. "You're right. I'm not very okay just now. I shouldn't do this. I don't know you, but I'm tired and scared so I'm doing it anyway. You may carry me to my car. I warn you now, though, if this ends up being the opening act to some sick game, I'm gonna fight you like hell."

The declaration made him want to smile, but Steve didn't allow himself the indulgence. Instead he inclined his head in a small bow and held out his hands.

She stared at his hand, drew a shaking breath and stepped into his open arms.

FOR THE FIRST time since he'd started drag, Chenco went out of character while still in women's clothes.

Flashes between personas like the one when Mitch had come backstage were common, and those instances always stemmed from Chenco growing too nervous or upset. As Steve hefted Caramela into his arms and carried her out the door of Club 33, however, it was she who did the abandoning. She held on for about five seconds in Steve's grip before sliding away, and Chenco had no choice but to move forward.

"We're heading into the parking lot now," Steve said as he rounded the building. "If you can't bring her back, do your best to fake it. You'll regret it later if you don't."

How had he known the difference in the personas? The exposure made Chenco feel dizzy as he let out a breath. "I can't." He tried again, but she was water in his hands. "She's gone."

Steve's grip tightened on him. "Breathe," he commanded.

Chenco did. "I think—I think it's because she hurt

Randy. She's threatened it before, but she's never actually done it until now." The white-hot moment returned, and he found the shadow he'd been trying not to look at. "She almost put it in his neck."

"Almost isn't doing. May be best, though, we let her rest. What would she do right now if she were okay?"

Chenco tried to think. He was in the arms of a hot leather daddy Caramela had sung her heart out to. Thinking took some work. "She'd wave and ham it up, blowing kisses and drawing hearts in the air. Except she wouldn't. No way in hell would she go off with a stranger."

"Would they think she would?"

Chenco considered. "They liked me singing to you. I think we're writing a new chapter for Caramela right now, so anything goes from a fan perspective."

"You're switching pronouns. Is she back, or are you getting lost?"

Chenco honestly didn't know. "Both, maybe."

He shifted his grip and leaned down to Chenco's ear. "Caramela," he said, his Spanish accent achingly perfect. "I want you to come back from here to the car. Chenco will hold you, but he needs you right now. We need you until we clear the lot, and then you can rest. Do you understand?"

Chenco shut his eyes, dizzy as the full weight of his battered queen filled his headspace. She wanted to cry, but she held on, for Chenco, for Steve. "Yes. I understand."

Steve's lips brushed Chenco's ear, bleeding the tension out.

It was Caramela who waved, but as he never had before, Chenco felt himself prop her up, aware of her limits, of his own, conscious of how bizarre the whole situation was and how much trust he'd blindly given Steve, trust based on a few glances, a conversation, and a projection of strength. Who was this guy who carried him? Why did he keep showing up? Why should Chenco trust him?

With no answers, Chenco couldn't calm himself. So as Steve climbed into the Nova and Caramela slipped away, Chenco went about getting some.

"How do you know Mitch? How do you know my dad?"

Steve pulled into traffic as he answered. "I knew Mitch when he was first out, which meant knowing Cooper a little. I know your brother a lot better than I do your father." He glanced at Chenco. "Mitch isn't his dad. Just looks a fuck lot like him. He's not a gay-basher. He's a gay, married man."

Chenco nodded, still processing that. Mitch was gay too, and married. The idea made Chenco's brain sort of shut down.

Steve continued to speak as he drove. "It was just Mitch and Cooper since Mitch was eight. Mom ran off, which has always been hard on Mitch. He went through a dark phase where he tried to bully his way out of his orientation. Hated everything and anyone gay in high school from what I was told. I would suppose that's when he wrote those journals."

Chenco rubbed his arms and stared at the dash-board. "They're fucking terrifying."

"Whatever you read in them, remember all that vitriol was how he thought of himself. You don't grow up with Cooper Tedsoe and come out with your head on right." Steve eased his hands into a casual position on the steering wheel. "By the time I met Mitch, he was out, at least to himself, though he was involved with some not-so-good BDSM. Some of us from the local scene found him, shaped him up as best we could, taught him how to play safely. He got into trucking and started coming and going from the valley, and eventually he returned with Randy. Shit, but they were a pair. Two north ends and nothing but trouble. I did my best to help, but I had my hands full with something else at the time."

So his brother was into BDSM too, and this Randy. And Steve, and Booker. Chenco frowned. Was there something in the water in the valley, or what?

Steve went back to his story. "Mitch left the valley, but he kept coming home, and he could not stop trying to get his dad's attention whenever he was in town. Take him out of the RGV, and he's strong enough to make most men bend just for looking at him, but bring him here and he's eight years old again, wondering why his mama didn't love him enough to take him too. Cooper made Mitch the reason for everything wrong in his life, and he put it all on him, right up until the day Mitch beat him down. Stopped short of killing him, and then Mitch left and never returned. Seven years he's been gone, but back ten minutes, he was the same as the day he'd left. The old fuck is dead, but he'll haunt his boy forever. Cooper was a brute, an ass, the kind of shit-heel who gives sadists a bad name."

Chenco couldn't see Steve's triskele from the passenger seat, but he knew it was there. He touched the place on his shoulder still burning from those fingernail indentations. "You're a sadist. A BDSM sadist. You're into pain."

Steve nodded, eyes never leaving the road. "I am. You're changing the subject, but if you need to go here, I don't mind questions."

"Well, there's a lot of subject matter flying around."

This brought out another one of those half smiles. "Do you have questions about BDSM? If your friends have given you a negative impression, I wouldn't mind a chance to clear things up."

No, Chenco didn't want to discuss BDSM, not yet. Did bringing it up mean Steve was into him, though? Sinking into the seat, he put his hand on his face and shocked himself when he felt the heavy makeup and fake lashes. "This is really weird, being me in her clothes."

"Just about to the flats." He switched lanes, heading for the exit into Donna.

"How much are they going to hate me for stabbing Randy?"

"Randy's already forgiven you, and he'll also respect the hell out of you from now on. He doesn't normally misjudge people's limits, and he'll want to make amends for reading you wrong. Mitch is in a little shock at finding out he has a brother, so I think Randy's shoulder is the least of his concerns now." Steve nodded at Chenco's lap. "Do you have your phone handy? You should probably let someone at the club know you're okay. That bouncer or someone else."

"Booker? Oh shit, I should." Chenco pulled his phone out of Caramela's clutch and fumbled with the keys, removing the gloves so he could manipulate the phone easier. He sent the text and put it away. "So Mitch and Randy are cool. What about the other one?" *Mitch's husband.* God, that would never stop being weird.

"Sam? He won't care for your hurting Randy. From the stories I've heard, however, he understands the impulse. I suspect an apology and a little explanation of why you were so scared to meet someone connected to your father would probably set everything right." Steve turned the Nova into the flats and grimaced. "This place has gone to shit since I last came through, and it stank then. Given the gangs it likes to produce, I suppose I should have suspected."

"It's mostly meth labs, I think. And yes, the crime is horrible."

He waited for Steve to ask why he lived there, but Steve didn't. He simply drove to the trailer, parked the Nova in the drive, and killed the engine.

Immediately, Chenco realized what he'd forgotten and began to panic.

"My hoodie," he managed to get out when Steve's

hand closed over his arm, bringing him back to earth. "I have to cover her up. If they see me—"

"I need to know where the hoodie is, Chenco."

"Backseat, but I always put it on before I get here, and I can't get the sweatpants on in the car, not here—"

"*Breathe.*"

Chenco took one breath, then another. Something hot and tight let go inside him, and a delicious pressure pierced his left arm. He looked down and saw Steve's hand on his arm, the skin white beneath his grip. It hurt, he realized.

It hurt, but it felt a little good too.

A different fear lit up in Chenco as he met Steve's gaze. "Why do you keep doing that? Digging your nails into me?"

The guilt on Steve's face surprised Chenco. "Instinct. And effectiveness. It keeps being the only thing to calm you down."

What, you can't try shushing me and telling me everything's fine like a normal person? Chenco replayed Steve's flash of…conscience? Embarrassment? Contrition? Was this a warning sign Chenco should heed? As discomfort leached back into Steve's expression, Chenco did worry, thinking *see, he is another psycho and I just called his bluff,* and then something else whispered at him, surprise stilling Chenco to his core. Surprise and a sense of…power.

It wasn't guilt he'd seen. It was vulnerability.

Flattening his lips inside his goatee, Steve reached into the backseat, grabbed the hoodie, and tossed it into

Chenco's lap. Vulnerability was gone now, as was the sense the reins had landed in Chenco's lap for more than a flickering second.

Chenco slid into the garment in a daze, drawing the hood up tight.

Steve nodded at the house. "No one is here right now, and I'll keep an eye out. I think your legs aren't a big deal, but without shoes I'll have to carry you unless you want to write off these stockings."

Chenco thought of the hundreds of dollars, maybe even a thousand, loose and lost somewhere at Club 33. Booker would pick up some of it, but…well, Chenco wouldn't get half of what was actually there. So much money gone, money he needed right now more than ever.

Not now. Don't think about it right now because you have enough on your plate as it is.

He swallowed hard. "If you could carry me please, I'd be very grateful."

A heavy hand came down on his shoulder, no pain this time, just gentle touch. "You're doing well, Chenco. You're being very, very strong. This is a lot to take in, and you're trusting a stranger, and you're being smart and strong and good."

You're a good, strong man. Chenco felt himself teeter, and he let out a shuddering sigh. "Don't, please—it breaks me when you're nice."

"I noticed. But usually I like to get to know someone before I start sharing pain without politeness first."

The comment made Chenco dizzy. "I think I need

to get inside."

"I'll come around to get you."

Chenco gathered his bag and his shoes from the backseat—his shoes! He'd forgotten they were there, and it was like finding an extra Christmas present under the tree. He slipped them on, and by the time Steve was at his door, he felt a lot better. Steve nodded approval at the footwear, but he still helped Chenco up the stairs and into the trailer, carrying his bag for him. Once inside, Steve addressed Chenco again.

"Am I waiting here, or do you want me to come back to your room while you change?"

Shaking his head, Chenco gave a half-smile. "Wow. You are *serious* about getting permission for every-thing."

"For the record, my asking for permission comes from the BDSM background you're so nervous about." He cleared his throat. "I need the answer. Am I'm coming back with you or waiting here?"

Chenco considered. "I think I want you to come." When this statement was met with silence, Chenco sighed, irritated. "Fine. I want you to come along. Part of me thinks I'm being stupid, but I still want you to come sit with me while I change."

This confession seemed to relax Steve. "First of all, it's natural and smart to be wary, and since I haven't had adequate time or opportunity to demonstrate my trustworthiness, I'll take it as a compliment someone as smart and careful as you has decided to accept me as safe on so little." His expression became gentle, very patient, and it was such a change Chenco almost felt lightheaded. "So it's clear—nothing about this is a setup to get you in bed or anything smelling like sex."

The damnedest part was every now and again Chenco *was* thinking about sex with Steve, in this distant, maybe-I'll-get-off-to-it kind of way. It was more humble pie than he cared for to hear the attraction wasn't reciprocated, but it was also a relief.

Chenco shook his head. "This is the most surreal conversation I've ever had."

Steve's whole goatee lifted in a grin. "It's probably the most *real* conversation you've had, especially about sex."

God, *that* statement was borderline arrogant. Bossy McBosserpants. Big old Dom, don't-you-fuck-with-me, I-run-the-room Steve Vance.

Except for the half a second in the car.

Even from a few feet away, Chenco could smell Steve, a subtle but intoxicating bouquet of leather and sweat. No more vulnerability now, not so much as a morsel. Chenco couldn't decide which he liked better. Bossy or not, this was hot, this *don't worry, I got the whole world* persona. He thought about the comment Steve had made about real conversations and tried to unpack it.

"Is that why you're a sadist? Because it gives you control of things?"

"I'm a sadist because it's who I am. It's as impossible to separate from my identity as being gay. Practicing BDSM gives me focus and structure, like being Caramela does for you, I'd imagine. In a world eager to reject people like me, BDSM gives my sadism a frame which not only works but makes me stronger. I may take the lifestyle more seriously than some, may extend it deeper into aspects of my life, but it helps me find myself, my center, my space, and it makes me a better person."

"You make it sound like a religion."

"For some of us, I think it is."

Chenco digested this. Unfortunately as he did so, his bladder reminded him it had been putting up with his bullshit since eight thirty. "This is the worst segue ever, but I have to pee."

Steve grinned, and Chenco decided he very much liked Steve's smiles. "Do you want some help, or are you explaining why you're about to run off?"

"No help, but could you stand outside the door and talk to me? I... Well, your voice is very soothing right now."

Steve nodded to the hall. "You lead. I'll follow."

CHAPTER FIVE

S TEVE LIKED CHENCO, which was fine. Except he
really *liked* Chenco, which wasn't so fine. Initially
he'd justified the attraction as a kind of do-over for
Gordy, yes, just as Jansen had accused. The problem
was Steve realized now the two men had nothing in
common except for life dealing them a shit hand.
Chenco was young only in the number of years he'd
been on the earth. In every other respect, the kid had
more than once made Steve feel foolish in the face of the
younger man's maturity. Something about being with
the boy kept ripping the floor out from underneath
him, and he didn't like it.

Except for those moments when he loved it.

"Do I have time to shower?" Chenco hung up his
dress and began to peel out of his compression garments. He paused with his hand on the edge of his
underwear. "Is it okay if I get undressed in front of
you?"

"I don't mind, if you don't," Steve told him. "And
yes, you have time for a shower."

"Have you heard from the others? Are they back at
your place? Is Randy okay?"

Steve nodded. He'd exchanged several texts with both Sam and Randy. "Their greatest struggle is Randy wanting weed for the pain, and Sam doesn't want him to have it. Oh, which reminds me. Randy says he's got your shoes, and they're fine. In fact, the dice heels made him laugh. If you want to shove one up his ass, he says he can take it."

Chenco continued to fight the elastic. "I stab him and he makes a joke?"

"That would be Randy." The elastic had rolled down enough to expose the jutting bones of Chenco's slender hips. "I think he almost means it. It's as I said, he feels bad he misread you."

"Why is it such a big deal to him?"

The dark flesh of Chenco's groin appeared—no hair, completely shaved. Steve's cock took notice. "He's a poker player. Professional. Reading people is, in every way, how he survives."

Chenco slid the underwear down to his thighs, and his cock sprang free, soft and springy and uncut, flopping twice before resting against low-hung, heavy balls, wrinkled from their confinement. "Well, tell him it's fine. I'm not stabbing him again, nor am I going anywhere near his ass, and I apologize for doing it at all. They aren't my shoes, so it's good they're not broken." Chenco caught Steve examining his body and paused. "I thought you said no sexy times." When Steve said nothing, he added, "You're watching my cock, and your package says you have something for me."

"I'm watching your cock because you're sexy and

hot and I like cocks. Being interested doesn't mean I'm going to do anything about it."

"So if I told you I was interested, there'd still be no sex?"

"Not tonight, no."

He couldn't tell if Chenco was annoyed, hurt, or simply confused. "Not even a quick one-off to relieve tension?"

"I take sex very seriously. I don't enter into it lightly."

"Me either." This made Chenco give him a wry smile. "Funny how it's probably why I almost feel like breaking my rule with you."

Steve was attracted too, so he figured they might as well lay it all on the table. "I need you to remember I'm a sadist."

Chenco stepped out of his compression underwear and reached into a drawer for a pair of briefs. "So when you have sex, there's pain? For the person you're having sex with?"

Nodding, Steve watched Chenco as he fell silent, clearly thinking hard as he climbed into jeans and a T-shirt.

"What does it mean, exactly? Sex with pain? I mean, I know a little of the lifestyle through Booker and a couple other friends, but you don't seem like you play the same as he and Trist."

"It means I take pleasure in inflicting pain on my partner while engaging in intercourse. Holding him down. Bites. Pinches. I enjoy flogging a great deal, but I love edge play and needles best of all. Mostly what I love, more than anything, is to fuck someone while he cries because of pain I've given him."

Chenco studied Steve critically. "I don't understand. I'm trying, but it frankly sounds scary and mean."

Steve appreciated the honesty. "Sex with pain can be scary—and I love that part. It's terrifying for someone to turn so much trust over to you. They give it to me, believing I can take them to a high they need so desperately but cannot find on their own. Giving that to someone is a gift I take seriously. It's power and control and terrible, crushing responsibility. It's chaos and danger, and I'm allowed to hold it in my hand and make it something beautiful."

Chenco had been putting on his socks when Steve started, but stopped and sat on a bench, listening. "Wow. I'm not sure it's for me, but you definitely make it sound good." Steve meant to shield his thoughts so Chenco couldn't read them, but Chenco gave Steve a little glare as he finished with his sock. "*You* think it's for me."

"I think you shouldn't ever dismiss something entirely without exploring it first."

Now Chenco looked triumphant, like he'd caught Steve on a technicality. "You said no sex. So I can't try it, not yet."

"And I told you BDSM isn't necessarily about sex. You want to test the waters, we can start right now."

Chenco startled, his gaze darting to Steve's hands. "I don't want to be tied up."

"I'm not talking about tying you up."

Chenco crossed his arms over his chest, hunching his shoulders. "Then what *are* you talking about? Tell me what you'd want to do. I'm not saying we're doing anything, now or ever, but I'll tell you one thing right now—I *hate* surprises, especially in bed. It's why I don't have sex often. Every time I let go, somebody fucks me over."

"BDSM isn't about surprises. In the lifestyle, *consent* is king. Even if play is about taking away control, none of it happens until the submissive *gives* the control up. What it can do, though, is offer a safe place to escape, to be. For example, if we were in a D/s relationship, after a night like tonight I'd ask you to do a scene with me, as I'd figure you needed it."

Chenco's eyes widened. "On a night like *tonight* you'd want to do BDSM?"

"I said if we were in a relationship, but we aren't."

"Except you said you could show me right now."

Fuck. This time he *was* caught on a technicality. Steve tried to hide his unease with an arched eyebrow.

Chenco tucked those arms tighter around him. "Fine. Then tell me what you'd have me do if we were in a D/s thing."

"D stands for Dom, and s for sub. Dominant and submissive." He gestured to the floor. "First thing I'd have you do if you were my sub is have you kneel in position. You'd go to your knees and put your hands behind your back, one wrist clasped inside your other palm. That alone would do a lot for you. Going to your knees for me would mean you were giving up control, so part of your brain would already be letting go."

"Weird, how BDSM is about safety." Chenco paused and corrected himself. "I mean, not weird. Good. Not what I thought, though."

Steve cocked a wry smile. "Most people think it's about tying somebody up and getting them off. Probably the same way people think drag is about putting on a dress."

Chenco laughed. "Point taken. So what would be next?"

"Next I'd let you sit there a bit, enjoying yourself. Everything after would be specific to you and our relationship, which is theoretical at this point." Steve rubbed his beard a minute before continuing. "I'd say first I'd walk some circles around you, not touching you, but letting you know I was there. This would narrow your focus to me, shutting out the rest of the world."

Chenco's stance had relaxed a great deal as Steve spoke, and while his arms were still folded in front of him, they'd slipped to something only casually self-protective. "That sounds kind of nice."

"Contrary to what you might be thinking, that's the entire point." Steve leaned over on his knees, his body posture open and casual—except the look on Chenco's face was doing him in. "I'd tell you that you were a good boy. If it were the kind of relationship we had, I'd assign you a punishment for what you did to Randy. I can tell it's eating at you, what happened at the club, and you're punishing yourself. If we were in a relationship, I'd want those sorts of things to fall to me."

Now Chenco looked intrigued. "Punish me how?"

"It'd depend on what I'd found out you liked. You're thinking spanks or flogging, but if you *enjoyed* such activities, it wouldn't be a punishment. You need to face what you did but also process it. You'd feel easier knowing I'd taken the responsibility from you, reminding you it wasn't yours to worry about anymore."

Chenco's body posture was fully relaxed now, and he looked still slightly wary, but mostly hungry. "That…sounds good actually."

"I could do it, if you'd trust me to. But it's okay if you don't."

Shit. This time Steve had pulled the rug out from under his own feet. What the fuck was he offering this for?

To make things worse, Chenco looked *ravenous* now. "I… Maybe. Can I think about it?"

"Of course." Steve cleared his throat.

"What else would you do? Right now, if we were in a relationship?"

Goddamn if he wasn't half under this kid. This sweet, smart young man who was just finding out he liked pain. "I'd want things to be all about you, about putting you at ease, making you feel good. I wouldn't use pain right now. This is about comfort. Not sex, even if that was part of our BDSM relationship."

"You mean some people have BDSM relationships without sex?"

"Yes. More than you probably think. But as I said, this isn't about sex. I'd praise you, remind you of your punishment, and then…" He scratched his beard. "Then I think I'd pull up my chair and pet you."

"*Pet?*"

"Yeah." Steve mimed stroking a submissive's hair, as if the sub knelt between his legs. "Pet. Bad as you got shaken up, I'd let you lean on my thigh, nice and close, my legs surrounding you. Making your world narrow for as long as you needed. Something tells me there hasn't been a lot of touch in your life for a while, and never anything so safe and simple with another man."

Chenco stiffened, the observation clearly hitting close to home. "I'd just sit there? Leaning on you?"

Steve could see it in his head, so beautiful it made him ache. "While I stroked your hair and said you were a good, smart, strong boy. Yeah. That's what I'd do."

Chenco stared at him a few seconds. "Could we…could we do it now?"

No, the last sane part of Steve whispered, but sanity died under Chenco's dark, beautiful gaze. Steve smiled, the rug not only pulled out from under him but rolled up and put away. "Absolutely."

Chenco hadn't planned on asking Steve to pet him, and knowing it was going to happen freaked him out. A lot. It also made him shake, he wanted it so much. Which freaked him out more. He wanted *this*? With this guy he'd known for ten minutes? What the *fuck*?

Except yeah, he really did.

If Steve knew how nervous Chenco was, he didn't let it show. Chenco worried he'd shout "on your knees" or something and wreck it, but Steve simply kept watching Chenco, like he had all the time in the world. When he finally spoke, his voice was so gentle it made Chenco ache.

"Nothing will happen which we didn't discuss. Is there something, though, you'd rather not do?"

Chenco had no idea he wanted any of it to happen. Only one thing stood out as a potential danger zone. "What about the punishment part?"

"I don't know you well enough to give you a punishment yet. But if you want me to take it over for you, if you trust me to read you and judge correctly, then yes, I'll take the responsibility for it and get back to you when I figure it out."

Never, not in a thousand years, would Chenco have thought he wanted someone to punish him, but holy shit, he did. It tore him up inside knowing maybe his brother wasn't the monster but rather the family he'd dreamed of, *and Caramela had slammed her stiletto into the chest of his brother's best friend.* If Steve could make the heavy regret and guilt go away? God, yes. Except… "Is it stupid of me to say yes when I barely know you, agreeing only because I really want to?"

There it was again, the vulnerability. Steve faltered, a weird look of guilt and unsteadiness all over his face. Which made no damn sense. Chenco was the one potentially getting the scolding or whatever. As he had before, Steve recovered quickly, going back into *ice, ice baby* mode. But Chenco couldn't unsee the moment when Steve, counter to his big, bad persona, had not been entirely in control.

"That's something only you can answer," Steve said at last.

Nice evasion, but Chenco truly needed this sorted out. "But what would you do, if you punished me? Let's say I said yes and you'd had time to think about it. What's a for-instance?" Chenco bit his lip. "I hope you get I don't like to be embarrassed, especially in front of other people. I mean, would Mitch and those guys know about it?"

"We'd negotiate whether or not it was public or private. If the others did know about it, I can promise you none of them would view a punishment as something you should be embarrassed about." Steve tilted his head. "Are you asking me, Chenco, to punish you for putting a heel through Randy's shoulder? Even though it was Caramela who did it?"

Tricky question. "Well, she's me. And she did it to protect me. But honestly, she's mostly the front I use to be brave enough to do the things I'd like to do. So I had her wig on and her makeup, and they were her shoes, but I…" He stopped, getting lost. "I don't know actually. Maybe it's not as simple as it felt, asking for this."

"If I decide Caramela needs to take the punishment, will she honor my decision?"

Chenco bit his lip as he stared at the floor, as if maybe the answer was in the carpet. "Well…no."

"But you want the punishment? You feel it's yours to take on?"

Did he? "Maybe." He lifted his gaze. "Okay, forget the punishment. Right now I'd like to stick with the petting thing. It sounds nice. And I'd rather nobody else knew about it for now. Is that okay?"

The amount of approval coming from Steve's expression made Chenco feel like jelly. No more of the weird indecision, the guilt or vulnerability or whatever it was, only Chenco feeling so safe. Steve smiled then said in the same gentle voice, but this time with a thread of command, "Get on your knees, Chenco."

Chenco went to the floor.

He did his best to take up the pose Steve had described, back straight, knees slightly apart, hands clasped behind his back. He kept his chin up, trying not to seem defiant but still attentive. Kind of a kneeling parade rest. He watched Steve, wary but mostly wondering if he'd done it right.

Steve smiled. "Very good. Now we'll see to your pleasure."

My pleasure. The words rolled around in Chenco's head, a delicious, forbidden treat Steve held out to him, promising to spoonfeed it into his mouth. Chenco held himself still, but it was hard because he was as excited as Lincoln's little Chihuahua when he knew he was about to get canned food.

"You were very good tonight, boy." Steve's voice was so soft, but so sure. Chenco closed his eyes and listened to the footfalls, to the sweet sound of Steve's praise. "You were so nervous, and we really upset you by showing up unannounced, but you didn't let us distract you from your show. You were amazing, beautiful. You have such good instincts, Chenco. You and Caramela both."

Steve stopped walking, and he didn't say anything until Chenco opened his eyes and looked up at him. When he caught Steve staring back, quiet but reproachful, Chenco realized he wasn't supposed to shut his eyes.

"I'm sorry. Sir," he added belatedly, feeling awkward with the honorific.

"I want your eyes open so I know you're listening. Also I didn't give you permission to close them. The point of submitting, Chenco, is to let go. The involuntary actions you get to keep. Everything else? Those are mine. Give it *all* up. To me."

Give it all up. Was that okay to do? He was distracted from having to ask by a logistical issue—he had no idea what he was supposed to look at with his eyes open. When Steve paced the part of the circle in front of him, Chenco knew what to do, but once Steve disappeared behind him, Chenco felt a little flaily.

"Watch me when you can, and when you can't, turn your head back to anticipate me. You're a smart boy. You'll figure out how to time it so you get your head turned in time for me to appear."

Actually, now as he tried this suggestion, it wasn't hard at all. But… "Steve—sir, I told you before. I'm twenty-four. I'm not a boy."

Steve laughed, a soft, easy sound. "Even if you were

fifty-five, tonight I'd call you boy. It's not about your age. It's your role. Being a man is tough work. Being a boy is something we all miss, and some of us never got it. Right now you get to be a boy. You can be tired, you can be petulant, you can be scared. It doesn't matter. I'm your man right now, the only one you need. You can lay it all down and be a boy. In fact, I *require* you to."

Chenco let out a breath from the bottom of his soul. Steve caught his eye and smiled as if to say, *I told you so.*

As he continued his slow walk, Steve resumed his litany of praise. Chenco listened, basking in the accolades, marveling at how much attention Steve had paid to even the little things he did. Nobody had ever done anything like that for him, ever. Chenco never wanted it to end, but eventually it did—Steve went back to his chair and spread his legs over the edges, creating a space between them.

Chenco stared at the gap, never so desperate to be anywhere in his life. He didn't go, though, just stared at the vee until Steve said, "Come here, Chenco. Crawl to me on your hands and knees, then sit right between my legs so I can pet you."

Crawl. Chenco did it, swatting away a flicker of resistance which said this was humiliating. No, it was the easiest way to get there. Plus, he decided, it felt good. A boy wouldn't feel bad about crawling. A boy would be happy to crawl because nobody would have told him it was bad. So Chenco crawled, slowly at first, then faster, eager to get to the place he longed to be.

Steve had him sit on his feet, knees tucked under the chair so Chenco's head was parallel to Steve's knees. His eyes fell right on Steve's crotch, which was a happy bulge in his jeans. Chenco could smell him—faint, but it was a nice whiff of dick all the same. Jesus. How long had it been since he had a mouthful of cock? Way, way too long. Except, *shit*, he'd taken it off the menu.

Steve chuckled. "No, no meat for you tonight. Are you ready, baby? Are you ready for me to pet you, good boy?"

A whimper escaped Chenco's throat as he nodded. "Yes. Please, sir."

Steve beamed at him. "Such a good boy. Such a good, good boy."

His hand came down gently into Chenco's hair.

The touch was so soft, so delicious, Chenco's eyes fell closed until he had enough wits to open them. He looked up at Steve, unnerved to do so at first, but once he locked in to the other man's gaze, he couldn't look anywhere else.

Strong. His whole world reduced, this time to the feel of those heavy, thick fingers working through his wavy black locks, teasing them out of the matting they'd endured under the nylon cap. Sometimes Steve massaged his head, sometimes he teased the very tips of his hair. Every single part of it was glorious.

"Such sensual hair you have. So soft."

Chenco opened his mouth to explain it was the cap, because all the sweat from performing was like a hot oil bath, but Steve put a finger to his lips, silencing him.

"Hush. This isn't the time for talking, boy."

He resumed his massage, sliding his fingers along the sides near Chenco's ears. Chenco had to work to keep his eyes from rolling back in his head. Where was he supposed to look now? His gaze kept defaulting to Steve's crotch, which wasn't a bad view at all, but he wondered if he should look up, maybe, meet his eyes?

All of a sudden the truth of what he was doing hit him, how he knelt between a stranger's legs, letting him tell him to be quiet, to crawl—

Steve kept petting, shushing him now as if he were a baby fussing. "Hush. It's fine, Chenco. This isn't a trick to get you to relax so I can shove my cock down your throat. So far it's been exactly what I said would happen, yes? There's only one more step in this dance, and you know what it is. Your head resting on my thigh. If you want to end the scene now, you can. Don't, though, think I'm playing you. I haven't lied to you. I haven't once manipulated you into anything. You chose this. You asked to submit to me. There's nothing in submission to fear or be ashamed of. No matter what anybody says."

Chenco felt like crying, which made him even more panicked. "You said sex had to be pain with you. So where's the pain?"

He realized too late he'd talked, which was against the rules, but they seemed to be in some kind of break because Steve didn't blink. "I've told you several times we aren't having sex tonight, yet you keep bringing it up. Are you telling me, Chenco, your experience has made you this jaded? You believe only someone who wants sex from you would offer you praise and gentle touch, that you absolutely cannot believe me when I say it's all I'm offering?"

Chenco couldn't answer. If he so much as opened his mouth, he'd lose it. He could only stare at Steve, hollowed out and raw, so cold, so ashamed he thought he would die. He swallowed over and over and over, trying to push the feeling down, but it overflowed inside him, and he couldn't make it go away.

Steve reached out to Chenco, his face full of sorrow, and he stroked Chenco's cheek. "Oh, baby. Oh, sweet baby, come here, right now."

A few tears leaked out of Chenco's eyes as his head lowered to Steve's jean-clad thigh. This was all, though—he stayed rigid for a few seconds, still guarding, but as Steve's heavy hand came back to his hair, he allowed himself to let go slowly. The touch was so sweet, like before, except now he could *really* smell cock, and he had his head against the sexiest pillow in the world…and nothing else was going to happen. He got to sit here, resting, enjoying.

This was actually happening.

"Hush." Steve's hand grazed his ear, trailing the outside of the fleshy curve. "You may shut your eyes, boy. Shut your eyes and know you're safe. Rest. Rest, let everything else go, and accept this safe space, this pleasure of being petted."

Chenco shut his eyes, relaxing into the touch, letting his worries, his fears, his anxieties flow out with each stroke of Steve's hand. Part of him still worried this wasn't smart, wasn't safe, but eventually this concern died down too, lulled to sleep by the lure of a master's fingers. Pulling a blanket over his worry, Chenco sank deeper into his trance and willed himself to memorize every single moment.

STEVE STARED DOWN at Chenco's pretty, serene face and thought, *You're in a world of trouble, Vance.*

The boy was still under, which turned Steve on all the way to the back of his balls. Stroking Chenco's hair a little more, he asked, "How are you feeling?"

The sweet, sleepy smile made Steve's whole body hum. "Good. Really good. Thank you." He started to drift off, but then his eyes snapped open as he added, "Sir."

Jesus, he was goddamned *precious.* Steve stroked the dark, silky hair, never wanting to let it out of his fingers. "I never gave you protocol on how to address me, and I've been sloppy about starting and ending the scene." Like now, ending it but not really ending it. He ran his fingers along Chenco's temple. "My apologies."

"I don't have any complaints." Chenco blinked slowly, trying to come out from under, but Steve was being a real prick, not letting up on the petting, therefore keeping him nicely in place. "Are we…done?"

With a sigh, Steve rested his hand on Chenco's shoulder. "We need to be. You still haven't eaten, and we have to drive all the way to my place on the far side of McAllen. Unless you want to put meeting your brother off until tomorrow?"

"No. I want to be introduced to Mitch properly, to-night." Chenco sat up, but he swayed, drifting to brush Steve's leg a couple times. He smiled, still easy and light. "Thank you. That was amazing. I won't ever forget it."

Steve lifted an eyebrow and ran his thumb along Chenco's cheek. Butter-soft, it was the color of Jansen's beloved Bailey's. "Seemed to me you enjoyed our scene." He ran his knuckles up to Chenco's temple, loving the way those long, dark lashes drifted closed at the sensation before popping open to obediently hold his gaze. *So. Fucking. Perfect.* "I did too. I think we should have another one some time."

God, Steve could drown in those soulful, hopeful brown eyes. Chenco didn't say anything right away, though he opened and closed his mouth several times before speaking. "Okay—I know you got upset before when I mentioned this, but…if we kept doing this, there *would* be sex eventually, right?"

Mayday. Mayday. "If it was something we both wanted, yes. But as I said, it's not required."

Also, it's been over five years since I've been in a rela-tionship of any kind, so this might not be a good idea full stop.

Chenco looked at him as if he'd grown a second head. "You'd seriously have a relationship with me without sex *or* pain?"

Leaning forward, Steve pinned Chenco still with his gaze. "BDSM, boy, is *not* about sex. Neither is pain an absolute requirement." He stroked his boy's jaw, distracted by the beautiful line of it. "Patience. There's not a damn thing wrong with taking our time."

He rose, offering Chenco his hands and helping him to his feet, steadying him as he wobbled. Chenco blinked, trying to come out of his trance. "I think I need to eat something."

"You went under pretty deep, which is your biggest issue right now, but yes, I'd like you to eat. Did you decide to skip your shower?"

Chenco looked down at himself as if surprised to see the clothes there. "Oh." He touched his hair, which was a little wild from being teased in Steve's fingers. Steve had to check an urge to delve in there.

Stop. Steve cleared his throat. "I don't think it matters either way, so if you want to take one still, I'll wait."

It made Steve sad to watch the last dregs of Chenco's serene bliss fall away, his usual worries returning, however muted. "I think I'm fine. Anyway, I'd rather eat." He let go of Steve, wobbling a second before heading for the door.

Steve followed Chenco down the hall, tracking him carefully to make sure his boy truly had his feet back. When Chenco headed to the kitchen and opened the fridge, Steve frowned. "I can take you through a drive-through, if you don't want the trouble."

Chenco's soft laugh rolled inside Steve and nestled in his belly. "I don't do fast food unless I'm very desperate." He pulled out a stack of sealed containers, each one full of vegetables. "My money goes to two places:

drag and food. I suffer in neither department. Every-where else, I'm completely impoverished."

It was an impressive array of high-quality food. "Are you vegan?"

"No, but I eat veg a lot. I'll occasionally do a bit of flesh, but only chicken and I keep it to a minimum. I simply find that when I eat the way I do, I have more energy, more focus, and my skin and hair are a lot better." He paused with a hummus-laden piece of cauliflower halfway to his mouth. "Well, the hair part isn't such a big deal, but Caramela will have nothing but healthy skin."

This, right here, this was the problem—Steve loved discipline in all its forms, and to see Chenco applying it so naturally to himself drew Steve in on a fishing line. He longed to compliment Chenco daily, to tell him he was good, to stroke him and preen him and make him slide into pleasure, to facilitate his natural self-discipline and make it stronger.

"Take all the time you need to eat," he said instead.

Chenco did, giving his full attention to the food, and after declining an offer to share, Steve watched him stuff himself with the vegetables and the hummus, finishing up with what appeared to be homemade nut milk of some kind. Chenco cleaned up after himself too, not only putting away all the food in tidy stacks, but also washing his plate and cup in the sink.

The entire trailer, in fact, was radically transformed from the last time Steve had seen it. Not a whiff of old smoke lingered, and every bit of Cooper's clutter and junk had been eradicated, replaced only with simple, serviceable, and above all clean markers of Chenco's residence. Chenco took pride in his home, humble as it was.

Goddamn it, but it made Steve a little hard.

As they drove back into McAllen, he tried to figure out what about Chenco had snagged him. Steve had always admired strength, and Chenco had serious steel. The boy wasn't just tough. He was tooled leather, yielding and bending while enduring. Some of Steve's admiration came from the way he could tell his dominance had made something bloom inside Chenco, something which had lain dormant—it massaged his ego to think he'd been the one to bring it out, and not another man.

He passed the cannery as he acknowledged this, and the building cast a shadow over his thoughts. There was a good reason for his celibacy and his solitude. Jansen and the others called him Monk as a joke, but for Steve, his removal was serious. Important. He had, quite firmly, closed this door.

Steve found he'd consider opening it for Chenco.

Nothing was settled yet, he reminded himself as he turned down the road to the ranch. Chenco had a lot of misgivings, and even handled patiently, those might never be eased. Yet despite this knowledge, Steve knew the fallout from Chenco turning out to be Cooper's secret son was nothing on what was going to go down between the two of them.

He was afraid, very afraid.

The fear, and the promise of what might lie behind it, tasted so, so good.

CHAPTER SIX

I NSTEAD OF LIVING in a development or in an older neighborhood as Chenco assumed, Steve lived on ranch property on the edge of town, a sprawling set of buildings separated from the road by a rusted metal gate. When they pulled up to the barrier, it was closed, but Steve pushed a few buttons on his smartphone and the hinges creaked open.

Chenco arched an eyebrow. "Nice."

"Thanks." Steve put the phone down on his thigh.

Glancing around the property, Chenco couldn't help notice it was a bit of a mess. Arid, unkempt land and sagging sheds surrounded them as they wound their way to the house. A few green ash and Texas olive trees stood like lonely sentries in the middle of fallow fields, but other than this, the ranch was a wasteland. "Was this an orchard?"

"Up until the freeze."

Chenco had heard of this, vaguely. "This the one in the '80s?"

Steve nodded. "There were two, actually. One in '83 and another in '89. They thought the first was the Big One, the hundred-year freeze as bad as the one in 1888.

Then came 1989 and made '83 look like a summer day. Killed everything and changed the economy of the valley forever." He gestured at the ruined land. "My parents were about done anyway, so they retired to South Padre and let me have the hacienda. We have an old cannery too down the road. Passed it on the way here."

Chenco tried to imagine the land as a thriving orchard, and it made him sad. "I was born in 1991. If Cooper were here, he'd tell me I brought the freeze because I'm a devil child."

"If you can control Arctic air masses, we'll hire you out." Steve shook his head. "Born in 1991. I was seventeen then. About to run off to school. A few years later I went to the Persian Gulf."

Chenco glanced at him. "Are you serious?"

"About being that old or in the Army?"

"Both."

"I was born in 1974. Joined the Army in 1991 and went off to keep the peace. Drove trucks mostly and dumped snakes out of my sleeping bag." He adjusted his wrist on the steering wheel. "Went back to college when I came home and learned computers. It's what I do now, that and selling scrap metal. Sometimes I fix bikes."

It was too bad they reached the house then— Chenco would have liked to hear more about Steve, or maybe even tell some of his own story. As soon as he saw the lights on above the front door, he remembered what he was in for, and all desire for small talk fled.

Steve pulled up alongside a big blue semi cab without a trailer and killed the engine. Before he opened the door, he turned to Chenco. "You still have the necklace?"

Chenco had it in his hand, in fact, and he looked down at it now. "You said this was Mitch's mother's?"

"Yeah. It was how Randy put the last pieces of the puzzle together. Mitch kept it in his room to remember her, and then one day it was gone. Cooper said he didn't take it, but Mitch always thought he had."

"Either he took it or Mitch forgot he'd hidden it in the bottom of a drawer in Cooper's bedroom."

Steve looked grim. "Such a fuck. I hope he's on a fat spit about now."

"I hope he's trapped in the skankiest gay club in history." Chenco let out a breath and closed his hand over the necklace. "Okay. So I'll give this to Mitch and hope it helps us start off on a better footing."

"From what I understand, it'll win Mitch and Sam both, and I already told you Randy's cool." He put a hand on Chenco's shoulder. "You ready?"

Hell no. "Sure. Let's go."

The house was bigger than Chenco's stepfather's, which was really saying something. It was old, though, a true hacienda with sprawling additions and adobe and a tiled roof and fancy windows. Like the rest of the ranch, it was run-down, but it wasn't as decrepit as the rest of the property. Clearly someone had put effort into keeping things put together as much as possible, but there was no escaping the overbearing sense of weariness the house carried.

The porch light was on, illuminating a rounded door. Light pooled from the first-floor windows, and occasionally shadows moved across them.

I'm about to meet my brother. Chenco's gut clenched.

Steve put a hand at his elbow and led him through the door.

The foyer was brightly lit by an ancient, beautiful chandelier, and it spilled open into a living room full of white leather furniture over heavy terra-cotta tile. Though old and showing wear, the furnishings were clearly high quality. In its day, this had been the show-place.

The room was full of plants and light—and people. Randy sat in the corner of a long couch, Sam beside him in caretaker mode. Mitch Tedsoe stood off to the side in the archway to a formal dining room.

He looked like a younger, healthier Cooper, except when Mitch saw Chenco enter the room, the associa-tions with his father ended. Mitch looked tired, wary…and hopeful. Reminding himself of Steve's stories about how Mitch had changed since those journals, and arming himself with what courage he could muster, Chenco crossed the room to his brother and held out his hand.

"I heard this belongs to you."

The fear his brother might be anything like Cooper evaporated as Chenco watched Mitch with his mother's necklace. It was exactly as Steve said—the grown man, who couldn't be a whole lot younger than Steve, stared down at the necklace with the eyes of a young boy. A wounded young boy, and Chenco tried to imagine what fun Cooper must have had with him. Nothing about this man before him matched the menace Cooper had promised Chenco would find in his elder brother, nor the hate and violence of those journals.

Once again Cooper had given him nothing but lies.

Still, it was harder than it should have been to put away his fear and face the man he'd been conditioned for so long to regard as an enemy. Not until Steve posted himself like a sentry at the wall near the fireplace was Chenco able to speak, and as he did his gaze kept flicking back to Vance.

"I'm Chenco," he said.

Mitch nodded gruffly, tucking his thumbs in his jean pockets. "I'm Mitch. Your…older brother. I guess."

He seemed about as stunned as Chenco felt. Their awkward silence made Chenco uneasy though, so he kept talking. "Chenco is short for Crescencio. My last name is Ortiz, but only because my mother made my stepfather adopt me legally. On my birth certificate it originally said Tedsoe, as my mother lived in hope for a long time." Chenco moved the necklace closer. "Here. I only took it because it was pretty and I had a feeling it belonged to someone who had hurt Cooper, which made whoever it was my hero. It should be yours now."

Mitch handled the trefoil as if it might dissolve at a touch. "It was my mom's. Her great-grandmother gave it to her. It came from Ireland." He drew a breath, and the next part sounded as if it came from the bottom of his gut. "When I was little and got scared because Dad hit her, she'd let me hold it."

God, Chenco wished he could bring Cooper back to life so he could kill him. "Where is she now, your mom?"

"Houston. Remarried, though I don't think she stepped up much."

Mom was clearly a touchy subject, so Chenco let it go. Trouble was, he didn't know what they were supposed to talk about now. "So. Anyway. It's nice to meet you. Sorry for stabbing your friend."

Mitch smiled. "Don't worry about it." He stared at the necklace for another minute, then tucked it in his pocket and squared his shoulders. "Right. I suppose we should do a proper introduction." He pointed at the couch. "You met Randy, and this is my husband, Sam."

Sam had been watching them, but at the mention of his name he came over and held out a hand to Chenco. "Hi. Nice to meet you."

Chenco accepted his hand, trying to decide how angry Sam was. Not as bad as he'd feared, which was good. He put forth his best effort at making things better. "It's nice to meet you. Sorry about that earlier. I learned to be wary of anything connected to Cooper, and I wasn't sure meeting my older brother would be wise." He turned to Mitch and shook his head. "It's creepy how much you look like him."

Mitch reached into the breast pocket of his shirt, withdrawing a beat-up pack of Winstons and a lighter.

He lit up a cigarette as he answered. "I get that a lot."

Chenco wondered if he should mention the journals, but instinct told him no, not just yet. Part of him worried speaking of them would bring the scary kid who'd penned the scree back to life. Instead he turned to Sam. "Is Randy going to be okay?"

Sam nodded, his frowning gaze lingering on his husband's cigarette. "It's literally only a flesh wound. It wasn't deep enough to need stitches, and I cleaned it out and put some dressing on. He'll bitch about it for a few days, but he'll be fine." He smiled a half-smile. "I'm an RN, so I know what I'm doing. He'll be fine."

Chenco glanced over at the couch. Randy looked a little pale, but otherwise he was much the same as he'd been the other two times they'd met—eagle-eyed and dangerous. He didn't smile as he met Chenco's gaze, though. If anything, he seemed guilty. "I'm very sorry. It just threw me when I put it all together. Plus *you* look like him too, you know."

Chenco wrinkled his nose. "I do?"

Randy nodded. "It's not so much your appearance as some of your gestures. They reminded me of Mitch and Cooper both. When I figured it out, I was so surprised I couldn't stop my mouth." He grimaced. "But knowing Cooper, I should have been more delicate about it."

"It's okay," Chenco said, and he meant it.

It was fine, he decided, being here. It still felt odd to trust strangers so fast, but…well, the same instincts had initially told him this was a bad plan. Now they switched their allegiances to sticking around, especially as long as Steve Vance was in the picture. He wasn't sure if this meant his instincts were seriously fucked or if things were okay.

It occurred to him that outside of a few texts, Booker had pretty much abandoned Caramela and Chenco both. The realization hurt—maybe Chenco was safe, but shouldn't his friend have followed up a little better? He'd expected Booker to be here, supporting him, but he wasn't. Probably he'd run home to Trist because he was upset.

What about me? You left me to strangers, to let them comfort me? And yet you ask me to surrender control of my career to you?

Chenco stilled himself, turning away into a quiet corner, pulling himself to center. It didn't work, though, not as well as it should have.

He felt a hand on his arm, and the sweet, perfect memory of being on his knees came to him, making him okay.

"Chenco?"

Chenco opened his eyes, smiling up at his host. "I'm fine."

Turning around, he took in the living room full of newfound family, then joined them.

THEY ENDED UP out on the patio. Mitch stoked the chimenea, Randy found the extension cord for the twinkle lights, and Steve passed around bottles of

Bohemia. Sam declined but accepted an offer of a margarita. Chenco only wanted water, though when he heard they had San Pellegrino, he gladly took one instead.

Steve hung back, watching and listening as the half-brothers got to know one another.

"My mom is illegal," Chenco began, when asked to tell his story of how he ended up living with Cooper. "She came over with her first husband in the mid-eighties because he had some big plan about making it in America. They'd been middle class in Saltillo—she worked at a bank and had a woman clean her house once a month. In the valley, she was the one cleaning houses and being spit on for being an immigrant. It broke her heart. One night she ended up at a bar, a handsome American flirted with her, and I happened. She had it all fixed in her head, I think, how she'd fallen in love and the guy would rescue her like a prince. It was Cooper, and he wasn't the saving type. She came to him when she was pregnant, and he called her a dirty whore and told her he'd kill her if she came near his wife."

"Sounds like the old man, all right," Randy said into the mouth of his beer bottle.

Chenco nodded, a curt acknowledgment. "It kind of worked out, though. She left her first husband in case I didn't come out brown enough. He's a first-class dick, so she was better off. She hoped for a few years, sending Cooper pictures of his baby boy, but it never came to anything. She was on her own, and it was bad, but then she met my stepdad."

When Chenco paused to take a drink, Steve hated the look of loss that crossed Chenco's face.

Clearing his throat, Chenco continued. "He owns a car dealership, and he has a big heart. I grew up in a nice house in Edinburg. I have a little sister and a baby brother, and we went to good schools, but Mom never let us learn Spanish. I always thought it was weird, having this crazy Mexican name to honor some grand-father I never met. But she named me before she decided I was going to be the one to make it, to be the big American star. I'd be a doctor, she said. I had everything I could want." He smiled sadly at his bottle of Pellegrino, running his fingernail over the label. "Everything except a trunk full of dresses and heels."

"So what happened?" Sam asked.

"What happened is she caught me in her makeup one too many times. I was in Catholic school, so they had me talk to the priests and nuns a lot. I think she could have handled the gay okay, but I was so fixated on the dresses, she flipped out. I can't understand her Spanish so well, but she'd be on the phone to her best friend and cry about how she was afraid I was going to get a sex change. Didn't matter that I told her I wasn't. All she saw was she'd given me everything in the world, and I was throwing it in her face."

Randy's smile was sly. "That's the problem with freedom. People tend to do whatever they want with it."

Chenco shrugged. "Basically I was a bit of a mess when I was eighteen. She told me if I wanted my college money and a place to live, I had to date a girl and submit to my stepdad inspecting my life, making sure I wasn't hiding any dresses or anything. I said no way, so she kicked me out, and I had to regroup fast. I thought, I'm going to find my father. I bet *he'll* love me for who I am."

"Shit," Mitch murmured.

"Pretty much," Chenco agreed. "Took me three months to convince him he was my dad, and this only after I stole a beer bottle and money enough for a DNA test. I don't know what I thought this was going to prove—like he'd all of a sudden have a personality transplant, but it kind of worked out in the end. Part of it was he was plenty sick then already. He'd had his first stroke, and he couldn't keep himself together. I needed somewhere to stay, and I was a little wild in the head over making it work. I kept telling him he owed me, and eventually I realized he couldn't walk well enough to throw me out of the house and wasn't strong enough to beat me, not badly. So I moved in."

Chenco paused to wipe his mouth, as if the gesture would take the dark memories away. "He swore at me every day, and I barricaded my door at night because I never quite trusted him not to fuck me up. He told me about you, Mitch, but he promised you'd come back someday and kick the shit out of me, which was why I was so nervous after I saw you at the funeral. That and—" Chenco cut himself off and glanced at Steve.

Steve nodded. This wouldn't be comfortable for Mitch, but it was important for Chenco to have this cleared up.

"That and what?" Mitch prompted.

Chenco bit his lip as he met his brother's gaze. "I found your high school journals."

Mitch averted his gaze to the patio tile, his face burning with shame.

"Why would this be bad?" Sam nudged his husband. "What did you put in—? Oh. You told me about this. How you bullied the guy I remind you of. You wrote in a journal too?"

Mitch looked like he'd love to crawl under his chair. "I wasn't in a great place then." Forcing himself to lift his gaze, he turned his focus to his brother. "I'm sorry you found those. I didn't think they were still around." He grimaced. "I *know* I burned the ones where I finally figured everything out. Probably should have left them so you didn't think I was as big a dick as our dad."

"It's okay." Chenco didn't appear entirely at ease, but he seemed a lot less tense than he had when Steve had first tried to explain about Mitch. "I can't imagine it was easy growing up with him."

Instead of answering, Mitch gave a sharp snort of derision and drained the rest of his beer.

Sam stroked Mitch's arm before turning to Chenco. "Why did you stay? Did he not treat you as badly?"

Chenco shrugged. "I had nowhere else to go. He treated me like a dog, but I gave as good as I got. Threw all his shit right at him. I didn't do drag at first when I lived with him, but when he found out, he came at me with a knife. I got it away from him, said I'd call the cops, and he laughed. I locked up the knives after that. It was grim for a while, but then he had the second stroke, and he had to move to the home. He didn't want to, but he couldn't argue or say no anymore. I paid for it because he said I would get the trailer, which turned out to be a big lie. I got him back, though. When he lay there drooling, I'd tell him all about my hookups because he couldn't stop me. I made up shit, nasty crap just to watch him squirm."

Randy stared at Chenco in open admiration for several seconds. "Crescencio Ortiz, I want to fucking have your baby."

Chenco grinned, a wicked split of his lips. "Bend over and I'll give you one."

Everyone laughed, and Chenco eased now that his story was out. He'd found his real family, the people who he was just discovering, who Steve knew even after this one night would lay down just about anything to help. Steve watched the connection unfold, glad for his friends, glad for Chenco.

He tried to tamp down the part of himself that wanted to join in, find a place in the happy family too.

At three thirty they headed for bed, and when Steve suggested Chenco stay over, he didn't fight. Steve gave him the last open bedroom, ignoring the quiet invitation in Chenco's gaze, then went downstairs to clean up.

Randy was in the kitchen, nursing a whiskey neat. He raised it in toast as Steve sat beside him. "Job well done tonight, Monk. Though from the look of things, we might have to get you a new nickname soon."

Steve reached for his packet and papers and rolled a cigarette. No, he shouldn't be turning in his cowl. But Jansen was right. He wanted to.

Randy ran a finger around the rim of his glass. "Haven't discussed it with Mitch yet, but I'm figuring we'll be staying longer now than originally planned. This okay with you?"

With a nod, Steve tucked the packet into his pocket and lit up. "Stay as long as you need." *Bring Chenco over as much as you can.*

"Can't help but wonder where he's going to end up living. He doesn't sound like he's made any alternative plans yet. Looks to me he could use some help finding a place. Probably has friends here somewhere, but staying with them doesn't answer the long-term. Which somebody's got to consider, even if the kid won't."

This was his cue, Steve knew, to say it was okay for Chenco to stay at the hacienda, to offer to help Randy find a place for Chenco to live full-time. This was when he could confess he was interested in maybe Chenco staying here after the others had left, with or without the hanky-panky.

Steve reached for the bottle of Jamesons.

Randy pulled a clean glass from the cupboard behind him and nudged it over. "I checked the feeds earlier. Gordy was okay all night. Nobody ever went near the cannery, and he seems pretty calm. He disappeared for a while—probably foraging or something."

As ever, talk of Gordy brought an additional cloud down on Steve's already murky thoughts. *There's your reminder of why you should steer clear of this.* Except he knew he wasn't going to.

He was pretty sure Jansen knew it too.

"Thing I need to know," Randy said as Steve sipped, "is how tight I can play this. There's a clear path here, I figure. Kid wants to be a showgirl, and I live in Vegas. Sam and Mitch come through regular now, and with Chenco there it'd get even more frequent. Of course, there are other considerations, like the uptight mom in the burbs he wants to reconnect with." Randy picked up his whiskey glass and swirled the liquid around the bottom. "There are a lot of angles. Obviously what the kid wants is the most important thing. Thought I'd ask what you wanted me to do, though, before I lay too much pipe."

Steve took a long, slow drag, watching the smoke curl as he exhaled. *Tell him you don't care. Tell him you don't do this anymore, that he's a sweet kid, sexy as hell. He'd make a great masochist for somebody else, but you're too fucked up to get into this anymore.* The voice of caution rung in his head, but as Steve remembered the way Chenco had looked in the firelight, the way he'd smiled and blushed when his gaze had met Steve's, need edged out sense.

"Play loose," Steve said at last, swirling the whiskey against the sides of his glass. "For now."

CHAPTER SEVEN

CHENCO TRIED NOT to get attached to his brother and his friends as he didn't harbor any illusions Mitch and Sam would stay in the valley for long. Still, it was great to head over to Steve's place for a barbecue after work several nights a week, to sit around the fire pit and listen to everyone tell stories. Mitch had a million of them, having traveled all over the country and into parts of Canada, even to Mexico on a few occasions. Chenco's favorite tale was Mitch's attempt at the ice roads in Canada, just like the TV show—clearly this was a sore spot between husband and husband because Sam became grim and left the room for that one.

Sam, actually, was one of Chenco's favorite parts of gaining a brother. He was only two years older than Chenco, and in a room full of men who liked to remind Chenco of the jobs they'd held when he was in diapers, Sam was an instant ally. Mitch's husband also turned out to be a huge pop-music nut, which made him interested in Caramela's set list. When he found out how little Chenco used the internet, Sam immediately sat his brother-in-law down in front of a laptop and gave him an education in pop blogs and message boards. Chenco didn't get as much out of it as Sam wanted him to, but he enjoyed hanging out with his new friend.

Sam never hesitated to enthusiastically drag Chenco into activities or conversation, but everyone else measured Chenco, welcoming but not wanting to overstep. Randy teased Chenco, but not half as badly as he did anyone else. He cooked for Chenco too, and took his dietary fussiness as a personal challenge. Every time Chenco came over, there was a new Chenco-friendly item in the fridge or pantry.

Randy told stories as well, but mostly Randy watched. Sometimes Chenco felt like a bug in a jar around the man, and he wished he knew what Randy had decided about him.

They went out together too, all five of them, to dinner, to bars, and once to Heide's show at Lasers. It was fun, appearing at the club in a herd. Better still, Lincoln seemed to love them when they all hung out together after Heide's show had finished, though Steve hadn't been able to hang around, saying he had to check on something back at the house. The next day he and Chenco got together at Taco Palenque after Chenco finished work, and Lincoln didn't hold back.

"They're good for you. They respect you, they clearly want to support you and help you, and the big leather daddy is so hot for you he's about to blow up."

The comment made Chenco sit up straighter in the booth. "He is?"

Lincoln rolled his eyes and swirled his straw into his

soda. "Yes. The eye fucking is intense, and if someone is ever stupid enough to hit on you while he's in the room, they'll be swallowing their teeth."

Chenco chewed on this, wondering if it could be true. He'd about given up on the idea Steve would ever be interested in him. "He's into BDSM. Like, way."

Lincoln's expression became guarded. "This is a problem for you?"

What did the look on Lincoln's face mean? That BDSM was bad, or Chenco was a prude for not wanting to be involved? "I don't know. I mean, Booker talks it up all the time, but Booker's a crazy crackhead."

"Have you tried BDSM?" When Chenco turned as red as the booth table, Lincoln laughed. "Okay, that's a yes. Was it good, or you don't know this either?"

Chenco stared at his hands. "It was only a little, but it was…good. I just…I don't know. I didn't think I was that person."

"Well, if you are, make friends with him. If you have an S&M streak in you, it'll probably go back to dormancy about as well as your queen would."

This was, actually, exactly what Chenco was afraid of. "I have enough going on right now. I don't need sex games too."

"Sex games aren't work, honey, they're fun." Lincoln tapped his straw up and down in his drink and stared wistfully out the window. "Damn, but it's been a while since I indulged. There's nobody here I want to play with, though. Maybe I should go read *Mr. Benson*, jack off, and call it good."

Chenco's jaw fell slack. "*You* do BDSM?"

"I have, yeah. Not much lately, but I've dabbled. I'm not full on in the lifestyle, but I like nosing around on occasion. For some people it's very serious. I dated a guy who was way into it once, and he took me to meetings and the whole thing. I couldn't go that far, and this realization bummed him out, so we broke up."

Chenco could see this happening with him. "I think Steve is one of those guys, the ones who take it seriously."

Lincoln narrowed his gaze. "Okay, hold on. I've been thinking he looked familiar, and now I suspect I know why." Lincoln rubbed at his jaw as he stared down into his drink. "I'm amending my earlier suggestion you explore your masochistic side. Do it, but not with this guy."

Wait, *what*? "Why not? What do you know about Steve?"

"Not much, I'll admit. Let's just say I've seen him in action, and I've heard stories." Lincoln shook his head with a grimace. "Be careful. When I said I was going to go read *Mr. Benson*—this guy as far as I can tell thinks he *is* Mr. Benson."

"Who is Mr. Benson?"

Lincoln waved an impatient hand. "*Mr. Benson* is a novel whose title character is to the leather community what Edward Cullen is to a teenage girl or her middle-aged mother, except most leathermen would knife me for saying so. The book was big in the early '80s. I think it's reached cult status in part because it couldn't be written now, not with AIDS and the whole LGBT politically correct parade. Benson is the Dom of Doms, the leather daddy everybody wants. Even now you catch men wearing shirts saying they're 'looking for Mr. Benson'. Which is great, but let me tell you, Benson doesn't exist. Fantasy is fine for a novel, but when it walks and talks, something nasty is waiting underneath."

Now Chenco's stomach hurt. "You're telling me Steve is nasty?"

Lincoln hesitated before speaking. "He used to show up at the local leather bar with this guy all tricked out in puppy gear. The puppy gear wasn't the problem, mind you, and neither was their play. It was all clearly consensual. It's just…the dynamic the two of them had. You could smell the mess."

"Mess?" *Puppy gear?*

It was clear Lincoln struggled to find the right words, censoring what he truly wanted to say. "Sex games are supposed to be fun, like I said. Whatever he had going on with that guy wasn't fun. I always thought they were playing out some weird, old drama, like every aspect of their lives together was a fucked-up scene they never resolved. I doubt they were dating, though the looks the sub gave Steve, probably they had at one point, or he wished they would." Grimacing, Lincoln slouched in his seat. "You know what, forget it. This was years ago. Be careful is all. Don't rush into anything with him. If he's still into what I saw him doing to his puppy? It isn't for you. There are a million flavors to playing, a million guys to play with. If he doesn't feel right, pick somebody else."

Something hollowed inside of Chenco at these words, making him feel lost and sad. Which was stupid, because it wasn't like Steve had made so much as a move on him. "Well, no matter what you saw, he's not interested, and we haven't done anything." *Except he petted me once, and I think about it all the time.*

Lincoln cocked his head. "You blush like you *have* done something, and you said you had. It wasn't with him then?"

Flustered, Chenco felt his ears burn. "I'm done talking about this."

Lincoln didn't look happy. "Fine. You're a big boy, you can play with Mr. Benson if you want to. Just don't be shy about using your safe word."

"Safe word?"

Lincoln threw up his hands.

THE CONVERSATION WITH Lincoln about Steve echoed in Chenco's head for days, and quickly it felt as if his whole life were perched on a pivot. It was as if he had to move, had to decide, except he wasn't exactly sure what his options were. On one side was darkness and uncertainty—finding a new place to live, contacting Cuevas to tell him he still didn't have a will, wondering how many times the lawyer would tell him, "It's all right, take your time," and when Chenco would be told to load up the Nova and get out.

On the other side was laughter and light, the happiness filling Steve's house and the men Chenco had hesitantly begun to think of as his family. They never brought up the trailer, and they made no move to return to their regular lives, except for Steve who often disappeared into his office to work. They invited Chenco to stop by whenever he liked, and if he went more than a day without contact, one of them would invite him over. Several times he'd stayed the night.

What caught Chenco up were Lincoln's warnings. He'd gone to the library and looked up puppy play on the internet, which had been an eye-opener. He'd have done more recon on BDSM in general, but a young mom and her kids came to use the computer next to him then, and he'd closed the browser before she'd have to explain things she probably didn't know the answers to herself.

Nothing sexual or otherwise happened between Chenco and Steve. Several times he caught Steve watching him, but this was all. Chenco felt as if someone needed to move, but he didn't know what play to make. Occasionally he was annoyed Steve didn't make the choice for him, but mostly Chenco hovered, waiting for something, anything, to happen.

One night in early March as he sat around the fire pit with the others, something did.

Randy had gone into the house to use the bathroom, but within a minute he had come back out, his face grave. "Monk. You've got trouble in River City."

Mitch stood without a word, watching Steve. Steve's

mask of anger scared Chenco. He disappeared into his office, came out looking angrier, then nodded at Randy and Mitch, who followed him out the front door, stopping to brush a kiss across Sam's cheek before he departed.

Sam seemed distinctly unhappy, but outside of a murmured, "Be careful," he said nothing, only watched the three men leave.

Chenco's hair stood up on the back of his neck when he realized Mitch and Steve had both left the house toting guns. Randy had a baseball bat. When Chenco turned to Sam in horror, ready to ask what the fuck was going on, Sam crumbled, sagging against the kitchen counter and hugging himself with a forlorn expression on his face. "I hate it when they do this. I wish they'd just call the police."

"What's going on? What are they doing?"

Sam's mouth flattened into a grim line. "Steve's family had a cannery next to the orchard. It's abandoned now, and the gangs love to torture a homeless man who lives there, an old friend of Steve's. Steve has a video feed set up to monitor the place, and when the gang comes, he goes over and shoots at them until they leave."

Chenco sank into a chair. "Are you serious?" He realized this man's husband, Chenco's brother, was out there risking his life—Randy too, and Steve.

Steve. Chenco's gut clenched in fear.

Sam ran a weary hand through his hair. "I've asked Mitch not to go, but he says I don't understand. He's right, I don't—this is insane, and I hate him doing it. The last time Gordy got hurt, and they asked me to stitch him up. Mitch and I got into a huge fight because I wanted to take the man to the mental hospital, but apparently that's a touchy subject. I wish we would leave so this wasn't an issue anymore." He shook his head, shoulders drooping. "Sorry. I don't really mean that."

Oh, he did. "Are you…are you staying for me?"

He felt self-conscious, like this had been rude to ask, but Sam only smiled sadly. "Of course. Mitch wants to get to know you, wants to help you. Everyone does."

"Help me?" Chenco repeated.

"Yes, help you. You're about to be thrown out of your home, you seem a bit frazzled and lost—they want to help. I do too. We can't quite figure out how to do it yet, but I think it's because you're not sure what you want."

No, *now* Chenco felt self-conscious. "But I don't need you to do anything for me. I haven't asked for anything."

"Yes, I know. I told them this, said we should let you know we wanted to help, but they said not to rush you." Sam tipped his head to the side. "Am I rushing you?"

Chenco had no idea what to say to this. "I don't need anyone to help me."

Sam's expression hinted he disagreed, but instead of contradicting Chenco, he said, "*They* need to help you, hon. I want to help too, but the others? Mitch and

Randy and Steve? They *need* it, even if you don't."

They sat together, awkward and uncomfortable while somewhere in the distance Mitch, Randy, and Steve shot at thugs. Insane didn't begin to describe the moment.

"I don't know what to say," Chenco said at last. "I don't know what you want me to say."

Sam shrugged. "I'm not listening for anything in particular. I only think they're wrong. You need to be prompted. I think Randy feels guilty about upsetting you when he figured out how you were connected to Mitch, Steve is doing backflips to avoid his attraction to you, and Mitch is so scared of losing his last real hope at family he's paralyzed himself."

"You think Steve is attracted to me?"

Instead of answering, Sam grabbed two glasses, a bottle of high-end mescal, a salt shaker, and a bowl of key limes. "I'm going to drink," he announced as he sat at the kitchen island and began cutting the limes into wedges. "I'm going to get drunk, yell at my husband and Randy, and then we're going to have wild monkey sex. You can get drunk with me, and I think it would be great if you helped me yell, but you have to find your own monkey sex. I'll do all kinds of kinky, but I'm drawing the line at incest."

Chenco sat across from Sam, poured a liberal amount of alcohol into his glass, and downed it.

"I have the lime and the salt," Sam pointed out, but Chenco only flipped him off and took a second hit.

By the third shot, Chenco's tongue came loose. "He

can't be into me." He watched the room slosh pleasantly while Sam sucked the juice out of a key lime. "He never does anything. He doesn't even give me heavy glances."

"Not when you're looking." Sam tossed the lime into a bowl and refilled his glass. "I don't know his whole story, but it's twisted and weird. Steve kind of makes me tired. I mean, a big, bad top is hot sometimes, but he never fucking stands down." He bit his lip, looking apologetic. "I mean, it's okay if you like it, but it's not my thing."

"Lincoln says he's Mr. Benson."

Sam clapped a hand to his mouth. *"Oh my God, he is.* I never noticed it, but you're totally right."

"Who the fuck is Mr. Benson?"

Sam led Chenco down the hall. In Steve's office, Sam went right to a bookshelf and emerged with a worn black paperback. "This is Mr. Benson. Go ahead. If Gordy has to go to the hospital, we'll be waiting awhile."

"You want me to read it right now?"

Sam shrugged and sank into a leather armchair. "Whatever. I'm a little drunk. I'm kind of open. And horny." He touched his fingers absently to his lips. "Numb too."

Chenco clutched the novel as if he had a bomb in his hands and he didn't want to set it off. "Lincoln said I wouldn't like this book."

"Well, read it and find out. You'll know pretty quickly."

"Do *you* like this book?"

Sam's look was inscrutable. "Parts of it. Sometimes.

I don't like the pain stuff at all. I don't do piss play, and I wouldn't lick anyone's boots, but—"

"Lick boots?"

Sam motioned at the book, then another empty chair. "Sit. Read. I'll go get us more to drink."

Chenco sat. He read.

He had no idea what to think of the damn book.

About twenty pages in, he almost tossed it across the room, but he accepted a shot of mescal from Sam instead. "*This* is what Steve wants to do to me?"

Sam shrugged. "I have no idea."

"But you said this guy was Steve."

Now Sam looked annoyed. "The way he *acts*, not what he wants. Though he is a sadist."

So this *was* Steve. Chenco read on, skimming sometimes, but mostly getting more and more upset. "If anyone was this cruel to me, this humiliating, I'd kick them in the face."

He'd expected Sam to commiserate, but to his surprise, Sam blushed. "The humiliation part is good. Maybe not as strong as Benson dishes out, but..." He took on a sly look. "Yeah. Some of it's okay."

"You'd let someone use you as a toilet?"

"It's a fucking book, Chenco. No, I don't want it so extreme. But to be used, let go so deeply? Yeah, it's okay." He waved a dismissive hand. "All those novels from the seventies and early eighties are full of piss and shit and crazy nastiness. Maybe it's all the repression and anger. Or maybe it's a different world. I mean, none of it could pretend to happen now. AIDS is only one thing to consider. Do you know how many STDs those guys must have had, if they were doing half this crap? Everything is too far, too extreme. I mean, wait until you get to the white slavery. I love how the day is saved by a secret sensor shoved up someone's ass."

Chenco didn't know how to respond, so he kept reading. He shut off his squick and tried to keep an open mind, tried to imagine Steve as this asshole and him as the idiot who let himself be used—and he couldn't do it. Eventually he put the book down and reached for the bottle.

"Lincoln is right. Steve isn't for me, if this is who he is. This isn't what I want. Don't tell me this is fantasy—Steve's hardcore. He said something once about edge play and liking needles. I can't do that either. I can't do *any* of this."

A funny look crossed Sam's face when Chenco said *needles*. "I don't think he does much with the edge play anymore. Not after Gordy."

Chenco couldn't get all those nasty scenes from the novel out of his mind. *Yet another goddamn place I'm not manly enough, not strong enough.* "I can't do this. I have to forget it. Steve's not for me." Which was an awful realization, as he hadn't acknowledged how quiet and deep a pleasure pining for the man had been until it was taken away.

Sam picked up the book and thumbed to the back before passing it over. "Here. Read the epilogue. I think it might change your mind."

Reluctantly, Chenco resumed reading—and then he

slowed down, digesting carefully. After a few pages he glanced up at Sam, who had a knowing look on his face, slightly naughty but mostly understanding, like they were both in on the secret.

This. This he did want. The love, the attention, the way Benson could *see* into Jamie as no one else could. The way he understood Jamie better than he knew himself.

If *this* was Steve…

Without consciously meaning to, Chenco went back to the point in the book where he'd left off. Eventually Sam murmured about being tired, and when he passed out in his bed, Chenco went with him to sit beside him and keep reading.

It was as if somehow the book had changed, a layer taken away. Instead of Benson being a cruel man making fun of Jamie, using rough sex and humiliation to expose his toy, Benson became a safe space, a leader, a guide. No, Chenco would never ask to be a slave, and he would *not* be someone's toilet, but…yes, a lighter version of some of this might not be so bad. He *wished* he could trust like that. Some of it…some of the taboo was thrilling in theory, filling him with dangerous want. But he couldn't imagine letting anyone, not Steve, not *anyone*, treat him that way. Even for fun. Even to let go.

Even if he wanted to.

What do you want, Chenco? He still didn't know. It wasn't as if the book had made the answer to the question any easier.

At some point he drifted off, and he didn't wake

until Mitch came into the room. Though his brother tried to leave, saying he'd take another guest bed, Chenco said no, he needed to brush his teeth anyway. He didn't go to the bathroom, though, or the room he'd stayed in so much everyone referred to it as Chenco's. He went downstairs, trying to find Steve. It was time they talked. About what, he didn't know. He hoped he'd figure it out when he got there.

In the doorway to Steve's office, Chenco stopped, stunned into immobility by the sight of the man before him.

This was not Mr. Benson. The man slumped in his office chair watching a black-and-white CCTV feed—this man was dirty, slightly bloody, and haggard. He was not a man in control. The person before Chenco was beaten, weary, uneasy and alone. Every muscle in his body spoke of tension begging for release, an escape he did not expect to find.

Normally Chenco found Steve's age an asset, a kind of vintage handsomeness, but it was as if the man had aged twenty years in the hours since they'd last seen one another, and not one of those hours had been kind. He had on glasses too, which Chenco had never seen before. The glasses weren't a big deal, yet somehow they increased his appearance of vulnerability and helplessness. This wasn't a big, bad top waiting for a bossy twink to offer himself properly as a bottom. This wasn't a man who organized raids on white slavers. This man was so far from Mr. Benson they didn't live on the same planet.

This was a man so lost, so worn down, he didn't bother to look up.

As he watched Steve swim in his sorrow, Chenco's heart flew out. Were he still young and foolish, he'd think himself in love, but it wasn't. It was something far more complex and personal.

Chenco stood in that doorway and *saw* Steve, saw him and knew him, understood the pain and hopelessness, comprehended it as only another who felt the same emotions could feel. He yearned to go to the man, to take him in his arms and hold him, to take the heaviness away. All thoughts of pain and humiliation and piss and degradation fell away—whatever Lincoln had seen Steve do, he hadn't seen this. Something told Chenco no one ever, *ever* saw this.

He'd seen it, and he wouldn't forget.

Leaving the room as quietly as he'd entered, Chenco went to bed. He could hear Sam and Mitch arguing, then as promised, heard them fucking. For the first time since overhearing his brother's sexual adventures, however, he wasn't jealous, wasn't frustrated Steve never came to his door or invited Chenco to his bedroom. Instead he lay there thinking about the look on Steve's face, playing it up against the moments in the trailer when Steve's guard had come down.

Those cracks in the facade were everything, he realized. Steve wasn't all tough guy and leather. There was another man in there, a man who bled, who knew sorrow and fear. A man who, when he saw those emotions in someone else, stopped to try and help them, who couldn't bear the thought of someone else hurting. A man who needed love.

A man who'd resist anyone finding out that weakness, who gave all his love away so no one would notice how empty he was himself.

A man who needed saving too.

This, Chenco decided as he drifted off to slightly drunken sleep—*this* was what he wanted. To be the man Steve was looking for, who could crawl under the tough exterior and make the man accept affection for himself. To not just love but be the safe space for the man at that desk.

To be *his* Mr. Benson.

SOMETHING HAD SHIFTED with Chenco, and Steve would be damned if he could figure out what it was.

It all stemmed from the night he, Mitch, and Randy had gone over to chase off the gang, and for a horrible second Steve worried Sam and Chenco had followed, had seen what "calming down" Gordy looked like. But no, Sam said they'd gotten drunk together and passed out in his bed.

The idea of Chenco and Sam making out, while theoretically hot, made Steve go cold with jealousy. When Sam had caught the flicker of irritation, he'd only smiled a sly little smile and said he only fucked one Tedsoe brother, thanks, and sauntered off.

Something had happened, though, because Chenco was different. Instead of hanging back and stealing moon-eyed glances, Chenco sat next to him and instigated conversation. Awkwardly more often than not, but he kept at it with a quiet determination that charmed Steve far more than it should have. He found himself opening up, easing around the young man, letting himself fantasize about relationships with Chenco he'd told himself weren't on the table. They danced politely toward an inevitable conclusion, and though Steve knew this course of action wasn't wise, he couldn't bring himself to stop.

One night as they sat alone on the patio, looking up at the stars, Chenco stopped being polite and went right to the point.

"So, you told me we weren't going to be done playing after the trailer, but nothing's ever happened."

The comment came from so far out of nowhere Steve had to take a second to form a response. "You've never asked for anything else to happen."

"Steve, I'd like something else to happen. Please."

Steve's head filled with crazy, carnal images of pressing Chenco down into the grass, tugging on his hair and taking his mouth in a deep kiss, swallowing gasps and groans. This wasn't the serene, no-sex control and comfort Steve had given before.

It was, however, what Steve wanted now.

He tried to deflect. "Are you talking about the punishment over what happened with Randy?"

"Not right now, no. I would like that sometime, though, if you're still willing. I see him wincing and touching his shoulder when he works in the kitchen, and it makes me feel bad."

Yes, and Steve had left it way too long. Really, it was almost too late. The thought that he'd maybe missed the window to comfort Chenco made him ache with loss.

Chenco ran a hand down Steve's arm. "I'm not talking about Randy right now. I'm talking about playing. With you."

Mayday. "Playing how?"

Chenco's smile sent shivers down Steve's spine. "However you like, Papi."

Steve sat up straighter in his chair and caught sight of Randy milling about in the kitchen. *There's your out.* "Everyone's still up. They might come outside."

"We could go somewhere else." When Steve kept quiet, Chenco's cheeks stained red. "Forget it."

Get a fucking grip, Steve. He swung his body to face Chenco. "I'm not saying no. But I need to know what you want."

"Well, *I* want sex, but I assume you'll still tell me no."

That's right, it's not happening, Steve wanted to say, but once Chenco looked at him, sauce mixed with shy, fire dancing in the back of those hesitant eyes, he was undone. He didn't speak, only stroked the side of Chenco's face. Those brown eyes softened, guards coming down.

Chenco nuzzled tentatively into Steve's hand. "Do you *want* to have sex with me?"

Yes, Steve did. He ached for it like nothing he'd ever yearned for, a want that terrified him. "I'm too old for you."

Steve almost laughed at the angry look Chenco gave him. God, to be twenty-four again. Thinking this, though, only made Steve remember how lost and helpless *he* had felt at that age.

"I do want you." Steve gentled his voice. "I just don't know if it's a great idea."

"What, do you think I'm going to be some kind of moony stalker? If we have sex, I'll assume I'm moving in? Why can't it be about having a good time?"

Because I'm an old, tired man who forgot how to be carefree a long time ago. Because I'd love you to move in, even if I never so much as touch you, and that's really fucking crazy. "I don't think you're a moony stalker."

"Okay." Chenco relaxed a little. "I meant what I said. I don't sleep around."

Steve couldn't hold back a smile. "I know. You're choosy. I like it."

"Booker says I'm a frigid prude." Chenco's face clouded. "Do you know, he hasn't called me since that night? We're due for another show soon, but we haven't rehearsed. He doesn't know about the trailer—hasn't asked." He ran a weary hand through his hair. "I think I'm going to have to move in with Lincoln. I don't want to, but I don't have any choice."

Yes you do. Come stay with me. Play or don't play, but stay. Let me make everything okay. Steve bit the entreaty back. "You always have choices."

"I had one choice—to let my mother turn me into someone I wasn't, or to go off on my own. I chose my pride, and this is what it bought me. I live the real-life version of those romantic stories where the duke's daughter runs off with the stable hand. They don't live happily ever after. They live in abject poverty, miserable, cold, hungry. They have each other and nothing more, and pretty damn quickly it isn't enough."

"Do you wish you would have gone the other way?"

Chenco shook his head. "I don't. But…I wish the fairy tale were real."

Steve couldn't bite his tongue anymore, not without taking it clean off. He couldn't stop this train, but if he schooled himself, if he did his job, he could keep it under control. Straightening in the chair, putting his hands on his knees, he looked Chenco dead in the eye.

"Kneel."

Pleasure curled in Steve's belly at how gracefully Chenco complied with the command. The boy was nervous, yes, self-conscious, afraid of rejection, afraid of being mocked—but he was determined too, and he was here, obeying. Playing. Brave, beautiful, proud Chenco, kneeling before a man.

When Steve's hand slid into that dark, curling hair, Chenco shuddered, and the reverberation rang all the way into Steve's soul. *So much want.* So much yearning, so much need, but so much *strength.*

This confident man wasn't Gordy. How had he ever seen the two of them as the same?

You don't deserve him. You don't deserve someone like this.

Jesus, nothing was ever more true, but when Steve

started to draw back, Chenco looked up at him, wounded, confused, and it was over.

With a sharp pull, Steve drew Chenco's face right into his crotch.

The sharp, hot breath of surprise against his fly was better than any caress. Steve watched, want and pure, red lust burning as Chenco's lips parted, as he stared at the bulge in front of him. The saucy bottoms Steve had tricked with in his youth would have leered up at him and reached for his fly. Gordy would have nuzzled in like a grateful bear cub, sucking up musk.

Not Chenco. He hesitated, yearning but holding back, wanting but not daring to take. There was fear there, but it wasn't of Steve. It wasn't even trepidation over kneeling, no hesitation of being caught giving a blowjob beneath the stars. Chenco feared being seen, period. Of being tough without his drag. Exposing his vulnerability to anyone, no matter how safe they were. Letting Steve take his control away, being the one who played *that game.*

He feared it, but he faced it. *Oh, baby.*

For the first time in fifteen years, it was Steve who choked. It was Steve who didn't have the guts to reach for his fly, who couldn't bring himself to force Chenco's face into his groin, though it was what they both wanted. Fucking hell, he wanted Chenco stripped *down* while he knelt, wanted to fuck his face so hard everyone came out to see what the ruckus was about. He wanted them all to see, wanted them to know this boy was his. He wanted—He wanted—

Steve gripped Chenco's hair, yanked it until his boy's hot breath burned against his leg, half of Chenco's face pressed into Steve's thigh. He kept him pinned there by his hair, clamoring for control.

He couldn't do this.

Chenco turned his face into Steve's leg and bit him lightly through his jeans.

Steve's hand tightened on the curly dark hair, and he felt Chenco's scalp fighting the pressure. This wasn't playing, this wasn't a scene—and if it was, Steve wasn't the fucking Dom. Was Chenco, though, or were they flying blind together?

With a whimper, Chenco bit harder. The more Steve tugged, the more Chenco cried out and the deeper his teeth went, until Steve could feel the burn of Chenco's jaw pressing through the denim into his thigh. God, but it was glorious.

With a choked roar, Steve crammed that wicked mouth to the hot length of his cock. What he should and shouldn't do was forgotten as he ground Chenco's face into his rod, fingers digging in as Chenco bit here too. Jesus fuck, but he wanted to pound into that mouth. He wanted to back Chenco against a wall and slam into his sweet face until Chenco came undone around him.

He could do it. He could take him right now. Right here. He'd asked for it, begged for it. Fuck, it'd be so good, so sweet, and Steve could show him, *really show him—*

"*No.*"

Steve wasn't aware he'd pushed Chenco away, not until he was standing over him, looking down at a red-faced, confused boy.

"Did…did I do something wrong?"

"No." Steve fought for breath, for control. *Give him an answer. Not the truth of why you stopped, but give him something. Anything.* "You didn't do anything wrong. But I'm not going to face-fuck you on the patio."

Chenco sat back on his heels, placing his hands delicately on his thighs. "Because I'm too young?"

"Because I said we're not. You want to play, you play by my rules, and I said we're done." He let out a shuddering breath. "I told you I play with pain. I don't know if I can ease you in."

"You mean you think you'll hurt me not in a good way?"

Steve ran a hand over his smooth scalp. "I mean I can't make it nice. You rile me up like nobody has in a long time, and I don't know that you're ready for zero to sixty. Don't tell me you are. You don't know what it is yet I'm talking about doing with you."

"I would if you told me. I could show you how much I'll surprise you."

Steve could not, could *not* answer, so he clammed up.

Chenco eased a little, reluctant but accepting. "Are we done, sir?"

God yes, get me out of here. "Yes. Get up and go inside."

It had been the worst scene ever, Steve thought as

Chenco rose. He had to give him another round, soon, if only to clear up this mess, but nothing more. Chenco was not Gordy. Chenco was fire and danger, and he deserved so much better. This was a bad idea, and Steve had to *stop*.

Chenco brushed Steve's shoulder with his hand as he passed by. "I would have, you know. I would have let you face-fuck me on the patio."

A howl of *pure need* clawed Steve's gut, driving an urge to pull Chenco back. Steve marshaled himself, but only just, and as he heard Chenco slide open the glass door to the dining room, he gave in.

"You can stay."

Chenco paused with the door half-open.

"You can stay." This time Steve was able to make his voice a little less rough. "In my house. However long you want. However long you need to, you can stay with me. Your brother is looking for trucking jobs, so he'll be around for a while yet. You should be here too. I have the room. I enjoy your company. Stay at my house, save your money, figure out what you want, what you need. Even if Mitch leaves."

For a long time Chenco didn't say anything. Steve waited for Chenco to ask if they'd have sex if he stayed, and honest to God, Steve wasn't sure what he'd say. Probably yes, probably he'd sell off any part of his soul if only Chenco would tell him he wasn't leaving. If they could have more nights together on the patio in the quiet, so he'd see that bright smile and those beautiful eyes every time he sat down to dinner. He'd give anything right then to make him stay, and he was terrified he had no mask and this naked need was written all over his face.

Chenco kept his expression carefully schooled. "I'll think about it," he said, and disappeared into the house.

CHAPTER EIGHT

T HE MORNING AFTER Steve told him he could move in, Mitch and Chenco went to breakfast. It had been Steve's idea.

"Get to know him," Steve suggested. "You haven't spent much time just the two of you. Don't take him to the trailer, though. It's not a great idea for him to go back to ground zero."

Chenco agreed, and fifteen minutes later he and Mitch went out in Steve's big black Ford F-150, Harley edition. Chenco whistled low as he slid into the passenger seat. "Damn. I should have gone into computer programming. My mother would still love me, and I could have bought this truck."

This made Mitch chuckle as he strapped himself in and fumbled with the keys. "Shit pile of money his family sits on helps a bit too. But yeah, computers are good." He fired up the engine, let it rev a minute then put it in reverse.

As his brother led the truck down the drive, Chenco thought of the big blue semi. "So you drive a rig, huh?"

"I do indeed." His drawl wasn't as thick as most south Texans, like he'd been away awhile, but sometimes it crept in with a vengeance, which it did right then. "Independent operator."

"So you travel all over the country?" Chenco couldn't keep the wistfulness out of his voice.

"Used to. Stick around hubs now more often than not, especially in the western states. So Sam can get a job." Mitch nodded and reached for his cigarettes. "I've seen the country. Right now I like seeing Sam."

Okay, that was about the most romantic thing Chenco had ever heard, and he didn't believe in romance. He settled into his seat as his older brother smoked. "How'd you two meet?"

This question made a slow grin spread across Mitch's face. "It's a long, wild story."

Mitch shared some of it as they made their way into town, about Sam dancing in an alley behind his aunt and uncle's pharmacy, about a long-distance drive which ended with Sam bringing Mitch and Randy together. Occasionally it seemed Mitch edited things out, and Chenco got the idea those missing bits were on the steamy side. He made a mental note to ask Randy about them later. Something told Chenco Randy wouldn't leave any meat to spoil.

Mitch told several stories as they wove their way through McAllen, some about him and Sam, some with him and Sam and Randy, one particularly crazy one about how Randy met *his* husband, who apparently was some big casino owner in Vegas—but in the middle of his tale, Mitch broke off.

"Forgot to ask if you cared where we ate. Normally

I'd say we should hit Taco Palenque, but I figure you don't want to go there since it's where you work." Mitch rubbed his chin and grinned. "I worked in a taqueria for six months when I first cut out of Donna. Lived in a piece of shit on Pecan Boulevard and worked next door." He took a drag and shook his head, smiling around the butt. "Had some of the best fucking times of my life in those six months."

"How'd you end up driving a truck?"

"Fucked a guy who taught me how." Now his smile wasn't just nostalgic, it was tender and sad. "Taught me my Spanish, my business, and how to not fuck myself up. He was a good friend of Steve's, which is how I met him too." He cut a glance at Chenco. "Steve's taken a real shine to you, and I can't help but notice it's mutual. You choose to go anywhere with it, I'll tell you this— you won't ever find a stronger, more loyal, more devoted man."

Remembering the fierce, conflicted look on Steve's face and the force he'd used to grind Chenco's face against his cock, Chenco swallowed hard. *Don't think about that.*

Mitch ashed out the window. "Can't fucking believe we both came out queer. I hope Dad got the fucking runs thinking about it."

"I'm fairly sure he did."

"Why'd you volunteer to live with him?"

Chenco shrugged. "At first it was some sort of fuck you to the universe, but then it became practical. You know how much money I saved with no rent? I don't work much at the restaurant, so I can practice and take jobs doing drag—I'd quit Palenque outright, but I like the extra cash to keep things flush. I kept trying to save up to move out when Cooper was alive, but he conned me into helping him out in the home, lying about leaving me the trailer, and I was dumb enough not to get proof. Booker's always wanting to take the show on the road, take Caramela up to Austin and the gay circuit there—hell, he wants to go to Filthy Divas—but it takes cash. Lots of cash."

Mitch smoked for a minute. "What's Filthy Divas?"

"It's an annual drag competition in L.A. Kind of like RuPaul's drag race, but no reality show broadcast. It's more about bringing your act and showing it off. The cash prize is only okay—covers your expenses and a good night out—but the real prize is being able to say you were there, you went down the runway, you stood on the stage. If you win, you pretty much won't ever beg for a gig again. Book wanted us to win and tour the continental U.S. as RuPaul & Company Part Two. It isn't going to happen."

"Never say never," Mitch drawled.

"Life says never to me every damn day. I like to flip it the bird, but I try to get myself into the best position possible first. I'll get to Filthy Divas someday, if I want to go. Maybe I'll do something else. It's just gonna take some time. Also, Book's either got to ditch his boyfriend or convince him he can actually leave town."

This made Mitch frown. "What?"

"His guy, his Dom or whatever—Tristan is a bit of a

shit as far as I'm concerned. Booker loves him, but he's mean sometimes. I've wondered more than once if all Book's bruises were from consensual play."

Mitch went quiet, and it gave Chenco the opportunity to realize they had wandered away from McAllen and were heading east. "You missed the turn for Palenque."

"Didn't think you wanted to go there." Mitch's voice was suddenly a bit sharper, more focused. "This Tristan have a last name?"

Uh-oh. "Shit, I stepped in something, didn't I?"

"I'm more a tourist in the lifestyle, but you tossed up a big red flag someone should check out. There's shit here, maybe, but it ain't yours."

"But—"

"You try telling what you told me to Steve and see what happens."

Chenco's sense of what Steve would say was very clear. "Fuck."

"He's not going to be pissed at you. But you can bet Booker's boyfriend will be getting a visit. Don't give me that look," Mitch said, his voice getting sharp when Chenco paled. "Unless you think it's a good thing for your friend to have someone fucking him over?"

"Shit. No." The more he sat with the thought, the crappier he felt. "Fuck. *Fuck.* I should have said something sooner."

"Unless you knew someone in the scene, no you shouldn't have. This is a self-policing community."

"What, they're going to rub Tristan out?"

Mitch gave him a *come-on* look. "They're BDSM, not mafia. If he's in the official scene and he's gone bad, he won't get laid again anytime soon, not local. If he's not, he'll get a swift education about what those letters really mean and the responsibility that goes with them." He took another drag and swore under his breath. "Everybody reads a fucking book or hops a few websites and thinks they're cool to play around."

Chenco, who had indeed read a book and visited a few websites, felt foolish. He wanted to crack the door a little more open, ask how he'd find out without books or websites, maybe before he got too comfy about the idea of letting Steve play with him, but then Mitch turned the truck off at the exit leading to the flats. "Oh shit. Steve said I wasn't supposed to take you back to the trailer."

Mitch grunted. "Yeah, well, he ain't my Dom, and neither are you. I want my fucking closure."

Chenco wanted to tell him that where Cooper was concerned, he wasn't ever going to get it, but he figured it would be a waste of breath.

As they turned into the trailer park, Mitch had much the same reaction as Steve about the condition of the neighborhood. He drove slowly, taking in the decrepit trailers, the aluminum foil on the windows to keep out the heat—it was too early for that yet, but some people didn't want to bother putting it up and taking it down, and there wasn't anything to look at outside anyway. Chenco liked the light, so he pulled it down in the winter and waited to put it up until the first

May day that tried to bake him raw. Rusted trucks stood on blocks, yards were weed traps. No kids ran the streets, no old men sat on lawn chairs. It wasn't that kind of neighborhood, not anymore. The flats were where lives came to die.

They pulled up to the trailer but didn't get out of the truck, not right away.

"Looks smaller." Mitch's voice was a little gruff. "Rustier."

"I thought about painting it, but I figured I might as well take out an ad saying *good shit to steal inside.* Except it'd say it in Spanish."

"*Buena mierda adentro para robar.*"

That wasn't just Spanish—it was Spanish with all the right moves and notes and a bit of valley for the cherry on top. Chenco gaped at Mitch, and his brother stared back at him, brow lifted in silent question, looking like a kinder, gentler version of Cooper. Speaking fucking valley Spanish.

"Fuck you." Chenco shoved him. "I'm half goddamn Mexican, and you speak better Spanish than me."

Mitch grinned. "Yeah, well, fuck wisely and you might learn to *hablar Español* too, gringo." When Chenco swore at him again, he laughed and cracked open his door. "Come on. Show me what you've done with the place."

IT MADE CHENCO feel good, knowing Mitch liked what his little brother had done with his childhood home.

Chenco gave him the fifty-cent tour, stem to stern, and Mitch paused a lot to smile and remember. Occasionally he didn't smile, pointing out a dent in the wall from one of Cooper's drunken swings or when he'd locked himself in the closet because his father's poker buddy had wanted to show him something in the bathroom. Mostly he liked how Chenco had reclaimed the space. "You healed it," he said more than once.

Partly due to this warm reception, Chenco allowed the tour to extend to his dressing room.

It was Cooper's old bedroom—Chenco still lived in Mitch's, and he'd been able to show him some of the childhood posters he'd found in the back of the closet. Chenco got a sick thrill out of putting on pantyhose in the room once belonging to his fuckhead of a father. With Mitch, he was revealing a part of himself he didn't hide but didn't share easily.

"How'd you get into drag, anyway?" Mitch asked as they settled down in the kitchen, Chenco making them breakfast.

"Sideways, pretty much. I kind of always had it in me, but I didn't know what I was doing with it. I wanted to be a girl, but I didn't want to *be* a girl. I'd watch Beyoncé videos and Nelly and JLo—God, Jenny, I worshipped her so hard—and dance like them and beg my mom for a sparkly leotard. Then one day I snuck into a gay club, saw a drag show, and it was over." He flipped eggs over with his spatula and smiled. "Heide and Lincoln helped me get my shit together, come out to my queen and she to me. Guided me through the ropes. Only trouble is, Caramela is all glam. God, but I wish she'd be happy with fifty-dollar wigs from the costume shop, but no. She wants to make JLo herself look like a bad copy."

"Well, you're good. She's good. Fucking amazing. I've seen drag all over the country. You could take any of them. Are you gonna perform again pretty soon?"

"I'm supposed to next week." Chenco tried not to melt under his brother's praise, but it was impossible. "Are you saying nice things about my act because we share a gene pool?"

"Shit, no. If you were crap, I'd tell you to knock it off and try to teach you trucking. You're good. You need to get your ass to the Filthy Divas thing."

"Well, unless you come with a trust fund you feel like sharing, honey, that's not happening anytime soon."

Mitch huffed a laugh. "I don't, but—well, let's say I bet Randy's already made some calls." He stood and stretched. "I'm gonna nip out and have a smoke, if I've got time."

"Sure. This'll be a few minutes yet." He smiled a little shyly. "Thanks for this, Mitch. For coming here, for saying nice things. It means a lot."

Mitch gave a gruff nod as he headed out the door. "Keep 'er warm for me."

Chenco smiled to himself as he put Mitch's omelet onto a plate and served himself up a bowl of muesli and almond milk. It was cool having an older brother who thought he'd done okay with himself. It had been a long time since he'd allowed family to matter to him, and while it still felt a little dangerous, it was also beginning to feel more than a little bit okay to let down his guard.

As if that thought had personally gone out and stirred up trouble, no sooner did Chenco think it than Mitch came tearing back in, his cell phone to his ear. "Chenco, we need to get you out of here. Right now."

The world shifted slightly sideways. "What? Why? We haven't had breakfast."

"We can't have breakfast. And when I say you need to get out of here, I mean you need to get *out of here.* Like, you can't come back. Ever."

"*What?*" Chenco's heart slammed at the top of his throat. He swallowed it back down. "No way. This is my life, my stuff—"

"*Chenco.*" Mitch pointed out the window. "Sometime in the hour since we've been here, somebody painted a gang symbol on Steve's truck."

"They do it all the time. It's our welcome wagon."

"Steve has a very distinctive truck. A lot of people in the valley know it. A lot of dicks in the flats know it. They enjoy bashing in the heads of homeless people for fun. Homeless people who live at the cannery."

Oh no. A cold, terrible wind whipped through Chenco. *Oh no, oh no, oh no.*

Oh yes, Mitch's face said. "They know this truck. They know Steve. They hate Steve. I just drove Steve's truck into their turf and parked it in front of your house."

For a horrible second Chenco stared at his brother.

Then he melted, slow motion, into a chair.

Mitch hauled him back to his feet. "*We have to leave.*"

Chenco was going to be sick. "If I leave, they'll trash the trailer. They'll trash my stuff, Mitch. *Caramela's stuff.* I can't leave her to them. It's her back there. It's not just my head, it's her stuff. I can't do this to her."

"Then start packing. If you have a gun, I'd appreciate knowing where it is."

"Under my bed. Bullets in the bedside drawer." Chenco headed for the dressing room, but he stumbled. "Oh my God, Mitch."

"Steve's on his way, and he called some of the guys."

"Not Randy?"

"Randy is at Steve's house, keeping my husband from coming along."

Chenco couldn't ask any more questions because Mitch disappeared into his bedroom. To get the gun. To defend the trailer against the Donna gang.

Chenco moved in a daze, at first simply spinning in vain, trying to decide how to start, then ruthlessly combing through from one side of the room to the other, identifying each item and deciding whether or not it was essential. It was extreme reverse hoarding—to each item he asked, *do I need this to live my life? Does Caramela?* The answers sometimes surprised him.

She rose up too, making it clear what was at her core, what she could not leave behind and what was frivolous. When he threatened to fall apart, she soothed him, reminding him all this could be replaced, that they were queens the both of them, that they were strong and nothing and no one could get them down.

Even so, when Chenco saw Steve filling the doorway to the dressing room, he couldn't stand it anymore. He broke down.

Without saying a word, Steve took charge of the room—a few other men Chenco didn't know had arrived with Steve, and they all moved to Steve's orders, taking Chenco's things, finishing the boxing up and moving his belongings outside.

Sitting on Steve's massive thigh, Chenco curled into his neck, calming, accepting strokes on his arm and thigh. The uncertainty, the wildness of the night before, was gone. This was the Steve who had petted him, the Steve who had carried him out of the club.

"I have control of this, Chenco. You do not need to worry about this anymore. I will take your things to my house, and I will keep you safe until you choose to leave."

Swallowing a sob, Chenco pressed closer. "Thank you."

"Thanks isn't a requirement. It's my truck, my past messing up your present, and I clean up my messes." Steve nuzzled Chenco, vulnerability leaking through. "I know you said you'd think about it, but for now, you need to say yes, baby. We'll talk the rest through back at my place. What you need to know right now is you're safe."

Chenco wanted to crawl inside Steve's belly and lie there, warm and curled and part of him forever. "Okay.

I'll move in."

Steve crushed him close. "Good."

The rest of Chenco's packing happened with Steve and Mitch and the other silent men as his personal pack mules—when he pointed to something and said it came along, they boxed it or bagged it and took it outside. They had him go through each room twice, closing the door on it when he was finished.

"This will never all fit in the truck," Chenco said at one point, starting to lose it again.

"That's not for you to worry about." Steve said this with another one of his hard grips on Chenco's arm. "Finish going through your things."

Chenco did. He sent everything out except for the cedar box with his mother's letters, which he said he'd carry himself. When it was all over, Mitch and the guys left the two of them alone in the living room, Chenco's back to the door, forehead on Steve's shoulder as Steve wrapped big arms around him and stroked him gently. Steve was a little shorter than he was, so he had to slump, but he felt about three inches tall, so it worked out in its own way.

"I'm not ever coming back here, am I?" Chenco whispered.

"No." Steve kept stroking his arms. "I'm sorry. The guys will stay as long as they can, stripping everything not nailed down, and they'll bring it to the house. But no, you can't come back here, ever. Not when they associate you with me. Even if things don't work out with us, you can't, because you are now connected with somebody they're aching to fuck over. You're a big, easy target. These assholes can't be taken out by stilettos. Not even in the neck."

"I know, I just—" One tear escaped, and Chenco wiped furiously at his eyes. "I worked so hard. I came here with nothing, I beat Cooper, I beat the gangs, and now—"

He started to break, and Steve dug in his fingers, staying him, but he nipped at Chenco's ear too, a baby bite, enough to make everything inside Chenco slow to a crawl.

"Hold on to the pain, baby. Be strong for me, carry your troubles home. Don't give them your sorrow. They don't deserve it. You save it for me, lover, and I'll show you things you can do with the heaviness you carry that will blow your mind. I'll take you so high you won't know pain from pleasure. These threats will be so far beneath you they'll be dust, and you'll laugh and blow them away. Keep it close, keep it real, keep it deep, because, baby, I'm going to ask you for it, and you're going to give it to me. You'll sob, scream, and you'll beg me for more, get down on your knees even as you cry big fat tears. It'll hurt, oh, it'll hurt—so good you'll never, ever let anybody cheap have it again. So hold on to that pain, baby. Hold on."

Chenco's head felt crazy, rotating lazily about six feet above his body. Steve's words filled him with terror and yearning, but above all they gave him, inside, the same kind of control Steve could leash a room with. In the distant landscape of his mind, Chenco could see a great big beast he hadn't known was there. It would have been scary, except he knew that darkness wouldn't come out until Steve let it. Steve would keep it in control.

He looked up at Steve. "Give me a preview, Papi."

Steve's eyes went dark, and his face split into a terrible grin, giving Chenco a glimpse of his own monster. Hand in Chenco's hair, Steve pressed a kiss to his lips before drawing Chenco's bottom lip into his mouth.

And bit.

Chenco cried out in surprise, but as Steve's teeth found purchase, the cry became one of pain, *real* pain. Steve fed on it, groaning pleasure and sliding his jaw back and forth, making it worse, making Chenco howl. He melted into Steve's arms, crying, not quite sobbing but so close, and Steve pressed him into the door, grinding an iron erection into his groin.

Sadist. *Oh. My. God, he really was.*

The beast inside Chenco lifted its head, and as it met its master, it shoved Chenco's sensibilities and the last whispers of his propriety aside. It lay down for Steve, lay Chenco open and wide.

He's ready. He's yours. Take him.

As his inner masochist came to bloom against the door of Cooper's trailer, Chenco felt like he'd pulled his chest cavity wide open and stood ready for Steve. He wanted this, he got off on this, not so much with his dick but with something so deep inside him it made dicks seem cheap.

Here at this door was where Cooper had called him

anchor baby and faggot and shitsucker. This was the door Chenco had kept coming to like a dog, where he asked Cooper if this was all he had, if he could hit any harder, because he wasn't impressed. Here was where he'd made his stand, where he'd taken the pain of his life and put a yoke on it.

Now this door was where another man, a better man, took the yoke for him.

His cock was so heavy and ready he fully expected it to bust out of his jeans and start whimpering and begging along with the rest of him. In fact, when Steve drew away, Chenco moaned more than he had for any pain. The loss of Steve's touch was the first pain from his papi not dripping in pleasure.

"We have to go, baby." Steve nipped one last time at Chenco's swollen lip, but it was so subtle it was worse than if he'd just kissed him. "The guys are waiting. We have to go." He stroked Chenco's arm. "It's time to say goodbye."

Chenco did. Holding on to Steve, still pressed to the door, he scanned the half-emptied room, seeing it as it was and as it had been in all its stages. He saw Mitch's uneaten breakfast as well as his own. He saw the cans of beer Cooper left for him to pick up. He smelled the stench of Cooper's unwashed body, saw it sitting slack-jawed in front of the television, half-rotten from a stroke. He saw it all, heard it all, remembered it all.

"Goodbye, Cooper. You fucker."

Steve nudged his elbow to move him and opened the door.

Outside on the trailer's lawn and all up the street were bikes and trucks, every last one driven by fuck-you leather daddies gleaming in the sun.

Chenco stared. "This might be worth it actually."

Steve's laugh was low and wicked as he reached down to openly fondle Chenco's ass.

Chenco had envisioned himself leaving the flats many, many times, but never had he imagined it would be riding bitch behind Steve on his hog as he drove with Mitch and a small squadron of badass men not just out of the flats but *through* them, brazenly revving their engines on the gang's home turf.

They had it timed right too. They did enough of a circuit to dig into the gang's side, a parade for the angry-faced, rough young men who had begun to crowd at the end of the street, but the bikers didn't stay long enough to get the gang so pissed they'd try to retaliate. When they swung out of the flats and toward the highway, a pair of black-and-whites was on their way in, and when Steve tossed a salute to them, they gave it back.

The ride away from the flats was like everything else about being with Steve—slightly nerve-wracking and ultimately thrilling. His cedar box was tucked into a leather satchel on the side of the bike, secured into place by a buckle, leaving Chenco free to wrap his arms around his papi and watch the world fly by. It felt fucking good to be able to slide his hands down Steve's thighs at stoplights and have Steve move Chenco's hands to his crotch, encouraging him to fondle the fat sausage waiting for him there. It should have been a shitty moment, but it wasn't, and it was all because of Steve.

He half-thought he'd get a chance to explore more of what they'd started in the trailer when they got back to the house, but all Chenco got was a reassuring grip on his ass before Steve started directing his friends where to put Chenco's belongings.

Well. He'd moved out.

The thought made him dizzy.

Sam came out to greet Mitch, and Chenco's brother got not just a motherfucker of a bear hug but a public grope and a hand down the back of his pants before Mitch called over his shoulder he'd be back down to help in about twenty minutes. Then he and Sam were gone. Chenco glanced toward Steve, wishing they could disappear too.

Randy smirked as he came onto the porch and read the expression on Chenco's face. "Yeah, none of that is coming your way soon. You, Princess, just put on the world's biggest cock ring. His nickname is Monk for a fucking good reason."

Chenco swallowed a whimper. "I'm not a princess, bitch, I'm a queen."

"Yeah, but you're my best friend's little brother I didn't know he had. I have ten years of ribbing to make up for." He squeezed Chenco's arm and nodded toward the house. "I'm making brunch for the masses. I could use a sous-chef for vegetable chopping."

"Fair enough." Chenco followed him.

"There's some good news," Randy said as they headed to the kitchen. "My husband got tired of hearing about all the fun we're having here without him, and he's coming down in a few days. He can't wait to meet you." He grinned over his shoulder. "He's bringing our gangster with him too."

Gangster? Chenco paused, wondering if he should ask for clarification, but given the amount of explosives his poor mind had already endured today, he figured it'd be best not to ask. If there was one thing he'd learned from his new family, it was that pretty much damn near anything was possible.

CHAPTER NINE

I T WASN'T LONG ago, Steve mused as the guys departed after delivering the last load of Chenco's stuff, that his life had been quiet and boring. Now he had a house full of people and the promise of more before too long. So many fucking people, and every last one of them needed something.

Once Chenco was settled in with Randy, Steve climbed on his bike and wound his way back into town, letting the wind carry away his tangled thoughts.

He still reverberated from the kindness of the guys who had helped move Chenco's things, the laughter and friendship as they'd worked together an unexpected balm. It had been a long time since he'd seen them, and it had felt good to reconnect with the community. All of them were leather, part of an unofficial valley club of sorts, but he hadn't seen any of them in years. Despite his absence, they'd welcomed him like the prodigal son, encouraging him to call them again, promising to help keep an eye on Gordy if he wanted extra hands.

Once upon a time they had been his family. When had that changed?

Except this was a question he knew the answer to.

As he headed home, Steve swung into the cannery's parking lot.

In Steve's youth this place had been a hub, full of trucks and tractors and activity. Steve remembered hanging out with his dad on the loading dock, stealing grapefruit from crates and eating them out back with Gordy, their legs swinging as they stared out at the fields and planned out their summer vacations. Usually when he stopped by like this, Steve tried to bring some citrus with him, but he'd forgotten today. This time he needed his best friend as much as Gordy needed him. He didn't want to cloud this with the idea he'd stopped by to stroke his pet.

"Gordy," Steve called as he climbed the stairs. During the day Gordy usually looked before he shot, but it never hurt to be careful. "It's Steve. You in, buddy?" A shadow shifted in the corner of the old sorting room. Steve moved toward the shape. "Gord, that you?"

What initially looked to be a pile of newspapers lifted its head. Gordy, face streaked with dirt and long beard tangled with sticks, glared up at him. "I was taking a nap."

"I can see that."

Steve crouched at the edge of the newspaper pile. Gordy looked good today. Stank like hell, but he seemed calm, almost happy. It made Steve ache, made him want to curl into the mess beside his friend, if it was the only way he could get him.

"Wondered if I could convince you into putting your nap off for an hour and chat with me instead."

Newspapers fell away as Gordy sat up straighter. "What do you want to talk about?" When Steve hesitated, running a mental filter over his recent exploits, Gordy rolled his eyes. "Never mind. I know. The kid. The one you're mooning after."

He knew about Chenco? Steve hesitated, trying to work out how. Randy and Mitch would never talk to Gordy about Chenco, which meant Gordy had been spying.

Maybe coming here was a mistake.

Clearing his throat, Steve tried to redirect the conversation. "I want to talk to you about the gangs. Some shit went down today, and they might be by."

Gordy's face screwed up in rage. "I'll blow them up. I'll get my guns and mow them down."

Steve held up a hand. "No can do. They'd take you out. I told the local police, and some of the guys will be by tonight to check on you."

Gordy's snarl was almost animal. "Fuck that shit. This is my home. I'll defend it myself. I'll shoot them in the fucking *balls*."

Definitely a mistake to come here. "This isn't your home. This is the goddamned cannery. Why do you have to be like this, Gordy?"

"Why do *you* have to be like this?" Gordy leaned forward, eyes sparking with anger, his rotten scent choking in its thick, caustic waves. "Why aren't *you* protecting me? Why aren't you sitting with *me* on the patio, making moon eyes and fetching drinks?"

Fuck, Gordy had been spying. "I *am* protecting

you." Steve gestured to the cameras. "I watch you all the fucking time, making sure you're okay."

"Fuck your fucking cameras. I don't want them, I want *you*."

Steve felt sick. This again. *And he knows about Chenco, so he'll be worse.* "Gordy, don't do this. Just leave it."

"*Fuck leaving it.*" Gordy's eyes were clear and sharp with rage. "*You* leave it. Leave me the fuck alone. You don't love me. You give me scenes, but you hate them. You hate me. Let me go."

"Where the hell is it you want to go?" Steve could taste his fury in the back of his throat, rising so easily to Gordy's bait. "To the flats, to get the shit kicked out of you? Back to the assholes who fucked you over, who broke you?"

"They didn't break me. *You* broke me, you asshole." Gordy's sneer was soul-deep ugly, an echo of the darkness haunting Steve's boyhood friend. "Fuck you and your new boyfriend. You'll never make it with him. You think I'm fucked up, cuntface, try looking in a mirror."

Steve slid a hand into Gordy's collar, tugged hard enough to cut off his air and said, "*Heel.*"

The move was automatic, an act learned from years of practice. Gordy fought him, struggling and clawing at the air, at Steve, but with a few more jerks on the studded ring around his neck and some bit-off commands, Gordy fell to his hands and knees, whimpering and nuzzling Steve's leg.

For Steve, however, hell had just begun. He hated this, hated when Gordy goaded him. It wasn't that he resented the puppy play—well he did, but because of what Gordy had done to it, not the play itself. He hated how angry Gordy made him feel, how helpless. He hated how out of control he felt, how manipulated, hated how Gordy always managed to get what he wanted and how the result always left Steve himself so empty and hollow inside. He resented himself for being this weak, for letting things get this far, for not knowing how to make them right again.

Worst was Gordy seeing this weakness. His comment about the mirror had been cruel, but it wasn't a lie.

Probably sensing the chink in Steve's armor, Gordy bent and kissed Steve's boot. "Can I have my hood?" All the spit was gone from Gordy's tone, but there was a smugness there, pleasure at having gotten what he wanted, a certainty he could get more. "Give me a scene, baby. Give it to me good and hard. Cut me, Stevie. Cut me good the way you used to. Make me bleed out. Don't make me do it myself. Hurt me, and we'll both feel better, same as always."

Steve felt furious, sick, trapped. This wasn't a scene. This wasn't the exchange he had with Chenco. This was manipulation, plain and simple. It was fucked up, fucked over, and it was wrong. Steve didn't want this. He didn't want to give until he bled, not anymore.

Not to Gordy.

"No."

The word echoed in the empty cannery. Gordy lifted his head and looked at Steve, surprised.

"No." Emboldened by his own defiance, Steve let go of Gordy and took a few steps back, feeling stronger with each one. "No. I'm not giving you a scene. You want me to be in charge, you let me set the rules. No scene right now."

"Too eager to go back to your cute little black bean?" Gordy bared his dirty teeth. "Bet you'll make him cry. You'll hurt him then you'll leave him, just like you do me. I'll make him a room for when you're through."

God, but Steve wanted to smack Gordy's cruel mouth. The only thing keeping him from swinging was the whisper of sanity reminding him this was what Gordy wanted. Giving in to the urge wasn't only wrong, it would let him win.

"No," he said a third time, losing track of what exactly he was defying. "Stay away from Chenco. Stay away from the fucking flats."

"Stay away from *me*, asswipe." Gordy threw a wad of rotten newspaper at him. "Go. Get out. Go fuck your toy. Make him as miserable as you made me."

Vibrating with emotion, clinging to the edges of his control, Steve left, ignoring the roars and smashes he heard behind him. He climbed on his bike and rode the wind, screaming down deserted roads until the terror of high speed gnawed off the pain in his heart. When he felt halfway human, he headed home.

He found Randy sitting in the office, frowning at

the screens, half of which were fuzz. "Something happened to the feed." When Steve didn't reply, Jansen did a double take. "Jesus. What the fuck happened to *you*?"

After shutting the door, Steve sat in the chair beside the desk. "I can't do this."

"This is Gordy, isn't it. He fucked the feed because he's pissed at you." Randy's expression hardened. "Let me guess. He knows about Chenco, and he's jealous."

Self-loathing, fear, and loss swirled inside Steve like a storm. "I should send the boy away with you. Right now. When Ethan comes, you should take him away from me, so I can't hurt him."

"You're not going to hurt him."

Steve curled his fingers into the chair. "He deserves better. He could have better, so easily. Younger, less fucked up. Take him to Vegas, take him to a bar, let him meet somebody better."

Randy gripped Steve's goatee and held him in place—the gesture shocked them both, and they regarded one another, surprised. Then Randy gathered himself, staring Steve down with a surprising thread of steel.

"He's poison to you, Monk, and you're poison to him. You need out of this. You've needed out for a long, long time, but now that you have something good in your hand, you *really* gotta get out of Dodge. I'll take Chenco to Vegas if he wants to go—but you gotta come too."

"I can't leave Gordy." Steve pulled back from

Randy's grip and sagged in the chair. "He'll get himself killed."

"You are not his husband, Steven Vance. Even if you were, at this point of the fuckery, I'd say you need to get a divorce."

"*I can't leave him.* It's fucked, you're right, but I can't let him stay here by himself. He's right, I did make him. I can't leave him. I can't fix him, but I can't leave him."

Randy's smile was so wicked, it could have ruined a saint. "Maybe I know somebody who can."

Every fiber of Steve's being went still. "What?"

Eyes dancing, Randy leaned forward. "Tell me what you want, Monk. Give me the words."

I want to be free. I want Gordy to be my friend again, not my cross to bear. I want Chenco. I want to look in the mirror and see a man who deserves him, not the man who might undo him like I've undone Gordy. I want what Mitch has, what you say you have too. I want the big pot. I want it all.

"I want out." Steve's fingernails almost pierced the leather arm of the chair. "I want out of this."

"Do you want Chenco?"

Like nothing else in the world. "Yes."

"Enough to leave the valley and go with him to Vegas, if it's what he wants?"

"Yes." Anything. *Everything.*

"Okay." Randy leaned back in his chair.

Steve stepped on the hope rising in his heart. "You can't give me that."

Randy chuckled darkly. "The fuck I can't. Hell, honey, this one isn't even hard. You're ninety percent there already. You just need one little variable removed, and then you need to bring those brass balls you used to be so proud of and put them back on your dick. This one's easy."

"*How?*" God, Steve wanted it to be true, but he couldn't see a way out, not for anything. "How can you make this okay?"

Randy put his arms behind his head as he propped his booted feet on the edge of Steve's desk. "You dear, fucked-up old man. I already stacked your deck."

CHENCO WAS *SURE*, absolutely sure he was going to get his sexytimes the night after the trailer fiasco, but in point of fact the first day and a half after he moved in, he barely saw Steve at all. He didn't push it because he was tired, but he woke the next morning full of determination. Unfortunately, Mitch informed him Steve had been up early and wouldn't be back until the afternoon.

Which, as Chenco had to work, meant he'd miss Steve. As he went off to Taco Palenque, Chenco felt frustrated and angry. He wasn't in any better of a mood when he got off and realized home was now Steve's place, which meant he had to be around a bunch of people when he was upset, one of them the person he was upset with. Grumbling to himself, he beelined to the shower across from his room and scrubbed the grease out of his hair. He wondered if he could talk Sam into getting drunk with him again.

When he got back to his room, though, Steve was there, sitting on the edge of the bed. He had a stack of papers in his hand.

"Hi." Chenco adjusted the towel at his waist, trying to play it cool. He shifted uncomfortably, aware he was naked, damp, and a guest in someone else's home—with no home of his own anymore. "Is everything okay?" His glance shifted to the stack of papers and saw the word *contract* in boldface. "Oh. You...you need me to sign something, like a lease?"

"What?" Steve followed Chenco's gaze and rolled the papers up. "No." He ran a hand over his bald head. He looked nervous.

Chenco sat beside him, resisting the urge to put a hand on his arm. "What's wrong? Did something happen?" He pushed past his own selfish desires and added, "If things have changed, if you need me to leave—"

"*No.*" Steve sighed and caught Chenco's hand, folding it into his palm. "The opposite, really. I came...I came in here to see if you were still interested in exploring something with me."

Jesus, the guy made it sound like they were going off to poke around in a cave. "Are you talking about a relationship? Sex?" *Do I get a headlamp?*

"Yes. Both." After clutching the papers, Steve thrust them into Chenco's hand. "Here."

Frowning, Chenco scanned the opening paragraph—then looked up sharply as he realized what Steve had handed him. "Are you serious? This is a contract about *sex*?"

Steve went tense and rigid. "I told you, I play rough. I want things very clear between us. No surprises, no one upset."

Chenco felt plenty upset right now. "I thought this shit was only in those kinky romance novels."

"It's not a requirement in the lifestyle, no. Usually it's for Master/slave relationships, which this isn't. But a contract is necessary for playing with me. Especially after—" His face clouded with pain, but then his rigid control was back. "I won't hurt you, not beyond what you want, but first I have to know what the breaking point is."

This was *crazy*. But when Chenco turned to Steve, ready to argue, he got a good look at the frayed edges of the man's control and stopped.

Look on the bright side. You'll be getting sex. With a sigh, Chenco picked up the paper. "All right, Papi. Lay it out for me."

Steve walked him through the agreement, starting with the preamble where he took Chenco directly down the rabbit hole of how Steve Vance got off on pain. Chenco quickly understood why the contract came into question, because apparently when Steve said sex without pain was food without taste, he wasn't fucking around, and man, did the guy like to eat.

"The first point I need you to clarify is whether or not we're breaking skin, and there's a distinction—

accidental and deliberate. If blood is a hard limit for you, if it can't happen at all, I'll take care never to come close. If you're willing to let accidents happen, I can push things a little. Now, I'm assuming this is all a bit new to you, and I want to make it clear—should we engage in any blood play at any time, I will take appropriate precautions. Our scenes will be clean, and if I spill you, part of your aftercare will be making sure you do not get infected or injured in a way outside of consensual play."

It was telling, Chenco decided, how much calmer Steve got as he outlined his kink. Calm was something Chenco couldn't quite get when he realized sex for the foreseeable future contained concepts such as *blood play*. Maybe the contract was a really good fucking thing, in fact. "I think accidental is okay for now. I'm not saying no to the other, but it might be best to walk before I run in this stuff."

This comment earned him a brief massage of his shoulder. "Before I can go to the next point, we need to come to an official understanding. You will trust me when I tell you to do something or not do something. You will respect my authority and yield to it at all times. You may ask questions, but you will not challenge me. It will be my job to make sure you don't feel uncertain about things. You have no need to double-check me, but if I ever miss something, I need you to speak up respectfully as you ask for clarification and reassurance. I will not be patient with sass or backtalk or bitching about whether or not I'm doing the right thing."

Yes, Mr. Benson. "Okay."

Steve handed Chenco another paper. "Here's your first test on that point."

Chenco scanned the paper—and found he was looking at his own confidential STD test from the McAllen free clinic.

"*What*—" He stood up, swallowing a string of curses. "How, *sir*, did you get this?"

"I told you. I'm very, very good with computers. There aren't a lot of secrets I can't uncover. I'm taking you at your word you haven't had contact since this, but I don't like contracts without the tests included. You'll find mine at the back. It's got an old date, but I've had no contact since then. I've played, but never penetrated, and there has been no fluid exchange of any kind. On the rare occasions I've done edge play, there have been gloves and proper precautions. If you want, however, I can get another test tomorrow, and we can put things off until you have proof I'm clear."

Chenco stared at him for several seconds, trying to find places in his head to stick everything. Was there something wrong with a fucking condom? Apparently for Steve there was.

It was a serious invasion of privacy, but did Chenco really care? Steve hadn't poked around in his private records to hurt him, he'd done it because he was a crazed control-freak. The only indignity here was proof of how long Chenco had been dry. "I'm fine. Thank you."

"You reacted a lot better than I thought you would.

I assumed you'd point out you could have called in and requested the results yourself."

The thought hadn't occurred to Chenco, which illustrated he was off his usual game, way too focused on getting busy. Control freak wasn't looking so bad, actually. "Nope. I'm good." He met Steve's gaze and said, with sincerity, "Thank you. For checking for me, for walking me through what to expect."

They finished the list with a practical calm Chenco didn't know he had in him when it came to kinky sex. He had to admit, it cleared a lot of snot out of the air over hooking up. For one, nobody had ever understood before Steve how in no way could any marks or signs of sex interfere with Caramela's ability to perform.

Steve had a whole page of the contract for Chenco to fill out for her, complete with diagrams of the body so Chenco could delineate where Steve could and could not mark him. The clarification of acceptable and unacceptable kinks was great too, because all the ones he hated had been tried on him without so much as a "do you wanna?" before engagement. Permission, Chenco began to understand, was an entire buffet of pleasure in its own right.

He was surprised to find Steve's hard limits didn't just include sass and backtalk. He had a few kink lines he wouldn't cross too. No infantilism, no age play, and no scat. He was open to watersports, he said, but it wasn't a requirement.

Chenco hesitated, his pen poised over the checkbox. He couldn't move, couldn't speak, and he felt abruptly strange, as if reading that question had stripped him naked and put him on a stage.

Watersports.

Piss play.

Peeing on someone during sex.

Jesus. Fucking. Christ.

Fingers threaded softly through his hair. "Chenco, you don't have to be embarrassed with me about anything you want or don't. And just because I'm open to something doesn't mean we have to do it."

Chenco tried to nod, but it was hard to make his body respond. He kept reading that line over and over. *Would you be open to watersports? Would you like Steve to piss all over your body?* Because he didn't have any illusions about who would be peeing on whom here. It made him think of *Mr. Benson*, of how appalled he'd been by the act when depicted there. No, he didn't want to be a toilet. That hadn't changed. Yet as he stood here, Steve touching him in reassurance, the menu of pleasure and sin in front of him…

All he had to do was check *no* and it would be over. Except the more Chenco stared at the question, the more he realized, for reasons blooming deep from his subconscious, he wanted to check *yes*.

For a moment his mind flashed him an image of fantasy, of him lying on Steve's bed, tied up and helpless, Steve looming over him in leather, leering with a knowing smile as he slowly unzipped his fly and aimed…

Chenco shivered and shifted the stiffy in his pants.

What the fucking fuck. Who the hell was he, and how was this happening?

Steve's hand began to knead at Chenco's neck. "Talk to me, boy."

He spoke gently, but with that edge giving Chenco space and safety. Chenco drew a deep breath and let it out, staccato and rough. "I...I don't know."

"I assume, since I've made it clear I do *not* require this, that your hesitation comes from realizing *you* do."

Gut churning, Chenco nodded once and gripped the pen so tight he feared it would break.

Steve brushed a kiss on Chenco's hair. "Sweetheart. There's nothing to be ashamed of in wanting that."

Chenco swallowed hard. "A lot of people would disagree with you. I would have, before. Except right now...I wouldn't. But I don't know why." *And I'm so scared by that realization I can barely breathe.*

Steve kept touching, stroking, caressing, with hands and mouth and the sweet, silky gentleness of his tone. "I'm honored you trust me enough to even talk about this, Chenco. That's what the act would be about between us. Honor and trust. Do you understand how much that means to me, that you would even *think* of allowing me that right, giving me permission to treat you in a way you wouldn't let anyone else?"

"H-how is letting you...do that about honor?"

"Because so many people say it's terrible. To most of the world, that we would consider engaging in that play is disgusting, inhuman, beyond the pale, an instant taboo. That you would give that act to me, allow me to turn it into something sacred, communion between the two of us?" He drew Chenco's back to his front and pressed a long, soft kiss to Chenco's hair. "I don't have words to tell you how pleased with you I am right now. I can only hope I'm able to show you."

Chenco sank into Steve's embrace, his breath coming short now as it took everything in him not to cry. Steve held him while he gathered himself, not rushing him, only comforting and supporting.

Eventually Chenco slipped out of Steve's arms enough to lean forward and, without so much as a tremble in his fingers, checked the box for *yes*.

Steve drew him back into the backward hug and nuzzled Chenco's ear again. "Thank you for sharing this with me. I truly am honored, pleased by your trust. When we decide it's the right time, I'll make it something special, something worthy."

It took Chenco a few swallows to be able to reply, and when he did, his voice shook. "You do know sometimes you nearly get me off by doing nothing more than talking to me?"

With a dark chuckle, Steve nipped lightly at Chenco's ear. "Yes."

Nobody was uneasy now. Steve seemed very relaxed, and having breached the most taboo and terrifying line item on the menu of permissive, kinky sex, Chenco filled out the rest of the form with ease. Soon they were finished with the contract, everything initialed but the last clause, which was about safe words. This was the only time Chenco argued, as he was upset he didn't get to pick his own.

Steve wouldn't budge. "Safe words are about being safe, not being cute. Yellow means slow down and red means stop universally in western culture. Why the fuck anybody needs to make safety complicated, I will never understand."

Chenco wanted to argue choosing his own safe words would make it personal and give him a sense of ownership over his security, which was also pretty important from where he stood. However, not only did he not care as much about it as Steve seemed to, but he also suspected these remarks would be construed as backtalk.

As he hovered with a pen, ready to sign, he stopped when he realized what was missing. "There wasn't anything about needles in the contract. You told me in the trailer those were your favorite, but they weren't mentioned once."

Whoa, but did this comment unleash *big* vulnerability. Only for a second, a cold, lonely shadow crossed Steve's face, but then it was gone, Papi back in control. "That's a different contract, and not for right now."

Though Chenco was disappointed at being deliberately left out of Steve's favorite kink, he put the thought out of his mind and concentrated on the fact that he was, finally, getting laid.

There were two contracts, one for Steve and one for Chenco—they each initialed and signed them both. When they were done, Steve handed Chenco his copy.

"What now?" Chenco asked as he tucked it into the

drawer in the bureau Steve had cleared for his clothes.

Steve settled back on the pillows of Chenco's bed. "Now you drop your towel, boy."

CHAPTER TEN

FROM HIS POST at the head of the bed, Steve regarded Chenco with a lazy gaze promising danger and pleasure and infinitely expanding horizons. It was Caramela's fantasy come to life, undressing for her man, but Chenco was the one here and now, and he was nervous.

Chenco let her slide into his skin, dropping the towel with grace and artistry, exposing his body with the confidence only she could grant. When she finished, when she returned to the shadows of his mind to watch how things played out, Chenco breathed heavily as he stood at the foot of the bed, wanting to demand Steve get this party started, knowing he couldn't.

Steve regarded the landscape of Chenco's nude body with a passionate rake of his gaze. "Come here."

Chenco went where he was told, and Steve watched him, coaxing him with his finger to move closer.

Then he leaned forward and took firm possession of Chenco's balls.

Chenco wanted to yelp and cover himself—the man had promised him exquisite pain, and he'd gone right for the part of him least interested in trying pain on. It wasn't a painful grip—yet.

Though he didn't flinch, Chenco had to breathe, focusing on Steve's promise that he knew what he was doing, how all pain would end in pleasure. Chenco reminded himself Steve could navigate the dangerous waters to the land of delights. As Steve held his sac, Chenco did his best not to freak out.

Steve squeezed.

This had been the pain Chenco had wanted to brace against, soft and sharp and raw. Steve constricted nerves and pinched sensitive, delicate skin. This touch was dangerous and wrong and should be stopped, said Chenco's balls. Yet even as the message arrived, it tangled with Steve's contract, which challenged Chenco to let go of the urge to protect himself, to give it over in exchange for transformation.

Wait, Chenco told his balls. *Let me sit with this for a bit, because I think if we hold out, we're going to get something incredible.*

Steve's grip changed slowly, alternating between pain and massage, scrambling the signals to Chenco's frantic brain until it didn't know the difference. He wasn't sure how long it went on—maybe minutes, maybe hours, maybe days—he only knew it began with his body tensed and ended with him breathing into the pain, riding it into waves of pleasure. While his cock never exactly got hard, he certainly began to understand what Steve had meant about getting off not necessarily being a physical thing. If he had a metaphorical cock, it was throbbing something serious right now.

He was so focused on his balls, he didn't realize what was about to happen to his left nipple until it was too late.

It began as a lick, a quick flick of the tongue, but Chenco was so sensitized to pain he read the lick as a bite. Gasping, he started to draw away, then stopped. It had caught him off-guard—two fronts at once was a trick.

Steve grinned, his expression making it clear this was why he did it.

This was how Steve played him, always changing the assaults and sensations—as soon as Chenco got used to the lick-nip-lick-bite of his nipple, Steve pinched his backside. A hand stroked Chenco's thigh, a loving gesture. Teeth scraped his abdomen.

Lips trailed over his foreskin—then teeth—

Fear getting the better of his determination to withstand the torment, Chenco jerked away from Steve's grasp, then opened his eyes, ready to apologize.

The words died on his lips as he saw the delightful savagery on Steve's face—right before he leapt at Chenco and pulled him, rolling, to the bed.

Everything happened so fast—Chenco went flat on his back, pinned, Steve's heavy body pressing over his, rough hairy chest and thighs grinding along his wiry frame. The tormenting had him keyed up, jerking and startling at every touch, and just when he would get himself calmed down, Steve would tweak a nipple, nip at his chin, grind his pelvis.

Chenco tried to withstand it, tried to bear up, but he

couldn't hold on. It wasn't about pain, which was what he'd readied himself for. It was that he never knew what was coming or from where. It had almost nothing to do with discomfort and everything to do with realizing Steve could and would hurt him, and he couldn't anticipate it, couldn't guard against it, not even in his mind. He had to hand over control, give Steve the power to decide what pain was and when and how it happened. It wasn't long before Chenco felt himself sliding, leaking out of his composure.

"Please," he said, first in a whisper and then in a whine. "Please—please—"

"Please what?" Steve sucked hard in the center of Chenco's chest.

Crying out, Chenco arced into him. "*Ngyh*. Please—please, don't…please stop…"

Steve chuckled at Chenco's sternum, licking it like a popsicle. "You want me to stop?"

Chenco didn't know what he wanted. He was starting to lose more and more of his mind every time Steve touched him. When Steve took Chenco's nipples in his teeth, tugging at them as he moved his head back and forth in rapid motion, Chenco began to wail. Not because it hurt, but because he couldn't stand to be lost anymore.

Steve slapped his thigh.

It was a sharp, stinging pain, and the shock of it brought Chenco up short. The second strike tingled. The third started to burn, and he gasped. On the fourth he cried out, and on the fifth he tried to wriggle away.

Laughing, a wicked purr making all the hair Chenco hadn't waxed or shaved stand on end, Steve grabbed Chenco's hips and flipped him over. Chenco had just enough time to acclimate to the new position when his thighs were wrenched open, knees apart, butt lifted. His libido pulsed as he imagined Steve looking at him, felt him tease Chenco's opening with fingertips and tongue.

Then Steve's lips brushed Chenco's hole, and he clenched, entire body ready to bolt.

Holding him down, Steve spread him wide and took the edge of his opening gently in his teeth.

Chenco screamed—it didn't hurt, not yet, but it would, it would *hurt*, and it was all he could think about. When Steve thrust his tongue deep, Chenco cried out as if he'd been impaled roughly with a metal plug. His sensors were broken now, his brain short-circuited, and he couldn't get away. When a real nip came, he shrieked and clawed at the sheets.

With almost no warning, he began to cry.

There wasn't much pain, not really, only the uncertainty of when the pain would come and to what degree. His brain didn't care. His brain spun and spit and made him howl, drew up every curdled bit of tension inside him and projected it out of his mouth. He cried, sobbed as if he were being beaten, no longer able to fake it, no longer able to be strong. He could pull the edge of his emotions back, keeping the tide at bay but only just.

As if this was what he'd been waiting for, Steve changed.

Oh, he still tortured Chenco, still teased and tormented his backside, his thighs, his hole—but he stroked Chenco's skin reverently too. He nipped and poked and scrambled Chenco's senses, but he petted too, and as Chenco tipped toward the edge, Steve crooned between tastes of Chenco.

"Let it go, baby. Let me have it. Don't hold back. I want you undone all the way." He licked, long and wicked, down Chenco's crack. "I got you. I'll catch you when you fall."

Chenco tried to fight. He didn't want to fall, not like this. This wasn't part of the deal—he'd signed up for pain, but not for this, not to be exposed like *this*—

Steve kissed the crease of Chenco's leg at his thigh, nuzzling the line of skin with his nose.

A deep, cracking sob broke out of Chenco, and his whole body went rigid as he resisted.

Steve sucked and nipped, dragging the flat of his tongue down Chenco's taint. He thrust his tongue inside a few times, then whispered against Chenco's wet, heated skin.

"Dance for your papi."

Chenco danced.

It was a dance of pain, of loss, of sorrow—he slammed back into the memory of the trailer, when he realized he had to go, when he knew everything had changed and would stay changed forever. Steve had instructed him to put the pain away, but it all returned now. He was homeless. Even without the gangs, the trailer would go, and not to him. Cooper had promised to fuck him over in death, and he had. Chenco had worked hard for his life, sweat blood and tears, and yet it was gone. Taken by his father, the parent he had dreamed since he was a little boy would someday love him.

He cried. Oh, how Chenco cried.

When the physical pain returned—blows to his backside, his thighs, rough grips at his nipples—he sighed, relieved, because thank God, at least he had something to focus on other than how lost he was. As the pain went on it began to burn, a sweet, aching yaw lighting a tiny flame inside his darkness and spreading through him, grounding him, showing him the way. To what he wasn't sure, but it was better than darkness, and he followed it.

All the while he struggled, Steve held him. Grounded him with whispers and with his touch, sometimes soft, sometimes sharp. When Chenco had agreed to step into Steve's sadism, he'd expected floggers and benches and ropes, titillating games and kinky thrills. He had not expected this, to be drawn so into pain, to be fucked by it—not by blows or bonds but by the pain itself, his own pain.

To be released.

This was no game, no kinky giggle. This was more reverent than a church service, more personal than any priest-led confession. This was closer to the bone than putting on a dress and wig and makeup and releasing his inner queen.

This was only the first time of playing this way, the barest introduction to a whole new world.

When Chenco felt Steve move behind him, felt the cock nudging his hole, felt Steve's hairy chest and thick pectorals rubbing along his back, his body crowding as he prepared to enter, Chenco shut his eyes. He reached back to clutch at Steve's neck and released the deepest, heaviest breath he had in him. When Steve thrust inside, unleashing a new burn, Chenco sobbed, finding a new pit from which to pull the pain.

Steve bit down on the back of Chenco's neck, holding him still like a dog beneath his thrusts, Chenco let go, and when Steve growled and laved the skin caught beneath his teeth with a rough, rude tongue, Chenco flew away.

There was pain, there was rough fucking, there was everything that had been, but now there was space and light and freedom. Oh God, so much freedom he started crying *again*, and he couldn't stop. He exploded, he turned into light, he danced with stars.

He danced for his papi all across the pain, so happy, so grateful, so free.

He lost time, somehow—the shift was subtle, a fuzzy burn on his brain, a space between being fucked like a dog and lying tangled in Steve's arms, surrounded by his heat and scent and strength, accepting soft kisses and strokes and the widest, brightest smiles he'd ever seen on the other man's face.

"Oh, honey." Steve nuzzled Chenco's ear as he kept petting, never ceasing his gentle and grounding attentions. "Sweetheart, you were so amazing. So brave, so wonderful, so beautiful."

It was amazing, Chenco tried to say, but he could only make a soft sound, his hand grasping weakly at Steve's rough jaw.

"Shh. Take it easy. You went in hard, deeper than I've ever seen anybody go on their first try. Take a minute to find your feet, baby. Just rest. There's no rush. I've got you, and I'm not going anywhere." He pressed another kiss on Chenco's forehead. "You're safe, *cariño.* I've got you. You're safe."

Okay, Chenco tried to say, but still couldn't. The rest, though, he fought for, swallowed several times and made his lips shape to say the words. "Thank you."

This earned him a kiss on his lips, slow and full of tongue and teeth. "It was my pleasure."

Chenco smiled.

CHAPTER ELEVEN

THE MORNING AFTER the contract and the best sex he'd ever had in his life, Steve offered to give Chenco his punishment for stabbing Randy. "If you still want it. It's been a while, and it's not usually good to leave things this long. I'm sorry I let you down in this regard."

"You didn't let me down, and yes, please, I do want it." Chenco leaned into Steve's warm, naked chest. "I don't feel bad all the time, but sometimes I catch him wincing and holding his shoulder, and it eats me up."

Steve tangled his fingers in Chenco's hair. "If I do this, it means you have to stop punishing yourself. If his shoulder bugs him, you don't get to be upset about it because you already paid. Got it?"

"Got it," Chenco said, but he worried he'd have to work on following through.

"All right. Then your punishment is spending six and a half hours with Randy, one hour for each inch of the shoe heel you put into him."

"That's it?" Chenco sat up and glared at Steve. "I hang out with Randy all the time. This isn't a punishment."

Steve tweaked his nose. "You've never spent six straight hours with Jansen when he knows you're his to command. It'll be punishment enough."

Uh-oh. "He can't… I don't want to have sex—"

"No sex. He won't try."

"Okay," Chenco said, but he wasn't sure it really was okay yet.

Steve laughed. "You don't get to agree to the punishment, baby. You just have to take it."

He rose from the bed, leaving Chenco to wonder whether or not this had been a very good idea after all.

A few days before his husband was supposed to arrive, Randy called in his hours, announcing he was kidnapping Chenco for a ride. "I need something to keep my mind off my man still being days away."

Chenco tried not to let on how nervous he was, wondering what Randy would make him do, hoping it wasn't too embarrassing, doing his best to trust Steve wouldn't put him in such a position. "What do you have in mind?"

"I want a Chenco tour of the RGV, starting with the beautiful fucking flea market in Alamo. Please tell me it's still there."

Chenco relaxed. "That's all you want?"

"I didn't say it was all I wanted." Randy linked his arm through Chenco's and hollered down the hall toward Steve's office. "Monk, I'm taking your truck and your boy, and I plan to get comfy."

It was the first time someone had called Steve Chenco's boy, and it made him feel slightly out of body.

He said nothing all the way to the truck. As he settled into the lush seats, Randy adjusted the mirrors, wheel, and seat, and he plugged an MP3 player into the stereo. Captain & Tennille began to sing, and Chenco couldn't help it, he laughed.

Randy flipped him off. "This is my day, so I get my music. Old school all the way, all the songs my uncle used to sing to me. C&T, Journey, AC/DC, Pat Benatar, Styx, and of course Queen."

Chenco noticed the way Randy's face softened as he spoke of his uncle. "Sorry. I won't make fun."

"Damn right you won't." Randy pulled onto the main highway. "It's been a long fucking time since I went to Alamo. Direct me, Princess."

It took a good forty minutes to get there, and by the time they parked, Chenco sang along with the golden oldies. In fact, as they crossed the parking lot to the main entrance, he hummed the chorus to "Open Arms". He was excited to be back at *la pulga*. He hadn't been in years, and it brought back good memories of when he'd sneak away with friends in high school.

The Alamo flea market was a mighty beast, sprawling ten aisles wide and probably a thousand feet long. Half of it was permanent, shops with wiring and even air conditioning in a few instances. Chenco drank it all in, letting it take him back. "My mom got so pissed when I came here. Once, on a dare, I got my hair cut in the barber shop. Mama pitched a fit, but the cut actually wasn't too bad."

Randy had been thumbing through some old vinyl

albums, but he looked up when Chenco told him the story. "She flipped out? Why?"

"She hated everything low-brow Mexican. You'd think being half Latino I'd get a pass from racism in at least one parent, but no."

"Damn, that had to bite." Randy crooked his finger at the shopkeeper, who was in the back of his booth reading an iPad. Randy asked him several questions in Spanish, something about did he have any other albums, as far as Chenco could tell. The man nodded, replied with something too swift for Chenco to translate, and rooted under a table for another box.

Chenco grimaced. "Jesus, do *all* of you have better Spanish than me?"

Randy flashed him an apologetic smile. "You can probably still beat Sam, but he's catching up fast. It's an asset for him to be a bilingual nurse. Maybe the two of you can learn together."

"I kind of suck at languages. I tried to learn in high school, sneaking CDs from the library, but it didn't really work."

"You'll get there. Mitch'll teach you. He's who taught me. But you have to ask."

He ended up buying three albums, and he seemed pleased with himself as they went on to the next booth. When they got to the shop with fancy prom dresses, Chenco beamed. "Oh man, this is where Caramela got her first costume."

"No shit?" Randy ducked inside, flipping through the racks. "Think we can find her anything today?"

"She's too refined for the flea market now." Still, Chenco had fun window-shopping, remembering when it felt wickedly dangerous to even dream of shopping for his alter ego.

"What color was the dress?" Randy asked as they gave up and went on to the next shop.

"Blue sheath, full of sequins. I bought it, a pair of silver heels, a blonde wig, and a gaudy necklace and earrings set. I was seventeen. God, I thought I was so fierce."

"Something tells me this story doesn't end well."

No, it didn't. "Mom found it and burned it all. Cried for a week. Both of us did, actually."

Randy shook his head. "Ah, family. Can't live with them, can't shoot them." He brightened as he saw the food carts up ahead. "Shit, do they still have those slushy things?"

They got mango slushies and tacos. Randy laughed about the live chickens a vendor sold, telling a story about how once he had Mitch buy one and they kept it as a pet until it shit on the carpet. He had a million stories about Mitch, some which involved Sam too. He talked some about his husband, though not much as he said it made him twitchy and homesick.

It amazed Chenco how carefree Randy could be so attached to somebody, and eventually he told him so.

Randy shrugged and took another sip of his slushy. "Everybody needs someone they can lay themselves down with. I never figured I'd get it, assumed I'd have to sort of cobble my release space out of other people, and then there was Ethan. Slick, my sexy man, the fool who wanted me, warts and all." He stirred his straw in his drink, frowning at it. "Honestly, I'm half afraid being away from me this long will make him come to his senses."

Chenco elbowed him. "He *married* you."

"Yeah, well." He ran a hand through his hair. "God, I wish he'd fucking get here."

Chenco smiled and jerked his head at the next aisle. "Come on. Tell me another story, and let's go find him a present."

They did find one—a truly ugly coffee mug reading *Welcome to Las Vegas!* with a 1960s stylized faded scene plastered around the sides. Chenco was dubious, but Randy only chuckled and declared it would be perfect.

"Yeah. He'll love this." He wiped sweat from his brow with his fingers. "Okay, I think I've had enough of this fucking heat. We still have an hour and a half. Let's get in Steve's air-conditioned beast, grab us some Starbucks, and soak up more RGV."

It was kind of fun to hear what had changed about the valley over the years—they had some overlapping memories, but Randy knew more stories of days past, most of them secondhand from Mitch, but they were still cool. "I should take this tour with Mitch sometime."

Randy shrugged. "He gets funny about this place. Loves and hates it at the same time."

"I know the feeling."

"We need to go on a field trip with Sam before we bust out of here. He's always going on about learning

Mitch's history, and anyway, the two of you need to bond."

"We could go get him now," Chenco pointed out.

"Nope. I want to see your home digs. Edinburg, you said, right?"

Chenco balked. "I don't want to go to my mom's house."

"Not into it, no. Just show me the outside."

The very idea had Chenco's insides churning with acid. "It's gated. We can't."

"Show me the gates, then."

"*No.*" Chenco's chest felt so tight he thought he was having a heart attack. He was about ready to jump out of the truck.

He couldn't do this—he didn't care if Steve told him he had to, he couldn't, he had to make it stop.

Safe word, his subconscious offered up, and he shouted, at the top of his lungs, "*Red!*"

"Fine, fine. We won't go." Randy sank in his seat, shaking his head. "Jesus, I'm gonna go make everybody use their fucking safe word, aren't I?"

Chenco unclenched a fraction. "We really aren't going?"

"No, hon, we're not." Randy glanced at him, apologetic. "Sorry. I got carried away. That's twice with you I've pushed too hard. I really fucking shouldn't be let out of the state without my husband."

"I don't want to go back. I don't know what I'd do if I saw them being okay without me."

"She still thinks of you, no matter what she says."

Randy rubbed at his jaw as he stared out at traffic. "Sent my mom a wedding announcement when I married Ethan. She never said boo to me about it, but my cousin told me Mom keeps the letter in her dresser drawer. Sometimes they love their pride more than they love us, but it doesn't mean they don't love us at least a little."

"Your parents don't talk to you either?"

"Not a fucking word since I was seventeen. Last thing my dad said to me was, 'Get the hell out of my house, you fucking faggot.' Don't remember what my mom said, just that she cried." He glanced across the seat at Chenco and gave him a crooked smile. "I guess I was hoping maybe your mom wasn't as much of a fuckhead as mine, but sounds like we both got the shit stick in that department."

Chenco traced his finger across the passenger window. "She'd freak if she found out about Steve. Older than me, and the BDSM thing."

"Yeah, well, shows what the fuck she knows, doesn't it? Anybody looks at Monk and sees anything but a loyal, solid-as-rock man, they need their heads examined. What he does in bed doesn't mean shit. It goes for you too with the drag thing. Hell, none of it should matter. You're a good person. You pay your taxes, you don't hurt anybody, and you make a hell of a lot of people happy. This is what life's about, not how well you fit into somebody's fucking box." He reached over and patted Chenco's leg. "Okay. How about instead of memory lane we find one of those drive-through convenience stores? Those seriously blow my mind."

Smiling, Chenco nodded to the exit coming up. "Get off here and turn left."

"You got it, Princess," Randy said, easing into the right lane.

THE FIRST FEW days of Chenco living at the ranch had gone about as Steve expected—Chenco alternated between feeling right at home and actively trying not to get attached to anything or anyone. Oddly enough, Steve struggled with the same poles. For so long it had only been him in the house, but now it wasn't just full of people, it was full of family living life. Mitch had taken a short-range job delivering within the RGV, and Sam had looked into part-time nursing at a local care center. Randy, having appointed himself the hacienda's personal housekeeper, kept them all fed, washed all the clothes, and hollered at people when they messed up his clean floors.

Chenco still worked at Taco Palenque and met up with Booker to rehearse, and on the night before Ethan and Crabtree were due to arrive, they all went to Caramela's show at Club 33. It was as grand a performance as the first time Steve had seen it, but Booker and Chenco felt it could use a lot of work.

They were relentless in their pursuit of the perfect staging, and when they weren't on the floor at the club working through numbers, they could often be found talking through plans and schemes in the old maid's quarters at the hacienda, which Steve had given over completely to the care and keeping of all things Caramela.

Steve kept a close eye on Booker.

The boy was one hell of a mess, and if it wasn't for Chenco's friendship with him, Steve would have happily washed his hands of the whole scenario. Brett, one of Steve's longtime friends he'd reconnected with during Chenco's rescue, had paid a visit to this Tristan, and he reported to Steve it hadn't been a productive meeting.

"Both of them are hotheads," Brett told Steve as they sat on a crumbling loading dock one afternoon at the cannery, where they'd met to talk after seeing to a bad episode with Gordy. "This Tristan idiot thinks it's fun to hurt people. This is about as deep as he goes."

Fucking amateurs. "I suppose when you tried to correct his ignorance, he told you to fuck off and mind your own business?"

"Oh yeah, but wait—it gets better. This Booker kid? Not just a budding sub, but he's got a clear kink for humiliation, and it's tangled up like hell with an abusive father, a family who kicked him out, and a series of other bad relationships. When I advised him to leave Tristan, he tried to punch me out and yelled at me for getting in his business."

Steve swore under his breath. This was often a snarl in the lifestyle—while BDSM identification decidedly did *not* come out of personal trauma or abuse, the two conditions shared an unfortunate and frequent correlation. No surprise, when most men and women who realized they enjoyed receiving pain were labeled as freaks and those who took pleasure in inflicting it monsters. Sadomasochism was a complex enough state—force it into the dark and make healthy, compassionate discussion about it difficult if not impossible, and fuckery would soon follow.

"I'm figuring the easiest thing to do is leave him under your watch, since he's all but living at your place." Brett said this carefully, however, and his beard lifted in a sad smile as he continued. "If you need someone else to mind Booker, given everything with Gordy, say the word."

Man, but Steve was tempted. *Everything with Gordy* that afternoon had entailed Steve checking in on the live feed to the cannery and catching his best friend carving into his skin with a piece of broken glass. Brett had come over right away, and they'd talked him into not just his medication but a trip to the doctor for some stitches—no way Steve was asking Sam to sew him up like last time.

After they got back from the clinic, Gordy had begged them for a scene, but Brett had been firm where Steve hadn't been able to hold his own. Brett volunteered to stand guard until the punishment time was over and get Gordy settled down.

"I can handle the Booker kid." He didn't let himself dwell too long over whether or not he was fit for the job.

Brett nodded, but the door had been opened on the conversation they'd been trying not to have, and there was no closing it now. "He's getting worse," Brett said, and Steve knew he meant Gordy.

Steve kept his gaze down. "Yeah. I know."

"Nobody would blame you if you called mental health. Everyone understands that's where it's going. It's not something we want, but it might be best at this point."

The knot in Steve's gut twisted. "I would blame myself. He'll never get better inside."

Brett was quiet a long time before he said, "Steve, I don't think he's going to get better anywhere."

Steve was back between his rock and a hard place, and nobody could help him, not unless they took the decision away from him, which he wouldn't ever forgive. Which was why Brett let it drop, though Steve knew his friend didn't like leaving things this way.

As Steve got on his bike and headed to the house, the conversation with Brett stirred dark thoughts. How was Steve supposed to help Chenco while babysitting his mentally ill best friend who wouldn't live in a house, would only burrow in squalor in the abandoned factory he'd played in as a kid? This was a question he didn't have the answer to. Soon he'd be deciding between pursuing a relationship with Chenco and serving out his obligation to Gordy.

The darkest thought of all was how, for the first time, he was considering not choosing Gordy.

When Steve returned to the house after meeting with Brett, Booker and Chenco had taken over the dining room table with blocked maps of routines, complete with setup of lights and props. They had some for Club 33, but they were working on a mirror version for a one-sided stage instead of a theater-in-the-round. Steve lingered in the doorway from the kitchen, just out of their line of sight, listening.

"We need to go to South Padre," Booker kept saying. "Trist says I can go this time, for real. The guy at the club had a cancellation for spring break, and if we act now, we can take the spot."

Chenco frowned at the plans. "I've told you, I don't have the money. We'd need a truck—not a pickup, a *truck*—to haul the stuff and get it back, and we'd need to buy some of the gels and things we always borrow from 33."

"You're saving money now, living here. You have spare change."

"*No.* I don't." Chenco sounded tired. "It's a different game now, Book, and you know it."

"If this is about needing permission from your new *daddy*," Booker began, his voice dripping with irritation, but Chenco cut him off angrily and redirected them back to their layout of a particular routine.

Once he was sure his lover had a handle on the situation, Steve removed himself from the doorway, drifting out to the patio. After rolling a cigarette, he smoked it leisurely as he pondered how to proceed. Chenco he knew how to work, but Booker was tricky—for as much as Chenco responded well to managing, Booker only seemed to like being told what to do when it was a bad command, when he was guaranteed a rotten outcome to reinforce the garbage he'd managed to get crammed into his head.

The sounds of a car coming down the drive interrupted his thoughts—heading around to the front, he arrived in time to see a sleek silver Mercedes come to a stop between Mitch's semi cab and his own truck. The driver's door opened to reveal a tall, sandy-haired middle-aged man in a casual suit and mirrored sunglasses who came around quickly to the passenger side to assist an older man. The passenger had white hair, a trim beard, and the ragged look of someone who had been sick and recently lost a great deal of weight. The older man also wore a suit, as well-cut and expensive-looking as the younger man's, but no amount of glamour could hide the fact that the gentleman was still very much recovering from illness.

The front door to the hacienda opened, and Randy came bursting out of it, grinning and calling to the tall man. "Well look at you, sexypants."

The driver smiled at him, a wide, welcoming beacon for his lover, and once the older man had shooed him off, the sandy-haired man took Randy in a full, possessive embrace. Steve enjoyed the tableau while thick emotions battled inside him. Then he crossed the yard to welcome his guests.

Randy had a light about him Steve hadn't ever seen before. "Steve, this is Ethan Ellison, the hottest fuck in Vegas. Ethan, this is Steve Vance, who could crack your casino open with a smartphone and a stick of gum."

Ethan cast a *down, boy* glance at his husband before smiling and extending a lean hand to Steve. "A pleasure to meet you. I've heard nothing but good things."

"Likewise." Steve took his hand, and they met firm grip to firm grip, steady gaze to steady gaze.

"And this," Randy said, extricating himself from his husband and indicating with a grand sweep the older man, who came forward with the aid of a cane, "is Crabtree."

This would be the gangster. Steve came forward a little more cautiously than he normally would, not having ever met a gangster before. Not much in life intimidated him, but something more than the whispered reputation of this guy made Steve's spine straighter. Even weakened, this man had a kind of self-possession Steve envied, and he wasn't exactly a shrinking violet.

Steve shook hands with Crabtree and gave a curt, respectful nod.

Crabtree's grip was firm but with a ghost on it, as if he'd once had great strength but had recently flagged. Something in the back of Steve's mind whispered about a heart attack possibly, but he'd have to check with the others to be certain. Whatever had felled the man, it hadn't dulled his steely blue eyes in the slightest. They were sharp as knives, and Steve suspected knives were a running theme with Crabtree.

"Thank you for your hospitality." Crabtree nodded at Ethan, who accepted the prompt and returned to the car, coming back with a cloth gift bag. He handed it to Steve, who withdrew a bottle of 1974 Dalmore.

Steve accepted it with a bow. "Thank you, sir. Please come in and make yourself at home."

"Well played," Randy murmured as they followed Ethan and Crabtree inside.

Steve watched the old man moving stiffly, clearly hating his weakness but unable to overcome it. "I've seen too many mobster movies."

"Probably for the best, since he *is* a mobster movie." He nodded to the bottle in Steve's hand. "That's over a grand, what you're holding there."

Fucking Christ. Steve slid the scotch into the bag. "Any tips on how to behave around him?"

"Be kind, but not condescending. The heart attack was pretty fucking serious, and he's not taking to his new lifestyle very well. He's lost about seventy pounds in a few months, and the weight had been keeping a lot of the world at bay. Now it's gone, and he's weak to boot. Lots of wounded pride walking around in front of you there. Tread respectfully."

Steve nodded. Respect he could do.

"Oh, and he loves cats. Like, crazy stupid loves them."

"I fucking hate cats."

"I used to too. You won't for long." When Steve grunted, Randy patted his arm. "Come on. Let's go inside so I can help you drink some of your scotch."

CHAPTER TWELVE

T HERE WASN'T ANY question, Steve decided as he watched Crabtree greet Mitch and Sam—Crabtree was in the lifestyle. The tell was there, a subtle vein running through the man and everything he did. As Steve studied the way Crabtree dealt with his physical limitations and how he maneuvered others, another suspicion grew in Steve's mind. He began to think not only did Crabtree actively practice, he might be a sadist too.

For as much as Sam seemed wary of Crabtree, Crabtree exhibited gentleness with the young man beyond what Randy gave him—and while Crabtree delighted in making Mitch squirm, he respected the bond between Sam and Mitch and never so much as taunted it. He regarded Chenco from a distance when he saw his initial overtures were met with wariness.

Crabtree also watched Booker.

"What's this you're working on?" Crabtree asked, sidling up to Chenco and Booker's table.

"New act." Booker pointed to the plans. "We've about got this blocked. A few days of practice, and we'll nail this bitch."

Chenco pursed his lips, looking slightly haggard. Crabtree regarded the plans, absently toying with the top of his cane. "This is the drag show?"

"This is Caramela's show." Booker nudged Chenco with his elbow. "Best fucking drag act in the RGV."

"Well." Crabtree smiled at Chenco, the gesture almost as gentle as the one he saved for Sam. "I look forward to seeing it. When's the next performance?"

Chenco started to answer, but Booker cut him off.

"There's another one at Club 33 at the end of April, but this is what I'm trying to tell him—I could get a show lined up for spring break—"

"Chenco?" It was impressive, the way Crabtree cut Booker off with a hard edge but gave Chenco a lot of soft space, all in the one word. "Will you be performing anywhere anytime soon? Perhaps in a more private performance, if a public one isn't in your lineup right now?"

Chenco glanced at Steve, looking for reassurance to speak his mind, and Steve nodded. *Yes. It's okay.*

"Well," Chenco began, "the thing is, I'm trying to save up. I want to perform big, but I want to be ready, and I want to do it up right, so I need the money."

"If you'd let me book these gigs, you'd have—"

"Booker." The edge in Crabtree's tone was much more pronounced and yet still veiled, a knife pushed discreetly into one's back. "Kindly let Chenco finish."

"I just…" Booker stopped, caught up in Crabtree's terrible stare.

Crabtree returned his focus to Chenco, gentle once

more. "What is your goal, young man? For what are you saving your pennies? I would love to hear all about it."

Chenco relaxed a fraction. "I want to take the show on the road, but not until I have better legs under me."

"And Filthy Divas," Booker interjected, grinning, though he faded at a hard look from Crabtree.

Chenco shot a *don't start* look at Booker. "Maybe I'll do a show like Filthy Divas, maybe not. Whatever I do, I need a little bigger name first. I'll go to South Padre and Austin, but I have to be ready. I won't go when it's not the right time."

Crabtree nodded sagely. "How long have you been performing drag?"

"Well, I got interested when I was sixteen, and as soon as I moved out on my own I started collecting costumes and makeup and hair, but I was twenty-one before I went onstage. So I'm heading into my fourth year now. I've only done regular shows for six months."

Booker looked as if he wanted to say something, but he swallowed and studied Crabtree carefully instead.

Crabtree didn't give Booker a chance to speak. "You're deliberate in your choices. Very admirable."

It warmed Steve's heart to see Chenco smile as he did, but it thumped an extra beat of pride as Chenco said, "Thank you, sir."

Though Crabtree didn't move, he might as well have run a hand over Chenco's head, the way he looked at him. Then the gangster turned to Booker. "And you, boy? What are your goals in this venture?"

This was actually fun, watching Booker try to figure

out how to behave around Crabtree. He wanted to sass, but even a headcase like Booker could read the writing on the wall that was Crabtree. From the other side of the room, Steve saw Randy watching the show too, biting back a cheeky grin.

Booker cleared his throat and did a kind of submissive head bob as he replied. "I want to make Caramela big. Bigger than anybody else. I like making her shine. You have to see her. She's fucking amazing. The best. I go on stage with her sometimes, but it's all for her. Caramela is my queen."

Chenco listened to this quietly, clearly hearing this level of devotion for the first time. He leaned over and bussed Booker on the cheek.

Booker said nothing, didn't look him in the eye, but he put a hand on Chenco's leg and squeezed before returning to a kind of slumped parade rest. He also cast another glance at Crabtree.

The gangster's focus returned to their layouts and schematics. "What holds you back is finances? Or do you not feel the show is ready?"

"It's mostly finances," Chenco said after a small hesitation. "I'll admit, I get a little fussy wanting things to be just so, but Book's right. We're there." He sighed and brushed his hand over the pages. "It's going to be clunky at first, no question. I'll do it someday—but it really is about having the money right first, about being ready."

"Proper financing is very important." Crabtree reached into his jacket pocket, pulled out a fine leather wallet and peeled out several hundred-dollar bills. "Consider this my donation to a good cause. If this pushes you over to being able to put on this South Padre show, then I shall be in the front row. If I like what I see, you can consider me an official sponsor."

Chenco gaped, and Booker's head jerked up to track Crabtree as he leisurely strode away.

The gangster slowed in his already sedate pace as he neared Steve, glancing at Booker before he spoke. "The boy belong to anyone?"

"To a shit wannabe. I've been keeping an eye on him while others sort the other end, but it's not going so well."

Crabtree's eyes narrowed, and then he nodded. "I'll help you in your shepherding. I don't think it will take, but I won't have him bothering your boy. Randy is correct. Crescencio is a treasure."

"I'd be very grateful for your help, sir. Thank you."

Crabtree ambled to the kitchen counter, where he stopped and examined fruit in a bowl. Waiting, Steve knew, for Booker to come over and thank him, engage with him. He only had to linger a minute.

Steve watched Crabtree work Booker—subtle, distant, feeling him out, but not only did he seem to expertly unpack and identify the damaged sub, he began, without prompting, without so much as a clarification for permission, to repair him.

It was all how he spoke to the young man. How he positioned his body as they conversed, how he commanded Booker to obsequiousness, how when Booker tried to sass him as he did Steve, Crabtree redirected him with only a narrowing of his eyes and a quiet threat of violence so sharp it was a blade in its own right. He succeeded where Steve and the others had failed because he *used* the threat, made it clear he played well beyond the edge, offering something twisted enough to catch Booker's equally messed-up interest.

Crabtree played the boy like an instrument, but not out of spite or malice or even glee. He played the boy because the boy so desperately needed to be played. He played Booker because it was what Crabtree did best.

A new light flared inside Steve's darkness, a lantern not threatening to burn down his world but possibly illuminating the way to rise from the ashes. Maybe Crabtree could help another messed-up man in Steve's life.

Steve stole a glance at Randy, saw the gambler's slow, patient smile. Randy had seen it too, and he wasn't in the least bit surprised.

Stacking the deck.

For the first time in a long, long time, Steve began to hope.

WHILE CHENCO STILL wasn't entirely certain about Randy, his husband Ethan was quickly a favorite.

Ethan was cool, smooth, and easy to look at. He wore suits a lot, which was weird, but hot—literally hot, with the heat wave hitting the RGV. Ethan said Vegas was worse most days.

Ethan ran a casino he'd won in a card game—how the fuck did you top that in the game of life? He had a quietness about him Chenco appreciated too, something probably essential for survival when dealing with Randy. Chenco's favorite trait about Ethan was the way he calmed his husband without doing anything at all, just by being present. With Ethan around, Randy was less like a loose ball bearing and more of a paddle ball on a string. Ethan clearly held the paddle.

Something about their relationship caught Chenco's attention, but he couldn't figure out what it was. Maybe Chenco was too new at the BDSM thing and wanted to label everyone top and bottom, but he couldn't quite work them out. If he had to pin them down, he'd call Randy the sub and Ethan the Dom, but only sometimes. Every now and again, when they weren't aware you were looking, they flipped. When Chenco studied them in public, he could sometimes catch Randy shoring up his husband or making a place for him in a strange situation. It was a complicated dance, and Chenco found he enjoyed it.

He enjoyed Ethan on his own merit, in part due to his subtle approach. Chenco kind of wanted to follow him around like a puppy—not for sex, but because Ethan made him feel even and okay. He talked with Chenco in such a quiet, easy way, giving him space to work things out.

Such as whether or not he should do the South Padre gig. Chenco asked Ethan if he owed Crabtree now. Ethan said no, not exactly, but he pointed out Crabtree didn't do such things lightly, so if this truly did mean the difference between no and yes, perhaps he should consider letting things move forward. Ethan had nudged him into letting his new family help him prep too—Randy took Booker to get the lighting set up, and Mitch had been offended Chenco hadn't asked him earlier to find a small truck to haul all Caramela's shit to the site.

When Chenco confessed to Ethan he was nervous to approach the owner, how sometimes Booker had bad judgments about contacts, Ethan offered to vet the man himself.

This was how Chenco found himself sliding sideways into the spring break show, taking Caramela to a bigger stage. He wasn't sure why it made him feel so panicked. One night, as he sat snuggled against Steve in Caramela's room listening to music, he confessed how he felt. Steve hadn't had any trouble understanding.

"It makes you feel panicked because you're taking a step forward. You've already been kicked out of your nest twice, and you've been flapping around, but now you're going to try to actually fly. It would be odd if you weren't nervous."

Chenco wanted to fake it, to buck up and be self-assured, but he didn't have it in him, especially with the next thing brought up. That morning Chenco had gone to his post office box and found the notice from the lawyer letting him know the trailer now belonged to the Ku Klux Klan. Chenco was officially homeless.

When he told Steve, his boyfriend said nothing, only pulled Chenco onto his lap, tucked Chenco's head into his shoulder, and began to pet his hair.

It felt good, but worry clawed at Chenco, fears formerly lurking in the dark working their way to the surface. He didn't lift his head, but he still tensed a little as he asked, "How long is it okay, really, for me to stay here?"

"I don't have any specific timeline in mind. I suspect you'll soon—" He broke off, pausing in his strokes on Chenco's hair. When he started up again, his voice had a careful quality about it. "Let's just say, things are fluid for you right now, and I understand. I can't give you any guarantees on what will happen, but I'll give you my word—if things don't work out with us, I'll never throw you out. If I had to ask you to leave, I'd work with you and give you time."

"Okay. Thanks." He shut his eyes, soaking in safety, feeling secure enough to add, "I love how you explain things so clearly and honestly. I don't feel like you'd ever lie to me. Even if what you had to tell me was grim, you wouldn't lie."

"I wouldn't, no." Steve's hand trailed down Chenco's back and began to rub in gentle, drugging circles. "You've had it rough a long while. Take your time to make sure you feel safe, but don't stop yourself from letting go with those you can tell care about you. Those people would be Mitch and the boys."

"But they barely know me."

"The blood tie counts for a lot. You fill in a piece missing for your brother by doing nothing at all. But you're making connections with him now too, all on your own merit. You have a new family now."

Does this include you? Chenco didn't ask. Instead he let himself slide under the pleasure of Steve's touch before lifting his face to brush a kiss across Steve's cheek.

Steve kissed him back, tightened his grip on Chenco's arm and led him to his bedroom.

Technically it was their bedroom now, Chenco supposed. He slept with Steve every night, in Steve's room not the spare room, and every night they had sex. Sometimes it was rough and wild like the first time—okay, mostly it was rough and wild, though sometimes it was simply a *hello, good to see you.* Some nights it was more. Increasingly Steve brought toys into play, gloves with wicked little spikes pricking and teasing, unbelievably soft fur gloves arousing Chenco like nothing he knew how to describe. Always, *always* Steve came inside Chenco—more consistently than pain, this was the man's kink, Chenco realized, coming inside his lover.

It was the vulnerability again, as if Steve couldn't quite accept he was inside of Chenco unless he was *inside* Chenco, part of him remaining behind after. A few nights he had Chenco sleep with a plug, adding a new load inside Chenco's ass in the morning. Sometimes Chenco thought Steve would keep him cream-filled all day every day if he could.

There seemed to be a steady arc, though, heading them deeper and deeper into heavy play, and tonight, the night Chenco officially lost the trailer, Steve brought in a flogger. He only used it lightly, sliding the leather tails across Chenco's skin.

"I'm going to use this for real on you soon," he promised.

He didn't yet, though. That evening was like floating on a cloud, the massage Steve had begun out on the couch resuming on the bed. It led into sex, but it was, for them, almost sweet coupling, and afterward Chenco lay sprawled boneless atop Steve's body. "God, you have amazing hands. You should have been a masseuse."

"I have been, at least on an amateur level." Steve trailed a lazy hand down Chenco's spine. "A friend had a bad bike accident a few years ago, so I bought a table and gave him regular treatments."

It was an innocent enough statement, but the idea of Steve giving him treatments of any kind made Chenco a little hard.

Steve shifted his leg to draw Chenco closer. "We could make it part of tomorrow's playing." He rubbed his beard against the top of Chenco's head. "I'd already been planning to take you into the playroom, if you were ready. We could make it the warm-up."

Chenco nuzzled Steve's chest. "I'm ready, Papi."

The gentle massage slid down to Chenco's hip, making goose bumps break out across his flesh. "I could strip you naked and give you a nice, slow, sensual massage." He bent down to whisper in Chenco's ear. "Then, when you were all relaxed, I'd strap you to a bench and flog you until you screamed."

The goose bumps across Chenco's skin turned electric as he gasped and buried his face deeper into Steve.

"Would you like that?" Steve pressed.

Chenco wasn't sure. He wanted to try, but the idea of someone deliberately striking him—*striking* him—until he cried out in pain wasn't yet something he associated with fun times.

The hand on his hip stilled. "Chenco?"

Taking a deep breath, Chenco placed a kiss on Steve's erect nipple. "Yes. I would." He ran his hand down Steve's arm. "I think maybe I need to work up to it."

He worried he'd wrecked the mood, but if anything, it made Steve relax, and in the end Chenco was very glad he'd asked to go slowly. Over the next few days more and more toys made it into their play—the floggers came regularly, never used very hard, but always there, a third party in the bed. They started using restraints too, at first in the bed, and then in the playroom itself. It was just a regular room, except it had several interesting tables and benches and a closet full of various BDSM implements, carefully cleaned and stowed. Steve gave Chenco a tour of them all.

Nothing was quite as delicious to Chenco as those sweet, beautiful floggers, even though he still feared them. Some of it was because he knew Steve would be using them on him, some because they really were pretty. Even when they weren't playing, simply thinking of them made Chenco hum.

It seemed to please Steve to see how much Chenco enjoyed his toys. "You should try to swing one a few times, get a feel for what they're like from the other end."

Chenco flushed with excitement at the idea. "Really? I can do that?"

"Of course you can. Here. I'll show you how to hit with them too."

It was a fun game all in itself, being taught how to wield a flogger. It wasn't, it turned out, as easy as hauling one's arm back and whacking. Steve instructed him how to use the proper muscles, how to pace himself, how to control the weight of the falls. They practiced at a padded support beam in the playroom, but Steve explained how it would feel against real flesh too, and eventually he had Chenco slap himself on his thigh. A few times Steve had him strike his own leg too, and Steve's jean-clad ass.

The idea of striking Steve sent a wicked thrill through Chenco, but it also made him self-conscious. "That doesn't hurt?"

"Oh, a little. But these are love taps. Not like the real thing yet."

Chenco had thought there was plenty of sting in the blows Steve had given him, and some of his test slaps had been quite uncomfortable. "How hard is the real thing?"

In answer, Steve had picked up a flogger, hauled back his arm, and whaled on the post with enough force to make it shudder.

Dropping the implement in his own hand, Chenco stepped back, eyes wide. That had been *intense*. Was this how Steve would hit him?

Of course it was. It was what he'd asked to see.

It was *awfully* intense.

Steve's hand came to rest on Chenco's shoulder, making him jump. "You okay, baby?"

Chenco didn't trust himself to speak, so he waited a minute. "That would *hurt*."

"That's the point."

It was, wasn't it? Jesus, suddenly it all seemed so serious.

They hadn't done anything more during the session, which made Chenco feel like a failure. He sulked all through work that night. When he got home at eleven, Sam was in Steve's room, waiting for him.

"Hey." He smiled nervously. "So, um, this is awkward, but I've been sent to talk to you about the flogging thing."

"Steve sent you?" Jesus, how badly had he messed this up?

"No—not Steve. Randy." Sam gave a helpless shrug. "He might be talking shit, but he says he's been watching you, and he thinks you're nervous. He says he'd just scare you more, but he thought I should talk to you. So here I am, talking."

Sam didn't look like someone who wanted to talk. "You don't have to do this."

Now Sam looked annoyed. "So Randy's full of shit? God, I'm gonna kill him."

"Well…no, he's not full of shit, not on this score. But you still don't have to do this."

"Oh?" Sam brightened. "Don't worry about it. God,

he was right? Damn. He'll be smug as fuck. Okay." He rubbed his hands together. "What do you want to talk about? What are you nervous about?"

Chenco sat across from Sam. "I don't know. He showed me how hard he was going to hit me, and it freaked me out."

"Yeah, I get it." Sam tucked his feet underneath his body as he sat on the bed. "I don't go for implements so much. I'd rather have a paddle than a flogger, but honestly, mostly I prefer a guy's hand."

"Hand?"

"Yeah. Spanking. It's…kind of my thing. I like hands because you can feel the guy working you. I can tell if it's Mitch or Randy or Ethan even when I'm blindfolded—" Sam cut himself off, his whole *body* blushing now. "Oh God. I hadn't meant to tell you about that."

Chenco had kind of figured there was something going on with Randy and Sam, the way the guy was always after Sam's ass, but he hadn't known all four of them were into each other. He didn't want to make Sam feel awkward, though, especially when he was being so open to ease Chenco. "Don't worry about it. I'm not judging here."

"Yeah, well…I don't want you to think I'm some kind of whore. Well—I am, I guess. But not a *bad* whore." He rolled his eyes at himself and cleared his throat. "Anyway. I don't think you need to be scared, not unless you're going to be dumb and not tell Steve if you don't like something."

Here they were, at the heart of it all. "What if he wants to do something and I don't?"

"Then you don't." Sam's tone brooked no argument. "I get what you're afraid of, but trust me, you don't screw around here. He'd be a whole lot more upset with you if you let him do something you didn't want than if you told him no. Here's the thing it took me a while to truly understand—letting him do something to you isn't proving you care for him. He wants to share this with you, not force it on you. And maybe there are some things you don't want to try today but do in the future."

"Have you ever told Mitch no?"

Sam hesitated. "Mitch seems to read my mind. Randy, I tell no to at least once a week. It's kind of who we are. Mitch wants to protect me, and so does Randy, but Randy likes to challenge me." He bit his lip. "Is it…is this okay how we're talking about how I sleep with more guys than just your brother? He's down with it, I swear."

"It's very okay." Chenco smiled to show he meant it, but he didn't wait long to go back to questioning Sam. "Have you ever been flogged? You said you didn't like it, but…have you been?"

"Oh yeah. I'm better at doing it than I am taking it, though I've only ever done Randy." He shifted his feet around on the bed. "You want to know how it feels. Obviously it hurts, but a lot of things do. I would say flogging hurts a lot like a spanking, but spankings have a different kind of force, plus there's so much about shame with a spanking—which is why I enjoy it. Flogging is about enduring. I never cared for it because I feel too disconnected. Randy loves it. He loves to be whaled on, and he loves to whale back. He says he wants the challenge of it, like he's duking it out with the pain."

Chenco considered this. "I think what I'm most nervous about is Steve wants to do it until I break down. I can't duke it out. He's going to make me lose."

"Oh, Randy usually ends up swearing and screaming and sobbing by the end. He says it's an emotional enema." Sam shrugged. "I don't play that fiddle. I like to float into subspace and hang out, let myself be a slut and nobody can look down on me for it. In fact, they tend to tell me I'm beautiful for doing it. There's not a lot to let go of there."

No, Sam wouldn't have a lot to let go of, period. He'd heard Mitch call Sam Sunshine, and he didn't have to ask why.

"Anyway." Sam slid to the edge of the bed. "That's about it. Don't do something you don't want to. If you're not ready, say so. Steve hasn't dated in forever as far as I understand, so you're special. He'll wait for you. What he won't do is put up with someone who won't tell him the truth about when they're ready."

"I think I am ready." Chenco rubbed his arms as he leaned against the wall by the door. "I mean, we've done plenty. But I can tell he's been holding back. At this point I'm scared, but I want to take it to the next level. If it's too far, I have to try it to find out."

"Then tell him so."

Chenco promised he would.

CHENCO DIDN'T SAY anything right away because he wanted to be sure. It wasn't until a week before the South Padre show, while he and Steve sat out on the patio. Steve commented on how tense he looked, how he thought Chenco needed a release. That was when Chenco realized an emotional enema was exactly what he wanted.

He turned to Steve, looked him in the eye. "When we play tonight, could we…would you flog me? For real?"

Steve's eyes lit with delight, but his reply was measured. "You mean you want me to flog you until you break down, until you cry?"

"Yes." Chenco was nervous, but he didn't falter. "It's what I want. In fact, I think it might be what I need right now."

Smiling, Steve brushed a kiss across Chenco's forehead. "You'll tell me when it's too much." It wasn't a question.

Chenco nodded.

Taking Chenco by the hand, Steve led him through the main floor and down the hall to the master bedroom suite. The hacienda wasn't some modern remake but the real deal, full of nooks and hallways and chunky add-ons. It had a second floor, but not much of one—it seemed to have been where the children were stowed back in the day. Now it was full of guests, Sam and

Mitch in one room, Ethan and Randy in another, Crabtree at the end of the hall.

Steve's bedroom was on the main floor, past the great room and kitchen and dining room, down its own hallway and spilling out behind the garage. It was a suite, not just one room—Steve's bed was in the first space and the room beyond it was the playroom. The playroom, however, could also be accessed from the garage.

Tonight Steve led Chenco through to the playroom, but he didn't order him to his knees. "We'll start with a full massage, on the table and everything, like I told you about." At a cabinet, he picked up a jar of oil and offered it to Chenco, indicating he should sniff. The oil smelled faintly of eucalyptus or spearmint. Maybe both.

"Nice," Chenco offered.

Steve set the oil on a shelf and went to a closet behind the St. Andrew's cross, digging inside before returning bearing a folded blue massage table. With deft motions, he assembled it, tested it, and nodded at Chenco.

"Strip and climb on, facedown first."

He went back to the closet and came out with a set of sheets as Chenco complied with the order. A fitted one went on the main table, a special small thing covered the face rest, and a flat sheet went over it all, followed by a thin white cotton blanket before Steve tucked the whole business away. The freshly made massage bed looked so inviting and cozy, Chenco got undressed faster.

"Have you ever had a massage before, like this?" Steve asked as Chenco climbed coltishly aboard.

"No," Chenco confessed. "It always sounded nice though."

Steve directed him into place, making sure the headrest was comfortable, tucking him beneath the blanket. "The general result of this is going to be increased blood flow and a more direct release of toxins. Given we intend to add pain play to this scene, I'm going to make sure you drink a lot of water, stick to your usual healthy diet, and rest. Serious aftercare is coming your way. If you try and skip any of it, I'm going to get very bitchy."

"Yes, sir. I mean, I'll do as you say." Chenco was glad his face was buried because it meant he could smile and have whatever ridiculous expression he wanted. He *loved* aftercare. It was when Steve held him and coddled him and petted him and told him how strong and brave he was. Even when their scenes weren't super intense, Steve always loved him up afterwards. The idea he'd be getting *more* aftercare made Chenco more eager to please Steve, to make him proud, and he vowed to take all the pain he could, to give him all the noises and sobs he craved.

Noises turned out not to be any kind of a problem. As soon as Steve put his oily hands on Chenco's body, Chenco started to moan.

"Oh my God, it feels so good." Chenco's eyes fell shut, his words slurred, and he felt himself sliding into headspace without so much as a whiff of pain.

"You're very tense," Steve said, and his tone made it clear he didn't care for this state of affairs.

"I'm so nervous about the show."

Steve's thumbs slid along the line of his shoulders, forcing the muscles to relax. Chenco took a breath, let it out, and his body surrendered to Steve's ministrations.

"You're not nervous about the show. You're nervous about what the show will mean, what it might change. You're worried it won't change anything or that it will change everything." He moved his hands lower and kneaded insistently against Chenco's shoulder blades. "Holding your tension in won't keep you safe. You need to let it go."

Let it go? How could he? What if he didn't impress Crabtree? What if he *did*? Would he and Booker go on the road? Did he want to go? Would he have to leave Steve just as things were getting good?

Chenco drew in another breath, but this one couldn't go as deeply since his nerves were up again. "It's tough. I feel so vulnerable."

"You *are* vulnerable. But being on guard makes it worse, not better. Let go." He increased the pressure of his massage, so hard it edged toward the pleasure-pain barrier, making Chenco moan more. "Let go with your body. We'll loosen it up first. Then we'll take you over to the bench and free your mind as well."

Chenco tried to let go with his mind right then too—his muscles couldn't stand up to Steve's manipulations, turning to limp noodles with every pass on his back, his legs, his arms. He'd half expected the massage to become a seduction—it was, but not in the way he'd anticipated. Steve lured Chenco's body into relaxation, coaxing it, luring it then demanding it yield to him. If only Chenco's mind would have come along for the ride.

All through the massage, Chenco did his best to stop thinking about the future, but it yawed before him like a terrible, sharp-toothed thing, ready to devour him if he went the wrong way. He worried about disappointing Mitch and Randy and Ethan and Sam, he worried about disappointing Crabtree and Booker—he ached at the idea of not being what Steve wanted him to be. There were so many ways to fail.

When Steve flipped him over to work his neck, Chenco tried to keep his face clear, not let his rabbit brain show in his expression. His body was loose, but his mind was a tougher sell. Steve sat him up and gave him a big glass of water, and Chenco was surprised to find an hour had gone by—and he was chagrined at how little progress he had made with his internal struggles.

Steve stood in front of Chenco, bare-chested, smiling wryly as he threaded his thick fingers through Chenco's hair. "Quit yelling at yourself for not being able to shut off your head. That's my job, to turn it off. I can tell already it's going to be a hell of a scene, baby."

Chenco leaned into Steve's chest, opening his lips over those familiar muscles. "I'm scared." His hands went to Steve's waist, holding on. "Of the show. Of the scene. Of letting go. Of everything."

The hand at the back of Chenco's hair kneaded gently. "Scared of me?"

Chenco shook his head. "No. I'm not afraid of you."

"Then forget everything but me. I'm the only thing that matters for the next twenty-four hours. You listen to me, you obey me, you please me. I'm canceling everything I have until this time tomorrow night, including a project for work. Everything is for you—if you're willing to give everything else up for one spin of the sun. We have a deal?"

Chenco nodded and clutched at Steve's waistband. *A whole day with Steve, in submission, in freedom.* "Yes, sir."

"Excellent." His hand slid to Chenco's naked ass and pinched it. "Head to the cross. I'm going to strap you down and flog every last bit of nervousness right out of your head."

CHAPTER THIRTEEN

I T HAD BEEN a long, long time since Steve had flogged a lover.

Tightening the last of the leather cuffs, Steve scanned Chenco's restraints then checked them again. He knew the cross was properly anchored and stable enough to handle the most violent recoils, but the compulsion to be completely sure was too strong to do anything else. They'd done extended play, they'd done rough play, but they hadn't yet done both together. Tonight this would change.

After making one final round of checks, when he knew his boy was as safe and secure as could be, Steve admired the beauty of the young man spread open and naked before him.

God, but Chenco was gorgeous. He still had the youthful, rangy appearance saying *boy*, but naked and exposed like this, Steve could see this was a man before him, not a child. The latter wasn't an appearance as much as a carriage, a self-possession flickering against the backdrop of insecurity. He didn't cringe from it, though—he faced it boldly, shoving his unease aside.

The idea of tearing down the fragile wall, of stripping Chenco down to raw—of watching him surrender to pain for real, being part of his transformation—the thought alone made Steve hard.

Steve took a swig of water and examined Chenco's naked back, trying to decide if he wanted to blindfold him. Probably best to do so, he decided, and fished a mask out of the drawer. He knew a fleeting yearning for a cigar as he spied them on a shelf—normally he would indulge during a scene, but Chenco took health so seriously, and Steve couldn't bring himself to poison the playroom's air. It was a consideration he would only give Chenco, he acknowledged, as he tied the leather mask into place.

Once he'd secured it, he examined the scene one last time and went to his flogger cupboard.

Steve weighed his options as he took in the racks of carefully stored and meticulously cared-for implements. Chain was out, as was rubber. He wanted some thud, wanted to knock Chenco so hard if he wasn't secured, he'd go across the room. At the same time, he wanted a stinger handy. Something to hold in reserve, so when Chenco was used to the big blows, a new sensation would come at him. That's when he'd come undone, when there'd be nothing between them but the pain. It had to be good. It had to be *perfect*.

Steve chose the twenty-inch bull with seventy tails, and the kangaroo. After closing the cupboard, he turned on some low, slow-burning alternative music. He dimmed the lights enough to suit his mood while still allowing for safety—low enough that when he removed

Chenco's blindfold, it wouldn't be too jarring. Putting the bullhide flogger in his right hand and the kangaroo in his left, he took up his position behind his lover and drew in a few centering, focusing breaths. He turned the bullhide around a few times, warming up his arm, letting the tails hit the floor occasionally with a soft slap. He grinned as each little sound made Chenco jump.

Moving silently, he stepped closer to Chenco, took aim, and thudded the right cheek of that beautiful, bare brown ass.

Chenco yelped and jerked. Steve grinned and enjoyed the shock as it moved through his bottom's body like liquid silver. Yeah, it hurt different than anybody thought. Not as bad and yet worse at the same time. Steve had put a lot of work into getting the trick of it. The right implement helped, but there was a skill about the wrist, the shoulder, the timing.

This is just a taste of what I can give you, baby, he thought, and hit him again.

Chenco was fun to torture—he clung so nobly to composure before folding with the grace of a queen. Steve could knock him off balance in thirty seconds, reduce him to sobs and begging and pleading, but he liked to draw things out, to toy with his prey and really mindfuck them. Liked to let them think they might make it, run them out to the edge of endurance, and then up the ante with the clear message he had hours of torture ahead.

He could also drive someone into their safe word, and after a solid two weeks of learning Chenco's limits, he knew exactly where the boundary lay. Sadism wasn't about taking people too far. It was about taking them *almost* too far. It was about not asking for but assuming control. It was about being strong and sure, a huge wall of absolute his sub crumbled against. It was about getting another human being to voluntarily submit to his will, knowing they could trust him with it. It was about, for an hour or two, playing God.

Tonight he played deity for Chenco, and tonight he was in the mood to knock flat the ridiculous paper wall Chenco had around himself. He'd show Chenco that this idea he could protect himself from the world by hiding behind petty fears wouldn't stand up to a mild wind. He'd lift the dark fear Chenco had himself wrapped in, to see the Chenco underneath. He'd watch the man rise up and overcome it all.

He'd knock that man down too, send him trembling into Steve's arms. Fuck him hard and long and beautiful, make the strong, amazing man his for a day—completely, utterly his. He wanted, when it was over, for Chenco to thank him for the ride.

He hit the same spot on the right ass cheek, three sharp successive blows taking Chenco up to the edge of wanting to get away, made his mind insist he not allow it to happen anymore. Steve grinned as his lover tensed on the third strike—he'd known that one was coming—then readied himself for another. Steve drew a breath, pretending it was his cigar, waited another half-beat to get out of the rhythm—and struck Chenco on his left thigh.

This game went on for twenty minutes. He peppered Chenco's body with slaps of varying weight, establishing a rhythm and pattern only to break it and switch to a new area. He would focus on Chenco's upper back and his arms, letting the *whoosh* of air taunt but never touch his face. He teased the falls against Chenco's tender, vulnerable sides then struck them roughly enough to choke out a cry. He focused twenty, thirty lashes in succession on the now very red and tender ass, making Chenco shout and buck and try, in vain, to move away.

Steve watched his lover battle the flogger blows, watched his face screw up in determination, watched deeper strength take hold. Steve admired it.

Then he gave Chenco his first real blow.

The cry tearing through his lover's body was so beautiful—a perfect mixture of surprise, fear, and true agony. Steve gave him another, so close to the edge he listened for the call that would slow or stop their play. None came.

Chenco was determined not to bend. It had nothing to do with Steve, he knew, and everything to do with life teaching him over and over again how bending led to bad, bad things. It had everything to do with a personality which, while it craved authority and attention and enjoyed playing with pain, was not as duck to water with submission as Sam Keller-Tedsoe or Gordy. No, someday Steve was fairly sure Chenco would wield a whip of his own.

Not today. Today, Chenco still had a great deal to

learn about pain, and Steve was his teacher.

The bullhide flogger was his pen, and Steve wrote Chenco's lessons across the tender, over-sensitized surface of his lover's skin. Pain was only part of the problem. Pain was what everyone who heard about BDSM thought they feared, but they were wrong. It was the loss of control, giving up *to* pain. Any fool could endure. It took a real man to deliberately walk into fire.

Chenco likely felt as if he were in flames—his skin was so raw and crazed Steve could skim ice down his back and it would burn. If Steve put the flogger down and fucked Chenco, the sensations of his skin would blend with the spearing of his flesh, and the rough pounding would turn into strange bliss only accessible during this kind of play. But Steve didn't put the flogger down and fuck Chenco. He whipped him harder, bringing the blows closer together as they became more and more erratic. He drew deep into the place inside him aching for a cigar between his teeth, smoke burning his eyes—this part of him turned the handle.

He stepped closer and slid the falls along Chenco's balls, his perineum, pushed the handle a few times over the crease hiding his hole. Chenco jerked and whimpered, a shiver of new fear whispering over him with a gossamer touch. Steve sucked it down like honey. *Yes, love. I could hurt you there too. I could hurt you any-where.* He let Chenco swim in the knowledge, let him anticipate Steve's hand on his balls, his cock, his fingers teasing at his hole.

Moving away without sound, Steve resumed flogging.

The music had shifted into something with a heavy backbeat, and Steve thrummed Chenco's body in time so he could feel it in his skin, his blood, his soul. He became so regular he knew Chenco had forgotten Steve's love for varying technique. He went on in rhythm so long that, when he paused, only Chenco's deepest subconscious was ready for the return.

Steve drew another breath, a toke on his imaginary cigar.

He raised the kangaroo flogger and brought it down with crushing force on the raw skin of Chenco's lower back.

Chenco screamed.

Steve hit him again.

It felt, Steve knew, like the sharp sting of cold snow on an already frozen face. Those blows were tiny bites beside a deep, throbbing ache—one or two slaps were bad, but in succession, they were maddening. Pain? Fuck pain, this was sensation now, leaving behind words such as *bad* and *good* and forcing Chenco into whole new atmospheres. His body was so thick with endorphins he had to leave it to make room for the subsequent rounds.

Except there was one problem. Chenco had to cling to those walls. He couldn't let go because only the walls were safe.

With throbbing pleasure, Steve burned those barriers down.

He was in a rhythm again now, alternating sting and

thud, hard and soft, heavy, and light. He gave nothing but patterns—bull, kangaroo, kangaroo bull for six bars, then kangaroo, kangaroo, kangaroo bull for eight more. He taught Chenco's body all it could crave about sting and thud, beating him into headspace, forcing him to leave everything else behind.

Chenco screamed, sobbed, swore—he struggled against the leather cuffs, tried to lift the cross off the bolts securing it to the floor. He shook. He cried, a terrified, little-boy sob. He fought Steve tooth and nail, with the conviction of one ready to go to the absolute edge—until Steve took the stinger up to the same second notch he'd already taken the bullhide. Steve teased him with a deeper level still, showing him, at the edge of Chenco's exhaustion, that Steve was just getting warmed up.

Chenco gave one last cry, a defeated gasp. Then he let go of the ruins of his walls, gave himself over to Steve—and soared into space.

They traveled to heaven together now—though they stood feet apart, Steve had never felt closer to Chenco. He moved through the air, through the music, through the haze of Chenco's pain as if they were living things he could manipulate. With his floggers, Steve conducted the orchestra of pain and pleasure, of sensation and surrender.

Time fell away, the world fell away. Division fell away. Chenco's skin was Steve's skin, his canvas, his space to carve and mold. Each gasp, each cry, each arch into the next blow felt like crystal etched in beauty only he could see and only Chenco could feel. In this separate space and time, Steve could see the future, could see the limits of Chenco's endurance as he'd never known them before, could see their stages and their progression. The chain flogger would come out someday. The rubber one too.

Not yet. Not now. But the potential was there. Chenco would want it all. Steve found himself aching at the thought, ready to do anything to be the one Chenco was with when it happened.

When a wind-down song came on, Steve sighed at the upcoming loss, hating that the roller coaster had to go back to the station. Chenco was tired—Chenco wouldn't call him to a stop, not now, not until he collapsed in a faint from exhaustion. He was so high he'd keep going until he burned against the sun. Steve brought him down slowly, expertly. He took Chenco a bottle of water—the kind fighters used, an angled straw bending into the mouth so Steve could squeeze a liberal amount inside. He murmured under his breath as he did so, stroking Chenco's sensitized skin with the falls.

Steve set the floggers on a nearby table and drew the table closer, balancing some lube and a heavy metal plug within easy reach. He stroked Chenco's side, murmuring his pleasure, then went to another drawer, coming back with a small clamp. He greased his cock, took more lube and pressed between Chenco's cheeks with insistent fingers. Around the edges of the mask, he could see Chenco's face. His lover was serene, lost in his headspace, drifting down from the highest planes, still strapped into the roller coaster.

One more time around.

Steve closed the clamp over Chenco's nipple, pushed his cock inside, and bit Chenco's neck.

He groaned in chorus with Chenco's cries, feeling them reverberate inside his own body as he drove them ruthlessly back up—this was the edge, the thinnest blade of it, and Steve gloried in the rush. He fucked hard, twisting and turning the clamp until Chenco's sobs were incoherent pleas, until his own thrusts were so rough they stole Chenco's voice. He let go of the clamp and jacked Chenco's cock, teasing inside the slit with his index finger as if he could extract the ejaculate by force. He took Chenco to the furthest point he'd ever taken anyone, and when he knew he could go no further, he gripped the clamp and pulled it taut.

At the same time he released Chenco, Steve whispered, "Come."

He dropped the clamp and fucked into Chenco as he came apart, holding himself back until Chenco fell, his body too over-sensitized to take any more pounding. Steve made him take more anyway, undid him until he was nothing but frayed bits, and then he came too, pumping himself deep into Chenco. He pushed the plug tip inside before he pulled out completely, straining Chenco, claiming one last gasp before shoving the toy home, wedging it deep inside.

The plug stayed in all night. He held it in place himself as he drew Chenco down, scooping him in and carrying him to the bed. As he gave Chenco more water and told him how proud he was, how beautiful Chenco had been, he nudged at the base, reminding Chenco he was still inside him, fucking him to keep the edge of over-sensitization alive.

He kissed Chenco, stroking his body, pinching the abused nipple. When Chenco was stable enough, he collected a set of clamps from the playroom—he wanted them on all night, all day, there for him to tease until this long, sweet scene was completely done. Chenco emerged from his haze enough to complain he had to pee—Steve made him hold it, keeping him semi-aroused so the need to piss became another edge to claim. When he did let him up to pee, Steve came along, holding the plug in place.

Then he had Chenco bend over the sink, and he removed the plug to fuck him again.

"That's two of my loads in you now," Steve reminded him as he led a wobbly-legged Chenco back to bed. "I'm going to keep filling you all day. I'm going to fuck your mouth, your ass, feeding you until my twenty-four hours are up."

Chenco purred and curled beside him, but he held on too, burrowing his face in Steve's shoulder, his fingernails sharp points of the anxiety Steve knew damn well shouldn't be left.

"I don't want to leave you," Chenco whispered. "If the show goes well, I don't want to leave you."

The confession felled Steve. His walls came down too, toppled with the barest breath from Chenco. "I'll go with you. Wherever you go, I'll go too."

For the first time since the flogging, Chenco tensed. "You can't. You can't promise me that."

Chenco wasn't the only one who'd been undone by their scene. Steve rolled Chenco's nipple between his fingers. "Don't you tell me what I can't do."

Chenco cried again, but it wasn't because of the pain in his nipple. "Nobody does this. Nobody cares about me like this."

Steve slid his hand down to Chenco's cock and gripped his balls possessively. "They do now."

Chenco wept, and Steve kissed him and fondled him, stoking their fires slowly, languidly, until they were hard once more. He jerked Chenco off, then turned him over and fucked him long and slow—he was so loose, so sloppy now inside he'd need a strap to keep the plug in place, and Steve would get him one.

He shoved Chenco's knees wide to the point of aching, teased his too-tender cock, dug his fingers into the welted flesh of his ass, and rode his precious hole until he leaked spunk and lube.

Mine.

Steve fucked until his cock went limp and raw. He put the plug back in, went to the playroom to find a strap, and locked the metal and his fluids in place.

Mine. For as long as you let me, boy, you're mine.

He wrapped his body around Chenco, knowing he was falling too hard, too fast, knowing there was no way he could ever keep someone like Chenco forever, knowing with certainty heartbreak was absolutely on his way.

He let himself fall anyway.

THE DAY AFTER his flogging was the most sacred day of Chenco's life.

It was a dirty, deliciously gritty day. He'd never thought he'd wanted something so raunchy, but everything they did, he loved. This was playing, they were boys, and sometimes boys played gross. They were little boys who knew exactly what to do with their penises and their holes, and they did all the fun, naughty things they could make them do.

Jesus, did they play with Chenco's poor little hole.

Once upon a time Chenco had looked up all the wicked, taboo gay sex terms on the net, and now he hadn't only read about them, he'd done them. Felching? Yep. This came with one hell of a hygiene regimen first, but yes, it had happened, and Chenco got hard just thinking about it. Fisting? Had happened a few days before the flogging. Today Steve put a ball with a string on it inside Chenco and *played his fucking ass like a violin*. Chenco came with such force he knocked the table over.

If there was a game to be had with his ass, he was pretty sure he'd played it. And yet there was one taboo, one secret, terrible thing he had not yet done, something that had nothing to do with his ass at all.

He couldn't stop thinking about the contract, about what he'd confessed he wanted. For the first time, however, he wasn't ashamed, wasn't afraid. Not about this—not with Steve.

Chenco couldn't do anything *but* feel safe and protected with Steve. There was no room for shame. Steve wouldn't allow it. Never had Chenco felt so owned. He had in fact, outside of Steve, never allowed anyone to feel they'd owned him even in the slightest, but everything about being with Steve was a category all its own.

There was something so *bone-deep, achingly pure* about Steve not asking what Chenco wanted, just taking from his body. He felt like a junkie, yearning for his next fix of contact, of play, of degradation or pain or whatever Steve wanted. The acts and any social meanings attached to them were gone. Everything now was about serving Steve, honoring that space he made for Chenco. Every surrender was another chance to be free.

Beyond that liberation, however, was another gift, one he never would have expected to find in being so rough and raw—Steve's caretaking. While *Chenco* was so high on his freedom he'd happily throw safety and smarts out the door, Steve was ruthlessly attentive to his care. Yes, he teased sensitive skin, but more than once he told Chenco no, they needed to rest for a bit before continuing to play. All the water wasn't just to torture his bladder, either. Twice Chenco had been delirious with begging, feeling lightheaded and happy, but something must have been off because Steve stopped play, grabbed water and made him drink it.

He stopped often to make Chenco eat too, always light things, but they ate a lot. Crackers, hummus, veggies, fruit. It was almost sexier than the actual sex, being fed. Sometimes he had to eat from Steve's sweaty, sexy skin.

Steve made food part of play too—Chenco's body was disgusting, and the bed was an unholy mess, stained with crushed strawberries, littered with cracker crumbs, damp with spunk and sweat and God knew what else. The hedonism, the wickedness of their play, made Chenco want to purr. Sometimes he did.

By the afternoon, Chenco had drifted down a little, and Steve encouraged him to nap. Once he woke, however, they were back at it—Steve took him into the playroom, where he shoved a cock gag deep into Chenco's throat. Chenco didn't flinch and was mostly annoyed he had to hold a hanky in his hand to drop as a replacement safe word. Even four hours ago, he might have refused to try the gag on. It was a nasty thing, ugly looking and uncomfortable, designed to humiliate, which Chenco still hated—except right now he wanted it. It was yet another way to serve Steve, to honor himself. Honor them both.

He thought again about what they had not done, that line in the contract, a dark, silky whisper in the back of his mind. The watersports permission he'd granted. The last line to cross, the thing he now wanted to happen today more than anything, the thing he was no longer embarrassed about or scared of. He only craved it, ached for it with a barren, hedonistic shamelessness he refused to self-examine.

Piss on me, Steve. Oh, it would be so perfect, in the middle of all this nasty, frothy mess. No one ever had to know, but he'd know. Steve would too. He didn't have to be ashamed. Steve was here. It would be safe. He would be okay.

It didn't happen, though, not yet anyway. Chenco did get a real cock at least—Steve took out the gag and gave him long, slow, deep fucks into his throat which never stole his air, though now that he thought about it, Chenco kind of wanted that. *Another forbidden act I can give to you. Please,* cariño, *let me give it all to you.*

Steve's smile said he could read Chenco's desire, and the love in his eyes said *patience, baby, I'll let you.*

He pulled out and came all over Chenco's face. It wasn't much of a spray—Steve's balls had to be in overdrive at this point—but it was enough to soothe the savage beast that had risen in Chenco.

Part of him, anyway.

Bending into a crouch, Steve stroked Chenco's face, his hair, his raw and ragged throat.

"You're such a good boy. You were so strong, but you gave it up to me, letting me have all your strength to play with. You're pushing your body so hard, right to the edge, but you're trusting me to keep you safe. You make me so proud, holding my loads, wearing one on your face. You're raw but you're letting me fuck you because you're such a good, obedient boy. You don't want to let go, but you do with me. You're so beautiful. You make me burst, I'm so proud."

Chenco started to hum in the middle of Steve's praise, a low, deep sound of pleasure and contentment he couldn't stop, and he nuzzled Steve's neck. He was so raw, he burned, but he wanted to burn more, longer.

Just one more thing, Papi. Please.

He needed an act wrong, forbidden, something only Steve was allowed to do. Something that would wash away the hurt of his mother's rejection, the fear that he wouldn't be good enough to make it out of the valley. Something that took the wounds the world gave him, turned shame and degradation on its ear, and made them communion.

He looked Steve in the eye, naked all the way to his soul. "Do it, Papi. Please, please give it to me."

Steve's countenance darkened in pleasure and power. He stroked Chenco's cheek. "Say it. Give me the words, boy."

Chenco knew no shame. None whatsoever. Only need.

"Piss on me, Papi. Please, Papi. Give it to me."

Bending down, Steve kissed him, crushing, claiming, biting.

Then he stood back and, gaze fixed on Chenco's face, set his stance, and aimed his cock at Chenco's face.

As the warmth hit him, Chenco wept.

Part of his brain acknowledged the care Steve took—nowhere near his eyes, mostly on his chin and cheeks, his chest—but mostly Chenco reeled from the knowledge that he'd let this happen, he'd *let another man piss on him, he'd allowed* this…and it undid him. It was ten thousand times more vulnerable than anything he'd let Steve do to him yet, more humbling. It was the kind of thing his father would have expected him to do.

Fucking faggots, always pissing on each other. Demeaning, debasing. So few people would understand why he would let anyone do this to him. How disgusting. How debasing.

How free are you right now, Crescencio Ortiz? What is left now for you to hold onto in this world but your own life?

He sobbed, his cries rushing out from the depths of his bowels, this release sacred in a way nothing else in the world could be. *I am this person. I have gone here, I have sung this song.* Though Steve had crooned praises all day, for the first time Chenco felt that pride, a river of power inside him, filling him with holy fire.

I am the one who has allowed this. I have faced this mountain, this judgment.

I can face anything.

He floated through the next hour. Steve led him to the shower and washed them both down, bearing Chenco up, kissing him, murmuring sweet things, but mostly he was quiet, acknowledging the sacred space Chenco had found. Once they were clean, Steve took an hour to pamper Chenco's skin, applying lotions and oils, checking welts. Every single inch of Chenco was stroked and loved, every part of him studied to be absolutely, completely sure the damage to his skin was what Steve had intended and no more. All the while Chenco drifted in the sweet, beautiful place he'd found.

The place Steve had shown him how to find.

Steve tucked Chenco into freshly made sheets and brought him food Randy had made for them—fragrant gyros and fruit and vegetables and hummus and pita bread and juice. Every bite tasted so sharp and perfect and wonderful Chenco felt like he could slip into subspace again.

When he woke in the morning, Chenco rose from the deepest, longest dream he'd ever had. Colors seemed brighter. Smells seemed sharper. He could feel, in a way he never had before, his center, his weighted anchor in the seat of himself, a small red fire burning with surety, telling him yes, everything was about to change, but he would be fine. He knew certainty with a conviction he'd never known before.

He shut his eyes and swam in it, grateful to Steve, to himself, to everything.

Caramela slid into place inside him, her strength and power coming back. It was time, she whispered to him, to rehearse. To plot. To plan. To blow Crabtree's mind clean out of his head. To take over the whole goddamned world, just like they'd always planned.

Chenco smiled. He couldn't wait.

CHAPTER FOURTEEN

As Booker and Chenco prepared to head to South Padre, thinking of what the performance might bring, Steve could already see their future.

Everyone liked Chenco and wanted him to live out his dream. Ethan and Randy had the means to see he at least got a decent shot at receiving it. One way or another the guys would make sure Chenco soon left the valley. If Steve wanted to go along, which he did, he had some housecleaning to do.

He'd dragged his feet over telling Crabtree about Gordy, but after the intense scene with Chenco he gave in and took the older man to the cannery. Steve had let Brett and Randy take care of repairing the damaged cameras, getting Gordy to take his meds, bringing him at least one decent meal a day. It was strange to be back, and Steve felt self-conscious.

He had to do this, though, if he wanted out. Parked in the deserted, weed-riddled lot, Steve stared at the rim of his steering wheel. "I grew up here. My parents ran the orchards and the cannery the same as my dad's parents had and their parents before. Since there have been orchards in the Rio Grande Valley, my family has been here, growing citrus."

"Yes," Crabtree agreed, speaking as one who clearly knew this fact.

Steve remembered what Randy had said about Crabtree liking to look into people's history. He glanced across the seat, wondering how much of this story he needed to bother telling.

Crabtree read his silent question with a quirk of his lips. "One can learn as much from the way the tale is told as one can from the facts themselves. Please continue."

Steve shifted uncomfortably in his seat, eyeing his packet of tobacco on the dash. He thought about asking if Crabtree would mind if he smoked, remembered the heart attack and changed his mind.

"Gordy and I knew each other from grade school. His parents both worked for us—mom the receptionist at the cannery, dad a driver. We were friends through high school too. After the freeze, though, things got rough—I went to college, the cannery closed. I left school and went to Desert Storm, then went back to Stanford. Didn't go local. I should have. I only saw him on breaks, and not then, not always."

Crabtree snorted. "You were at a prestigious institution making top grades. You had job offers before you left for the Army. The idea that you should have been in McAllen in case something might have happened to your friend is foolish, and you know it."

"We were friends. He thought we were lovers. My being gone so long made him think I'd abandoned him."

This excuse only made Crabtree wave a dismissive hand.

Steve swallowed against the rawness of his throat. "I heard about it through my sister, from one of her friends from the valley. How he couldn't hold a job. How he was 'messed up in sex', as she put it. We'd been playing casually before I left, so I knew she meant BDSM, but I didn't yet get it was bad shit until I came through again."

He shut his eyes, remembering.

"It was bad. He'd been caged, beat, passed around like a fucking toy. True cruelty, taking advantage of his loneliness and vulnerability and…well, they ruined him. And it was all because I left him. So I moved back here. I tried to undo some of their shit, and for a while it was almost okay. But he wanted me to be his boyfriend, and I couldn't. One day I couldn't find him. I searched and searched, but it was a friend who found him by accident at the hospital. There was Gordy, beat to a piece of meat. The tats were the only reason Brett knew him."

Steve still stared at the cannery, but his gaze was unfocused now, lost to memory. "He wouldn't move in with me. He went to the cannery on his own—I'd been about to sell it to a developer, but once Gordy moved in, I pulled out of the deal. I've set up surveillance so I can keep an eye on him, make sure nobody hurts him, make sure he doesn't hurt himself. Brett wants me to commit him—he's on enough meds to fell a horse, when we can get him to take them. I can't turn him in, though. They wouldn't understand him. He wants scenes, punishment, play—they'd tell him it was bad, and I can't stand the idea of anybody else telling him he's wrong."

He watched Crabtree, but the old man gave away nothing, only stared hard at Steve, as if his gaze could peel away layers of skin.

Finally, Crabtree spoke. "What is it you want from me? I assume you want advice, or help, or possibly some kind of miracle, which I'd argue you'd know better than to hope for, but I can see Gordy isn't the only one unhealthy in this relationship."

"I know I have work to do on myself. I'm trying." *You think I'm fucked up, try looking in a mirror.* Steve stiffened and looked away. "Randy said you could help, but if this is too much, I won't blame you."

Crabtree sighed and put his hand on the door of the truck. "Children. You're all children. Come now, boy. Let's go see what kind of mess you have for me."

They went into the cannery together, Steve slowing his steps to match Crabtree's halting gait. The cane seemed more accessory than tool while they were in the parking lot, but once they were inside the building, the older man needed it with every step to navigate around the rubble. It took everything in Steve not to reach out and steady him.

Crabtree cast him an impatient glance. "I'm man enough to clean up after you, but not to walk across an uneven floor?" He aimed his cane at a closed door. "I assume he's in there?"

"Yes, sir." Steve didn't anticipate this meeting would

be a good one. "I think—"

"Knock on the door, announce us, and then get the hell out of my way."

Gordy didn't answer when Steve called out, not even when he knocked a second time and called out louder. Before he could knock again, Crabtree shoved him neatly aside with the point of his cane and turned the doorknob.

"Gordon Weste?" Crabtree called out, swinging the door wide.

In the deep shadows, a nest of newspaper moved.

Crabtree's expression flickered before settling into his impassive, determined countenance. "I won't stand here all day waiting for a little brat. You have until the count of three to come out, or I'm coming in after you. One, two—"

Gordy's head popped out of the newspaper. He regarded the gangster warily. "Who are you?"

"I am the man who will master you, which is what I have heard you want, but watching you sit there thinking you're interviewing me, I'm not sure you're worthy. I'm thinking I'm wasting my time."

As Crabtree turned around, Gordy leaped forward. "*No.* No—please. Sir. Wait."

"Wait for you? Why on earth would I do that?"

Gordy's gaze flickered to Steve, but Steve had nothing to give him. A dim part of him understood what Crabtree was doing. Mostly, though, Steve felt lost and panicked and ready to bolt.

When Steve hesitated, Gordy drew back. "You're

giving me away?"

Guilt lay Steve low, but before he could speak, Crabtree murmured in irritation under his breath and dug into his pocket. "Here, boy."

He held out a dog biscuit.

Crabtree called again—his voice had changed subtly, full of rich command and entreaty, so much so something in Steve curled up and longed to be petted. Crabtree kept calling out, his tone eager but patient, as if he could stand there all day and call a puppy. It was intoxicating, his patience, and it filled the crumbling room, mesmerizing Steve and Gordy both.

Eventually it also brought Gordy out of his nest. His gaze darted between Steve and Crabtree before settling on the gangster. Crabtree continued to encourage him, and when Gordy made it all the way to his feet, Crabtree praised him and handed over the biscuit. Gordy accepted it with joy, gobbling it down, still uncertain but clearly longing to rub his face along Crabtree's leg.

Crabtree raised an eyebrow at him. "No, no rubs, no pets. Not until you've earned them. I don't play with puppies until I know they can behave."

Gordy looked as if he longed to bark, clearly loving the treat. It was beyond any play Steve had ever witnessed, and he'd seen plenty. Neither Crabtree nor Gordy shared Steve's revulsion. In fact, Gordy's eagerness to please Crabtree boiled over, but something about Crabtree kept him in check. He didn't bark.

He did glance at Steve, however, and when he saw Steve's face, he snarled. He swore at Steve, grabbing loose garbage and small clumps of crumbled concrete from the floor and tossing them across the room.

The cane moved so fast Steve jumped—it *thwacked* Gordy on the side of his knee before returning to its original position. "Puppies do not speak unless they have permission, and they certainly don't throw things. You are a bad dog who needs to be disciplined, and if you're lucky, I'll stay to give you the punishment you deserve. Otherwise I will leave you here to rot alone, filthy and stinking and sulking in your pile of garbage. Do you understand, boy? Do you understand if you break the rules with me, if you don't show me *right now* you deserve my attention, I'll leave you and not look back? Speak once if you understand. Otherwise please continue with your tantrum, and I'll be on my way."

Gordy whined in the back of his throat and lowered his head. He barked once, soft and sorrowful.

Crabtree's posture eased, but only a little. "Very good, puppy. Now. Would you like to play with me awhile? Speak again, if it's what you want."

If Gordy had a real tail, it would have been wagging. Lifting his head, he barked, only once, and beamed at the gangster.

"Very good. Perhaps you aren't as bad a puppy as I thought." Crabtree favored Gordy with a brief smile then glanced over his shoulder at Steve. "You may go."

Steve blinked. "What?"

"Leave. I'll take the keys to your vehicle, as I'm not yet certain when I'll be finished. If I need anything, I'll call Ethan."

Steve didn't move. While this was what he'd wanted, Crabtree taking control, now Steve wasn't so sure it was the best thing. He opened his mouth to voice his reservations.

Crabtree looked him dead in the eye.

Any doubts Steve had harbored over whether or not Crabtree had been a killer, a ruthless mobster, died in the glance. At the same time, though, he saw why Ethan and Randy trusted him, why though Mitch didn't like him, he had faith in him too. Steve saw Crabtree the man, the lines he had crossed and the ones he never would.

Steve realized how much he'd failed Gordy, not being this wall or finding safety for his friend sooner. His gut knotted so hard he hunched forward a little. He wasn't forty-one, he was fourteen, realizing how far his life choices would echo, knowing he'd accidentally hurt the ones he loved.

Crabtree's expression gentled. "It's all right. He'll be fine, and so will you. You've done the right thing. I know what I'm doing here much better than you imagine. Better yet, go ask Randy about my history. If I know my boy, he's had this in mind from the minute he found out Gordy existed."

That actually did sound like Randy. It gave Steve some ease, but it was still hard to head out into the parking lot. He stood in the empty center for a long time, thinking.

Eventually he started back to the ranch, the past closing behind him as a strange, uncertain future expanded exponentially ahead.

CHAPTER FIFTEEN

THE CLUB ON South Padre was called Crave, which apparently was also the name of a gay bar in Las Vegas. It wasn't anything, Randy said, like the real Krave.

"When we get to Vegas, I'll take you," Randy promised Chenco. "Then you'll understand."

Chenco frowned. "When am I going to Las Vegas?"

Randy only winked and went to help Booker with the setup.

Booker had been funny lately—ever since Steve and Mitch had looked into Tristan. He'd been better once Crabtree had started hanging with him, but there wasn't any question he'd changed. Chenco had thought maybe he and the gangster were sleeping together, but when he asked Book about it, Book got all funny and tense. "It ain't like that," he said, as if Chenco had stepped in something holy.

Sometimes, when Crabtree wasn't around, Booker showed up high. Seriously fucked-up high, and more than once Ethan or Steve had sent him off instead of letting him rehearse. One day Crabtree caught him stoned, and the two had a very bad fight. Chenco couldn't hear what happened, but Booker was worse now—not high as often, but jittery, especially around Chenco. He got the feeling Crabtree wasn't doing anything with Booker, not anymore.

Which made an already tense situation much worse. Ever since Chenco had agreed to the South Padre show, he and Booker had fought, and Chenco involving Ethan so heavily made Booker really jealous. Which was stupid, to Chenco's mind—the man ran a fucking casino with a theater attached. Why in the world would they *not* want to get his opinion on things? Somehow to Booker, Ethan's inclusion was a betrayal, and when Randy came over to help him set up, Booker threw down the gauntlet.

It was hours before opening, but there were three other acts there as well, and the owners. He got right up in Randy's face, shaking a clutch of cords in his face. "This is *my* show. I got this gig. The lights are my thing. *Mine.*"

Randy put up his hands. "No sweat, buddy. Just offering to help."

Yet even as Randy stepped back, Ethan came quietly closer. Randy's husband was having one of those moments when he looked like he'd been hanging out with gangsters a lot more than investment bankers.

Chenco hurried to Booker's side. "It's fine, Book. It's our show. They're just helping."

"We don't need no damn help." Booker loomed over Randy. "I've been doing her lights since the first fucking day. This is my show. My lights. *My job.* Get out of my fucking way and let me do my job."

"We're not here to take anything away from you." Ethan kept his voice calm, but everything about him said *tiger, ready to strike.* Mitch stood now too, and several of the Crave employees watched the exchange from a distance.

If Booker saw any of the warning signs flaring up around him, he ignored them. He got right into Randy's face and bellowed, "*Bullshit.* I worked for this. I worked hard, this whole time, and you come in and start calling the shots. You get up in his head, and now it's all what *you* want, not what I want—"

"When the *hell*," Chenco said, his own tiger roused, "did this start being about *you*?"

Booker whirled on him, all the fire formerly aimed at Randy turned on Chenco. "I work this shit for you. I get you the gigs. I make sure everything runs. I hold you up when shit goes down. *I* do that, not these assholes. They showed up at the end and took all the fucking credit, and you fucking let them."

Chenco shook his head, as if he could dispel this craziness. Caramela rose too, adding her fire to his words. "What the fuck have you been smoking? You've lost your goddamned mind. We work together, asshole, and don't you forget it's my ass out there on stage, me in the killer heels, *me* risking getting knifed in my trailer for wearing a wig. You run the lights, but it's me on the stage. We make decisions together, not you beat me down until I agree to whatever you want. I want their help. I want—"

"You owe me, bitch."

Chenco took a step back, and to his horror Booker raised his fist. *He's going to hit me,* Chenco realized, and he held his breath as he waited for the blow to strike.

A pale hand caught Booker's arm a foot away from Chenco. Booker's eyes widened in surprise then contracted in acute pain. Steve stood beside him, holding the other man's arm, impassive, not appearing to exert any energy.

"You're out of line." His vocal inflections were mild, as if Booker had stepped on his toe, not tried to punch Chenco. But the fire in his eyes promised Steve was anything but mellow.

Booker's struggle played out on his face—clearly he longed to lash out, to take Steve down, but he deflated significantly, and he didn't attempt to struggle out of Steve's grip. "They're gonna take him away, and you fucking know it. They're going to take him to Vegas, they're going to tell him what to do, and he's going to *fucking listen.*"

"To them instead of you, yes. He has the right to make that choice, and you have no right to hit him. And if you try…" Steve's voice became quiet and dangerous, "…I will make you sorry."

Everything went from bad into a suburb of hell. Booker swung at Steve, and Steve blocked him and twisted Booker's arm at a painful angle. Ethan grabbed Booker's other arm, and in seconds Mitch was there too, helping herd Booker out a side door into the bright afternoon sun.

Chenco stood staring, head spinning, gut knotting. It wasn't until Sam asked in gentle tones if he wanted to sit down that he realized he was shaking.

"What just happened?" Chenco whispered, but Sam didn't answer, only made him sit down and asked someone from the Crave staff to bring water.

Chenco drank, but he felt wooden and disconnected, the voices around him echoing oddly in his head, Sam a quiet blur before him. It wasn't until Steve's lower half moved into his field of vision, his bare, hairy arm reaching out, that Chenco came back into himself—he drew his breath in on a sharp hitch and leaned into the touch.

Ethan came into his vision too, crouching between Steve and Sam to take Chenco's hand in his. His tie was undone, and he looked like he'd been in a mild struggle. His gaze was calm and steady, however. "How you doing, sweetheart?"

"Booker," Chenco choked out, and it was all he could manage.

Ethan remained steady. "Booker won't be with us tonight. There's no need to worry," he said when Chenco tensed. "I've seen your rehearsals, so I know what's involved. Randy will work the lights. The club is giving us an extra half hour to set up and rehearse too. Everything will work out. You'll see."

This wasn't happening. *This could not be happening.* "But why—Booker—*why*?"

Steve's grip on his shoulder turned into a gentle kneading. "Baby, you can do this. The guys can help you too. It will all work out, just as it's supposed to."

"But—I don't—" Panic began to snowball inside Chenco, and he went stiff as he realized how close he was to coming apart.

The grip on his shoulder turned sharp, and he eased, but only a little.

Steve murmured something, and the next thing Chenco knew, Steve led him toward the side door to the stage, into an alcove with dark curtains shielding them. Steve's big body moved in front of him, trapping him, keeping out the world, and Chenco pressed against him, burrowing his face in Steve's chest, fighting sobs.

"Hush," Steve ordered, his hands gliding over Chenco's body, claiming it, demanding he calm down by sound and touch. "None of that. Not now."

"What did I do?" Chenco whispered. "Why—?"

"You didn't do anything. You and Booker have been coming at this for weeks. Months. Maybe years. He wanted things his way. You didn't share his vision."

"But I did, sometimes—"

"He's not healthy, baby. You held back because you're smart, careful."

"He's right, though—I trust you and the others, and I barely know them."

"You trust me and the others, particularly Ethan and Crabtree, because you look at us and can tell we're stable and strong and able to help you. This is his failure, *cariño*, not yours."

Chenco knew this was true, but it still hurt. "I don't know how to do this without him."

"Yes you do. Caramela does. Don't you tell me she can't get on stage and own it."

"But I was going to do 'On the Floor', and I need someone to play Pitbull."

"No you don't. Caramela's the star. Not him. That's why he's so upset. He liked the idea of controlling you, of having a star in his pocket. He never really had you, but in his mind, strong people need to be pinned down."

It sounded so ugly. It didn't fit with the Booker in Chenco's heart, which made him wonder if that Booker had ever been at all. He felt as if he were mourning someone who hadn't ever really existed.

Steve stroked his hair and made soft shushing noises. "It's going to be okay. You're going to go out there on stage, sweetheart, and you're going to kill them, you'll be so good. You're strong and amazing and talented. Later Crabtree will be here, and he'll see it too, and then, mark my words—he'll make all your dreams come true."

What good were his dreams if they came at the cost of losing his best friend? Chenco swallowed another sob and burrowed his face in Steve's chest.

"The thing you said about Booker," he began at last, "about him wanting to control me or whatever. How is it any different from the way you guys fuss over me? From the way you and I...?"

He half-expected Steve to get mad, but to his surprise, Steve only stroked his back and pressed a kiss to the side of his head. "The difference, Crescencio, is we fuss and control and set you up so you can fly—in the way we see as best for you. Which isn't much different than what Booker tried to do, except if you were to tell us no, we'd let you go."

What he said made sense, except it made Chenco sad. It felt like Booker was really gone, forever. "I'll miss him."

"Of course you will." Steve kept stroking him. "But I wouldn't count him out. Not completely."

Maybe Steve was making it up just to give him hope, but Chenco appreciated it anyway. "So what do I do now?"

"Now you go splash water on your face, pull out your queen, and you knock this gig out of the park."

KNOCK IT OUT of the park was exactly what Chenco did.

It was rocky at first. Randy knew what he was doing with lights, but it took a long time to try and explain what Booker had done and at what times as so much of it had been instinctive. For the first half hour of practice, Chenco wasn't sure it was ever going to work. He felt like he was performing naked and missing an arm and a leg, especially when Pitbull sang and there was no Booker there to play him. By the time they got to the top of the hour, though, he and Randy had a rhythm going, and Caramela had filled in all the gaps Booker's absence made from the routine. When their extra half hour of rehearsal closed, Chenco thought this might work after all.

As the club opened and the floor began to fill, Chenco went back to his dressing room and began the ritual of putting Caramela together. It was strange to not do it in the trailer or at Steve's house, to hear people milling about in the hall, knowing Steve stood there, ready in case Chenco needed him. He wondered if he should have asked Steve inside.

This will never work, Chenco thought, staring at his half made-up expression in the mirror.

Stop whining and let me do my job, Caramela replied. Since he didn't know what else to do, Chenco did.

She wore red tonight—a single shoulder strap, sequined piece of honey with a slit so high she had to wear a high-cut compression panty. It hugged her body and made her look like a glistening drop of blood with legs. She wore the long flowing wig with red piano striping, red silk opera gloves, and the fuck-me Pleaser pumps with a lipstick point heel and ribbon wrapped halfway up her leg. When she finished, she took a look at herself in the full-length mirror, drew a deep breath and went out into the hall.

There they were, her lineup of strong, sexy men. Even Sam looked as if he'd take on anybody who got in Caramela's way. When they saw her, they stood up straighter, eyes widening in surprise and pleasure. Everyone but Steve, who only looked approving, proud.

Unable to help herself, Caramela preened, touching her hair and smiling. "So. I'll do?"

"More than." Randy came forward with a leer and drew her into a careful embrace. Into her ear, he said,

"You're going to rock this house, sugar, and make all the boys come in their panties."

"Thank you for all your help," Caramela whispered back, squeezing his arm.

"Anything for you, Princess." He kissed her cheek. "You're the closing act, so we have a little time."

She blinked. "But I thought I was second?"

Randy grinned. "Yeah, but then the owner saw us warming up. He moved the order around. Slick saw the way the wind was moving too, which was why you had your own dressing room."

"Slick?"

Randy laughed. "Sorry, that's Ethan." He nodded at his spouse, who stood off to the side, looking very smooth and slick indeed. "You're all set up, honey. Just chill, mingle a bit, and get your game on, and when it's time, I'll come and find you."

"Mingle? You mean, go out into the club?"

"Hell yeah." Randy jerked his head at Steve. "You got a big sexy daddy to escort you, and the rest of the posse will be close behind." He pointed at Sam. "Except you, Peaches. You're gonna be my assistant for the night."

The club was packed, with dancers in cages and on the bar tops, with hundreds of young college men let loose and liquored up. The other drag queens worked the crowd too, staying on the edges close to the door. A few were comic, not glam, but several were stunningly gorgeous. Caramela wavered.

Steve put his hand on her elbow, and she found herself centered again.

Drawing a deep breath, she pulled herself into her game—she flirted with men who glanced her way, touching their faces, playing coy or vixen depending on what they wanted. A few looked like they wanted to dance with her but changed their mind when they saw Steve holding her arm. She ran her hands over Steve's body—his exposed body, as he'd changed into leather pants and a vest, leaving his sculpted, sexy torso visible for everyone to admire. She petted him, cooing and calling him papi, and the crowd ate it up, begging for more.

Soon she had a small crowd of admirers—they were there for both of them, for Caramela and her papi, and it was a joy, a rush to give them what they wanted. Steve stood like a soldier, his face deliciously expressionless, but he put his arm possessively around her waist and bore her up and protected her as she worked her boys— stem to her petal. She had a great time—a perfect, wonderful time.

When she had to go backstage and get ready, she remembered Booker, and it made her sad. She saw how good the other acts were and grew nervous, thinking she couldn't possibly compete against them, wondering why the owner had made her go last. Steve sensed her nerves and held her closer, saying nothing, just grounding her and keeping her from spiraling away.

Then it was time.

The lights went down, and she took her position in the center of the stage, back to the audience. Pitbull called out, and she answered in lip-sync into her mic. By the time she got to her first verse, she was feeding off the crowd. They pressed against the stage and called her name. Some shouted JLo, some Caramela—they were with her, inside the song, inside the performance, inside of her.

She gave them everything she had.

While she didn't deviate from the routine, she punched it up, her hip snaps sharper, harder, her knee-bends deeper. Randy had given her a long, ornate cane reminiscent of JLo's from the song's video, and she used it with relish, leaning on it, twirling it like a baton, aiming it at her audience, ordering them to dance along. They did, shouting and cheering, some of them weeping.

Was this as good as it felt? Was the magic bubble real, or a figment of her imagination? She wasn't sure how much of this was her own fantasy come to life—getting even an inch out of the valley—and how much of it was truly this good. She didn't know, and she didn't care, she only poured herself out from an endless well until the fire flew from her fingers, her eyes, her mouth.

This was what she'd wanted, what she'd craved when she'd watched recordings of JLo perform. This was her dream, right here, and she couldn't believe it was happening for real.

When the song ended, they roared.

There were so many of them, twice the crowd she'd ever had in McAllen. They tried to tip her, but security had come out to hold them back. Ethan and Mitch had moved to the other side of the human wall, holding out their hands to accept offerings in her stead. The crowd was insane, whipped into a frenzy and calling out. When the chant began, though, it wasn't her name, and it took it a second to congeal enough so she could hear it.

Papi. Papi. Papi.

She stilled, shocked, and glanced offstage at Randy, who stood grinning like a cat in a roomful of trapped mice. How had they known about "Papi"? Were people here from McAllen? But how did they *all* know? She was only meant to do the one song by the agreement with Crave. Was she supposed to perform another one? Now?

Randy glanced over his shoulder and nodded. The thumping backbeat of a "Papi" remix pounded through the loudspeakers, giving way to the familiar synthesizer identifying the specific arrangement. It thrilled her and sent her into panic all at once. Was she supposed to perform it? This version? She never did *this* one.

Apparently she did now.

She looked at Randy, who only stared back, encouraging. The mix was on loop, never going into the chorus. It wouldn't go until she gave the line for cue. She didn't give it. Not yet.

She looked out at the still-chanting crowd. *Papi. Papi. Papi.* Ethan and Mitch remained at the front, taking tips. Off to the other side, Crabtree and a man in a leather mask stood in the shadows. Crabtree nodded in approval, and Caramela glanced back at Steve.

He met Caramela's gaze, and he smiled a slow, proud smile.

Caramela drew a deep breath and let it out. No, *this*. This was what she wanted—to perform, to shine, but…with family. She wanted them all—Ethan, Randy, Mitch, Sam, even Crabtree. And Steve more than anything or anyone else. Chenco rose up to stand with her, and they were one, yearning and craving together. With one dream expanding beneath their feet, another one opened, and the need for it burned.

I will have it all, then. Caramela closed her eyes, absorbed the music into her soul, found her rhythm, her place in the song. She lifted the microphone to her lips and switched it live.

"Baila para tú Papi."

The crowd became so loud it was a wave of sound, a deeper rush and thrill than she had ever known. The music moved forward, onward into the song, into the future. Caramela danced—for her papi, for her family, for herself, for Chenco—for everyone.

She didn't remember the set ending—she only knew she was on stage, and then she was off, surrounded by Randy and Sam and the other queens, everyone fawning and gasping and congratulating her. Somewhere in the middle of it Chenco fell forward, mingling with her, absorbing the praise.

"Come to Vegas with us," Randy said. "Come back with us and knock them dead. Let Ethan and Crabtree help you."

Sam stood beside Randy, beaming. "Let us all help you."

Yes, Chenco wanted to shout, but he couldn't, could only look over at Steve, who was still fighting his way through the crowd.

Randy squeezed his shoulder and pressed a kiss on Caramela's hair. "We'll bring your papi too, honey."

"Come on." Sam bounced a little on his heels. "Say yes."

"Yes," Chenco said, then became so dizzy he had to hold on to them both to simply stand.

Steve shouldered his way through the last of the crush, Crabtree and Ethan behind him. Chenco saw his brother too, looking happy and proud. Mostly he saw Steve, his pride and admiration lifting Chenco higher than the adoration of a thousand crowds.

He'll come too, Chenco thought, Randy's promise echoing in his ears.

Yes, he realized as he looked into Steve's bright, proud face. His papi would follow him anywhere.

CHAPTER SIXTEEN

For over a week, Steve hadn't seen Gordy once. Not from the feeds—Crabtree had those taken down. Gordon was in Crabtree's exclusive care now, and he required he make every decision regarding his sub. His very first decree was Steve be removed from the equation unless Crabtree expressly asked for his return. It was the right thing to do. Intellectually, Steve understood this was what had to happen, that it was best for everyone involved.

Emotionally, Steve was going absolutely out of his fucking mind.

Three days after Caramela's South Padre show, Crabtree invited him to see Gordy's progress. The gangster had moved Gordon to a rented house in downtown McAllen a few days after he'd taken him over. At first, Steve had been impressed, even relieved. Gordy was clean, to start—his clothes unsoiled, his beard trimmed. His skin didn't look quite so sallow, and his eyes had a new light to them.

Ten minutes with Steve, though, and Gordy went to pieces.

It started subtly, Gordy growing agitated, fidgeting.

He didn't have on puppy gear, which apparently displeased him, and he begged to be allowed to put it on. Crabtree told him no.

Gordy whimpered and turned to Steve, pleading for his hood and his paws. Steve said to listen to Crabtree, and this led to a full-on meltdown where Gordy revealed his trump—a knife he'd pilfered from somewhere and stowed in his jeans pocket. He got a good long cut in along his arm before Crabtree had him disarmed and on the floor, but the real damage was the crazed, evil grin he'd thrown at Steve.

Come play in the blood with me, baby.

He left before Crabtree had Gordy secured—awful of him, beyond terrible, but it took everything in him to text Randy and let him know the old man might need backup, and then he was off on his bike. He drove so fast he wasn't just a danger to himself but anyone else on the road, tearing up dusty roads along the border, helmet off, wind screaming at his eyes until he couldn't see for tears.

It wasn't enough.

He stumbled into the drugstore as if he'd been drinking—what the poor clerk who checked him out must have thought, he didn't know. Stuffing his purchased supplies into the saddlebag, he tore off down the road, head spinning.

Swimming in irony, Steve went to the cannery. He'd used needles more there than anywhere else, after all, and it was Gordy who'd driven him to this, who'd thrown him so hard he had to go here. Unlike Gordy, however, he was sane enough to practice universal precautions. He laid out the beach towel he'd bought for this purpose and scrubbed his arms with the wet wipes until his skin was raw and red. He gave his hands the same treatment then put on latex gloves.

Drawing in a deep, tortured breath, he picked up a 22 and shut his eyes.

The first time he'd used a needle he'd been seven, and he'd been an idiot. He'd stuck his arm full of his mother's sewing sharps, no cleaning them or himself, and he'd been so proud he'd left them in when he'd gone out to play. When Gordy had wanted one, he'd simply pulled the first available out of his skin and slid it into the thick meat of Gordy's shoulder. To their mutual shock and delight, he'd gone too deep, and blood had run down Gordy's arm. They'd watched the red stream trickle between Gordy's freckles, trapping in the roll of fat above his elbow.

Gordy had looked up at Steve with worshipful eyes and said, "Do it again, Stevie."

They had, and until they were well into middle school they'd tempted fate with every prick, never washing a damn thing, never cleaning up after. AIDS was in full rage while they played, but they didn't give a damn.

Steve remembered those first times now as he slid the needle under his skin, deliberately going shallow, taking no blood.

Gordy loved blood. He wanted it every time, couldn't ever get enough. It was why Steve had stopped playing with him in high school, had felt a release as he'd left for college. What had been fun had become a little frightening. He'd given himself needles when he first went to Stanford, but sometime during the war he'd stopped. He'd never seen anything too grisly, not driving trucks across the desert in 1991, but so many things had changed during those eighteen months he'd been deployed. The world had been big and bad enough while he'd tried to find his way in California, but the Middle East? Steve came home far too aware he was an ant against a mountain.

Then he'd found out Gordy was in trouble, and suddenly he didn't have to be an ant anymore.

He'd restarted needles with Gordy—in fact, they were how he'd drawn his old friend back out of the dark, with Depeche Mode and a trio of 15s leaving beautiful trails down Gordy's pale, hairy skin. They'd taken needles together, a communion of mutual pain. As were so many things with Gordy, though, their sessions soon turned too dark and intense. Steve had walked away a second time—and Gordy had nearly died.

It had been several years since he'd given himself sharps, so he took things slow. He kept his phone out, ready to dial Mitch or Randy if something went wrong. As messed up as he felt inside, he didn't want to leave anything to chance. He wasn't so fucked up he couldn't take care. Order, discipline, and caution—it was what he craved, so he'd give it to himself.

That and a good, hard sting.

He let the second needle go deeper, a 25 this time, but no blood. It burned, but the depth gave it an edge of throb that soothed raw edges of his soul.

Once the third needle was in, he stopped thinking, just let himself float. Alone he couldn't let go too far—he made himself drink water, made himself touch his wrist every few sharps, testing his pulse. After twenty needles and four different gauges, he began to feel slightly human, so he gave himself a few fourteens and a hard poke that bled as a reward.

He was better by the time he cleaned up and headed to the house, a long shirt hiding the evidence of his indulgence, but he still felt off-center, especially when he found out Ethan and Randy were with Crabtree, still trying to bring Gordy down. Sam was shopping, and Chenco was at work, but Mitch was there. He took one look at Steve, grabbed his cigarettes, and motioned to the orchard, declaring it was a nice day for a walk.

They walked, and Steve talked, more than he would have if he hadn't given himself a session. They smoked like chimneys. Steve unloaded everything freaking him out, and Mitch listened. Steve confessed too what truly had begun to eat at him—he didn't really know this man he'd given Gordy to, didn't know he could trust him, yet didn't have any other choice.

Mitch grunted and tapped out a new Winston. "I'll be the first to tell you I hate Crabtree more than I love him. You want to bitch about him ever, I'm your man. But I'll also testify he would have your back even if it meant his own was on fire, once he takes you in. And

Crabtree does know his way around a wounded sub. He plays harder than you, and he's been doing it longer. Jesus, Monk, he's been doing it with *gangsters* since we were fucking babies. He's lost a lot too, and the reason he rides Ethan so hard is he had to give Ethan his baby. The casino is the most precious thing in his life, everything he's stood for, all his dreams. He had to give it away, and he couldn't have done better in Ethan, but it still makes him lose his goddamned mind."

Steve snorted, kicking at a clod of dirt.

Mitch laughed softly and continued. "Yeah, well, go ahead and enjoy that. Point is, he knows what you're going through. I know it sucks, but this probably is for the best. Honestly, buddy, we could all see as soon as we got here you were at the end of your rope over Gordon. I know you don't want to hear this, but it's the truth."

Steve didn't want to hear it, no, but he didn't doubt the truth of it either. "Figured you'd ride me for focusing on Gordy instead of your little brother."

"What? Oh hell no." Mitch paused to light up a new cigarette before passing his pack over to Steve. "Before I could be square with Sam, I had to sort out my past with Randy. Three people in bed is a trick and a half. You gotta have your shit together, all your demons out of the closet." Mitch pocketed his cigs again and took another heavy drag. "Shit, *Ethan* plays with us too. It's such a fucking nightmare ready to happen, and I always think, today's the day it's all gonna go to hell."

Mitch drew in his cigarette, sending the smoke out in a sharp exhale before he continued.

"My point is, I had to deal with my past before I could get to my future. That's part of why I'm staying so long here, trying to heal the last of my crap so I don't fuck things up with Sam. I figure it's why you're sorting out Gordy, so you can be with Chenco."

Steve exhaled his own cloud. "You shouldn't encourage me to be with your brother. I'm way too old."

Mitch rolled his eyes and blew out smoke. "Fuck, Monk, you're only a little older than me, and I'm with Sam."

"I was on my way to the goddamned Persian Gulf when Crescencio was *born*. The first fucking Gulf war, the one nobody fucking remembers anymore. When the second one started, Chenco wasn't a teenager yet, and I was *thirty*."

"Well, way to fucking add. He's not a teenager now, as you might have noticed, and he's about the most solemn, sober twenty-four-year-old I've ever met. Age matters, sure, but sometimes it ain't that simple. Sometimes the difference is good."

Steve snorted and took another drag.

Mitch grimaced at the dirt. "What's eating at you is what eats at me. You know the one getting the better deal out of this is you. You're the one old and tired, and here's this bright young thing smiling at you like you're not old or tired, and you want it so bad your teeth hurt. You tell yourself you should burn them and run. You do everything you can to throw them off the scent. Except they keep coming, partly because for every road you burn, you throw out breadcrumbs too. Me, I got lucky. Fucking *lucky*. Maybe I'm guilty of wanting this to all come together tidy and nice, get my family and friends in one basket, but I'm hoping you get lucky too."

Steve considered this awhile as he finished his cigarette. Eventually he ground it out and sighed. "It's not only age. You saw how I fucked up with Gordy. How can you let me play with your little brother, knowing what I've done?"

Mitch shook his head. "Monk, you're the only one in the whole world who believes the fault there was with you."

Steve said nothing. He couldn't. He looked away, out over the orchard, over the barren fields toward the cannery.

Mitch clapped him on the shoulder. "Come on. Let's head to the house." He coughed, spat up some phlegm, and grimaced. "Shit, that was too many cigarettes. I can't seem to stop lately, since I know I'm about fucking out of time."

Steve turned to his friend, alarmed. "Are you sick?"

Mitch laughed ruefully. "No, man. Ball and chain's making me quit. I was supposed to by our anniversary, but then the old bastard kicked off and I got a reprieve. June first, though, it's all fucking over."

They headed to the house, and all the way there Steve thought about what Mitch had said, about the age thing, about Gordy, about Crabtree. What rang in his head most, though, was his friend's last confession—shy, sweet little Sam had Mitch Tedsoe, who swore they'd take his cigs out of his cold, dead, cancerous hand, obediently kicking his habit.

If Mitch could learn to bend, if he could give just to make his partner happy—well, maybe somehow this *could* work.

If only Steve could be strong enough to believe.

THE MOVE TO Las Vegas happened faster than anything Chenco could have predicted.

Apparently Mitch, Randy, and Sam really had been hanging out for Chenco, because the second he agreed to let them turn him into a Las Vegas casino act, they started making arrangements to go within a week. Except it turned out this wasn't as simple as getting in Mitch's rig and Ethan's incredibly sexy car and driving. First of all, it turned out the Mercedes *wasn't* Ethan's incredibly sexy car, it was a rental.

"Seriously?" Chenco said when he found out.

"Seriously," Randy replied, putting a heavy hand on Ethan's shoulder. "I told him he should get something sexier than an Infiniti, which is what he actually drives."

"An *Infiniti*?" Chenco was crushed.

Ethan gave Randy a hard look. "It's rated third in its class. It has excellent handling, and its lack of a brand name only brings down the price, making it a good bargain."

"This is the moral of the story, Crescencio," Crabtree said, his cane *thunking* the floor. "Ethan has one of the few profiting hotel and casino outfits in Las Vegas during an economic downturn. He didn't get there by spending his money foolishly."

Ethan rolled his eyes. "And you wouldn't let me drive you here in it."

Chenco couldn't stop feeling bummed out. "So you guys are driving it back, then turning it in?"

"No." Crabtree tugged at his cuffs. "There has been a change in plans. We'll be turning the car in here instead. Randy is finding us an alternative means of transportation."

Chenco turned to Steve. "How are *we* getting to Las Vegas?"

Steve glanced at Crabtree. "I'm not certain, but I think you might be riding with Sam and Mitch."

While the idea of riding in the semi with his brother sounded fun, he couldn't help but ask, "Not you?"

"Steven will go with you as well," Crabtree said. "Mitch will need a relief driver, after all, and I require Randy with me and our additional guest."

For some reason this upset Steve—it was the first time Chenco had seen him flustered. "But I thought—"

Crabtree's cut-off reply was so sharp it made Chenco startle. "You handed the matter to me, Mr. Vance. You will not dictate how I proceed." When Steve started to turn red-faced, clearly biting back a retort, Crabtree jerked his head to the side yard. "Shall we move somewhere more private for this discussion?"

Steve didn't say anything, just headed out the front door.

Chenco turned to Randy and Ethan, who appeared to be waiting for his question. Chenco threw up his hands. "*What?*"

"You'll need to talk to Steve about it," Ethan said, before Randy could.

Randy snorted. "Steve's not going to tell him."

"Oh yes he will," Ethan replied with heat. "He's long overdue as it is."

Chenco thought he'd go crazy, trying to figure out what this talk would be about. Who was this additional guest? Why was Steve so upset about riding with Chenco? He tried not to jump to conclusions, but until Steve did come to him, saying they needed to talk, he was a mess.

They rode in silence together over to the cannery, and they sat in the weed-riddled parking lot as Steve told his story.

"There's something I haven't told you," Steve said, his voice tight. "Something important. It doesn't affect the two of us, but it affects me personally a great deal, and you deserve to know about it."

Play it cool, Chenco scolded himself, but he felt anything but. "What's that?"

Steve sat in silence for a full minute, clearly reluctant to have this conversation. "There's this guy, an old friend of mine."

Chenco's stomach lurched. *There's another guy.*

The weariness and guilt on Steve's face as he closed his eyes reminded Chenco of the night he'd caught him in his office looking old and tired. "It's not like that. If it were, this would be easy. I'd tell him to go. Gordy isn't easy, though. He never has been."

Gordy. "Wait—this is the homeless guy?"

Steve turned to him, alarmed. "How do you know about Gordy?"

"Sam told me. But not much." Chenco tucked his hands under his armpits and tried not to hunch his shoulders. "Please just explain." *Are you sleeping with him? Are you cheating on me?*

"Jesus, I wish I knew how to explain Gordy." Steve stared across the empty lot. "We grew up together. We figured out we were gay together. We found pain together. He's my best friend, or rather, he was. He got messed up, though. Fell in with a bad crowd, and I came back too late to help him. It's…" He ran a hand over his head and grimaced. "I know this is cliché, but it's complicated. It's really fucking complicated."

Chenco glanced around. "Is he home?"

"Oh—no, he's not here anymore. Crabtree has him in a house not far from downtown. He's trying to…settle him." He rubbed his head as if against an oncoming headache. "I'm coming with you to Vegas. But I can't leave Gordy behind. I don't…I don't know what to do with him, but I can't leave him."

Chenco was starting to think it'd be easier if Steve *had* been sleeping with someone else. Then Caramela could just stiletto them and move on. "So what are you going to do?" *What are we going to do?*

"I'm not doing anything, as I've been told to stay out of it. Crabtree's bringing him along to Vegas, keeping him at his house. Gordy can't do a plane, though, and neither can Crabtree, so they're taking my truck, the four of them together."

Steve had started giving himself a massage on his neck. Chenco displaced his hand and took over, loving the way Steve melted into his touch without thought. "Well, he's not a madwoman in your attic anymore, Mr. Rochester. I think it's a good start." Steve looked at him like he'd grown an extra head, and Chenco slapped lightly at his neck. "Hey. I'm not so stupid I can't make a *Jane Eyre* reference."

"I've never thought you're stupid, nor am I surprised you alluded to Brontë." Steve frowned, but then he sank into Chenco's fingers. "That said, I'm feeling like eight kinds of hell that I'm Mr. Rochester in this scenario. Because I am. *Jesus.*"

Chenco shifted so he could kneel behind Steve and use both hands for his work. Goddamn it, this Gordy guy didn't get to fuck things up for him, not when they were just starting to get good. *You can't take him away from me. This is* my *papi.*

"Don't be so hard on yourself. I'm sure there's more to the story than this, but from what I'm hearing, you did your best. You weren't hiding him away. You were protecting him the only way you knew how. You didn't lock him up and burn him down. You set up surveillance video and turned him over to a guy who gives casinos away."

Steve leaned against Chenco's body and said nothing else, but he was calmer now, more centered and relaxed. Chenco felt proud, as if for once he wasn't the kid who needed saving but the boyfriend who could save right back.

ON THE DAY before they left, Chenco agreed to a ride with Steve over to Edinburg.

It had been Chenco's idea. His freak-out over the almost trip with Randy had been gnawing at him, and now that he was *leaving*, he felt he should return. He was terrified all the way over, but while Steve made it clear they could turn around at any time, Chenco stuck to his guns. He owed himself a farewell.

They sat outside the gated subdivision—the gates were open, forgotten by someone entering or exiting, and honestly even if they were closed, Chenco could hop the rail with no trouble if he wanted to get inside. However, as he clung to Steve's waist and huddled against the safety of his broad back, he knew that he didn't want to go in any farther. He knew how this scene would play out. He had no delusions his mother would weep with joy for having found him—she'd known where he was for years. He hadn't changed his cell phone number since he left. If he tried to see her, she'd make him feel more lonely and scared than he already felt. He'd come here, though, and now he faced his fears, his demons, his sorrow at being turned away.

He said his farewells silently, and then he whispered for Steve to please take him home.

Chenco said goodbye to everyone at Taco Palenque—they weren't close friends, but he would miss some of them—and he gave Lincoln a tearful hug on their last night out at Club 33, promising to keep in touch. Lincoln said Chenco had better or he'd be cashing in some vacation time to check in on him in

Vegas.

"Maybe I should check in on you regardless." Lincoln waggled his eyebrows. "It's been a decade since I was last in Sin City."

"You're welcome anytime."

Lincoln's expression turned serious, and he touched Chenco's arm. "Be careful, okay? I know things are going well with Mr. Benson, and I'm glad for you. But be safe. If you ever need me, I'm a phone call away."

With another hug, this one piercing deep into Chenco's belly, he promised he would be careful.

He really was leaving. Not just the valley, but everything and everyone in it. Maybe forever.

Of course, Steve was leaving too, which still blew Chenco's mind. At the same time, it didn't seem that big of a deal, not as much as it was to Chenco to get out of the RGV. When Steve packed up his house, he said goodbye to his friends and handed his keys over to a caretaker—the friends clearly hadn't seen him much except for the day in the flats. They seemed more glad for Steve than sorry to see him leave, and unlike Chenco's parting with Lincoln, nobody shed a tear.

Mitch seemed excited to take a road trip with his husband and brother and Steve—Sam was positively giddy as he gave Chenco a tour of the cab and showed him how to turn the fold-down bed into a couch and raise the dining table.

Sam seemed eager to have a traveling companion. "We can sit back here and play cards while they drive."

"Do you ever drive?" Chenco asked, and almost

laughed at Sam's shudder.

Chenco kind of wanted to drive. Obviously not now. But he found himself hoping one day Mitch would offer to teach him.

When they finally pulled out of McAllen, Chenco sat in the front seat of Old Blue, leaving the only place in the world he'd ever been. He'd never traveled farther north than Austin, never crossed the border to Mexico. Now he was going all the way to Las Vegas.

He wasn't just leaving the valley, he was leaving with his brother. And his brother-in-law.

And a card shark, a casino mogul, and a gangster.

And his boyfriend and his madman fresh from the attic.

Once they were out in the brush country, Chenco moved out of the passenger seat, surrendering his place to Sam so he could sit with Steve on the couch. Steve pulled him in close and rubbed his arm.

Chenco sank into him. "It seems stupid, feeling sad for leaving. Nothing good ever came of being here. Why am I sad to go?"

"You lived your life here, and change is always hard."

"I didn't get to see Booker. I tried, but he wouldn't answer my calls."

Steve kissed him gently. "It's okay. He'll come around. Or he won't. But you're going to be okay."

It was such a sappy, stupid thing, but he couldn't keep himself from saying it. "You'll be with me?"

"For as long as you'll have me," Steve promised.

"For as long as you want me there."

I'm going to want you with me forever, Chenco thought, but that was *really* sappy and stupid, and he kept the words to himself.

CHAPTER SEVENTEEN

M ITCH DROVE NORTH to San Antonio, then headed
east on 10 toward Ciudad Juarez—they didn't
ever dip into Mexico, only skirted it via Fort Bliss, and
to get that far took eleven hours. Part of Chenco had
been hoping to see some of those great big leafy trees
he'd seen in movies and picture books, but of course
they were going from brush country to short grass to
desert. In addition to the scenery not being much—and
only visible if he sat up front with Mitch—there was
precious little to do. Chenco had grown tired of cards
with Sam well before then, and he was relieved when
they indulged in an extended break at a truck stop. It
had absolutely nothing he wanted to eat, but Sam had
stocked the mini fridge in the cab with fruit and veg and
hummus, and Chenco made a small picnic with Steve
under the shade of a mesquite tree.

"I can't believe we're not out of Texas yet," he said,
leaning against Steve as he twirled a grape between his
fingers.

"Nearly there now." Steve popped a piece of hummus-laden carrot into Chenco's mouth. "We'll get to
Arizona before nightfall. I don't know if I can get us all

the way to Phoenix—been a few years since I drove a rig in a big city. Mitch might well be rested enough to drive again by then, since he's used to driving long distance."

"I can't believe I have a brother *and* a boyfriend who can drive big rigs." He settled into Steve's arms and stared out at the interstate. "You drove a truck in the Army, right?"

"Slightly different kind of truck, but yes." He stroked Chenco's arms idly. "Man, I was younger than you when I did that."

"What were you doing sixteen years ago when you *were* my age?"

"It was 1998, so I was just about done at Stanford. Had big dreams of running a tech company." He laughed, the sound tinged with regret. "Hell, I knew Larry and Sergey pretty well. I can't say they'd have brought me in on the ground floor, but…well, things went a different way, so none of it matters."

"Larry and Sergey?"

"Larry Page and Sergey Brin. Google founders."

Whoa. "You left all that for Gordy?"

"I did."

Now it was Chenco stroking Steve's furry arm. "How's he doing? Have you heard?"

Steve's reply was careful, but Chenco could feel the mild tension in his body. "Crabtree has made it clear I'm out of the loop for a while. He's told Randy and Ethan to simply report everything is fine. Randy did leave a tracking app on for me, so I can see where they're at. It's all I get, though."

"That's harsh."

"It's smart." Steve caught Chenco's hand and twined their fingers together. "Gordy's relied on me for a long time, and he's pretty messed up."

Chenco was starting to think when it came to Gordy, Steve was messed up too. "So what's he doing, exactly? Crabtree, I mean. Is he…maybe this is a stupid question, but are they having sex?"

"I doubt it, but…well, I don't know. Like I said, I'm not privy to much information." He rubbed his thumb along the inside of Chenco's wrist. "Mostly he'll be setting boundaries, trying to give Gordy a routine. Making sure he takes his meds. Crabtree probably has to pull pretty hard on him sometimes, and travel isn't going to be easy. They'll take an extra day at least to get to Vegas. I think I heard Ethan and Crabtree talking about making time for a scene, though I doubt Ethan or Randy will be part of that."

"So he's using BDSM to do this rehabilitation, right?"

"Yes, but probably not the way you're thinking. It's not about tying him up. It's about giving him what he needs. Much like you, really, except your needs are different. More like the first scene we had. Rougher, but that kind of connection."

It was hard for Chenco to think he had anything in common with a man who holed up in an abandoned building. "You always seem to find things I need I didn't know about."

"That's my job." He nuzzled Chenco's ear briefly.

"Crabtree's doing the same thing—reading Gordy, trying to find out what he needs to feel safe and strong. It's what I should have been doing, what I tried to do, but I was blinded by my own feelings, my guilt."

"Why should you feel guilty? It's amazing you gave up a career to help your friend, but nobody would expect it of you."

"Gordy did. I did."

That was tough to argue with, especially since right now Chenco was the recipient of some pretty generous and wildly unnecessary aid. He watched the interstate some more. "I suppose we should head to the truck."

Steve lifted his phone from the blanket beside them and shook his head. "Not yet. Mitch said he'd text me when he's done."

"Done? With what?"

"Fucking the ever-loving shit out of his husband."

Chenco glanced at Steve to check the veracity of this. A sly smile played on Steve's face.

"No shit?" Chenco's head was full of images of his brother and Sam that made him a little bit tingly inside.

When they did finally go to the rig, it swelled with the smell of sex and freshly brewed coffee. Mitch—naked from the waist up and wearing low-hanging boxers—handed a travel mug full of black brew to Steve and went over some of the readouts and implements on the dashboard. His arms, Chenco couldn't help notice, were full of hard, red lines.

Fingernail trails.

Chenco tucked his feet under his body as they drove

onto the interstate, watching the ribbon of highway roll out before them, thinking about sex. He watched Steve work the gears, expertly shift lanes, a hot shock of man driving a big, sexy truck.

Once Chenco got up to use the bathroom and get a glass of water, and he couldn't help steal a gaze at Mitch and Sam, tucked in their bed, a bed that looked barely big enough for Mitch yet somehow held the two of them. Sam was clearly naked, Mitch's arm wrapped around his waist, hand cupped over Sam's cock and balls. His heavy leg swallowed Sam's thigh, and his face, slack with sleep, was half-buried in Sam's messy hair. The sight arrested Chenco, made him happy and lonely at once. It made him horny too.

Steve noticed.

At first he didn't say anything, but it wasn't long after Chenco buckled into his seat, his erection making him squirm, Steve said, "Take it out and play with yourself."

Chenco hesitated. Steve didn't look at him, but it was clear he waited for his order to be obeyed. Chenco felt weird. He hadn't ever masturbated in front of anyone before. He'd done a hell of a lot with Steve, but not this. Not with Steve sitting there driving. Not with his fucking brother ten feet away, asleep or no.

"Chenco," Steve said, a hint of warning in his tone.

Swallowing his nerves, his awkwardness, Chenco undid his fly.

He may have felt weird, but his cock still could see the fucked-out look on Sam's face, those scratches on

Mitch's arms. Chenco wanted some scratches. He wanted to feel the burn echoing through his skin, that soft heat. He wanted Steve's teeth on him biting hard into the meat of his shoulder.

Chenco cried out softly at the thought, jerking himself.

"That's right." The acrid smell of a match filled the air with a sharp hiss, followed by the scent of seared tobacco. "Should have put a plug in you at the rest stop. Should have stripped you down in the men's room, made you spread your legs and stuffed you up."

Chenco's cheeks burned scarlet fire at Steve's words, and he couldn't help a glance backward at the curtain.

"They'll hear you, boy. Not yet—they're still asleep. But when they wake up, I'm going to bend you in half on the floor, and they'll hear everything I do to you."

Something ugly and scary turned inside Chenco. His hand stilled on his cock. "Yellow."

He'd never used a word before with Steve, just the one blind-fear scream of *red* with Randy on the way to Edinburg, so he was almost more nervous after he spoke.

Steve didn't seem to share his anxiety. He relaxed a little and reached over to stroke Chenco's arm. "Tell me what part was yellow."

Chenco didn't want to talk about it, but he made himself. "Them hearing. Knowing what you're doing."

"Because Mitch is your brother? Or because someone will know?"

Both? Except as he thought about it, the *someone*

will know part was what felt so gurgly and dark. He swallowed and cupped his penis protectively. "Because they'll know. I'll let go like you make me do, and they'll know."

Somehow this pleased Steve. He didn't smile, but he had this look about him as if this was a road he knew well. "There's no sin in letting down your guard. Not when you're in a safe space. It's not shameful to let someone see you when you're vulnerable."

Chenco knew this, and he agreed in theory, but… "It's not shame. It's…" He wet his lip. "It feels dangerous."

Steve stroked Chenco's arm again, this time the touch a long, sensual caress with his thumb. "Do you trust me, Chenco, to keep you safe?"

Was it bad Chenco had to think about it? It wasn't that he didn't trust Steve, it was…Chenco didn't know what it was. Fear, maybe. Old, deep, nameless fear attached to something but long since tethered, snarling nastily in the darkness of his soul. Fear of being exposed and injured. Fear of not stepping onto the stage deliberately in Caramela's armor but dragged out unexpectedly into a harsh glare in the middle of jeering laughter. It made Chenco's breath catch, his erection wane, his heartbeat quicken.

"Chenco?" Steve's strong, sure voice cut through the fog like a lighthouse. "Do you want me to pull over so we can talk?"

No, Chenco didn't. "Keep—" His voice broke, and he swallowed. "Please keep moving. It's…something about the road. Everything moving. Makes it okay."

"I understand."

Steve let the silence expand between them now, and Chenco stared into the sunset, off to the northwest. The soft colors moved Chenco, soothed him. Eventually, he spoke.

"Nothing ever happened to me." His voice was soft, and it seemed to come from far away. "I don't have a story like Gordy's. Nobody ever hurt me. I never thought about playing until you."

"It's not a contest. You don't have to have been hurt in your body to be wounded. Sometimes all they have to do is ignore you."

The tears pricking Chenco's eyes shocked him, and he blinked them back with a terror. Once they were beaten down, he said, "They didn't know they were ignoring me. I wouldn't let them see. Not my family, not Cooper, not my friends. Not Booker." This time the tears got him in his solar plexus, and it was tough to sit upright. He made himself do it anyway, his eyes trained on the distant horizon. "You saw me, though. In the alley. You looked at me and you saw me. I was hiding, but I couldn't hide from you."

He swallowed several times, letting those words echo inside of his head. They echoed for a long, long time.

When he finally emerged from his strange meditation, the sun was almost gone. Dust colored the sky with rich, blood-red hues.

I want to bleed for him, Chenco thought, but he

didn't say. Not here. Not yet.

He heard stirring from behind the curtain, the soft murmurs of Mitch and Sam waking. In his half-trance, he felt their connection, and it made him ache. *I want that.* The yearning was a whisper in his head. *I want to feel that connected to Steve, not just about sex but about life. I don't have any right to it, but I want it so badly I could sob right here in this seat, if I let myself feel.*

The problem was, he couldn't seem to stop feeling tonight. He shut his eyes.

"They can hear you take me," he said, very quietly, "but I can't bear to let them hear me cry."

"Don't push yourself for me. Not out of fear. Don't you ever, ever yield to me in fear."

Chenco wanted to deny this, but he made himself examine his reactions anyway, just in case. He shut his eyes, drew a deep breath as he felt inside himself, then shook his head. "Not fear. More…more like I want to beat fear. I want to show you I'm strong. To show me I'm strong. Them too."

"All right," Steve said.

Doubt crept in. As Steve pulled the truck over at a rest stop, Chenco hastily did himself up and left the cab, wrapping his arms around his body in the evening chill, dark voices whispering in his ears.

He's never going to give you what Mitch gave Sam. He thinks you're going to get tired of him. He thinks seventeen years age difference is too many for anything more than fun and games. He might be right.

Chenco didn't want him to be right. He wanted his

papi to wrap him up and steal him away. To make all his dreams come true and keep him safe. He shouldn't want this, shouldn't be dependent on anyone else. It was too dangerous. But he couldn't stop wanting that and more.

Chenco didn't just want Steve to see him. He wanted Steve to see him—and keep him.

It was wrong to ask for this. Wrong to fixate on someone, to decide they were the one. Steve was right, they could play together, maybe for years, and then Chenco could find someone his age, or closer to his age, someone who hadn't been fighting a war when he was a toddler. It was smart. It was logical and safe.

It made Chenco want to rend his hair.

I want to stay with the one who found me when no one knew to look. It's the only thing I want.

Chenco could never let him know.

When they got back to the truck, Steve laid him out on blankets on the floor, folding him in half as promised, securing his hands and ankles together and fastening them to bolts on either side of the captains chairs in front. The curtain hung down, but Chenco could see underneath it. They'd be so close. They'd hear every sound he made.

Except no sooner did he think this but Steve squeezed his jaw open and forced a thick ball inside and fastened it at the back of Chenco's neck.

Chenco swallowed around the gag, his tongue playing helplessly behind it, beneath it, around it. He stared up at Steve, who looked down at him in wicked pleasure. Chenco felt himself go slack in mind as well as body, his ass and cock exposed, his belly, his heart.

Steve pressed a hanky into Chenco's hand. "This is your safe word."

Just like the time after the big flogging, with the penis gag. Chenco nodded. He gripped the hanky tight in his hand, hoping he didn't have to let it go.

Steve tortured him slowly. He teased Chenco's nipples, his abdomen, his cock. He fondled his balls, edging close to but not quite giving Chenco the aggression he wanted. He drifted soft fingers over Chenco's groin, his hole, maddening Chenco until he grunted behind the gag and thrust up desperately against Steve's too-gentle hands.

The door to the truck opened, and Mitch climbed inside.

Hot, terrible embarrassment flooded Chenco as he watched his brother settle into his seat—he clutched the hanky tight.

Steve sucked on Chenco's belly, and he moaned, shocked, delighted, and it was loud enough there was no question Mitch heard. Sam's voice, soft and questioning, floated over him, and then Sam gasped too. Chenco watched under the curtain as Mitch hauled Sam onto his lap and began to undress his husband.

Steve thrust a slick pair of fingers into Chenco's hole as Sam tipped his head back to let Mitch attach himself to his chest. Chenco moaned.

When he felt a hot mouth on the inside of his thigh, biting and sucking, Chenco looked down, groaning at the image of Steve feasting on his splayed apex. Something thick moved inside Chenco's ass, metal and bulbous and unyielding, and he clenched around it, crying against the gag as Steve sucked on his balls. If he'd had a voice, he'd have been begging for a bit of burn, a bite of pain. *Pinch me. Rake me. Mark me.*

Steve only teased him, thrusting something deeper and deeper inside Chenco. Whimpering, Chenco tried to squirm, as if he could wiggle his way into something more, but Steve wouldn't relent.

In the front of the cab, Sam cried out, and something squished. Chenco peered under the curtain—he shivered as he saw Sam, naked from the waist down, facing the windshield and splayed grotesquely over the wheel, knees on the door and the dash as Mitch idly shoved two fingers into Sam's swollen, slutty hole.

Chenco's eyes rolled shut, and he humped mindlessly against whatever Steve had in his ass.

He gave himself over to the wickedness of it all, to being tied down on the floor of a semi, spread naked and wide while Steve shoved shit in his ass and Mitch finger-fucked his husband over the steering wheel. Chenco felt a connection to Sam, thought about how they were both being used, objects of their masters' sexual whim, and he shivered.

A sharp slap made him jerk, but he felt no pain— the sound came again, this time with a whimper, and he peered under the curtain to see the red imprint of Mitch's hand on Sam's ass—an ass speared now on three insistently fucking fingers.

This time Chenco growled, the sound coming from the very base of his throat.

The next crack came on his own skin—his left butt cheek, sharp and delicious. He purred and tried to lift his ass higher, displaying it for Steve, making it a target. His reward was a sharp, stinging blow on whatever was in his hole. Then another. Then another. Then a stinging bite, a pinch that didn't end against the inside of his thigh—he cried out at the gag, and then another sting came, and another, and another. He looked down to see small plastic clamps lining the inside of his leg. He met Steve's gaze, and Steve grinned, so dark it was terrifying. He held up another clamp.

He lowered it to Chenco's balls.

Chenco cried out, bucked, thrashed—then screamed behind his gag and clutched the hanky so hard he feared he might turn it to dust as Steve put the clip in place, the pain white-hot and so wonderful he tripped, briefly, right out of his head. He rode the wave of a second clamp, and then a third, and then he lost count. He heard the sounds of sloppy, raunchy sex behind the curtain, slaps of flesh and the thick squish of Mitch playing in Sam's ass, Sam making incoherent, desperate pleas. Chenco heard, but he couldn't look, too lost in his own bliss.

The plug inside him came out, leaving him empty and clenching, but soon something else went in—something cold and thicker yet, and so long it made Chenco grunt and lift as Steve drove it home. It felt obscene and frightening.

Steve tugged on Chenco's nipple clips—when had those happened?—and made a soft sound of approval, clearly admiring his own work.

Then he fumbled at the opening of Chenco's ass, and whatever was inside him began to hum.

Chenco grunted and bore down, but Steve fumbled and the thing vibrated more, rubbing raw along Chenco's prostate. It made noise—Chenco could hear it buzzing, beating inside him, and he fucked back, lewd and mindless, without shame.

Tears ran down his cheeks.

He was crying—sometimes he had to take sharp breaths in through his nose around a sob. He felt more clips attaching to his body, pain on top of pain, and he fucked himself on the beast inside him, riding it, riding the pain, sobbing. He was so far gone right now he'd let Steve line up greasy, ugly truckers to watch him be played. Chenco was so out of control, but he was safe. Steve would never, ever hurt him, and Chenco knew this in his soul. He loved this, what Steve did to him. While what was happening to Sam was hot, it wasn't what Chenco wanted. He wanted the pain only Steve could give him.

He'd let Steve fuck him anywhere, any way, so long as he gave him this. So long as he stayed.

When Steve pulled him up by the hair, as the light from the lot sliced over his face, illuminating it, Chenco looked up at him and let it all show. *You, you forever, please, please.* He let it all shine.

Steve stared down at him, struck dumb.

Chenco's body hummed, the dildo inside him still mindlessly gnawing at his prostate and his bowels, and somehow the humility of it made it all the more perfect. *I will never run out of ways to be vulnerable for you, and I'll never grow tired.* If the gag wasn't in his mouth, he'd have said the words out loud.

Something moved like a ghost over Steve's face, something profound that seemed to reverberate to his center. His free hand stroked Chenco's face, trailing lube and musk.

He caught the edge of the gag and pulled it down.

Tears still flowing, Chenco looked up at him, lost in his high. "Steve," he whispered, ready to confess. But suddenly words were stupid, worthless. "Please," he begged. "Please."

Steve cupped Chenco's jaw so tightly it hurt.

He bent down to Chenco's face, his eyes wide and burning.

He sealed their lips together.

Chenco gasped and opened, inviting him in. Steve took him, plunging deep, gagging him with his tongue. He pressed his heavy body over Chenco's, frotting through his jeans, rubbing the zipper and the button along Chenco's naked cock. He sheared the clips off of Chenco's body, swallowing his cries of pain as they released. He undid his pants and thrust his dick against Chenco's own.

He pulled out the dildo, leaving it humming and rumbling beside Chenco's ass, borrowed some of its lube and speared Chenco in one deep thrust.

The cry almost escaped, but not quite—Steve caught it and swallowed it whole. When his thrusts made Chenco's eyes water, he clamped a hand over Chenco's mouth and licked the salt away.

He made Chenco come, then took his time in finishing, riding Chenco long and slow and deep, pushing the tears out of him from the inside. He filled him, coating Chenco's passage then pushing the plug back in before untying Chenco and gathering Chenco's slack body to his own.

"You're *mine*."

"*Si, Papi,*" Chenco whispered, arching, wedging the plug deeper. "All yours."

They slept there on the floor—eventually the truck began to roll, but they stayed there on the sheets, in the narrow space where they couldn't even spread their legs, Chenco pressed naked to Steve's body. At one point Sam stepped over them to use the bathroom, and when he came out, Steve made Sam stand there as he pushed his cock back into Chenco and filled him again. Chenco watched Sam the whole time, dazed, lost to his pleasure. Sam didn't look too far behind.

Chenco drifted to sleep as Sam went to the front of the cab, but as dawn broke, it was to the sounds of Mitch's low voice and Sam's muffled whimpers—bare knees on the floor told him Sam was blowing Mitch, but the soft, plaintive cries made him peek behind the curtain to see Mitch was fingering Sam at the same time.

He shifted beside Steve, hoping to wake him too.

He did get fucked a third time—this time over a picnic table behind a public restroom. He looked around, wild-eyed, as Steve pumped into him, barely touching him, making it clear this was all about filling Chenco's ass because he liked it stuffed full of his come, and he said he sure hoped somebody saw since he was fucking pretty good in Chenco's sloppy ass. This comment made Chenco come, and Steve plugged him up before kissing him deep, pushing on the metal end and making Chenco feel all the mess inside him.

Chenco went to the bathroom to clean up—not his ass, he promised Steve—and he met Sam there.

They were quite a picture together in the mirror. Sam's mouth was swollen, his neck full of hickeys. His nipples stood out on end, and he had the exhausted look of somebody who'd endured a lot of fucking. Chenco looked worse. He felt the burn of the clamps lingering all over his skin, felt his dick howling from overuse, felt his ass burn with pride around the heavy plug.

Sam smiled shyly at him—but wickedly too.

The rest of the ride was, in relation, rather boring. Chenco slept on the floor, Sam in the bed, and even when Chenco woke he lay there, listening to the soothing low voices of his lover and his brother.

Then Mitch said, "Here we are, Chenco. Las Vegas."

Chenco climbed to his knees, rising up to a crouch so he could see over the dash, wincing as the plug shifted inside him. It was true—there it was. Las Vegas. Sprawling roads and houses and buildings and casinos and the mountains rising quietly in the distance. It was huge. It was everywhere.

He was here. He was really here.

Steve pulled him closer and kissed his temple. "You're going to be great, baby."

Chenco leaned into him and held on. Maybe he would be, maybe he wouldn't. He almost didn't care.

That was when he realized the game had changed. It wasn't about whether or not he made Caramela a star. It was about whether or not he could make Steve his. For good.

Chenco watched the city expand before him, drew on his queen for courage, and got ready for the ride of his life.

CHAPTER EIGHTEEN

Wʜɪʟᴇ Sᴛᴇᴠᴇ ʜᴀᴅ anticipated the pleasure of Chenco discovering Las Vegas for the first time, reality was much more exquisite than he'd imagined. Everywhere he looked, Chenco's eyes were wide. Every turn around a corner was another discovery. The boy who had wanted to get out of the RGV had indeed—and Steve had helped get him there.

He took his lover on an extended tour on the back of his bike, which had come along in the trailer of Mitch's rig. Mitch and Sam kept bikes at the same distribution center where Mitch parked the trailer, and the four of them, Sam, Mitch, Steve and Chenco, had gone on a tour of the city before they went to Randy and Ethan's house, where they'd all be staying. They took in the Strip, drove by Ethan's casino, had a tour of the desert. When they stopped for a drink at a bar called the Watering Hole, Chenco was wide-eyed and dazed as they entered.

"We'll have to get you your own bike and set you up with some lessons," Steve said as he ordered Chenco a club soda.

Chenco did a visual sweep of the room, his dark

eyes cautious and intense. "Is this a gay bar?"

"It's an open-minded bar." Steve handed him his drink and did a sweep of the room too, but he didn't see anyone he knew. He hadn't been to Vegas in years, and even then he hadn't stayed long. Mitch and Sam, on the other hand, were making their social rounds, telling stories to friends. He turned to Chenco. "Anywhere else you'd particularly like to see?"

"I don't know." Chenco leaned into Steve. "I feel kind of dumb. Honestly, I want to go to Randy's house and rest. I spent twenty years wanting to get out of the valley, and now that it's happened, I feel weird."

"I know what you mean." Steve pulled Chenco closer, wrapping an arm around his waist and drawing Chenco snug to his front. "California was everything I wanted, but it terrified me too. Used to go to this isolated park where I could practice getting rid of my accent so they didn't look at me as if I were some dim-witted good ol' boy all the time."

"You know, it's funny—I hadn't really put my finger on it, but you *don't* have much of an accent. Mitch has more than you, and he hasn't lived in Texas for years." He settled deeper into their seat. "My mom was always harping on me for my English. I couldn't sound like some dirty Mexican. I took debate in high school, and when I was in middle school, she had me in these sessions with a vocal coach. She picked my clothes out for me too—we'd drive to San Antonio or Austin sometimes just so she could make sure I was an all-American boy. Then I gave her Caramela."

Caramela, named after his mother, Carmelita. That was everything about Chenco in a nutshell, wasn't it?

Steve stroked Chenco's arms. "You should send her video of the show. And tickets."

Chenco went rigid. "No. She won't come."

Steve let it drop. For now. "Would you like to see where you'll be performing?"

"Yes," Chenco said, though it was clear he was nervous too.

"I'm curious to see what Ethan's done with the casino. I've been to Herod's, but only under the former management." He slid his hand to Chenco's hip and squeezed lightly. "I'll see if Sam and Mitch are ready to head on over."

When they pulled up to the parking lot, Steve could already tell things were different. For one, they parked their bikes in a private side lot reserved for VIPs. The lot staff waved and smiled at Sam and Mitch and treated Steve and Chenco as if they must be important too. When Mitch proudly introduced Chenco as his brother, however, the boy received a very warm welcome and many enthusiastic handshakes. By the time they entered the building, a pretty older woman with upswept hair stood in the foyer with a clipboard, smiling and welcoming them with handshakes and kisses on their cheeks.

"You must be Mitch's brother." She smiled brightly at Chenco, enfolding him in a polite hug. "Welcome, Mr. Ortiz. I'm Sarah Reynolds, Mr. Ellison's personal assistant. If there's ever anything you need while at

Herod's, I'm the one you let take care of you. I assume you'll want to see the theater?"

Chenco looked a bit shell-shocked, but he nodded, dragging his eyes away from the circus of the casino floor and back to Ms. Reynolds. "Yes, ma'am. That would be wonderful, thank you."

"Right this way." She led them past a row of poker tables toward a gilded archway. "There might be a rehearsal going on, but nothing more. None of the shows start until seven, and the theater isn't open to the public until six."

Steve couldn't get over how much the entire casino was transformed—he rubbernecked all the way across the main floor, taking in the refinished red drapes, the new paint. No one could miss the demon statue in the center of the room. The floor overflowed with gaming tables and happy, helpful staff encouraging tourists to have fun. Several hosts, he noticed, had subtle rainbow flag pins next to their name badges, and from the way the guests paired up, it was pretty clear the word was out—Herod's Poker Room and Casino was LGBT friendly.

The theater was a charming thousand-seater, not as ornate as some Steve had seen but fancy enough to feel special, something between ornate opera and gilded old-school vaudeville. He'd listened to Sam wax rhapsodic about seeing Kylie Minogue perform there, and Steve could imagine any performance in this venue being both exciting and intimate. As the theater manager came up to greet Chenco, Steve fell back, content to observe Chenco as he received his tour.

He was proud of the way Chenco pushed past this and took advantage of the new experience. His boy not only listened attentively as the manager explained when he'd be allowed rehearsal time and who'd be helping him, but he asked questions about the kind of audience they usually had, what other acts were regular, and what they anticipated for a solo unknown drag act from the Rio Grande Valley. This led to a meeting with Caryle, the casino's marketing manager, who had already put together a portfolio of possible ad spots and marketing concepts for Chenco's debut.

Through it all, Chenco kept his cool, but when it was over, Steve didn't ask, he excused them from Mitch and Sam and took Chenco straight to the bar. He ordered Chenco a double of Abuelo 12 on the rocks and a Bohemia for himself, pleased to see they not only had it but kept it on tap.

"That's Mr. Jansen's favorite beer," the bartender replied, when Steve remarked on it. "When he's not having a Dirty Whiskey."

"Is that what this is?" Chenco took another sip of his drink. "It's good."

"You're drinking a top shelf Panama rum." He massaged Chenco's neck with his right hand. "You looked as if you could use it."

Instead of answering, Chenco sagged against Steve. "I don't know if I can do this."

"You can. You will. There's no rush."

Chenco looked up in concern at Steve, who stood

beside him. "But you can't stay here forever."

"I'm not going anywhere. I brought half my house up here."

I'm not leaving you.

Chenco relaxed, but only a little. "We're to stay at Randy and Ethan's, though. Do you mind? I thought we'd be with Mitch and Sam. I guess that's all one and the same here. Is this okay?"

"Mitch and Sam always stay with Randy when they're in town. When I last visited, Randy's house was significantly more low-key than where we'll be heading now." He hesitated over the next part then decided what the hell. "If you'd rather have more space, I understand they still own the old place. We could set up there, just the two of us. It's not as fancy, and the neighborhood's colorful—granted, it has nothing on the flats."

"Maybe. I kind of like the idea of being with everyone, if you don't mind—unless we'll be underfoot."

"It has six bedrooms from what I understand. We're fine."

"Okay. Then I'm fine with staying for now—if you are. Will Crabtree and Gordy be there too?"

Steve had been wondering the exact same thing. "I don't know. Crabtree doesn't live very far away. I think he stayed at their house when he was recovering, but…well, I don't know."

Chenco took a better look at Steve's face. "Are you worried about Gordy?"

Yes, Steve was terrified, though he couldn't for the life of him figure out of what, exactly. "It'll work out."

Chenco said nothing, only squeezed Steve's hand as he went back to his drink.

RANDY AND ETHAN'S house truly was impressive. Located in Henderson, it was in a newer development near what had been a pretty swanky area in the 1960s, as far as Steve could tell. The house was about ten years old, in a rather uptight little part of town. From the outside, the house looked like any other slightly ornate display of ostentation. Once beyond the front door, however, it was clear Randy Jansen had made his mark.

It had always amused Steve how Jansen fussed over his house, cooking and cleaning and playing hostess whenever he had guests. While he'd never shown much interest in having a fancy place when Steve knew him before, he'd made Ethan's home into a showplace for whomever he chose to entertain. In the absence of the official homemaker, Sam gave them a grand tour—the great room, the dining room, the theater room, the side patio bleeding into the backyard which had a long, narrow pool with raised hot tub and wet bar.

Everything looked as if at any moment the home might break into an elegant party. The walls were painted deep hues of red and brown and green, the floors gleaming hardwood or stone tile. Heavy crown molding accented the ceilings with an echo of ornate kick boards. The furniture was leather and luxurious, except for the patio, where it was weatherproof fabric nestled inside dark wicker matching the high, rock-and-wood walls shrouding the property.

The kitchen was gigantic and acutely functional, not just a showpiece that looked nice when caught out of the corner of one's eye from the dining room, but a working heart where Randy could make his gourmet meals, fancy desserts, and legendary Christmas cookies. It stood as a bridge between the elegant, in-your-face design of the front half of the house and the smaller, more intimate and comfortably furnished rooms beyond. In the cozy nook off the kitchen, for example, Steve recognized some old furniture and knickknacks. Farther on was a game room and laundry—outside of expensive equipment, these rooms might have been found in any house.

There were cats also, he saw to his dismay, a black-and-white one sitting in the middle of an ornate cat gymnasium in the sunroom and a slightly larger calico somehow managing to take up the entire six-foot couch in the den. Sam stroked and cooed at each one as they passed through on the tour, and both times the animals simply squinted at him and nodded as if yes, this was the kind of adoration they had been put on earth for.

Jesus, Steve hated cats.

"They're so precious." Chenco crouched to love on the calico's belly. "I always wanted one, but my mom said no, and of course Cooper would have killed it for fun."

Fuck, Steve was going to have to get a cat.

The black-and-white came in to receive attention too, and Sam bent to stroke it. "This is Salomé, and the one you're petting is Daisy. Crabtree gave Ethan Salomé as a kind of test during the whole casino thing, but he adopted Daisy on his own. He trained them with a clicker to do all kinds of things. I'll show you later."

"I'd love to see it." Chenco looked around the room, shaking his head. "This is the most amazing house I've ever been in."

"They fought forever about moving," Sam explained as he led them up a set of back stairs, a stark contrast to the curving, open air ones in the foyer. "At first Randy kept saying Ethan needed somewhere fancy because he owned the casino, but Ethan refused. He said a small house kept him grounded. It started to become an issue, though, when he'd want to entertain city officials and other bigwigs, and he'd have to go to Crabtree's place. Then Randy admitted *he* wanted a nice house. So they bought this one. It wasn't their favorite, but it's centrally located with enough growth they could shroud the backyard and have some privacy. They spent a ton of money on renovations. Added these second stairs, redesigned the whole rear half of the house to make it more intimate." He blushed as he led them toward a closed door at the end of the hall. "They did some remodeling up here too."

Sam opened the door, leading them into the biggest wet dream of a playroom Steve had ever seen.

Jansen had been at work in here as well, and at this point Donna Reed had on a bustier and carried a whip. The walls were painted a deep red, contrasted with a rich brown that managed to say *dungeon* and *elegant* all at the same time. Heavy wood and steel beams criss-crossed the ceiling with sturdy hooks arranged at appropriate places for rope work. Various benches and chairs decorated the periphery of the room, as well as dark-colored chests of drawers and a tall cabinet in the far corner. The lighting was recessed, the ceiling high enough to allow not only full range of arm motion but a flogger's arc. In the center of it all stood a king-sized Folsom bed, overflowing with pillows and satiny dark gray sheets.

Sam stood off to the side, cheeks coloring, but his expression made it also clear how proud he was of this part of the tour. "They let Mitch and I help design it. Honestly I think they mostly play in their bedroom, but when we…" He cleared his throat. "Anyway. I know you guys play, so feel free to use it anytime."

Steve and Chenco were given space two doors down, a spacious, open-air room with its own balcony. This was on the more formal side of the house and had clearly been the master bedroom once. It didn't just have its own bathroom—it had a sitting room.

"Randy says all this in here can go to storage if you want to move your things in," Sam explained. "It's always the guestroom, so it's a little impersonal. Ethan thought you'd like the sitting room for Caramela. She'll have her own space at the theater, but he figured this would be good too. If not, let me know. Or them know, or something." He stuck his hands in his pockets, looking unsure.

Steve gave Sam a smile to ease him. "It's fine. Thank

you, Sam."

Sam's shoulders returned to the proper latitude. "Mitch went back to the distribution center in Randy's truck. He'll grab your suitcases and a few things he can tote easily. We'll get the rest when you know where you want to be, he said." He nodded toward the downstairs as he headed into the hall. "I'll go make some dinner and let you guys get settled."

Shutting the door behind him, Sam left them alone.

Chenco stood at the window to the balcony. He hadn't said much of anything during the tour, and he'd even been guarded in the playroom. Steve watched him for a minute, trying to read him, then gave up and slipped his arms around Chenco's middle.

"Talk to me, *cariño*."

Chenco laughed, a quiet, almost sad sound. "I don't know what to say."

Steve continued to hold him, swaying slightly when the tension in Chenco seemed to need bleeding off. Chenco stopped tensing and moved with him, a subtle back and forth, and eventually he began to speak.

"I feel stupid," he said at last in a whisper. "I shouldn't be here. This house, that stage—I don't belong here. This isn't me. I'm a stupid kid from the valley." He bit his lip and shook his head. "I know what you said about family, but it still makes me nervous. I should be happy, but things like this *don't happen*. I should be back in the trailer, afraid of getting killed. Or I should be losing my home and having to go live with Booker or Heide. All I did was go yell at my dad's lawyer, and now I have this new life. I'm such an idiot. It's a good life, *amazing*, more than I ever wanted to dream of. Why can't I just accept it? What in the hell is wrong with me?"

Steve stroked Chenco's arms, pulling him in tighter, and deepened the sway. "Maybe this is too fast. If you want, I'll help you find an apartment of your own—here, back in Texas, wherever you want. Not something you owe to someone else—you could get a job here, anywhere, and earn your own way. Tell me what you want, what you need, and I'll help you get it."

By the end of this speech, though, Chenco had tensed again, and when he spoke, his voice shook. "This is the worst of all—how I get more upset the nicer you are to me. Why am I like this? Why do I feel easier when you hurt me? Why can't I just let you be nice? Why can't I let you say you'll help me, let them try to help me, but if you ask to hit me, beat me, whip me, piss on—" His voice broke, and he hung his head.

Steve pressed his face into Chenco's hair. "Bodies are easy. You endured physical pain and humiliation before you met me. It's never scared you. Nobody ever loved you for you before, though. None of your family ever saw you wearing Caramela and loved her as much as the boy they wanted you to be, the boy you never were, but Mitch did, and he did it without blinking. Nobody ever accepted you simply because you were somebody's brother, took you in as adoptive family."

He nuzzled Chenco's ear, slipped the soft lobe between his teeth, biting down, giving Chenco what he wanted at last, bleeding the edge off those emotions Steve knew were killing him.

"Nobody ever looked at you and saw things you needed you didn't know you longed for."

Chenco started to cry softly, his body still tense, everything in him telegraphing he couldn't take anything more. Steve swallowed the rest, knowing it was too much, too intense of play even for his brave Crescencio. He whispered the remainder to his own heart.

Nobody ever loved you like you were a goddess, like a jewel, ready and willing to lay everything down to please you, make you happy, to leave his life behind and follow you, watching out for you, guarding and protecting you. Nobody ever loved you without expectation of being loved back, loved you for your pride and strength and all your secrets.

Nobody ever loved you so much they scared themselves with the weight of it, knowing nothing mattered anymore but taking care of you, because loving you lifted them out of a darkness and fog they hadn't been able to see anymore. Nobody ever wanted to worship you so badly they were willing to give you whatever you needed, to watch carefully and figure out those needs before you did.

Nobody ever loved you like I do.

Steve let those words fall into the quiet. "You're strong enough for this. You can go to the RGV, or we can slow down—but I know you, Chenco, and I know you want this. This is the real deal, what they—what we—are offering you. I know it's tough to accept, so take your time with it. But I promise you, it's real." He wrapped his arms tighter around his lover. "It's real."

Chenco turned his head and pressed his forehead against Steve's own. Tears still ran down his face, but he'd come back from the edge. He shook as he spoke, and his voice was a whisper, the words falling from him in jagged shards. "Stay. Please." His fingers dug into Steve's arm, his nails small, blunt daggers. "Whatever happens—right now, just for now, please, please stay."

Deep oceans of pleasure rolled out of Steve, and he drew Chenco so tight to his chest he knew the boy could barely breathe. *Always, baby. I don't ever want to leave.* "You got it," he said, and pulled Chenco's sweet, soft mouth down for a kiss.

CHAPTER NINETEEN

B Y THE TIME Randy and Ethan arrived in Vegas, Chenco had himself so worked up he'd nearly taken Steve up twice on his offer to go back to Texas. If it weren't for Booker gloating and Lincoln being terribly disappointed in him, Chenco might have. When Ethan took him to the casino for his first rehearsal, however, his armor of pride had worn down to a worthless nub.

The theater staff at Herod's set him up with a rehearsal schedule and a dressing room, though the first few weeks were mostly planning and blocking for Caramela's mid-May debut. Ethan had hired her a choreographer, who while she was good gave Steve a run for his money on being a sadist. Ethan had also instructed Chenco to order a full set of costumes, wigs, and makeup, and when Chenco told him he'd pay him back out of his wages, Ethan had waved a dismissive hand and said not to worry about it. Caramela had her first interview with a local YouTube celebrity, which she ate up with a spoon. Sometimes work was sitting with Ethan, talking about career plans and trajectory—those meetings often included Caryle too.

At first Chenco was uncomfortable with how much

Ethan invested in him. He felt bad saying so to Ethan, but one afternoon as he sat with Randy at the River, he confessed his unease.

"I mean, I'm not making any money right now. I've earned a paycheck since I was sixteen. Now I'm living at your place, eating your food—I'm totally dependent."

"You're earning your keep, from what Slick tells me." Randy elbowed him. "Ease up, Princess. You'll feel better once your first performance is under your belt."

"They're not just talking about this show. Ethan wants to bring in a scout during the first of June. He says I could do a tour, if things played out right and it was what I wanted." Chenco stirred his sparkling water with a straw. "Which is crazy. Everything is happening so fast."

This only made Randy smile. "That's my boy. He loves a wild, impossible hair. I think you're candy to him. But if this is too much, say so, and he'll slow down."

"It's not…" Chenco stirred his water faster, turning the ice into a series of collision courses. "I don't know. I'm so fucking tense I could climb a wall."

"Well, if it's tension eating you, I know a sexy leather daddy who'd love to make you let go."

God, and that was the *other* problem. "Yeah, well…not so much lately."

Randy sat up straighter. "Is this new? You two seemed good to me."

"I can't really tell. I don't know it's me. I think it's…*him*. He's worried about Gordy. I wish Crabtree would let him go over. I think not knowing makes him worse." Chenco's force on the glass was threatening to knock it over. "Or it's not that at all, and I'm being a jealous bitch."

Randy took Chenco's glass away from him. "Lay it out a little better, babe. Is he ignoring you, or distracted? I know he's giving you scenes because I heard you howling your head off last night. You don't feel like he's into it, or what?"

Why had he brought this up, exactly? Chenco traced the wet spot where his glass had been. "Distracted, I guess. Or it's nothing. I don't know, and I can't tell. It's probably that I'm—"

He'd cut himself off, but of course Randy pushed him. "Probably that you're what?"

"Nothing. It's nothing." When Randy opened his mouth to press the issue, Chenco cut him with a glare. "Hooker, I have a sick heel in this bag I would *love* to shove down your throat if you keep talking."

Laughing, Randy slapped a poker chip on the bar and stood. "Well played. Except that gives me an idea, come to think of it." When Chenco gave him an incredulous look, Randy only waggled his eyebrows and brushed a kiss on Chenco's hairline as he passed by. "Nope. I'm supposed to stop talking. Catch you later. Stop fussing and let things go well already."

Chenco tried to let go, but it didn't work. Most days were so full of people and information that when he finally called Steve for a ride home, he was so overstimulated he shook all the way back. Those days Steve was a rock—if Chenco truly needed release, his lover never failed to provide it. The problem, what Chenco hadn't wanted to admit to Randy, was that scenes with Steve, even heavy ones, were rarely enough to pull him all the way back down. It made him feel lousy, and it made him panic. What if Steve figured it out? Would he leave? He'd said he wouldn't, but people always said that. People said all kinds of shit.

Like *I love you no matter what* and *I love you just the way you are* and *yes, I'll leave you the trailer.*

The plus side of the chaos of living with Ethan and Randy was he still had Mitch and Sam too. Chenco went with Sam on bike rides around town, showing off his favorite places. Sam picked up a job too, a full-time, non-temp gig which was apparently a very big deal as usually they only stayed somewhere a few months at a time.

Mitch took jobs, but they were always local runs, and sometimes he was home for days at a time before leaving again. He took Chenco on Vegas tours as well, but most of the time they just went out to dinner. Mitch was always full of interest, asking about Chenco's life, his plans. He told Chenco about his own life too, not just what he was doing but what he worried about. When he worried about what to get Sam for his birthday, Chenco was able to tip him off about a new Xbox game Sam had eyed the last time they were out shopping. The birthday party itself had been great too—for the first time since he left Edinburg, Chenco didn't go to a bar for someone's birthday—he stayed at home, ate some of the best tamales he'd ever had, and kicked everyone's ass at *Dance Central 2*.

Still, the longer time went on, the more he didn't just think, he *knew* something was wrong with Steve and that it had to do with Gordy. The good news was Chenco hadn't upset him. The bad news was there wasn't a damn thing he could do about it. He could only keep being frustrated, going out of his mind and trying not to let it show, which was what he did.

Until one night in late April after rehearsal, Randy met him in his dressing room with a wicked grin on his face. "Hurry up, honey, because you and I have an appointment in the boss's office."

Chenco paused with his shoe half tied and frowned. "I do? We do?"

"Yep. Cleared it with your papi and everything, so don't fuss. Meet me upstairs as soon as you're done. Don't stop at the bar, and if you do, grab water. In fact, have them send up a pitcher."

Once he was dressed, Chenco did as he was told, and when he gave the order for a pitcher of water to be sent to Ethan's office, the woman tending the bar grinned.

"Oh yeah? Well look at you go, handsome. Playing with the boss man."

Playing with the—what? But though Chenco seemed confused, she laughed and refused to explain.

When Chenco arrived at Ethan's office, Ethan was absorbed in the screen of his laptop. Randy stood at the large picture window, bouncing eagerly on his toes.

He wasn't wearing a shirt.

"Don't mind him," Ethan murmured without glancing up from his work. "He's overeager, as usual."

"Overeager for *what*?" Chenco asked.

Ethan glared at his husband. "You didn't *tell* him? Or ask?" When Randy only grinned, Ethan pursed his lips. "You're terrible. I should send you to bed without any supper."

"So long as you come with me, honey, I wouldn't care." He turned to Chenco. "I knew you'd obsess, and I didn't want to distract you while you were working. I also knew it would all be fine."

"Bossy and arrogant," Ethan remarked in singsong.

"You love it," Randy sang back.

They were adorable, but they were so connected when Chenco felt so cut off, and that didn't endear them to him right now. "You still haven't told me what's happening."

Randy grinned. "What's happening is Ethan is going to give you a lesson in flogging."

It was on the tip of Chenco's tongue to say he'd been flogged plenty—then he looked at Randy's naked chest again. "Wait—you want me to flog *you*?"

"I do indeed." Randy gave him an impatient look. "Come on, Princess. You've got switch written all over you. Yeah, you'll bottom, but you want to swing a whip too sometimes. Monk's not the man for that outlet." He grinned like a Cheshire cat. "I, however, am."

Dimly Chenco remembered Sam remarking about how he'd flogged Randy, which was the only way he knew this wasn't a joke. "We're going to do this now? Here? In Ethan's office?"

Someone knocked on the door, and when Ethan told them to come in, a handsome young man just a bit younger than Chenco entered bearing a tray of a pitcher of water and three glasses. He glanced at Randy's naked chest so many times he nearly spilled the whole business on the rug. Randy ogled him right back, and once the boy was gone, he turned to Ethan. "Slick, honey, I think we need to interview your new busboy together."

"You're a slut." Ethan said this idly while he sifted through papers, but then his gaze flicked to the door, and no one could mistake the banked heat there. "I'll make inquiries to see if he's interested. I don't want to scare him off. Sarah says he's very good."

Randy sniggered. "I'll be the judge of that."

Chenco recalled the way the bartender knew what the pitcher of water meant, the way the busboy had seemed to be in on the game too. "So, what, you guys do this all the time? Bring in guys to flog Randy?"

"No, it's only for family." Ethan shut his computer and shrugged out of his jacket before fumbling in a bottom drawer. "Ace, get your sassy little ass over the couch, and not another word, or I *won't* teach him how to flog you."

"Yessir." Still happy, Randy knelt backward on the lush red couch across from the desk as Ethan produced a beautiful black flogger from the desk. It was a cowhide with thin, medium-length tails.

"Another time we'll work you up to some thud, but

Randy is particular with how he takes his heavy blows, and you need to work up to that kind of artistry. Steve said you've handled floggers a few times, but I want you to practice on a pillow first." Ethan paused before adding, "This assumes Randy is correct and you *do* want to try this."

Randy was, but Chenco still wasn't sure he should. "Steve knows? He won't be upset?"

"He thinks it's a great idea, though I understand if you want to talk to him first. Do you wish to call? He's working in my office at the house."

Chenco wasn't sure. He was actually a little annoyed with Steve for not bringing it up. In a perfect world, he'd rather Steve were here, a part of the moment. Since Steve had deliberately *not* been a part of it…well. Put bluntly, yes, he felt like flogging someone right now.

"I'm good," he told Ethan, and the lessons began.

Like Steve had, Ethan showed him how to swing the flogger and not injure himself, making a figure eight in the air, but he focused much more on taking proper aim, measuring the weight of the blow. He had Chenco strike a suede pillow for several minutes and critiqued his form until he felt satisfied Chenco had the hang of it.

"Blows on a pillow aren't the same as hitting flesh. When you first strike Randy, you'll be nervous, but it's important you maintain your control. That's the key to this side of the whip—whether or not you feel in control in other aspects of your life, you *will* be in control here. Take some comfort in the fact that I'll be here the entire time. If you're unsure or anything goes wrong, I'm in control too. You need to let go, however, the same way you do when Steve takes you under—this time to the other side of the coin. Let go to control, to creating a safe space for Randy to enjoy what you give him." Ethan raised an eyebrow at him. "Questions. I know you have them."

Chenco did, but—"I think my questions are stupid."

"God, sometimes he reminds me so much of Sam, it's creepy," Randy murmured.

Ethan swatted him lightly on the butt. "You're about to hit my husband with a flogger, Chenco. I wouldn't count any questions you have as stupid. Ask them."

"It's not about flogging him, though. It's—well, Randy, why are you doing this? Are you being nice or something? This feels a little weird."

Randy eased up from his position and glanced over his shoulder. "Sweetheart, I *love* getting hit. I like it when Slick does me, but I really dig a young, sweet thing working me over. Weird kink, maybe, but it's mine. What I love is giving it back to the same sweet young thing after, but I prefer my teeth straight and all in my mouth, so that's not happening with you."

"You're saying Steve would hit you if you flogged me?"

"No, but he would if I had sex with you. Or even thought about it. He's batshit possessive of you."

Chenco flushed. "Sometimes I don't know."

Randy snorted. "What the hell did you think him making you wear those big plugs to stop up his come was about?" When Chenco sputtered indignantly, Randy rolled his eyes. "Please. You have a stopper in you half the time you're at home, and sometimes when we're out. I know a plug walk when I see one. Plus I know how Monk falls. Hard and deep and jealous, that's our Steve."

"Enough talking." Ethan's tone was stern, and Randy shut up. Ethan gave him a look both loving and weary, then turned to Chenco. "Yes, Randy enjoys this. What other questions do you have?"

"What if I hurt him—too much, I mean?"

"He'll use his safe word—cactus—and you'll stop. Or I'll stop you, if I think you're about to do something dangerous."

"But I don't want to hurt him, not like that."

"It's the risk you take, Chenco. You might. That's why this for you, tonight, is about control. Not giving it but claiming it."

He was going to make Chenco come out and say it, wasn't he? "But what if I *can't*?"

"Then you'll stop. I agree with Randy, however. I think you'll shortly find this is the part of you that you hadn't known had been missing." He handed Chenco the flogger. "Take your time. Warm up your arm. When you're ready, give him a tap and see if I'm right."

Chenco took the flogger. He held it in his hand, measuring the weight, then swung it around a few times, feeling the rhythm and scraping up his courage. He stared at Randy's broad, naked body, focusing on the subtle muscle, grateful Ethan had given him a pair of leather gloves as he was sure the flogger would have slipped from his hand otherwise.

Control. Control. Get some fucking control. Centering himself, Chenco stood his ground and let the falls land on Randy's back.

Smack.

Leather connected to skin, sending the reverberation into Chenco—he gasped, staggered backward, and almost dropped the flogger. As soon as it started to slip from his hand, however, he caught it fast and tucked it into his jeans.

Oh, *hell no*, he wasn't letting that go.

Ethan leaned in and said in a wicked, velvet whisper, "Would you like to try again?"

"Yes," Chenco replied, in a rough voice he barely recognized as his own.

This, Chenco decided, was better than sex. He loved subspace, yes, but holy *crap* this was fucking awesome too. He was *hitting Randy*, striking blows on him that left angry red lines across the perfect pale skin, skin that marked like a dream, and it felt *glorious*. He was fucking *hitting*, and it was okay. Chenco hadn't so much as taken a swing at anyone in the valley since he'd never been big enough to not end up a smear as a result. He sure as hell was swinging now. Control—oh fuck yeah. He could feel it curling around him, catching in his teeth, a contained, violent version of how Caramela managed a stage. This wasn't Caramela, though, this was *Chenco*. This was his stage. His moment.

Holy *shit*, he had to do this again.

When Ethan's quiet command called him to stop, Chenco felt dazed, like he was coming out of a room just north of subspace—not as disorienting, but still sacred and close. He hated to leave, but he realized something important then, something he'd forgotten: Randy. He felt a bit sick—if Ethan hadn't been there, he'd have kept going, sailing away on the high of hitting. What if Randy had been too far under too? What if he'd sent him to the hospital? What if—?

"Stop nagging yourself," Ethan ordered gently. "Yes, I saw that you forgot him, but I didn't. It was your first time. I got a bit lost too until I had it under control, though I suspect if you'd have been working him alone, you wouldn't have let yourself go like you did. You knew I was watching you. You have more control than you think." He nodded to Randy. "There's lotion on my desk. Give him some water and smooth out some of those pretty red lines, so I don't hear him moan and carry on all night long about how they sting."

Chenco gave Randy the water, which he took with a slightly trembling hand. It thrilled Chenco to see him undone like that, lost in the same place he'd been so many times—but when he started rubbing in the lotion, suddenly Randy was moving, twisting his body and pinning Chenco flat on the couch. He opened his mouth to say *what the hell* then froze, arrested by the heavy, intense heat in Randy's gaze. Chenco's dick, still half-hard from the thrill of flogging, rose to full mast.

Grinning lewdly, Randy ground his hard cock against Chenco's. At a sharp word from Ethan he laughed and drew back, though he kept Chenco in place. "I know, I know. No turnabout with this one." He ran rough knuckles down Chenco's cheek and gave him a grin that made Chenco's insides dance. "You just think about this, baby, when you put in those sexy little plugs, and everything you monogamists are missing."

Chenco could barely breathe, let alone respond, but then Randy was gone, rising away from him and moving to Ethan, who murmured something in disapproval before taking Randy's face firmly in hand and capturing his mouth in a greedy kiss.

He watched for a bit, but pretty soon Chenco's phone found its way into his hand, and before he knew it, Steve was answering his call.

"Papi?" Voice cracking, Chenco cleared his throat and deliberately turned away from the two sexy, sexy men flashing him knowing looks. "I think I need to come home." He heard Randy groan and swallowed hard. "Right now."

"I'll be there in twenty," Steve promised silkily, and hung up.

"There's another office next door." Randy gasped. "Unlocked. *Shit. Slick.*"

Chenco climbed off the couch and headed there, grabbing a glass of water on the way.

CHAPTER TWENTY

As Caramela's debut at Herod's drew closer, as Chenco's nerves began to settle and he found his feet in Vegas, both as a performer and as a member of the motley Tedsoe/Keller/Jansen/Ellison family, Steve admitted it was time he faced a hollow, uncomfortable truth—Chenco didn't need him.

He made himself sit with that revelation one afternoon in early May as he sat on the patio, taking a smoke break while a project uploaded to a client's server. Everyone else was at work—Ethan at the casino, Mitch on a run to L.A., Sam at the hospital, Chenco at rehearsal, Randy teaching a poker clinic. Even Salomé and Daisy were absent, off sleeping in their cat condos. More and more lately these were his days, with the house to himself, working out of Ethan's home office. It was not at all unlike his days had been in the RGV before Cooper's funeral, except he didn't have the feeds to watch and his internet connection was faster. There were better delivery options, and Randy kept the fridge stocked with gourmet-level snacks and quick meals. Not for five weeks had he worried about gangs at the cannery or whether or not he'd find Gordy dead and bloody in his nest of newspaper. It was the kind of quiet and peace he'd longed for.

Steve had never felt so rudderless, so irrelevant, so lonely.

The evenings when everyone returned were both better and worse. He'd grown accustomed to the chaos of living with five other men, had come to like it, but with everyone else happy and living their dreams, watching them joke and laugh and share the insights of their day, their challenges only served to make him feel more outside. It wasn't that they excluded him—quite the opposite. Their drive and focus, however, in achieving the goals they'd set for themselves, wasn't something Steve could share. For so long all he'd wanted was to help Gordy. When he first met Chenco, he hadn't considered a relationship, only helping someone who clearly needed a leg up.

Except the more he got to know Chenco, the more he realized his boy hadn't ever needed anything. Oh, he'd been in a tight spot, and he hadn't been happy, but he'd have figured something out. Ethan's cats didn't land on their feet as well as Chenco. This "rescue", Chenco's airlift out of the RGV, was simply a bonus round, a well-deserved assist for a young man who had been effectively sewing silk purses out of sows' ears since birth.

Chenco didn't need Steve. Their sex was still fantastic, except ever since the night Chenco had flogged Randy, it seemed to Steve his lover was a bit more distant. Chenco wasn't nervous, though, not the way he'd been before they left the valley, not like when they'd first arrived in Vegas. Gordy, from the few reports Steve had received, was making significant progress. Steve's clients had less they required of him lately, to the point he'd had to actively seek out more to keep himself busy during the day.

No one needed Steve, and he didn't know what to do about that.

After extinguishing his cigarette in the ashtray Randy had left out for him, Steve went to the kitchen to make himself some coffee. Jansen had one of those fancy single-serving makers with the coffee pods, which on the one hand made excellent coffee but on the other often made him a bit melancholy. He missed the homey waft of auto drip and the constancy of a twelve-cup carafe waiting for his next refill. He supposed that was a backward thing to pine for, but then it was how he felt lately—an irrelevant throwback, just like an automatic drip.

Realizing he'd compared himself to a coffee maker, Steve vowed to seek out a gym membership. Clearly he needed something to challenge him or he'd be seeing philosophical statements in Jansen's litter genie next. Shaking his head at himself, he collected his mug and headed to Ethan's office.

He had just sat at the desk and put his glasses on to work when the doorbell rang. Figuring it was someone's delivery, Steve grimaced in irritation and rose, sipping his beverage before answering the door.

It wasn't a delivery person on the other side. It took

Steve several seconds, however, to recognize who it was.

"Gordy?" Steve opened the door wider and stood in the center of the frame, as if a more direct angle could disrupt the illusion. But yes, this was his old friend, neatly trimmed and washed, smiling the familiar smile that had been home in so many ways since Steve was seven.

"Surprise." Gordy laughed. "The look on your face. Are you going to let me in or stare at me?"

Dazed, Steve stepped back and watched Gordy saunter into the foyer.

Jesus, Gordy looked *good*. His skin almost glowed, probably because he'd been eating decent meals and not sleeping with rat feces. There was a fullness to Gordy, a sense of humanity he'd been missing for years.

Heaviness eased in Steve, weight he'd carried since he'd turned his friend over to Crabtree's care. This had been a good move. He hadn't dreamed to see Gordy looking so well. Gordy, standing in the foyer of a nice house, clean and smiling and normal.

When Gordy turned around, Steve realized those blue eyes were a little *too* bright, and his shock gave way to quickly ripening caution.

"Gordy, where's Crabtree?"

The mean, angry face Gordy pulled told Steve all he needed to know. "Fuck him. He has a house full of guys to play with. He won't notice I'm gone. I miss you, Stevie. I want to be with you again." With some effort, he smoothed his face into a smile. "I'll be good. You'll see." The smile turned up, a bulb set too high. "It'll be just like you wanted in the valley—I'll live with you in a real room and everything. No feeds. I'll be down the hall. Or at the foot of your bed, if you'll let me." When Steve tensed, Gordy's coldness returned in a swift wind. "What? It's not like you don't have room here."

"This isn't my house." Steve thought about reaching for his phone to text Crabtree, Randy, anyone, but it was on Ethan's desk next to his coffee. The foyer, clean and neatly appointed, suddenly seemed fraught with weapons—a vase could be smashed and used for its sharp edges, a hall tree could make a fantastic club. A crystal bowl was heavy enough to render Steve unconscious if Gordy swung it at his head.

Gordy caught his inventorying and sneered. "God, look at you, freaking out because I might break something. Is that who you've become? A big pussy worried about me messing up someone else's stuff? Like you couldn't take them all out if you wanted. You don't need to be afraid of them."

"I'm not afraid of them, Gordy. I'm respecting Ethan and Randy's home. Which I can't invite you into without their say-so."

"They invited *him* in." The vitriol in Gordy's tone made it clear it was Chenco he referred to. "Your little boy toy. God, what a fucking stick insect. What the hell do you see in the scrawny little shit?"

"Watch your mouth," Steve snapped.

Gordy curled his lip in revulsion. "You shouldn't be with him. You should be with *me*."

As Steve realized how serious a threat Gordy had

become, rage gave way to cold fear as too many ugly futures rolled out potentially before Steve. What if he tried to hurt Chenco? He held out his hands, entreating. "Gordy, this isn't who you are. If you're upset about not seeing me, we can talk to Crabtree—"

"*I don't want Crabtree.*" Gordy's fury rendered him ugly, his clean, well-kept appearance making his rage that much more revealing. "I only went to him to get back at you, to make you want me again. But I can't get you to look, can I? All you see is the stupid twink who trusses up like a full-on fairy."

Parts of Steve's brain scrambled for control, for a way out of this scene, but he was too full of sorrow, hurt—*fear*. "Gordy, we haven't had sex in over twenty years. You've seen me date before too. Why are you like this now?"

"You're choosing him over me. You care about him." Gordy spat the words as if they tasted bad in his mouth. "You love him."

Steve did. Loved the way he shouldn't, like he loved nothing and no one else. "I love you too."

"*Bullshit.* If you loved me, you'd be with me. You'd give me what I wanted, the way you give *him* what he wants." Gordy's eyes were almost wild, everything about him too bright, too intense. "If you loved me, you'd give it to me, and you'd enjoy it, not act like I made you sick. If you loved me, you wouldn't be ashamed of me."

Guilt sideswiped Steve like a machete through brush. "I'm not ashamed of you."

Lie. It was a lie, and Gordy knew it. His hands

clenched into shaking fists at his sides. "You are. You're ashamed of me, and you're scared of me. You lie to me and tell me you love me, that you'll take care of me, and you don't. You can't, can you? You're weak and scared, not just of me but of everyone, everything. You always were." The rage bled away, Gordy's emotional tide shifting from fury to pleading in the space of a breath. "Why can't you give me what I need? Why do you push me away, lock me away, give me away? Why do you pick him and not me?"

"*Gordy.*" Steve's chest and shoulders ached, and his legs felt like jelly. "Gordy, stop. Please."

"Why should I?" Gordy took several steps forward, backing Steve into the wall. "Why the *fuck* should I, Stevie? You want me to trot over to Crabtree's house and play nice with the other puppies? You want to come watch me beg? Make me sit there whining because you won't fill me, won't treat me like you treat him?"

"You said you wanted other—" Steve could feel sweat running down his head, into the collar of his T-shirt. "You told me you hated being alone."

"*I want to be with you.*" Gordy pressed his hands against Steve's shoulders.

The touch was light, yet Steve felt like shattering glass, every wall he'd constructed falling away, every guard, every lie he'd told himself about who he was crumbling under those heavy palms. Gordy's hands were cleaned of their dirt, yes, but Steve found himself yearning for the veil now. Dirty, homeless Gordy he could pity, but this…*this*…

The front door burst open, and with the outside light came a rush of thick, burly young men wearing guns on their hips and shouting orders at one another as they pried Gordy off Steve. It was surreal, like a scene from a movie, except it actually happened, Gordy shouting, demanding to be let go as the men silently led him away. When Gordy began to swear and shout too loudly, a gag slipped into his mouth, and Steve's stomach turned as their eyes met, Gordy's wide in terror. The door closed and the din of the men's exit reduced to a muffle, then nothing, but Steve stayed slumped against the wall, staring at the place where they had been.

The door opened a second time, and Crabtree, his countenance as unreadable as a rock, came into the foyer. After crossing the tile, he stood before Steve, leaning on his cane as he spoke in quiet, careful tones.

"My apologies for allowing him to get away from me. I can see Gordon upset you."

Upset him. Steve shut his eyes for a second before he was able to face Crabtree. "What—what happened?" *What happens now?*

Anger flashed briefly before vanishing into Crabtree's cool gaze. "Gordon is a clever man. I believe he bided his time, lulling me into relaxing his security. My house isn't exactly guarded, but I had several minders watching him. Since he came directly to you, I suspect he's plotted this for a while, and I can see he's been here long enough to cause some damage."

Steve glanced around the foyer—it looked almost as

if nothing had happened. A vase on its stand was slightly askew, but beyond this the only thing upset by Gordy's entrance was Steve.

Crabtree's mouth flattened into a line before he continued. "We have reached a gray area, my boy. If I cannot convince him to remain willingly in my care, if he declares his intent to leave—well. Things become delicate. Even without his shouted threats to Crescencio before I asked the boys to silence him, I've been afraid of this happening. I cannot allow the young man to be placed in danger by letting Gordon go free."

This was the terror, Steve realized, banked deep within him. What if Gordy went after Chenco? What if Gordy refused to be kept by Crabtree and went off on his own, determined to take out his rival? What if this mad creature that had once been his friend, the beast Steve himself had helped make, destroyed the only good thing in his life?

What if Crabtree had Gordy *taken care of*? What if Steve had to live with that, his selfish, arrogant desire to follow Chenco leading to *this*?

A hand rested on Steve's shoulder, but unlike Gordy's heavy pressure, Crabtree's touch was light, steadying. "I must go and see to him. Despite his angry outburst, he'll be frightened, upset now that he's been tempered. You and I will speak soon, however. For now know I have him in hand and Chenco will be protected. Gordon will not escape me again."

With a gentle squeeze of Steve's shoulder, Crabtree left. After the car pulled away, Steve remained at the wall, slumped, breathing heavily, staring blankly across the foyer. His gaze fixed on the cream-colored vase on its stand, tilting sideways, nearly falling but saved by the silk flowers inside them, the sturdy, wispy wands bending against the walls of the nook they rested in.

Numbly, Steve pushed off the wall and righted the vase. He straightened the flowers, fingers brushing the rust-red petals. Nudging his glasses higher on his nose with a trembling hand, he drew a deep breath, caressed the flowers one last time, and returned to the office where he sipped, uncaring, at his stone-cold coffee.

CHAPTER TWENTY-ONE

The night of Caramela's first show at Herod's, Chenco nearly threw up from nerves.

All his boys were there, rallying for him—Randy kept up a constant banter, and Sam rubbed his back and said soothing things. Ethan appointed several staff members to see to him personally, fetching water, eyelash glue, anything he needed. Mitch stood sentry in the hallway, not allowing anyone in.

Steve never, not for one minute, left Chenco's side.

The last few days his papi had been unusually reserved, making Chenco wonder if he'd done something wrong. Tonight all hints of any trouble were wiped away. Steve was a solid, secure presence, full of quiet reassurance and support—exactly what Chenco needed. As the butterflies died down and Caramela emerged, Steve remained. Dismissing the others, Caramela turned to him, studying him with an equal quiet before finally speaking. "Thank you for being here, for helping me get here."

His smile seemed a little sad. "You didn't need me to get here, didn't need any of us. Maybe we helped things along, but I don't doubt you'd have made it to the Vegas stage someday, if that's what you wanted."

"I do need you." Caramela squeezed his hand, drawing it close to her chest before kissing it, careful not to smudge her lipstick. "If I would have left the valley on my own, it wouldn't have been for a long time, and it would have been with Booker making me crazy." She let his hand fall to her lap, sadness seeping in. "I do miss him, though. He always told me I was strong, I was a queen, right before I went on. In Spanish, to set the mood. For all his flaws, he was good sometimes."

Steve caught both her hands, bowed his head, and kissed her knuckles reverently. "*Eres fuerte, mi reina.*"

Caramela shut her eyes. "If you make me cry, I'll ruin my makeup."

His slow smile filled her belly with heat. "Save your tears for me, *cariño.*"

She laughed, but even as she did, she felt the same anchor that held Chenco begin to tether her too. She kissed his cheek and whispered in his ear. "*Soy fuerte.*"

For you, my king, she added silently. *I am strong for you.*

He led her out of the dressing room to the wings of the stage. Ethan was the only one remaining, the others having gone out to the audience to claim their seats. Her opening act was just finishing up—a magician who from the crowd's reaction was a known favorite. Ethan smiled at her as she approached, holding out his arms and taking her hands as he looked her up and down.

"Caramela. Enchanting as always." He pulled her alongside him and nodded out to the crowd, which they could barely see between the panels of a side curtain. "Caryle did her work well—a full house."

It was indeed full, much more so than Caramela had expected. "Why did they all come to see some hick drag queen from southern Texas?"

"Caryle is an amazing promoter, and I have a reputation for only hosting quality acts. If you're on my stage, you must be good."

Caramela would have taken a deep breath to steady herself, but the silver sequin dress she wore required some pretty serious Spanx, especially after a month of Randy's cooking. "I'll do my best to live up to your reputation."

"I have no doubts, my dear. None at all. You'll conquer Vegas, then the world." Kissing her hand, he gave her a wink. "If you'll excuse me, I'm going to take my seat so I can properly enjoy the show."

Ethan left. Caramela kept her knees flexed, rotated her shoulders, and mentally mapped out her opening routine, which she'd done a thousand times, almost fifty times on this stage alone.

Steve put his hand on her shoulder. She shut her eyes, absorbing his strength.

The lights went down, the manager gave her a nod, and she began.

It was, in so many ways, the same show she'd always done and yet it was entirely different. For one, it wasn't just a few numbers—she did a full hour of performing, with one break while backup dancers allowed her a moment's reprieve and an extensive costume change.

That was the first distinct difference—she had dancers behind her. Not just Booker, the sly show-stealer, but six strapping young men who made Booker's body and dancing skills look rather paltry. Caramela had come to know and respect each one of her dancers over the last few weeks' rehearsals, and having them onstage with her now was nothing but an honor.

She opened with "Starting Over", which felt good on so many levels—the title sent a positive internal message, but the song itself had a magical, floaty quality while still carrying enough energy to give the show a club vibe. The applause at the end of her number lifted her up, and the banter she'd planned between the first and second songs came easily, so she riffed a little, adding some flirts for strangers and plenty of nods to her family in the front row.

Steve was there now too, her papi standing guard. She blew him a kiss and swung into the next song. So *many* songs—they began to bleed together, dances, lip syncs, breaks to flirt. It was odd to not walk the perimeter and take tips. Ethan had been firm, insisting it wasn't how he ran things. The audience tonight came for free, because all first-time acts were set up this way at Herod's, but Ethan said he had no intention of letting them leave without gambling much more than her show fee away.

It was wonderful, she decided, to not have to work her *cojones* for cash, to simply pour herself into the music, the dancing, the audience. The difference between wheedling money out of them and simply serving them, thanking them for making her night so special, was profound, and she decided then and there she never wanted another tip, no matter how much Heide would be appalled.

When she went into Steve's arms at the break, she was breathless, vibrating with energy and smiling so wide she thought she'd crack her face.

The second half was entirely non-Lopez songs. This had been Sam's suggestion, to help Caramela not be simply a Lopez impersonator. He'd helped pick the songs as well—Kelly Rowland's "Commander", Nelly Furtado's "*No Hay Igual*", and as a special surprise, Kylie Minogue's "Aphrodite" for Sam. It didn't quite fit, but apparently the room was full of fans because not only did they love the song, they cheered at the way Caramela's backup dancers came out in full-on replicas of costumes from the Australian diva's most recent tour.

When the riotous applause died down, she made the transition into the finale, Nicole Scherzinger's "*Puakenikeni*", complete with a braided wig, a skimpy cowgirl outfit and plastic six-shooters. When Caramela struck a pose and the lights went down, the theater went wild.

She savored the roar, the sweet rush that rolled from the theater and over her body. She closed her eyes, drank it in deep.

Then she ran offstage, let her assistants change her clothes and hair. As the rising siren signaling the beginning of "Papi" rang across the stage, she grabbed her microphone, strode out in her five-inch red heels, and threw herself into the song with every ounce of everything she had. She reached into the bottom of her soul and pulled out a little bit more because she was *that* happy.

Baila para tú Papi.

He watched her as she danced. He was there in the wings when she came away, and she went into his arms, kissing him. She didn't care what about her makeup she wrecked now.

She'd done it. She'd come to Las Vegas, put on a dress and made a thousand people weep with joy. All because of Steve. The others had helped, had made the space, but it had been *he* who held her up, and she would never forget it.

When she came up for air, he smiled at her, his secret, wicked smile just for her and for Chenco. He stroked her face. "Are you ready to hit the town, *mi reina?*"

Caramela kissed his nose. "Yes, Papi. Let me change my clothes and take a quick shower, and I'm all yours."

"Why change? You're fine as you are."

Caramela almost forgot to breathe. "Papi—" she began, but that was all she could manage.

His smile deepened, full of trouble and promise. "Ethan has a limousine waiting. The others are already inside." He patted her on her padded bottom. "Get what you need, and let's go."

"But I can't—I don't pass, not good enough to go out," she whispered.

This time he put his thumb on her bottom lip, pressing his fingernail into it as he held her chin. "Get what you need, Caramela."

She kissed him so hard she drew blood. When she lifted her head, she was shaking. *Oh, he sees me. He sees every inch of me.* "I'll be a few minutes," she said, hurrying down the hall to her dressing room. "I have to fix my face, and I really, really fucking have to pee."

IT TOOK CARAMELA ten minutes to decide she'd been born for luxurious limousine rides down the Las Vegas Strip.

Her boys celebrated her as if she were Lopez herself, as if she'd just finished a concert and now would go out on the town. Champagne flowed inside the limo, all their eyes shining as they congratulated her over and over, recounting favorite moments of the performance, passing on reactions they'd heard from the casino floor after the show. Steve had taken her out via the front door, and she'd been so rushed by fans, casino security had to step in and help her into the limo Ethan had arranged for her. By the time she got to the car, she was breathless—not from fear but from excitement and a sense that oh yes, she'd had this coming, she was *owed* this kind of response.

The limo itself was incredibly swank—it was the new kind, half Hummer/party bus and looked like a rap daddy had tricked out the inside. Neon piping outlined the ceiling, offset by recessed lighting and spotlights over the shallow side bar. Sam saw to the music, which was Lopez heavy, but when Kylie came on, Sam beamed at her and thanked her for the song, which was as good as the real thing, he said.

When they got caught in slow traffic on the Strip, Randy opened the moonroof and stood with her as they toasted the town.

They went everywhere—bars, casino lounges, exclusive clubs—Caramela quickly lost track of where they were and had been and simply let herself flow. At first she hung back, needing to hold on to Steve as they entered a new place, but she soon stopped hesitating. He was always there, always at her elbow, glaring at anyone who dared look at Caramela with anything other than a worshipful eye. She did glean a lot of looks, but they were not, to her surprise, ever negative. Wide eyes, yes, and lots of whispering behind hands, but to her delight they treated her as if she were a star, not a boy in a dress.

"They think you're JLo," Sam told her as they entered the dance floor. They were at Krave, the real one Randy had mentioned in South Padre.

"I don't look like JLo," Caramela argued back, though she was secretly thrilled.

"You do, though." Sam indicated her with a sweep of his hand. "It's not just your hair and makeup. You hold yourself the same way a star does, and you look close, so people fill in the blanks. They want JLo to be partying in Vegas. It's a great story. You set it up, and they finish the job."

That was what Heide had always said about drag—it wasn't simply the performer's fantasy. A man in a dress, a woman in a beard with a pair of socks down her trousers—convincing impersonation allowed everyone a space to be free. She had felt that before, but never quite like this. Never this loud.

What had changed? Was it Las Vegas? Was it the magic of the show going so well? Whatever it was, it felt as if pieces of Caramela's soul were sliding into place, Chenco and queen merging in fuller harmony than they ever had.

Caramela watched a pair of tourists whisper to each other, and then, cautiously, one of them came up and asked for her autograph.

"I'm not—" she began, but Sam cut her off.

"She doesn't have a pen. Do you?"

The cute blond twink with spiky hair fished wildly in his pocket. "I'll get one." He turned to Caramela, worshipful. "I saw you at Herod's. You were *amazing*. I'm switching my plane ticket and staying an extra day so I can see your next show."

"*Amazing*," the man's partner said, touching her arm, then pulling away as if embarrassed he had dared.

Caramela felt dizzy. She didn't know what to say. Thankfully Ethan appeared with a pen, and as she signed programs—her program, advertising her show— Ethan put his hand on the small of her back and spoke to her admirers, asking them how they'd liked the show, where they were staying, handing out complimentary drink tickets to his bar. When the boys went away, they made it about ten feet before they began to melt down and grip each other's arms as if they couldn't believe what they'd done.

Caramela definitely knew the feeling. She'd just never been on this end of the exchange.

Ethan deftly took his pen from her hand and replaced it into his vest pocket. "Well done, my lady."

"I still can't believe this is happening," she confessed.

"Yes. I remember this part. If I might make a suggestion? Don't waste too much time wondering if it's real. Enjoy the ride. It won't take you anywhere unpleasant. You have my personal guarantee. In the meantime—" He turned to her, catching her hand and making a slight and formal bow. "May I have this dance?"

She laughed and took his hand. "Absolutely." Even so, she glanced over her shoulder, collecting Steve's nod of permission before she let Ethan lead her out to the floor.

Ethan, it turned out, was an amazing dancer—he didn't simply writhe against her but led her into something that made them seem like they were performers on *Dancing with the Stars*. He held her in a sturdy frame, tipping her back and running his hand down her cleavage before spinning her out again. Though he smiled at her, he was nothing but cool, and she let herself acknowledge that, had things been different, he'd have made an excellent papi. He seemed to think so too, and for the span of three songs, they indulged in the fantasy of what might have been, playing against their audience and their own pleasure. It was another unexpected thrill in a night so full of delights she had to breathe them in to make room for herself. Their fellow dancers made space for them, and a circle formed so people could watch. It was a scene right out of the movies and Caramela's deepest imagination.

Taking Ethan's advice, she let go of her self-consciousness and her fears, and allowed herself to fly.

Randy took a turn with her too—he was raunchy where his husband had been elegant, grinding against her ass and palming her crotch until she laughed and swatted him away. Sam came to dance also, and she found herself in the middle of a very pretty boy-sandwich. It was pure, honey-sweet heaven.

Steve danced with her as well, but he pulled her off to the side, into the dark, holding her close and whispering naughty things into her ear. He was so naughty, in fact, that eventually she had to point out erections hurt a great deal in compression panties, and ruined the line of her dress.

His only reply was a wicked grin and a lascivious tongue in her ear.

They danced all night, in bar after bar, club after club, heading to Herod's so Randy could teach Caramela poker and Sam could sing karaoke with Ethan in the bar. When they finally returned to the house, the first fingers of dawn were reaching across the eastern desert. Caramela lay in Steve's lap in the limo, exhausted, sore, and blissfully happy.

Then she realized something, and she turned her head so she could look Steve in the eye.

"Crabtree wasn't there." *Or Gordy.* She touched Steve's face, questioning silently.

It hurt her to see how sad he looked, how much he tried to hide it. "There's a little trouble."

Oh, Papi. She stroked his face. "You can go to him, you know. I'll understand."

The pain on his face was like nothing she'd ever seen—not his usual stoicism, but deep, weary, guilty pain. "I can't."

She rubbed her fingernail along his stubble. "Let me help *you*, Papi. Tell me what I can do." He said nothing, and it made her ache, so much that she brought Chenco up, drew him out of his sleepy soup and begged him *please, please help our papi.*

Chenco sat up, pulling off the wig and the nylon cap—hair wild, his face now a crazy mix of male and female, he hiked up Caramela's dress, straddled Steve's lap, and took his lover's face in his hands.

"Steve," he whispered.

Steve shut his eyes.

Chenco sealed them closed with a kiss, one on each. Then he held his papi, whispered silly things, stroked his skin, and promised everything would be all right. When they arrived at the house, he took Steve straight to their room, bringing him along into the shower, kissing him, loving him.

They didn't make love, they didn't play, and yet as he lay naked and wrapped around Steve's big, strong, familiar body, Chenco didn't think he'd ever loved anyone more. Caramela, wrapped along with him, agreed.

CHAPTER TWENTY-TWO

T HE DAY AFTER the show, Steve went to the casino. Sarah Reynolds met him with a sad smile and led him up an elevator to a small, cramped office stuck in the 1970s and decorated with jarringly off-tone and faded kitten posters along the walls.

Crabtree sat at the olive-green metal desk, but he rose as Sarah ushered Steve inside. "Please, sit. Sarah, would you bring us some coffee?"

"I'll send someone up with a carafe directly, sir."

Steve took the sagging vinyl chair across from the desk when Crabtree pointed to it. Before he had himself settled, a heavyset busboy entered bearing a tray of coffee and mugs, blushing when Crabtree thanked him and passed him a casino chip. After pouring the coffee and adding two sugar cubes to Crabtree's cup, the busboy disappeared, leaving the two of them alone.

Crabtree cradled his cup in his hand. "So. I hear last night went well."

Steve reached for his own mug, but his fingers felt fat and clumsy. "It did. Caramela was a big hit. We took her out afterward."

Crabtree nodded. "Good."

Silence fell between them, and while Steve yearned for a cigarette, he didn't ask, simply sipped at his coffee and tried to unclench himself.

Eventually Crabtree sighed, sounding bone-weary. "My deceased lover, Billy Senior, used to say to me, 'Evelyn, you snotty old bastard, someday you're going to take on a bear that's too much of a handful even for you, and I hope to God I'm there to see your pompous ass go down in flames.' Well, I'm fairly sure I've found my handful. I might have seen it coming, though, if I'd known it'd be a *pair* who brought me to my knees."

This comment made Steve look up, and he was surprised to find the gangster giving him an accusatory glare. "What—are you talking about *me*?"

Crabtree's eyebrow arched. "Boy, you're as damaged as he is, possibly more so." When Steve sputtered, Crabtree set his mug down and waved a dismissive hand. "Oh, yes, the theatrics are commendable, and I'll admit they had me fooled. Gordon Weste is not entirely sane, but then so few of us truly are. What he is, I have come to realize, is cunning, conniving, and selfish. He's a high-functioning sociopath—so high functioning, in fact, he can distract one from noticing until it's too late. Mostly, however, he's selfish. Intensely, passionately selfish. Everything that has happened to him, I believe, he has asked for. And it all works—so long as you let him keep blaming you."

Sociopath? "But I *am* to blame. I left him. I didn't help him."

"And are your parents to blame then for abandoning you, for not seeing you when you felt lost and untethered before and especially after the war? If I interview them, will they cry me more rivers, blaming *their* parents? Or perhaps your parents didn't help you because the mailman put them under a magic spell, made them travel too much? Perhaps a wicked witch gave them a potion?"

What the *hell*? How had Crabtree known about his parents' travel? And what the *fuck*, he didn't blame anything on being abandoned. He hadn't been…

Abruptly dizzy, Steve dug his fingers into the arms of his chair, the creak of the vinyl like a gunshot in his overloaded mind.

Crabtree sighed. "Oh, my dear boy. You didn't think anyone would ever see you, did you? You hide behind your leather, you hole up in your rotting castle deep in the wilds of the abandoned orchard, but you never expected anyone would come to slay your dragons. Certainly the others never caught on—you gave them something else to see. Gordy would have been enough, but you found your dear Chenco too, and they latched on to him. He's so darling, so pretty, with such a charming connection to Mitch, such a beautiful dream. They're so busy with Crescencio they don't bother to study you."

Steve's palms began to itch. He wanted to leave, but a quiet voice warned him that wouldn't be very wise. "I don't…I don't know what you're talking about."

"Yes you do. You simply don't want to hear it. But you must. You would have been content to go slowly down the drain with Gordy, but then you met Chenco and you woke up, Sleeping Beauty. *He* woke you, and you couldn't bear to go to sleep again. Now you want to live your dreams, but you can't. You have a monster in your past. The question is, do you know who the monster is?"

Steve stared down at his legs. "Chenco called Gordy my madwoman in the attic. Except he said I was protecting him."

"Yes, I imagine that's what he'd say. What do *you* think about it?"

Steve made a rude noise through his nose, but Crabtree waited him out. "I think I'm a horrible, selfish bastard," he said at last. He worked his throat then said, the words scraping past his teeth, "I think *I'm* the monster."

"Then you have a significant problem. If that's how you truly see yourself, eventually you won't be able to hide it. They'll see too, and they'll take Chenco away from you. Or worse…" Crabtree's voice dropped to a dangerous pitch, "…they won't be able to pry you away."

Steve began to sweat, a cold, sick perspiration born of terror and misery. "I need to fix this." *I can't lose him.*

"Yes you do, boy."

Steve leaned forward. "Please. Please, tell me what to do. How to make this right."

"Open your damn eyes, Vance. Open them all the way and see, look at the truth right in front of you." When Steve only stared at him, lost and confused,

Crabtree threw up his hands. "Honestly. What *did* you do at Stanford, knit?"

Steve caught his breath coming in short, panicked gasps, and he tried to take deeper draughts of air, but he couldn't. "*I don't know what you want from me.*"

Crabtree gave him no quarter. "You need to face the monster, boy. I know you're scared to do it, afraid of what you'll see, of what *he'll* see, but you need to open the door and face the beast down. You need to find it isn't you, only the ghost of very old, very weary pain. You must face this one way or another. You cannot continue as you are. You're either going to fix this, or you're letting Crescencio go, and you'll return to your Texas cave alone."

"I don't want to be alone," Steve whispered.

"Then fix this. As much as Chenco deserves this to work—so do you, Steven. So do you."

I have no idea how to fix this, Steve wanted to say, but he only nodded and stared down at the desk, hoping this interview was over so he could leave, go to Ethan's office at the house, shut the blinds and drown in silence.

Crabtree picked up his coffee again. "Now, the other matter we need to discuss is your employment. I'm aware you do freelance web security in addition to general programming, but you need something steady. With increasing cyber attacks on high-profile business-es, I'm concerned about the safety of Herod's servers. I would like you to examine our systems and provide me with a quote for necessary repairs, including sugges-tions for reliable contractors for any work you cannot complete yourself. You will, of course, be adequately compensated. Sarah has a dossier prepared. Sarah?"

He'd pushed a button as he said the last, and Ms. Reynolds entered the room, smiling and bearing a spiral-bound file which she presented to Steve. "Here you are, Mr. Vance. Let me know if you find anything is missing."

Steve blinked at Crabtree. "You want me to…what?"

"I want you to do your job," Crabtree said, staring him down.

He wanted…to hire Steve? Crabtree? Not Ethan? *What?* But as those flinty eyes bore into him, Steve remembered who this was, what he had done, what he could do, what Steve had seen him do only days ago with Gordy.

He also realized Crabtree had, several minutes ago, told Steve his first name, which Randy had said the gangster never told anyone.

He flipped open the file and began reading, and within a few lines he found himself sinking into the write-ups about code, about firewalls and system managements. This, actually, he did understand. And yeah, Herod's needed a cyber tune-up.

"I can do this," he said, his voice much steadier than it had been since Crabtree had started stripping him away. After pulling his glasses out of his vest pocket, he pushed them up the bridge of his nose and went to work.

As the weeks after Caramela's first performance went by, Chenco became more and more convinced something was wrong with Steve, but he couldn't figure out what it was. All he knew was Steve had gone from quiet to subdued to nearly scary. They hadn't slowed down in the bedroom and the playroom, and Steve still came to every show, always wrapped Caramela up in his arms at the end, but the more Steve tried to act as if nothing were wrong, the more Chenco knew something absolutely was. He had no idea, however, how to make things right.

He decided to talk to someone about it.

While Ethan was most often working at his casino, he never seemed to mind interruptions, and when Chenco asked if they could talk, he didn't hesitate to dismiss Ms. Reynolds and call up a car to take Chenco over to Bellagio for an early lunch.

"I didn't mean to use up so much of your time," Chenco said as the driver closed the door behind him.

Ethan waved this objection away. "That's all right. I enjoy your company, and I could use a break. Besides, I enjoy checking out my competition." He eased into his seat, his suit coat undone, his long limbs splayed around him. "Is everything going well? Are things in place for your performance next week?"

"Yes. We're doing a new JLo number, and Caryle is looking into some mild pyrotechnics. I think she has Crabtree greasing palms for a special license."

"Good. Now, tell me what's bothering you."

The car was a sedate black town car, but it resonated

in Chenco's head the same way the exotic limo had the night they'd taken Caramela out. It was extra plush and lush and had a smoked divider between the front seat and the back. Chenco huddled in his corner, feeling dirty and small and self-conscious. "It's Steve, actually."

Ethan said nothing, but he sat up a little straighter.

Chenco fixed his gaze out the window, watching the big, busy city go by as the driver wove them slowly down the Strip. "Something's wrong, but he won't tell me about it. I think something happened the night of the show. But I don't know."

"You asked him about that, and he said he wouldn't talk about it?"

Suddenly this plan to ask Ethan for help didn't feel like a good idea. Chenco hunched forward. "I haven't asked him anything. I'm pretty sure not only will he tell me nothing is wrong, he'll work harder to keep me from ever being able to find out." The air conditioning wasn't on very high, and yet Chenco felt cold to his bones. "I don't know. Maybe I'm making it up. I can't tell anymore. It shouldn't *be* like this. Everything was going so well. Then the night after Caramela's first performance…I almost didn't catch it. Like he's been hiding a limp, and I caught it when it was bad, and now I'm always seeing it." He tipped his head onto the headrest and stared at the ceiling. *So cold.* "I don't know. I shouldn't have said anything. I can't explain it."

For a moment, Ethan remained quiet. Then he said, "Chenco, how do you feel about heights?"

Heights? Chenco shrugged. "I don't really feel about

them much in any direction. I'm not scared of them, but I don't bungee jump or anything."

Ethan hit a button and lowered the divider. "A change of plan, Mark. Please take us to the Stratosphere."

"Yes, Mr. Ellison." The partition went back up.

The casino was on the north end of the Strip, and as soon as Chenco got a good look at it, he realized he'd heard of this one. The casino with the needle tower and rides on top. Ethan led Chenco through the lobby, waving to several people on the way and exchanging pleasantries, and when they came to the ticket counter for the tower, the cashier simply ushered them through with a cheery smile. They got to take a VIP elevator, and on the way up the attendant chatted familiarly with Ethan.

"My husband has a long-standing affection for the Stratosphere tower," Ethan explained as they exited to the sky lobby. "As an anniversary gift last year, I wheedled the owner and got us a kind of extra bells-and-whistles season pass. Randy usually brings me here once a week, but honestly I think he gets here every day when he can." He pointed to a side door and led Chenco away from the rush of tourists heading to the main outdoor deck. "We have access to a private observation area."

The whole needle swayed a bit as they walked through a small hallway to a plain metal door, and Chenco wondered if this was such a good idea. Once Ethan opened it, however, Chenco gasped and followed him up to the rail. The view was stunning, a panoramic of the city and the desert beyond. The sun beat down hot and bright, and the wind whipped around them, reminding them how precarious their position was. Chenco held on to the metal, and Ethan leaned on it, looking down at the city below as he spoke.

"I know you've heard versions of my story, of how I came to own Herod's, how I met Randy. What you don't know is what I was before all this happened."

"You were an investment banker or something."

"Broker. That's not what I'm talking about, though." Ethan's gaze became distant, and it was clear he wasn't seeing the city anymore, but his past. "I was a mess, is what. I came here after quitting my job, selling everything I had, and breaking up with my long-term, married boyfriend. He'd taken money meant for the two of us and used it to rescue his wife and kids. It upset me, so I decided I'd gamble my money away, then blow my head off in the front seat of my car."

Chenco couldn't breathe.

Ethan smiled a sad, weary smile. "I lost my last twenty on roulette at Herod's, and Randy saw me. I'd already decided I didn't actually want to kill myself, but I truly had washed myself out to absolutely nothing but the clothes I stood in, a ring from Nick, my car, and the gun. I was just starting to wrap my head around the fact when Randy came up and started annoying me. *That* is what led to Crabtree wheedling things so I ended up with his old lover's casino, what led me to Randy, or Randy to me, depending on how you want to look at it."

It took everything in Chenco not to call bullshit. "I don't understand. You're so…I don't know what the word is. Put together. Smooth. Amazing." The rest of it fell into place in his head, and he couldn't censor himself now. "You're like Steve, I mean. Dominant and strong."

"Sometimes I am. Sometimes, though, I'm faking it so no one realizes I'm still the man from American Fork, Utah, who was fool enough to love the wrong man and bet all his money on black like it owed him." Ethan turned his head toward Chenco with a wry smile. "Randy says I'm fine until I slow down. That's still true—if I stop and think about how much responsibility I have, how much can go wrong, how little I can truly control it, I start to panic. Crabtree sits on my shoulder, always second-guessing me, always ready to swoop in and tell me where I've screwed things up. Sometimes I do make mistakes, big ones, and I'm glad he's there. Sometimes he stifles me and I have to push on him to let me make my own way. It's not unlike having a parent who wishes he could fuck my husband."

Chenco blinked, full of a vision he really didn't want. "He wants Randy?"

"They used to date. He actually helped set us up, but…well, it's a complicated story." He threaded his fingers together over the edge of the rail and resumed staring at the city. "Steve is my age, almost exactly. He's a good man, and he's successful in his field, in his own way. He is strong, and loyal, and devoted to you. He's much better, I suspect, at hiding emotions he doesn't want people to see. Sometimes, though, especially now that he's here in Las Vegas, I look at him and I see the man I was when I arrived. I see the uncertainty, those demons. I don't care how dominant someone is in life or in bed, how toppy or bossy a man is—he's still a man, and he's going to have cracks in his surface. The issue isn't that he has flaws. The issue is how does he manage them. How in tune with them is he. Nobody comes out of the womb with a whip in their hand. Half of mastering another man in the bedroom is knowing how to master yourself first."

Chenco digested this. "So what is it you're saying about Steve? I'm not allowing for him to have flaws?"

"I'm not saying anything about Steve, except I think he's going through something similar to what I did. I doubt he has a gun buried in his truck, and if he does, it's not to shoot himself with. There's something going on there, though, and that you've picked up on it tells me he has work to do. What I'm saying to *you* is if I'm right, he needs you as much as you need him."

"But I thought that was the *point* of this whole D/s thing." It was getting hard to keep the whine out of his voice, and Chenco forced himself to calm down. "I thought he was supposed to take care of me, to—" He cut himself off, sensing thin ice.

"Randy and I play differently than the two of you. We switch, to start."

"So you think I need to switch with Steve?"

"Maybe. That's part of a relationship, finding the pattern that works for the both of you. Switching is the pattern that works for Randy and I. Mitch and Sam have their own style, and it's not necessarily always what you're thinking. You'll find your balance between the two of you eventually. Remember, though, this will take time, and yes, terrifying as it may be, you'll have to find a way to get him to talk to you about it." Chenco's belly knotted, but before the fear could take root, Ethan reached over and put a light hand on Chenco's shoulder. "You're not alone, Chenco. No matter what happens with Steve, or doesn't happen, you're never alone. Mitch, Sam, Randy, and I are here for you, always."

Chenco felt sweaty and sick, and it had nothing to do with the way the tower swayed in the wind. "Everything keeps changing. Every time I think I have something settled, it changes. Why are you different? If Steve can fail me, why—?"

"Who said anything about Steve failing you? The man didn't move up to Las Vegas to live in my spare room. He's here for you. Even if you don't work out as lovers, he loves you."

"That doesn't make sense." *If you don't work out as lovers.* The thought hadn't occurred to him until now. His chest felt tight. This had been such a bad idea.

The door behind them opened, and before Chenco could turn, a familiar voice called out, "Slick, what the fuck are you doing coming here without me? Didn't text me, just let me find out when Stalker App said you were—Oh."

Chenco gripped the rail and shut his eyes. God, not

Randy. He didn't need Randy right now, he really didn't.

"Sweetheart," Ethan said, sounding weary, and Chenco missed the rest of it, hearing only soft mumbles as they conversed in the corner. Then Randy came up beside Chenco.

"Please go away." Chenco would *not cry*.

"Not a chance. I'm not leaving, and you're wearing the wrong shoes to stab me." His hand rested on Chenco's arm, and when Chenco tried to pull it away, Randy took firmer hold. "Hey. It's okay."

"It's not." Chenco shut his eyes. "It's *not* okay."

Randy laughed, but it was a softer sound than Chenco had ever heard from him. He had a mental image of armor falling away. Maybe in Randy's example, it was a cake of mud.

"I think," he said at last, "it's time you let *me* give you a tour of Vegas."

"I don't want to talk about this anymore."

"Who said anything about talking? Slick covered that, and from the looks of it you have more than enough to chew on. You need some air."

Chenco nodded out at the thousands of feet of open air around him then turned to Randy with a quelling look.

This time it was the usual Randy laugh, right from his belly and full of mirth. "Okay, let me rephrase. You need shopping, good food, and poker. What do you say, Slick? Are you in?"

"I didn't say *I'm* in," Chenco complained.

Ethan shook his head. "No, I think he needs some Randy one-on-one. I have to go over some reports with Sarah at three anyway, and something tells me this will be an epic Jansen event."

"Hello, I'm *right here*," Chenco said, "and I *haven't said yes*."

"I know where you are, Princess, and you bet your ass you're saying yes." Randy tweaked his nose, grinning when Chenco swatted it away. "See? You're better already. You looked ready to go over the edge when I got up here, and now you're spitting mad. Excellent progress."

"I'm not Ethan. I don't find your annoying personality endearing."

"He didn't either, not at first. I'm definitely an acquired taste." He held out his arm and waggled his eyebrows. "Come on. You can insult me all the way to the door. But I bet you twenty dollars I have you laughing before we leave the lobby to get on my bike."

"I'm not betting you," Chenco replied.

"I'll take that one," Ethan said, buttoning up his coat. "You won't have him laughing until you take him shopping."

Randy's eyes glinted. "*Fifty* says you lose within an hour."

"Fifty plus a lap dance in my office says you've misread this." Ethan winked at Chenco. "Good luck. Text if you need me."

Randy stared at the door after Ethan, an odd expression on his face. Then he shook his head and turned to

Chenco. "Sorry, distracted there for a second." He lifted his arm. "Come on. Let's go get lunch, and you can tell Uncle Randy all about it."

Chenco looked at the arm, trying to tell himself he wanted to refuse it. The truth was he was tired, overwhelmed, and lonely. Randy was right. It'd be fun to hate him for a while instead of feeling panicked and crazy.

"I'm not telling you anything." Chenco tucked his hand into Randy's elbow. "And there's no way in hell you're winning that bet."

Randy said nothing, just laughed as he led Chenco to the elevator.

CHAPTER TWENTY-THREE

O NCE RANDY FOUND out Chenco hadn't eaten, he headed straight for his bike.

"Does this mean you lost the bet, since we're leaving the Stratosphere? Or was it a time limit now?" Chenco was confused as to why Randy would do this on purpose.

"It was a time limit, but yes, I'll lose. Nittaya's Secret Kitchen is way over in Summerlin, and unless riding through stupid traffic cracks you up, I'm toast."

"It doesn't bother you that you won't win?"

"I lose almost all my bets to Slick. He's the only one it happens with, by the way, so don't get any ideas." He flashed Chenco a wicked grin. "Besides, I don't lose when I play against Ethan, no matter how the cards fall."

Chenco thought to what Ethan had confessed on the top of the tower. "Did he really try to kill himself the night you met him?"

The way the light fell from Randy's face answered the question. "He says he wasn't going to by the time I met him, but yeah, I got rid of a gun from under his front seat." He ran a hand over his wild dark hair.

"Ethan's always been a moody thing, though he hides it from everybody else for the most part. Crabtree figured out before I did that he does best when he has something to chew on, something legit to worry about."

"Like running a casino?"

"Like running a *two-bit* casino next to a line of mega-corporate enterprises. Me, all I want is a decent poker table and somebody to warm my bed."

"And a top-of-the-line kitchen."

"And a top-of-the-line kitchen." He nudged Chenco's arm as they went the last few feet to his bike. "So, fussy-food boy. I'm taking you to this kick-ass Asian fusion place, and then I'm taking you to Town Square. Your alter ego's had plenty of shopping, but there's a boy in there who needs dressing too."

"I don't have any money with me."

Randy tossed a withering glance over his shoulder before straddling the bike. "Whatever. Get on. Let's fill your belly with wholesome goodness."

The restaurant was very nice—amazing food, light and tasty, excellent atmosphere—but what Chenco enjoyed most was the way Randy didn't pester him, just let him eat and relax. They didn't talk any more about Ethan or Steve or Caramela. In fact, mostly Randy told stories about his own past, which started when Chenco asked him how long he'd lived in Vegas.

Randy twirled his food on his fork, frowning at it as he thought. "Well, depends on your perspective. I first came here in about 1997, but Mitch and I didn't buy a house until 2005. That lasted about a year before we pissed each other off and he left with the truck. I've been a permanent resident since then. We were kind of in and out of the city before that, even when we bought the house, but I always knew I'd live here."

"You and Mitch dated?"

"Mitch and I fucked each other in the head, is what we did. I don't think it really counts as dating." Randy reached for his water. "We were in the RGV a lot too. That's how I met Steve and your batshit father. I still can't believe you lived with him. I got the hell away from my dad the second I could."

"And that's in Michigan?"

"Yes. Detroit. All my family's still there, lamenting how the homosexuals are hastening Armageddon."

"I didn't think people were as prejudiced in the north."

"Depends on the north. I'll admit there might be extra concentration of asshole in my gene pool." Forking the last bite of his entree into his mouth, Randy patted his belly. "Damn. I'd been meaning to try this place, and now I'm coming back. You feeling dessert, or are you ready to shop?"

"I'm good. Very full." Chenco glanced at a clock on the wall and raised his eyebrows at Randy.

Randy followed his gaze, grinned and pulled out his phone. "Time to tell hubby he's getting a lap dance tonight." He made a low noise of pleasure in the back of his throat as he texted, then slipped his phone into his pocket and put bills on the table. "Okay. Shopping it is."

Chenco didn't argue. He planned to simply not let

Randy buy anything for him. It was a good thing he hadn't said this out loud. Randy probably would have made a bet, and Chenco would have lost. It turned out Randy was *good* at shopping, and he had read the secret fashion desires Chenco hadn't realized he'd written on his heart.

Town Square was near the Strip, an open-air shopping center with plenty of parking, palm trees, and ostentation. Randy knew the place like the back of his hand, and he took Chenco from one store to another, a man on a mission.

"You're all about the plain tees and jeans, which suits you, but you're not dodging bullies in Donna anymore. You're in Vegas now, and you're young and cute. Play it up. I know you're wanting to." He held up a weathered shirt with black designs along the hem curling up toward one armpit like a kind of fabric tattoo. Randy looked between the shirt and Chenco then replaced it on the rack. "No, it's too much. You need something understated. Probably best to stick with plain on top. We'll do quality basics for shirts, jacket, and jeans, and save the party for your feet."

"My feet?"

"Oh hell yeah, honey. You wait until I show you what you're wearing out tonight."

Chenco started to protest—and then Randy showed him the boots.

For several seconds he could only hold them in his hand, hypnotized. Usually it was Caramela falling for shoes—he had no experience looking at men's footwear and feeling the yearning pull in the base of his gut. These were brown half boots with a long, sassy curve, rustic aerated leather and a buckle whispering steampunk but mostly said *oh, honey, you gotta buy me.*

Then he saw the price tag, and he almost cried, because these shoes weren't happening.

Randy turned the tag over and reached for the mate. "Come on. You're obviously getting them."

"I *can't.*" Chenco couldn't stop looking at them. "You can't spend this much on me—I won't let you—and I can't afford it."

"I hate to break it to you, but I already dropped four hundred on you in the last store. These are special, and you're right. You should make the purchase, a kind of symbol to yourself you're listening to all your needs, not just your drag persona's. Pay me back when we get to the house. Don't give me that look. Why can't you buy them? What have you been spending money on?"

"I have to save for—" Chenco cut himself off, not sure what he was saving for, actually. "I need to find my own place eventually. Plus I shouldn't let Ethan buy all Caramela's clothes. She needs—"

"*You* need clothes, bitch." Randy put the second boot in Chenco's hand and glared at him. "You've been throwing all your energy at Caramela and precious little at the boy who lets her run that stage. All except for the lovely afternoon you stripped the skin off my back."

Chenco went hot with the memory Randy conjured, and he couldn't say anything.

Randy moved in close, pressing the boots between

them. "Yeah, baby, I know you've been thinking about that, about asking to do it again. You haven't, though. You've been working and worrying about why Steve's being weird."

"Why is he being weird?" Chenco's voice was almost a whisper, and he hated how it wavered.

"I don't know. But you need to find out, and to do that, you have to confront him. And believe it or not, to find the courage, you have to do things like buy yourself fabulous shoes. *You*, not Caramela. Teach yourself to wear Caramela whether or not you have a wig on."

Chenco clutched them to his belly. "Why? *Why* are you buying me clothes and lunch and making me buy shoes? Why do you *all do this*?"

"Princess, take a look around. We're the fucking lonely hearts club. You're Mitch's little brother. You're goo-eyed over one of our longest-standing, loneliest friends. You need a family, we like adopting people. That's it." When Chenco sputtered, Randy put a hand on his shoulder. "Right, I know—it's more than taking in a stray. We're helping you with your dream. I'll try another angle. Why do you do Caramela? Not the shit you say. Not because you want to prove yourself or whatever. What made you put on the wig? What called you to the stage?"

Chenco didn't have to think about his answer. "When I go out there, when I put her on, I feel alive all the way to my toes. It's not about being a girl or saying *fuck you* to gender politics. It's about *being*. Living. Breathing. Existing in a way I can't by any other means.

It's better than anything in the world. Better than money. Better than sex. Better than love."

Randy nodded, not quite smiling, but there was a light on his face, an understanding. "That's how I feel when I play a particularly good run of poker. That's how Ethan feels when he makes the casino work. We took one look at you on your stage in McAllen and all we wanted to do was make the light you give off shine brighter. It's fun to watch you succeed. Other people helped us find our happiness, and it's time we returned the favor."

The floor that had felt so absent began to flood back beneath Chenco's feet. Feet which were itching to put on these damn shoes. What was Steve's dream, he wondered? What was it he dreamed to have? What was his Caramela? He thought maybe Randy knew, but he didn't want to ask. He wanted to discover it for himself.

Though he did wonder about something else. "What's Mitch's better-than-love?"

Randy snorted. "He and his slut-bunny husband are those disgusting nougat-center people who just flat out like being in love best. And fucking. Which, I gotta admit, is hot as all hell to watch."

Chenco, remembering the view beneath the curtain in the semi cab, blushed as he silently agreed.

Randy's eyes darkened, and so did his grin. "Somebody owes Uncle Randy a dirty story. Time for a tea break where you spill the dish. First, though, we're buying those shoes."

"Yes." Something deep inside Chenco eased as he

said the word. He grinned, hugged the boots against his chest and laughed. "First we're buying these shoes."

WHEN STEVE ARRIVED at the theater at six to pick up Chenco, he was surprised to find not only was Chenco not there, he hadn't been in all day. He was in the middle of texting him when Ethan appeared and explained Chenco had gone off earlier in the afternoon with Randy.

"To do what?" Steve demanded.

"Randy things," Ethan replied.

Had they done another scene? Without telling him? No, one look at Ethan told him this wasn't playtime, whatever Randy and Chenco were doing, but he couldn't work out what the hell was going on. They stared at each other for several long seconds in silent communication, Steve telegraphing he wasn't pleased, Ethan reflecting back he wasn't exactly happy, either.

"What's going on?"

Ethan's expression didn't change. "He came to me this morning, wanting to talk."

About you was heavily implied. Steve glanced around, half expecting to see angry big brother waiting in the wings. No Mitch, but the theater had quietly cleared out, and it was just the two of them now. Steve glanced up at the security camera and raised an eyebrow.

Ethan waved a dismissive hand. "I'm not Crabtree, and you're not going to end up as dry bones in the desert. But yes, I wanted to talk to you. Chenco is upset. We had a talk, but I don't think I helped. Randy showed up, and from what I hear, they're having a good time. Lunch. Shopping. Sam met them to collect their purchases, and now the three of them are on their way to a party, as I understand."

Randy things. Steve wanted to be annoyed, but the only person to blame was himself.

Ethan seemed to agree. "He has this idea he's somehow made a mistake and upset you, except he can't think of what he's done wrong. Thankfully he's got enough presence of mind to realize if this were the case, *you* should have told him." When this bald scrutiny got under Steve's skin, Ethan bared his teeth—and then he really did look like Crabtree. "Don't insult us both by saying this isn't any of my business. I haven't involved Mitch or Crabtree yet, for now."

"Crabtree already knows," Steve confessed.

Ethan's expression turned grim. "That's not a good sign. If he's not actively pushing on you, he's written you off."

Was Crabtree pushing Steve? He'd given him plenty to do on the security upgrade, but nothing else. Steve didn't know what to say to that, so he looked away.

Ethan sighed, frustration leaking out in the sound. "If you're giving up, don't stay here and fuck with Chenco."

Now Steve glared. "I'm not giving up."

"Then get your shit together." Ethan put his hands on his hips, fanning out his suit jacket. "Is this about

Gordy?"

"Partly." Steve pursed his lips and held up a hand. "Look, I've got this. You can stand down."

"The hell I can." Ethan aimed a long, elegant finger at Steve's chest. "I don't know what's going on, but consider me officially on a mission to find out. If Crabtree's willing to invest in Chenco but will write you off, this is serious. I like you, and I know Randy and Mitch feel you're family. You're well on your way to being that for me. You can fight me if you like, but you won't win. I won't insult you by explaining why. You have my attention, Mr. Vance. What do you wish to do with it?"

Steve drew a deep breath, pushed aside his pride and said, "I want to fix this."

"Good answer." Ethan pulled out his phone, punched in a text then waited a second to see the reply. "I'm told I can bring you at nine."

"Where is he?" Steve asked, trying not to demand. "Where is Chenco?"

"An old friend of Randy's is having a leather party, and Chenco is there with him and Sam. We're to come and bring Mitch." Ethan glanced at his watch. "We'll leave from the house at eight thirty, so you'll want to get ready, perhaps grab a bite to eat. I'll finish up here and join you shortly."

The idea of waiting two and a half hours to go to Chenco when something was clearly wrong made Steve crazy, but he did as he was told. He went back to the house and took another shower, standing with his eyes closed under the hot spray, calming himself down. He put on his side-laced leather jeans, his vest, and put a polish on his motorcycle boots. The black-and-white cat came in to supervise him, and while he glared at it, he didn't kick it out, either. *Be good,* he told himself, and he tolerated the animal. If he convinced Chenco to stay with him, he'd have to get used to them eventually because Chenco wanted one. Chenco deserved to get what he wanted.

Out on the patio, Steve lit up a cigar and settled in to wait. Mitch joined him before too long, looking good. Mitch favored Levi's over leather jeans and stuck to his well-worn cowboy boots, but he wore chaps and a thick leather band on his left wrist. He accepted the cigar Steve offered him, though he murmured something about *only a few days left* under his breath. He sat lounging as he savored the initial bouquet.

"Been a while since I put this getup on," he said after a period of silence. He nodded at Steve. "Everything going all right with your work? No trouble with the location change?"

"No trouble," Steve said. Mitch was very carefully, he knew, not asking about Gordy. Steve sipped the mescal he'd brought out with him and passed the bottle and a clean glass over to Mitch.

Mitch accepted but only poured a small finger of liquid. They spoke of idle things, Mitch reporting on some of the jobs he'd taken lately and ones he hoped to find in the future. The two of them were talking about moving in formally to Randy's old house, renting at first and then maybe buying it. Steve listened as Mitch confessed how a faltering economy hurt a long-distance driver, how jobs had become tougher for Sam to find. How he wanted to settle somewhere for a bit, how Sam hated the desert but loved being near the boys. How Mitch hated being tied down but hated feeling like he wasn't taking care of Sam and making him feel safe.

Steve listened, and he let himself yearn. *This is what I want, this struggle, this love, this life. I want it, and I want it with Chenco.*

Just before eight thirty, Ethan appeared, and Steve had to give an admiring smile when he saw Ethan Ellison in gear. He was in full leather—a close-fitting black polo with side vents and a line of grommets along the sternum, soft, elegant black leather jeans, and a pair of half boots looking as if they had come out of an Italian showroom.

Ethan, however, frowned as he took the finger of mescal Mitch poured for him. "Mitch, does this outfit really work?"

"Fuck yeah. Randy wouldn't have picked it out for you if it didn't. That boy knows poker and clothes like nobody I've ever met." He leaned back in his chair and waggled his eyebrows at Steve. "From what I hear, he dressed our boys."

Steve could feel the other man watching him closely. He raised his glass in toast. "Then let's go see what they look like."

They went in Ethan's convertible, top down, and Steve took the backseat, letting the wind caress his skin.

The party was in the historic district, so they had quite a bit of a drive ahead of them given evening traffic, and by the time they pulled into the neighborhood, it was almost nine thirty. As they parked on the street and walked toward the door, Ethan caught Steve gently by the elbow. "Are you doing all right?"

"I'm fine," Steve ground out. "I'm here to see Chenco."

"You're here to have a good time with your friends and make new ones," Ethan corrected, and led him inside.

The house was as grand as Ethan and Randy's, but it was an older home, its construction style dictating it was no newer than the 1960s. The whole first floor was nicely appointed in the same way any higher-end home would be—open seating plan, nice furniture, a sunken lounge area with an active bar off to the side. The guests were all men in leather, most with drinks in their hand as they chatted and milled about. There was a bit of everything—young twinks in short shorts and harnesses, older bears looking like aging Toms of Finland, bulked-up early thirty-somethings trying not to show they were still feeling their way around a whip.

There were several men in puppy gear too, some on leashes and some bounding about with their paws. They were happy, playfully enjoying a role, a game, expressing themselves. None of them used the gear to hide, the puppy mask to terrorize. They were boys playing and nothing more. One stared at Steve, and it tugged at his heart, making him think of Gordy and what could have been. What *should* have been.

Ethan introduced Mitch and Steve to their host, Ricky, a man who looked slightly younger than Crabtree and who boasted a harnessed bear cub on each arm. He welcomed them with a smile and a heavy wink as he suggested they head out to the pool area where he was fairly sure they'd find some pleasant entertainment.

The entertainment, as it turned out, was Chenco and Sam.

They stood on a platform constructed at the far end of the lawn, dancing to club music under soft spotlights. Sam wore tight leather boy shorts, a studded collar and heavy eye makeup, his hair looking like it had already been tousled by rough sex. Chenco was something of a foil. He wore a mix of brown and black leather—brown shoes, black captain's cap with silver studs, brown suede vest, black fingerless leather gloves, brown chaps over dark jeans with a pouch designed to highlight the bulge of his cock. Like Steve, he wore no shirt under his vest, but he also sported a pair of nipple clamps with a long, silver chain between them.

Chenco looked like an ad for the leather he wore, and he was beautiful.

What caught Steve, though, was the way Chenco moved. He'd seen him dance a million times, but never before as a man. Heels and sequins, wigs—yes, but Chenco the man had not danced.

The man danced now. Chenco held himself differently than Caramela—Steve could sometimes see the drag queen flickering on and off inside the boy, snapping his hips harder, making him bend deeper—but the dance was Chenco's, not hers. He danced with a confidence that had nothing to do with the clothing and everything to do with himself.

Mitch's husband was clearly halfway under his dancing partner. Chenco pulled Sam to him, and Sam melted against his brother-in-law, raising his hands and clasping them behind Chenco's neck to let Chenco's touch roam over his mostly naked body.

He slid his hands over Sam's skin, down his body, skimmed leather-clad hands down Sam's bare thighs. Steve had seen Sam dance—on official dance floors and while he did the dishes—and he was no slouch, but next to Chenco he looked a little bit bumbling. Even here, Chenco was generous. He led Sam, easing him into the moves, altering his own undulations to match what Sam did. Sometimes Sam turned to him, and then they danced together, bodies merging, arms tangling. They were fluid, they were free.

They were so far from the farce Steve felt inside, they made him ache.

The song shifted, and while Chenco motioned for him to stay, Sam held up his hands in surrender, indicating Chenco should perform solo. The crowd cheered and called out requests. They were right on the edge of rowdy, which almost pulled Steve forward, but that was when Jansen stepped in, deftly pushing them back, checking on Chenco to make sure he was okay. Chenco didn't seem upset—probably this was nothing compared to the crush at Club 33. He played the crowd, winking at them as he kept out of their reach. He struck poses, flashed nipple, tipped his hat rakishly and let his jaw hang slack while his mouth formed an inviting O. The crowd drank him in, hungry either to possess him or be him. Chenco handled them with grace and deftness, sliding into the next song with a smile.

He was marvelous, he was beautiful—but it was the dancing that made Chenco beautiful, not the clothes. It was the naked, confident honesty, and it wrapped around Steve's heart and held him like a vise.

Except sometimes there was a flash, a moment of pain Steve only saw because of how closely he studied his lover's face. Chenco continued to dance, his face lit, his smile bright. It took someone who knew him well to see beyond the mask.

Was Ethan right? Was Chenco upset because of him? Was Steve the one who had given Chenco this pain?

Was Chenco better off with him or without him? Bitterness choked Steve's throat—what a dumb question. *Absolutely* Chenco was better off without him.

Except as Steve watched Chenco dance, as he felt his own heart rising, aching to connect with the beautiful man before him, Steve acknowledged something else— *he* was not better off without Chenco.

Chenco didn't need Steve. But Steve needed Chenco.

The impact of the realization made Steve sway on his feet, left him raw and open and terrified. When this had happened, he wasn't sure, but happen it had. He didn't simply prefer being with Chenco, he wasn't sure how he could exist without him. Going back to McAllen, going anywhere without Chenco as part of his future, left him feeling so hollow and bleak he couldn't let his mind wrap around the concept. He didn't know how to be on his own.

He didn't *want* to be alone. He wanted to be with Chenco.

I want you. I need you, Chenco.

The song ended. Steve went to the edge of the stage, in a daze, grateful when Chenco came to meet him. He was stiff, uneasy. And hurt.

Steve took him by his hands, squeezing them tight. "You're beautiful. Amazing."

I love you.

Chenco's smile didn't reach his eyes. "Steve, we need to talk."

"Yes." *Let me fix this. Let me make this right, because I have to make it right.*

Chenco smiled again, a real one this time, and the gesture was like a sun to Steve.

Maybe this will work out. Maybe I really will be able to fix this, to make him happy, and everything will be okay.

Before Steve could speak, though, Chenco's smile faded, his expression first surprised, then wooden.

Steve turned to follow his lover's gaze and saw one of the puppies had come up beside them, hood pulled back to reveal a wild, flushed, and angry face.

It was Gordy.

CHAPTER TWENTY-FOUR

E VEN BEFORE STEVE'S whisper of the man's name, Chenco had known this was Gordy. Who else could he be, to make Steve so tired, scared, and guilty? As Chenco watched the silent interplay between the two men, he saw the same quiet torture Steve underwent every time he spoke of his friend.

This was what had Steve so distant, Chenco realized.

He wasn't what Chenco had expected, and for a moment he could only stare at the small, squat man with wild eyes and hard jaw. The way Steve had described his friend, Chenco expected someone sad and pathetic, but that wasn't who stood before him now. This man had a wickedness, a coldness to his gaze that froze Chenco's blood. It wasn't a desperate soul facing Steve down, glaring with seething hate at Chenco.

This wasn't a poor soul at all. This was the devil himself.

Mitch and Randy appeared, flanking the scene, and once Gordy saw them, he transformed from a short, scruffy little man with a neat beard into an animal, screaming wild accusations of being held against his will, of torture, rape, every dramatic piece of bullshit he could spout.

For a heartbeat Chenco doubted, wondering if he was projecting. He watched Gordon struggle, alternating between rage and pleading. No—there was no question. This guy played Steve, plucking his strings until they threatened to break. Maybe Gordon wasn't entirely healthy, but he knew what he was doing. Chenco did too. He'd seen this nasty creature many, many times, had known him intimately.

He'd lived with a man like this, after all.

Gordy wasn't a poor, broken, pitiful thing. Gordy was a monster. An asshole. A user, an abuser, a selfish son of a bitch who enjoyed tearing other people down. In a way neither Chenco nor Mitch could ever be, Gordy was the son of Cooper Tedsoe's heart, a cold-hearted abuser down to his core. This was an Oscar-level performance for sure. But there wasn't any question in Chenco's mind. This was an act. This was a game.

This was fucking ending right now.

As Mitch and Randy dragged Gordon off, helped by a cache of burly leathermen, Chenco stopped them, stepping into their path and meeting Gordy's gaze. He watched the man still, seeing him, measuring him.

Chenco channeled his father and gave Gordy a cold, ruthless smile.

I know you. He didn't dare speak the words out loud, but he willed Gordy to hear the furious vows of his heart. *You can fool them all you want, but I know you. I'm stronger than you.*

I will never let you have him again.

Gordy swore, spit, and kicked. Randy reached out to pull Chenco away, but Chenco had already stepped clear. He walked backward, aiming a finger at Gordy before turning on his heel, putting heavy sass into his hips as he sauntered off, Gordy sputtering in rage behind him.

Chenco smiled.

But then he saw Steve standing off to the side, ashen, visibly shaken. Smile faltering, Chenco found Sam and drew his friend aside, ducking to his ear so Steve couldn't overhear them. "I need to get him out of here."

Sam produced keys from his pocket. "I have my bike, but you still haven't finished your lessons."

No, Chenco hadn't, and he was sorely sorry now that he only sort of knew how to drive a motorcycle. Grimacing, he took the keys. "I'll fake it. Maybe it'll distract him, the way I lurch and hesitate all over the street."

"You'll be fine." Sam brushed a kiss against his cheek. "Call if you need anything. And good luck."

Chenco nodded, pretty sure he was going to need all the luck he could get.

He didn't think it was a good sign when Steve let himself be led like a lamb out of the house and into the driveway, but he was heartened that he balked when Chenco straddled Sam's bike and indicated Steve should climb on behind him.

"What the hell?"

There you are, Papi. "You need to get out of here.

I'm driving you."

"Do you know how to drive a bike?"

No, not really, and Chenco wasn't in the mood to argue. "Why don't you get on and find out?"

Steve looked ready to argue, but a series of angry shouts told them Gordy and his entourage were exiting the building too. When Steve blanched, falling into the scary space Chenco had seen him in before, Chenco found his steel.

"Get on this bike, Papi, right now," Chenco ordered.

Steve did.

He hadn't bothered to put on Sam's helmet, and neither had Steve, which was especially stupid given how rough Chenco's driving was. It was a strange moment all around, Chenco as the boy-toy white knight stealing away with his rescued leather daddy. He got about a block before he lingered at a stop sign and glanced over his shoulder.

"I don't know where I'm going," he confessed. "I don't know the way home, or to anywhere, really."

Steve, who was still tight from the scene at the party, relaxed somewhat and smiled, running a hand over Chenco's thigh. "Take a right here. It'll lead you to 159."

"That's not an interstate, is it? I don't think I'm ready for prime time."

"It's not an interstate." The brush of a goatee against his neck thrilled Chenco. "You'll be fine."

Chenco did fairly well, and while it was a little weird to be the one driving Steve, he didn't dislike it. Though Steve didn't wrap his arms around Chenco's middle the same way Chenco did when he rode bitch, he did rest his hands on Chenco's thighs in a comfortable, possessive way that made things feel just right. In fact he was starting to relax when at a stoplight, Steve leaned down and spoke directly into his ear.

"You would do better without me."

It was a damn good thing they were stopped since Chenco was sure he would have wrecked if he were driving. As it was, he about tipped the bike as he glared at Steve. "What the hell?"

He *hated* how tired and beaten Steve looked. "You heard me, and you know it's true." When Chenco started to argue, Steve nodded at the stoplight. "It's green."

Chenco went back to driving, but he was furious now, and he boiled all the way to Randy and Ethan's. When he pulled into the drive, he threw the kickstand, climbed off, and faced Steve with every ounce of anger he'd banked on the way home.

"You *son of a bitch*. You fucking *asshole*, if I had a fucking stiletto on me, I'd put one through your shoulder, or maybe through the middle of your goddamned heart." His nostrils flared with his anger, and tears of rage pricked his eyes, but he *refused* to let them fall. "Is this about the fucker back there? Are you breaking up with me because of *him*? The way you were looking at me before he showed up, I would have said we were going in a very different direction."

Steve glanced around. "Let's not do this in the middle of the driveway."

"Oh, I'll do this in the middle of the *goddamned Strip*, you fucker. You're so fucking tough, you think you can hide all your pain from me? *Fuck. You.* I may not speak Spanish for shit, but I've still got all the Latin blood, and I was raised by a woman who fed me tough love for breakfast. I'll give you a serving anywhere I damn well want to dish it up. Tell me, right fucking now, why you're doing this, why you're keeping yourself from me. Because of Gordy? You're letting him fuck you over because you believe the bullshit he throws at you?"

Ugh, but he hated the way Steve shuttered. "It's my fault. I let—"

"He's a fucking manipulator," Chenco shot back, not letting him spin the tired line again. "Oh, maybe he didn't get himself beat up to torture you, but you know what? He's not quite the victim he wants you to believe he is, not all the way down. I have lived with that asshole. I've dated plenty of guys like him too. He's a fucking user. Maybe he was your best friend then, but he's a piece of shit now. He's not a sorry little thing who needs to be saved. He's a goddamned monster, and he's eating you alive *because you're letting him.*" The tears threatened, choking his throat, and he hissed to keep them at bay. "So help me, if you break up with me because you'd rather let him tear you apart—"

Though Chenco groped for a suitable threat, he found only air. Crying out in angry frustration, he launched himself at Steve, not sure if he was tackling him, pummeling him or what, only knowing he had to knock sense into him somehow, and if that was with his thick fucking head hitting the pavement, then so be it.

Steve didn't go down—he wavered slightly, but when Chenco hit his lover, he found himself immediately wrapped up in those thick, handsome arms, pulled to that half-naked chest, against the open leather before Steve's lips came crushing down on his. They went to the ground, yes, but it was Chenco's back hitting the pavement, the force knocking out a gasp of air. Steve drank it down as his tongue stole deep into Chenco's mouth, tangling with him, claiming him, his big hand sheltering Chenco's head as he bruised him with his kiss.

"Steve," Chenco whispered when Steve let him up for air.

Steve cradled Chenco's face in his hands and stared down at him, all his shadows gone, all his weariness washed away, the vulnerability no longer a burden but a shining, open portal into his soul. He stroked Chenco's cheeks with his thumbs, his eyes shining as he said, his voice rough and overflowing with emotion, "I love you, Crescencio Ortiz."

Chenco couldn't help it—he did cry then, a sob escaping before he wrestled it back to simply tears streaming down into his hair. "I love you too, Steven Vance." Punching him in the chest, he added with a heavy whisper, "You big idiot."

Steve kissed him, lingering, nuzzling. "I have something I want to show you. To share with you."

Anything. Everything. "Okay."

"I need to pack a bag. Then I want to take you to Randy's old house so we can be alone. This is sacred, what I want to show you."

He loves me. Chenco was pretty sure his smile had sunbeams in it. "I'll help you."

"I have to get ready alone, but you can drive us over. I think, actually, I should let you drive more often." He tweaked Chenco's nose and added, "But this time we're wearing helmets. Both of us."

Laughing, Chenco nipped his chin. "Whatever you say, Papi."

THE DIFFERENCE BETWEEN the house Steve directed Chenco to and the one Randy and Ethan lived in now was staggering, and yet even with the two-bedroom ranch barely furnished, Randy's echo remained. It lingered in the way the trailer, despite what Mitch had said about Chenco healing it, had always harbored plenty of Cooper. Randy's ghosting, however, felt comforting tonight, as Steve unpacked the duffel he'd brought along. At the same time, the presence reminded him it was well past time he stopped living in other people's castles and went off to build his own.

Rubbing at his arms, Chenco moved closer to Steve as he fussed at the kitchen counter. "What are those?"

"Hypodermic needles."

Chenco's heart did a tiny flip. He'd given up waiting for Steve to bring them up, and now here they were before him. While needles were delightfully wicked in theory, as Chenco took in the spread of sharps before him, he worried this was a kink he wasn't going to be able to share with his lover.

As Steve continued to arrange his supplies, he began to speak.

"I first played with needles when I was too young to know what I was doing. I think probably every kid liked to slide pins under their skin to see what happened, to marvel at the way you'd pierced yourself but didn't bleed, how it hurt but not really. Not many people I knew then got into it the way I did. I couldn't say why I did it. There was simply something magical about piercing. Playing with an edge, flirting with a taboo. I didn't have the words for it then, nor the sense, but the thing I kept playing with in my head was that it was sacred, sliding something sharp under your skin. I couldn't get enough of it. And the only thing better than doing it to myself was doing it to someone else, having them pierce me back."

Chenco thought of all the things he'd let Steve do to him, all the taboos he'd claimed ownership of. "I understand."

Clouds passed over Steve's countenance. "Usually I played with Gordy. That was how we learned about each other, how I liked to hurt and he liked to be hurt, but he pierced me too. Needles were how it started. By the time we were in high school, every summer vacation was an amateur foray into BDSM, usually doing shit we shouldn't have known about, let alone tried. Needles were always there, though. Needles were communion between us. Piercing was how we spoke to one another, how we shared our love."

Steve ran a hand over the bath towel he'd arranged his supplies across. "Needles were the trouble too. It took me a while to figure it out, but Gordy had a different kink about them than me. Rougher. More dangerous. He didn't just like the edge, he needed it. What I've never let myself see, not fully, is that he loves emotional bleeding too. To bleed himself. To bleed me. I wanted to help him, to save him, but he never wanted to be saved."

Steve shut his eyes. Chenco stepped closer, running a hand down his arm. "No, he wanted to pull you into hell with him."

"Yes," Steve said, his voice rough.

Chenco kissed Steve's shoulder, then lifted his arm and kissed his triskele. "Show me needles, Papi. Show me how you want to pierce me, how I can pierce you."

Quietly, reverently, Steve showed Chenco the different sizes of needles, explaining how the widths would feel, telling Chenco where he could pierce and where no one should ever break skin. He told Chenco about the varied kinds of stabs, how deep he could go, how he could draw blood or not. He explained how important sterilization was, and proper disposal, and how even by taking all the precautions in the world, there was still a level of risk he needed to understand would always be present. He pulled out his phone and showed Chenco an online photo of someone pierced with needles and then laced up with ribbon around the sharps.

There was no contract this time, no wall of paper between them, but this act felt ten times as intimate as anything they'd ever done. Chenco's heart swelled with pride to think Steve trusted him *that much* to believe their contract ran so deep now mere words would never be enough.

"You don't have to do this," Steve said. "I won't lie—I want you to want this with me, but you can say no. This isn't a make-or-break deal. It's enough to tell you about it, to share how I feel about this kink."

Chenco shook his head. "No, it's not enough. You need to share more than just talking about this. But it's okay. I'm open to trying." He held out his forearm. "Show me, please."

"Lie down on the carpet, after we both strip down. And first you're going to drink some of this water."

After taking a heavy swig of the bottle Steve handed him, Chenco hurried out of his clothes. His heart felt like he harbored a racehorse behind his ribs as Steve cleaned off Chenco's chest with the antiseptic wipe.

"I'm going to start with something shallow that won't bleed. I want you to get a feel for what it's like. I'm leaving it in—you'll be wearing my needle, and you'll feel it burn there, right there on your skin. If you freak out, you'll cut yourself. It's important if you want to stop, you use your safe words. Yellow to slow. Red to stop. I'll get them out right away on red, but I'll go slower if you say yellow. Use those words, though. Let me take the needles out. Don't do it yourself, even if you're panicked."

"I can do that," Chenco said.

Steve held his gaze. "It can be very intense. It's heady but it's weird, having sharps inside your skin. If you let me, I'll put twenty, thirty of them into you. I'll put you on your knees and make taking the needles feel like surrender, like giving me the pain is your job, your calling. It's good, but it's intense." He stroked Chenco's face. "Then when you're recovered, I'll show you how to give it back to me."

Chenco leaned into Steve's hand, his heart feeling like it bloomed inside his chest. "This is your church. Not the needles, but the exchange. The understanding. The trust."

Steve pressed a soft kiss to Chenco's lips. "It's the place I can let go like nowhere else. Where I can put my troubles down. Where I don't have to be tough. I can just be."

That's what he's sharing with you. This is how much he loves you—enough to be weak. Chenco, swimming with the weight of the realization, pulled his lover's head down for one more kiss.

When Steve withdrew and turned to the sharps, Chenco felt no fear, only the dark-chocolate anticipation of pleasure coursing through him as he settled onto the towel, as if he were about to sunbathe instead of take a needle under his skin. "Please pierce me, Papi."

That pleasure began to evaporate, though, when Steve crouched beside him, resting one hand on Chenco's shoulder, holding a small hypodermic in the other. Though Chenco tried to see what color the cap was, it was too dark to properly tell, and honestly he couldn't remember which color meant what sensation anyway. He traced the trajectory of the point, his breath quickening.

"I'm not putting it in yet." Steve tipped the needle away from Chenco and rubbed his pinky across his abdomen. He smiled, slow and easy, clearly enjoying himself. Anticipating. "Relax. When you're ready, I'll do a count of three, and that's when it'll go in. I don't do surprises with needles, especially not when we're first starting."

"I'm ready," Chenco said around a tight breath.

Steve laughed. "Baby, you're not ready. Quit trying to drive. You're about to let me slide a sharp object under your skin, and you're going to lie there and let me. At this point holding on to the idea of control is pretty stupid."

Chenco couldn't take his eyes off the tip. "It's weirder than I thought, knowing you're going to stick me. I'm not saying I don't want you to, and I'm not using my word. I guess I'm surprised at myself. I thought I was stronger than this."

"All you have to do is be strong enough to trust me this hurt will be good, that I won't harm you. I'm going to take care of you, even while sliding a needle under your skin. I hope you believe I'm worthy of that kind of trust."

"You *are* worthy. This is just really hard."

The lamp from beside the sofa lit Steve's smile, made it strange and wonderful and haunting. "I know.

That's why it's so cool." Steve's expression softened. He pressed the flat of the needle against Chenco's chest. "One."

Chenco quivered and let out another breath.

Steve's pinky flicked across his nipple, teasing it. The sharp dipped closer to the flesh of his pectorals. "Two."

Chenco made himself breathe deeper, pushed his air out more slowly.

"Three."

At the last second Chenco glanced up—Steve's gaze trained on Chenco's face, eyes full of intensity, passion. Love. Chenco looked back, waiting, terrified, hopeful, determined.

The needle went in, then out.

Chenco's eyes widened then closed, his mouth parting on a silent sigh.

He had one moment of bliss, the sharp, sweet burn of the needle, the weight of the metal inside his skin— *inside his skin, inside him.* He was just starting to spiral in his head when he felt lips at his own, demanding entrance. Chenco whimpered and opened his mouth, eyes still shut, still savoring, still sipping at sensation, trying to decide if it was as good as it seemed or if he was trying to make it more than it was.

"Please," he whispered, surprised to hear his voice so raw, so shaken.

Steve smiled against his mouth. He sat up, but not far. He looked Chenco in the eye as he uncapped another needle and held it an inch away from the first one. "This one on two. One. Two."

In. Out. Chenco gasped again, louder this time. He kept his eyes open, but only just, and he stared up at Steve as if he were looking through watery glass. Another burn. Another bite, another weight—it was nothing, really, *nothing* compared to a flogger, but it was a needle, a needle in his skin, and it was altogether different. He'd lain there and let Steve do that, twice. He still had the needles in. He could feel them. If he sat up too fast, he might bend wrong and prick himself.

He wanted to whimper. He wanted to cry.

He wanted *more*.

Grinning, Steve gave Chenco another kiss then reached for another needle.

"I'm not counting this time," Steve said. He held a needle to the other side, his eyes trained on Chenco's face.

It took everything in him not to arch into the tip, but when it went in, he shut his eyes and lifted off the towel, groaning, begging for more.

More. More.

He did beg—like a whore, *please, please, Papi, please give me more*—and Steve smiled, wickedly, kissing all over Chenco's body instead of sticking him, licking him, stroking his dick while Chenco growled and whined and almost sobbed. He felt slightly stupid, as if his reaction were out of proportion to his actual experience, but he couldn't stop.

"I want to give one to you," he whispered against Steve's skin as he nipped at his neck, the burn of the needles driving him crazy. "Please, Papi—show me. *Show me.*"

He did. First he gave Chenco more water and spoke softly to him, easing him down, and then he gave Chenco an antiseptic wipe and had him clean off Steve's forearm, right above the triskele. "Try a small gauge," he suggested. "A 22 or 23, and do a shallow stick this first time. Give me a count like I did for you, and then go. Don't hesitate, don't doubt yourself."

"Control," Chenco said. "Like flogging." He looked up at Steve and caressed his face. "I wish you had been there. I want you there next time."

Something dark and beautiful passed over Steve's face, and instead of answering, he kissed him. "Give me a needle, Chenco."

It was more nerve-wracking to pierce Steve than it had been to flog Randy, but it was ten times as powerful. The bliss Chenco felt reverberate through his lover as the sharp slid through his skin, the white-hot pleasure he knew his papi felt, the sensation *he*, Chenco, had given him—flogging didn't come close, didn't compare.

They went back and forth for hours, one needle, two, three into Steve, then as many or more into Chenco, until their bodies were pincushions. At first they laughed and nuzzled as they shared, but as the euphoria built between them, so did the passion, and soon Chenco felt himself start to go under, sliding into subspace, yearning for the familiar, safe place with his lover.

"Please," he whispered, and bit at Steve's shoulder,

shuddering as he saw the needles decorating his papi.

Steve turned him around with the deliberation one handled a drunk, and Chenco went on his knees, presenting his flexing hole like a dog waiting to get humped. He didn't get fucked though, not right away, taking more needles first, down his back, on his thighs, and four across each sides of his ass.

Steve's hand scraped his balls, and Chenco whined in sweet, sharp terror. *Yes.* "Give it to me, Papi," he all but growled.

He screamed when that needle went in—it was a cry of pain-pleasure like nothing he'd ever felt, leaving him raw inside and out. He spread his knees wider. He began to babble, not even begging anymore, simply speaking in tongues.

Steve stroked his hip. "Doing so good, baby. You're so pretty, all full of my needles."

And you're wearing mine. Chenco began to cry.

He shivered as he felt Steve's tongue along his crack, as it entered him, toying with him. He grunted and thrust into it, whining, whimpering. Steve's hand brushed his thigh. His balls.

Chenco started to shake.

Fingers moved in his ass, and he began to grunt through his tears, and when Steve's cock slid almost raw inside him, he burned and buzzed and flew.

He barely remembered coming down. The plug went in, and he squeezed it, drooling, moving his lips, trying to thank his papi, to reassure him he was glad for his gift, but he couldn't keep himself upright, let alone speak coherently. He wanted to fall, but he couldn't, not with the needles.

Steve pulled a needle out, and Chenco gasped in displeasure—then sobbed as Steve's kiss sealed the wound.

He removed all the needles, kissing each inch of flesh as they departed, and there was a lot of flesh needing that kind of attention. A few times Steve stopped to give water, then continued on. Before he turned Chenco over to tend to his front, he slid antiseptic wipes all over the now-naked flesh, stopped to cover a bleeding wound with a bandage. Then he lay Chenco down on the towel and gave the same treatment to the front.

He took the needles from Chenco's cock last, and when he was done cleaning up, when every needle was gone and safely tucked away, when every wound that needed covering was covered, when there was no blood left to wipe away, Steve drew him tenderly into his arms.

"I need to take care of you," Chenco slurred, gesturing to the needles between them, all around them in Steve's skin.

"In a minute. I want to wear you a little longer." Steve kissed his brow. "I love you. I love you more than anything in the world, anything or anyone I ever thought I could love. Stay with me, please. Marry me, live with me—here, Texas, on the moon, wherever you want."

Steve kissed him again, on his lips this time, a desperate kiss that made Chenco hum to the bottom of his soul.

"I love you more," Chenco said when he was able, shutting his eyes as he floated happily on his bliss. "And yes. I'll marry you whenever and wherever you like."

CHAPTER TWENTY-FIVE

W HEN Steve and Chenco returned home late that night, they found everyone still up and sitting in the kitchen, grim and sober. Crabtree was there too, and Steve knew where this was going before anyone told him.

"Gordy ran away from the party," Randy said when the silence went on too long. "We tried to chase him down, but he got away."

"I have reprimanded my staff for letting him go—twice now." Crabtree's voice was tight, as if each word were painful to get past his lips. "I am deeply sorry for my failure, and I assure you I'll do everything I can to correct it."

Steve nodded, not sure how to respond. In fact, he felt strangely numb about it all. He didn't feel guilty, which seemed strange, but good. At least he thought it was good.

Tired, that's what he was. Very, very tired.

When Chenco led him to bed, he didn't fight. His soul was weary, but his body hummed with remembered pleasure, of the needles Chenco had given him, of those Chenco had taken. As they spooned together naked in their bed, his hand stole down to feel the butt of the plug his boy still wore for him, and the heaviness inside him eased. He fell at once into a deep, peaceful sleep, where his dreams were nothing more than floating on a soft, sweet cloud with Chenco snuggled sweetly in his arms.

He stayed there, happily ensconced, until the shouting started.

By the time he stumbled into sweatpants and headed into the hall, everyone else was awake and stumbling out too. When he tried to follow Randy and Mitch down the stairs, though, Chenco stopped him with a tug on his arm.

"Don't." Chenco stared over the railing toward the front door. "It's him, and this isn't going to be pretty."

"The police are on their way," Ethan said from the bottom of the stairs, a cordless phone in his hand. "So is Crabtree."

"Stevie, come out here right fucking now, or I swear to God, I'll kill myself."

Bile rising in his throat, Steve gripped the railing and shut his eyes. "He will," he bit off when Chenco's arms went around his waist. "He's not bluffing. He'll do it. As soon as the police or Crabtree's men get here, he will."

"Then let him."

Chenco's words made the hair on Steve's arms stand up. The grit in his lover's tone, the complete and utter lack of mercy—it startled him, yes, but it made him shudder, not in fear, but in a bone-deep sense of relief.

Immediately, guilt washed that release away. "Chenco—" he began, but his lover cut him off with the same steel he'd faced Steve down with in the driveway the night before.

"If he's that far gone, if he truly will go to that kind of length to manipulate you, then *let him go.*" When Steve's knees began to buckle, Chenco pressed him to the wall and held him up by his shoulders, staring him squarely in the eye. "This isn't your fault, Papi. This is all on him."

"I can't—"

Chenco kept tight hold of Steve. "You can. You must."

"*Stevie!*" The anguish in Gordy's tone tore at Steve, made him want to push Chenco aside and tear down the stairs, to go out the front door and make it stop. He didn't though. He only clung to his lover, as if he could draw strength into his body through the contact.

"Hush." Chenco pulled Steve's head down on his shoulder. "It's going to be all right."

Steve sank into him. "How?"

"Whatever happens, it's nothing you did. You're going forward, not backward. The choices he makes are not your responsibility, and at the end of the day, no matter what we promise to be to one another, no matter how much we want to save the ones we love, we can only ever save ourselves." Chenco kissed Steve's hair. "Save yourself, Papi. Save yourself."

Steve swallowed around the truth, willing it to go

down, not choke the life out of him. "That's hard."

"Tough love, baby. It's the most painful, wonderful kind there is." He drew Steve closer. "Just let him go. Stay here with me, keep yourself safe. *Let him go.*"

Steve stared at Chenco, wanting to argue. But the steel he saw in his lover's face wouldn't allow him to say a word, didn't give him space to run away. *I see you,* Chenco said without uttering a breath. *I see you, Steve Vance. Your weakness and your strength.*

I see you, beyond all your walls, and I love you.

Steve exhaled a shuddering breath and buried himself into Chenco's embrace.

As if he could hear and see Steve's surrender, Gordy's frustrated scream rent the air. "You *fucker.* You're choosing him over me? A goddamned *fence fairy*?" There was a pause, and Gordy's next shout was tearful, desperate. "Come on, Stevie. *Come on.* Don't leave it like this. Come out, please, and talk to me. *Don't leave it like this.*"

"Don't you dare let him get to you." Chenco held Steve so tight he could barely breathe.

Steve was going to be sick. His guts churned. He buried his face in Chenco's shoulder, nipping at Chenco's bare skin because he couldn't take it, couldn't bear this. He wasn't strong enough for this.

"I've got you, Papi," Chenco promised, his teeth grazing Steve's ear. *I'll be strong enough for you.*

"He's going to do it," Steve whispered, choking on the words. "He's not making it up. He'll do it."

"I'll hold you the whole time. I won't let you go."

Chenco kissed Steve gently on the temple as another incoherent cry came up from the drive. "You cry all you want, boy. I can hold all your pain."

Tears streaming down his cheeks, Steve clung to Chenco and waited, Gordy's cries shaking him to his soul.

When the crack of a gunshot cut through the night, he jolted and the tears came faster, but he didn't move, only kept holding on. The door opened, and Steve could hear others talking with the police—shaking, he didn't look up, didn't open his eyes, just kept holding to his rock, his solace, his only safe space in the world. In the distance someone spoke to him, but he didn't listen, didn't acknowledge anything but the beautiful *thud-thud* of Chenco's heartbeat, the soft *whooshes* of his breath.

My boy. My Chenco. My Crescencio. My Caramela, my queen.

Steve clung to them all, to the man who was so young but so wise and so, so strong, the only one in the world who could have ever carried him past this dragon.

When Chenco brushed his lips to his ear and whispered, "He's gone," Steve wept.

Right there on the stairs, where anyone could see, he sobbed like a baby, bleeding out all the pain he had carried for so, so long. Every frame of the movie of his life with Gordy, the good and the bad, the sacred and terrible, the wonders and the mistakes—he lived them all, and he bled for the friend he had loved, who had chosen to go away. Steve let it all flow, every ugly, awful drop, gave every last bit of his sorrows over to his beloved, to Chenco. Because he'd said he could bear it.

Because Steve knew he could.

There at the top of the stairs, Steve Vance let go. To the man who had come to save him. To the love he had for Chenco. To the sorrow of what he hadn't been strong enough to stop. To the hope they had, together, for the future. He let go and he listened as Chenco repeated, over and over, that this was not Steve's fault.

He couldn't believe in the words by themselves, but he could believe in Chenco. He could follow him anywhere, and he would, as long as his boy would allow him. Maybe Chenco only sometimes needed him, but Steve needed Chenco every minute of every hour of every single day.

As the last of his burdens fell away, as Chenco expertly scooped them up and insisted he could take even more, Steve followed the promise of hope, of happiness, of joy.

He followed his heart up the stairs as his lover enfolded him in his arms, Chenco's strength bearing him up, carrying the pain.

With Chenco there to keep him safe, Steve let himself be loved.

CHAPTER TWENTY-SIX

I N September, on the day of his wedding, Chenco got an email from Booker.

He'd been fooling around on the internet while Randy did something with Chenco's tie, and there it was, right in his inbox. Chenco almost didn't open it because he didn't want anything to spoil the day, but he clicked anyway. He was glad he did.

Booker, it turned out, had gone to L.A. He'd run away from Trist after a bad fight, hopped a bus and left, determined to get his own fresh start. Of course he'd ended up getting high and in trouble, and then he met a guy.

We're not fucking, Book wrote, but he said this guy was super-solid, a total ace who'd kept him up all night talking on Malibu beach and the next day got him into rehab. The email, it turned out, was one of his steps. He said he understood if Chenco didn't want to talk to him, but he wanted to apologize for what he had done wrong, and then he proceeded to list, in painful detail, all the ways he felt he'd let his friend down. It went on and on and on, and by the end Chenco was crying.

Randy got worried and tried to go get Steve, but

Chenco waved impatiently at him and said stop, he was fine. Then he wiped his eyes, squared his shoulders, and wrote back to Booker, saying of course he forgave him. He said they needed to set up a Skype chat or something soon, whatever his clinic allowed, and then he wrote, *OMG, I'm about to get married, bitch. Can you fucking believe it?* When he finally sent the email, he felt whole, as if a jagged piece of his life had begun to move into place.

He bustled around with Randy and Sam, getting the house ready for the ceremony. Tonight he and Steve would go to their new home down the street, in the place *Chenco* had bought, or at least put a mortgage on with his first two checks from Ethan and a significant loan from Crabtree. It *was* a loan, though, he'd told the gangster. This was his castle, and he'd build every brick of it himself.

Crabtree had seemed very pleased with that declaration and told him to take his time paying him back.

Lincoln had come, and though he was staying at Herod's, he was at the house today, helping Sam put up decorations. Only fifty people were coming, and half of them were already there helping, but Chenco loved the family feeling of it all.

Married. He was getting *married*.

To Steve. *Today.*

It wasn't going to be a fancy ceremony, but it would be special. Ethan had gotten himself ordained so he could officiate, and Mitch and Randy and Sam stood up as their attendants. As they got ready to start, however,

Chenco noticed his brother was a little twitchy, always looking at the front door instead of toward the patio, where the ceremony was all ready to go.

"What's going on?" Chenco demanded at last.

"Nothing," Mitch replied, obviously lying. He turned to Sam with a frown. "Will you…?"

Sam kissed him and hurried down the hallway. "I'll put Crabtree on it."

Chenco tried to press Mitch about what he was doing, but before he got anywhere, Steve found him and told him they needed to go get ready.

"He's up to something," Chenco said as they fussed with each other's ties.

"Yes, I think he is," Steve said calmly. "Let him. He's your brother, and he wants to do something special for your wedding day."

That was obvious, except something about the whole scenario had Chenco's belly full of butterflies. When he came down the stairs to get ready for the processional, he glanced out at the lawn, saw who was sitting in the front row on his side, and he fell against Steve, stunned out of his ability to stand.

"*Mama.*" His throat became horribly thick. "Is—is—?"

"Yes, Carmelita is here." Steve rubbed Chenco's back reassuringly, speaking in gentle tones. "Mitch's last run wasn't to Los Angeles, it was to the valley, and he made a stop in Edinburg. Part of his cargo was a DVD of your performances." He nuzzled Chenco's temple with a chuckle. "I wish I could have seen it. He has to look just like Cooper did when she met him."

Chenco couldn't stop staring at the front row, at the familiar, beautiful head of dark hair, now streaked with gray.

She came. For me.

Chenco's gaze moved from his mother to his brother, who gazed at him with such pride he seemed in danger of exploding with it.

Mama. Here at my wedding. Mitch brought my mama to me. Chenco's fingers dug into Steve's arm. Had she forgiven him? Was she truly okay with this, with his getting married to a man, performing in drag in Las Vegas? Could this be real?

"I'm going to bawl like a baby."

"That's fine." Steve squeezed him close. "Just not yet. Pull yourself together, honey. We're going to go get married."

They did. He walked up the aisle with Steve and stood before Ethan, signing a whole new contract, one that would go in his cedar box, with the now-outdated BDSM agreement and the letters from his mother.

The letters from Carmelita, who was here, watching him get married.

When he'd come down the aisle, Chenco had lingered at his mother, unsure if he should hug her, thank her, or what. He couldn't believe everything was completely okay between them just because Mitch had convinced her to come. Yes, there was work to do between them, he could see this, but when he smiled at her, she smiled back—slightly tentative, but it was a smile.

The biggest challenge came after the ceremony. *Chenco's* surprise for everyone was performing his new number, the one he'd cancelled in June when he'd told the L.A. agent he was grateful for the chance to meet her, but his partner was going through a difficult time, and he'd need to either pass or reschedule. He was due to fly down to Los Angeles later in the month for the rescheduled performance. Chenco still wasn't sure he wanted anything more than what he had, a nice house, a husband, and a regular gig on the Vegas stage.

But as Ethan often said, it certainly couldn't hurt to see how far he could fly.

Performing was fine, except now his mother was here. Chenco wasn't ashamed, and in fact if anything he was sorry he'd elected to give the performance *not* in drag—he wanted her to see the whole thing, the real deal. He was nervous, though, in a way he hadn't been on any stage. Not once had his mother seen him dance and done anything but tell him he had to stop.

You won't stop me, Mama. Not today. Not ever.

Gathering his courage and taking strength from his husband in the front row, Chenco motioned to Randy to start the music, assumed his place on the stage Mitch had arranged at the end of the lawn and let his queen fly without a single sequin to hold her up.

He sang "Live It Up" since he hadn't performed it for anyone yet but Ethan and his team. He wanted the people he loved most to see it first. A few of his regular backup dancers accompanied him, but they had none of their pyrotechnics, no lifts, glitter cannons, only themselves, the stage and the music.

It was strange, almost surreal to play himself, not Caramela, but within a few beats of the song, he was so, so glad he had. For one, he sang both parts, Pitbull and JLo, moving fluidly between man and woman. He shook his booty with a vengeance to make the diva herself impressed, and when he sang the line about knowing they liked her bumper, he winked at Randy, who clapped and laughed—and waggled his eyebrows.

Ethan joined him on stage for the middle section of the song, leading him through a seductive ballroom dance. This was in the show as well, and Randy said he couldn't wait to see how green everyone was when the hot casino owner got to dance with the sexy goddess, then go home with the grungy poker player from the shadows. Dancing with Ethan was as beautiful and erotic as it always was, and Chenco had to agree, it would be wicked fun to do it in full costume onstage.

When he finished, the small crowd erupted in whistles and wild applause. Ethan patted him on the back, Mitch beamed, and Steve—*his husband*—drew him into a tight embrace and kissed him hard, telling him he was wonderful.

Chenco accepted all their praise, thanked them for it—then turned to Carmelita.

She had tears in her eyes as she came forward, hands pressed together in front of her mouth. Behind her Sam wept openly, sinking into Mitch's waiting embrace. Chenco couldn't focus on them, though, couldn't see anyone but his mother, his mama who was here, who had come to him after all.

"Mama," he whispered, his throat raw, his heart aching.

Please, please have liked it. Please, please love me.

With a determination and strength that made Caramela look rather flimsy, Carmelita came forward, took Chenco's face in her hands and squeezed.

"Crescencio," she said, her voice quiet but strong, her soft, beautiful accent curling around Chenco's ears. "*Cariño.* I am so very, *very* proud of you."

Joy beyond Chenco's imagining filled his heart, his whole body humming with love and pride as she smiled at him.

"Me too," Chenco said, and hugged her tight.

ABOUT THE AUTHOR

 Heidi Cullinan has always enjoyed a good love story, provided it has a happy ending. Proud to be from the first Midwestern state with full marriage equality, Heidi is a vocal advocate for LGBT rights. She writes positive-outcome romances for LGBT characters struggling against insurmountable odds because she believes there's no such thing as too much happy ever after. When Heidi isn't writing, she enjoys cooking, reading, playing with her cats, and watching anime, with or without her family. Find out more about Heidi at heidicullinan.com.

Did you enjoy this book?

If you did, please consider leaving a review online or recommending it to a friend. There's absolutely nothing that helps an author more than a reader's enthusiasm. Your word of mouth is greatly appreciated and helps me sell more books, which helps me write more books.

MORE BOOKS IN THE SPECIAL DELIVERY SERIES COMING SOON

SPECIAL DELIVERY

Sam knows he'll never find the excitement he craves in

Middleton, Iowa. Then Sam meets Mitch, an independent, long-haul trucker. When Mitch offers to take him on a road trip west, Sam jumps at the chance. One minute Mitch is the star of Sam's X-rated fantasies, the next he's a perfect gentleman. And when they hit the Las Vegas city limit, Sam finds out why: Randy. Sam grapples with the meaning of friendship, letting go, growing up—even the meaning of love—because no matter how far he travels, eventually all roads lead home.

HOOCH AND CAKE

All Sam and Mitch want to do is get married, but between their busy schedules and the judgment of a small town, it's not as easy as it should be. Then their best friend Randy shows up, and the wedding that almost wasn't is about to become the wedding Iowa never even dreamed to see.

DOUBLE BLIND

Randy can't stand to just sit by and watch as a mysterious man throws money away on roulette. The man's dark desperation has him scrambling for a reason—any reason—to save his soul. Ethan has no idea what he's going to do with himself once his last dollar is gone—until Randy whirls into his life with a heart-stealing smile and a poker player's gaze that sees too much. Soon they're both taking risks that not only play fast and loose with the law, but with the biggest prize of all: their hearts.

THE TWELVE DAYS OF RANDY

Randy and Ethan are ready to enjoy their first Christmas at home together, but when Crabtree ropes Randy into wily holiday antics, Ethan feels left out in the cold. When Herod's new owner discovers his husband only plays at being an imp to hide a Christmas spirit bigger and tackier than Las Vegas, Ethan vows to find a way to have his cake and eat it too. Especially if Randy's the one jumping out of the middle.

OTHER BOOKS BY HEIDI CULLINAN

There's a lot happening with my books right now! Sign up for my **release-announcement-only newsletter** on my website to be sure you don't miss a single release or re-release.

www.heidicullinan.com/newssignup

Want the inside scoop on upcoming releases, automatic delivery of all my titles in your preferred format, with option for signed paperbacks shipped worldwide? Consider joining my Patreon.
www.patreon.com/heidicullinan

THE ROOSEVELT SERIES
Carry the Ocean
Shelter the Sea
Unleash the Earth (coming soon)
Shatter the Sky (coming soon)

LOVE LESSONS SERIES
Love Lessons (also available in German)
Frozen Heart
Fever Pitch (also available in German)
Lonely Hearts (also available in German)
Short Stay
Rebel Heart (coming fall 2017)

THE DANCING SERIES
Dance With Me
also available in French, Italian coming soon

Enjoy the Dance
Burn the Floor (coming soon)

MINNESOTA CHRISTMAS SERIES
Let It Snow
Sleigh Ride
Winter Wonderland
Santa Baby
More adventures in Logan, Minnesota, coming soon

CLOCKWORK LOVE SERIES
Clockwork Heart
Clockwork Pirate (coming soon)
Clockwork Princess (coming soon)

TUCKER SPRINGS SERIES
Second Hand (written with Marie Sexton) (available in French)
Dirty Laundry (available in French)
(more titles in this series by other authors)

SINGLE TITLES
Antisocial (coming summer 2017)
Nowhere Ranch (available in Italian)
Family Man (written with Marie Sexton)
A Private Gentleman
The Devil Will Do
Hero
Miles and the Magic Flute

NONFICTION
Your A Game: Winning Promo for Genre Fiction
(written with Damon Suede)

*Many titles are also available in audio and more are in
production. Check the listings wherever you purchase
audiobooks to see which titles are available.*